# THE ORB OF CHAOS

## Volume I: No Rest for the Wicked

A Novel by
M. Ray Allen

Lucky Duck
Publishing
2013

Kim,
I hope you enjoy this story
as much as I have :)
~ M. Ray Allen

The Orb of Chaos -
No Rest for the Wicked
Copyright 2013 by M. Ray Allen
ISBN-13: 978-1499142204
ISBN-10: 149914220X
Lucky Duck Publishing

Front and back cover art:
Copyright 2013 by Mattijs Buma

## *Acknowledgements*

This story wouldn't have been possible without a lot of help from my friends and family along the way. While there are far too many to list, here are a few that I would like to recognize for their exceptional help and encouragement: Mark Blauser for making me do this to begin with; Crissy Fleming, Victoria German, Judy Nguyen and Kristine Schwartz who were instrumental in editing out all my mistakes; Navilla Bagga, Bob & Judy Clark, Jonathan Allen and Sean Fleming who all kept pushing me to get this done and listening to me talk about it (All-The-Time); and finally Mattijs Buma and Leigh Lowe who are responsible for the fantastic artwork and cover design.

# Table of Contents

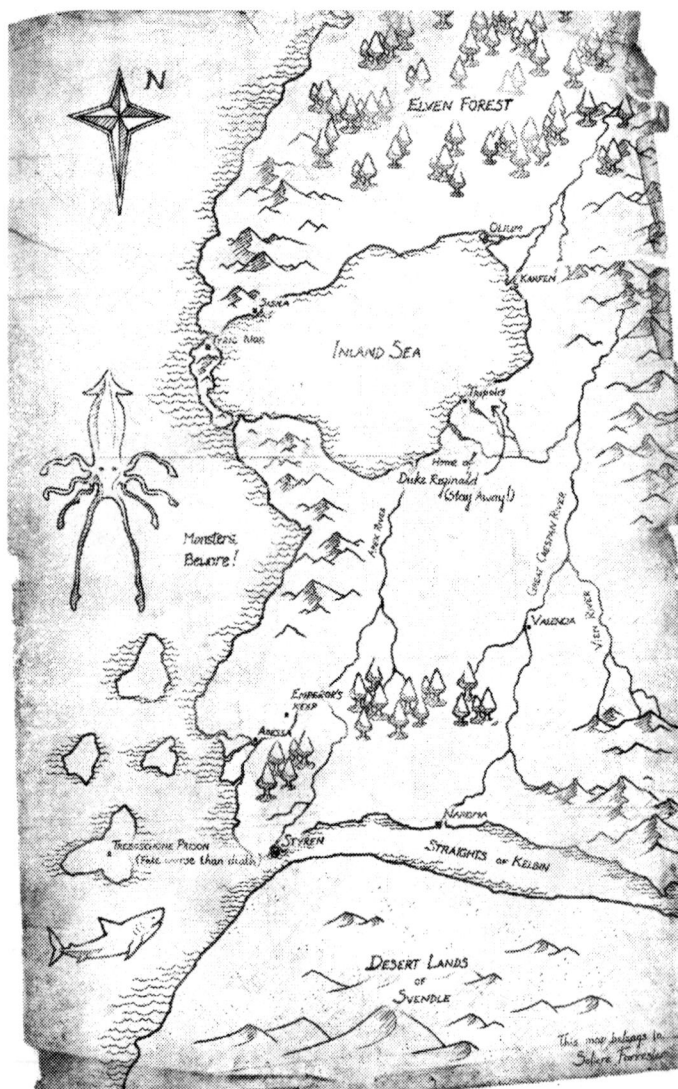

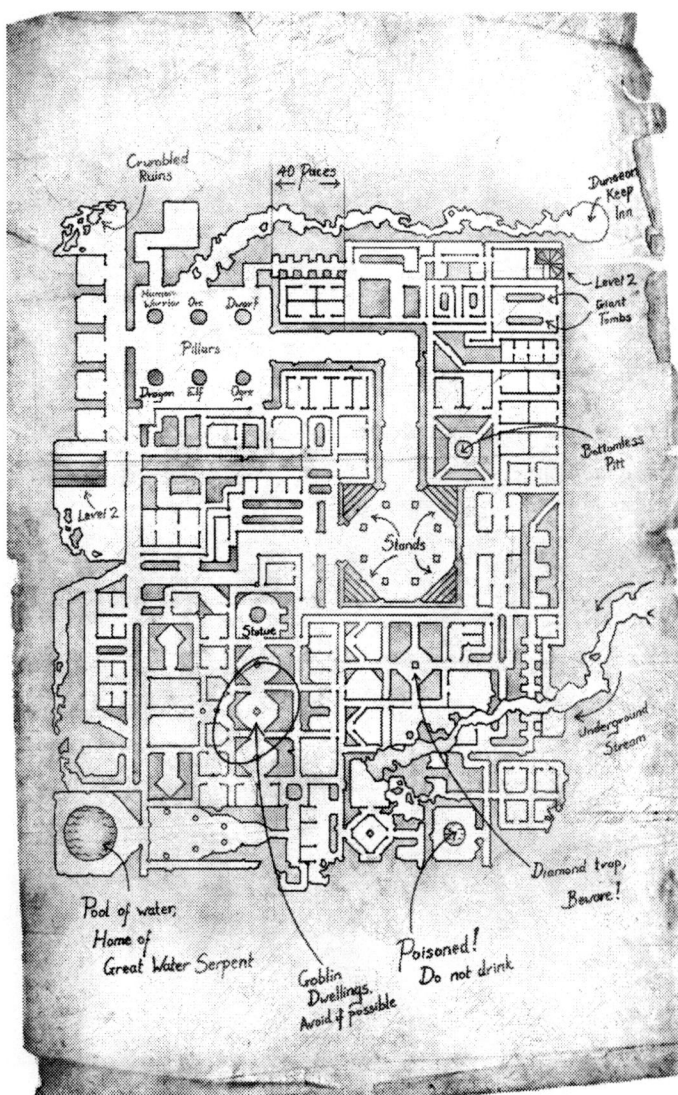

Crumbled Ruins

40 Paces

Dungeon Keep Inn

Human Warrior    Orc    Dwarf

Level 2 Giant Tombs

Pillars

Dragon    Elf    Ogre

Bottomless Pitt

Level 2

Stands

Statue

Underground Stream

Diamond trap, Beware!

Pool of water; Home of Great Water Serpent

Goblin Dwellings, Avoid if possible

Poisoned! Do not drink

## *01. Oather and the Blacksmith*

"G'morning, Oather," greeted Jasser Dalmon, the local glass-maker. Oather smiled and waved back. Normally, he would have talked to Jasser for a while but he had a lot of things he needed to do and he had very little time left.

The sun was barely above the horizon and the shop owners on the street were already quite busy preparing their shops for the day ahead. Oather hoped this was a good sign that the blacksmith would also be open. He really needed to get his sword repaired before he and Sol could get underway.

Oather reached the end of the street and began to turn the corner when he almost ran into a stubble-bearded man with several missing teeth. The older man was leading a cart pulled by the most ragged looking mule Oather had ever seen.

"Oh," the man said and quickly stepped back. "Excuse me, I didn't see you."

"It's okay, Calin. I should have been paying more attention."

"Oh, Oather," the old man replied. "It's you. It's good to see you again."

The old man was Calin Lulkoek. He sold manure in town and occasionally sat around with Tanner at the *Lucky Duck*, telling stories to each other and drinking. By the smell of it, today was a day he was in town to sell.

Oather started to step around Calin and his tired old mule when he saw Calin's eyes light up.

"Oh, Oather, you have to see this new mix I created."

Oather really wasn't a fan of manure, especially the way it smelled today, but he decided to humor Calin. "Oh, really?" he asked politely.

Calin's face brightened as he motioned for Oather to follow him. Calin quickly scooped up some of the foul smelling concoction with his bare hands and shoved it towards Oather's face.

"Here, take a good whiff."

That was exactly what Oather didn't want to do, but he took a quick smell anyway to appease the old man. The stink was absolutely horrid. To Oather, it smelled like sulfur mixed with spoiled cabbage and possibly a dead animal, and instantly made Oather's stomach queasy.

"Hmmm," Oather replied, trying his hardest not to wince.

"Isn't that some of the richest smelling stuff you've ever smelled?"

Oather tried not to inhale. "It's…it's…certainly strong," he finally managed to say.

"When people buy this, it's going to make their crops go wild. They'll be growing tomata's the size of your head."

Calin continued to talk while Oather took a couple of steps back. Calin seemed to be quite proud of his newest recipe. When he was done beaming, he motioned for Oather to step closer to him. Oather didn't really want to, but he also didn't want to be rude, so he leaned towards Calin.

"You wanna know the secret to making this batch?" Calin whispered.

Oather was about to tell Calin that he'd rather not, but he was too late. The old man reached into a bag and pulled out an apple. It was brown and black in color, nearly rotten, and looked terrible. Calin drew it closer and took a big bite out of it.

"Rotten apples," Calin said with his mouth full. "Feed'em to the horses and before you know it they're givin' you gold!"

Oather wasn't sure what to say, so he just nodded and tried to step back again.

"Granted, you gotta be careful, give'm too many and it'll make'm sick, but mix a couple in with the ones you're already gonna feed them and it's not too bad."

"That's good to know, but I really need to go. It was nice seeing you again, Calin."

"You too, Oather," Calin said. He waved as Oather began walking away.

"Oh," Oather heard Calin call from behind him. He stopped and turned around to see what else the old man needed. "Is Tanner up yet?"

"I think so, why?"

"I wanted to know if he'd let me set my cart up in the alleyway behind the tavern again…do you think he'd mind?"

"I don't think he would. He's never minded in the past."

"Okay, thanks," Calin said. He waved to Oather again, then grabbed the reins of the mule and started walking towards The *Lucky Duck*.

Moments later, Oather finally arrived at his destination. As luck would have it, the blacksmith shop was indeed open. Plumes of black smoke bellowed from its chimney. The shop was a large round building lined with open windows that resembled a large mushroom with a smokestack coming out of the top. Oather could feel the heat pouring out of them as he approached the building.

Oather pushed open the thick wooden door and stepped inside. As soon as the blacksmith saw him, the man's eyes popped open with excitement.

"Oather!" the blacksmith called. The blacksmith waved for Oather to come to him and began to retrieve something from behind the counter.

The blacksmith was an old friend of Oather's named Omar. Omar pulled out a long object wrapped in fine royal blue silk, which he set down on the counter and slowly unwrapped. Oather first got a glimpse of the hilt, which was very ornate and done in perfectly shined brass. Then the blade was unveiled and it was beautiful. The steel blade was polished to a mirror-like finish, with symbols etched down the center.

"May...may I hold it?"

"By all means, my boy," the blacksmith said with a wide smile on his face. "I've been waiting to show it to you ever since I finished it."

Oather cautiously picked up the blade and held it in front of him. With slow movements, he cut through the air and tested the balance of Omar's latest creation. The fire in the forge roared hotter as the blacksmith pumped the bellows. The shining new blade reflected the light and made it dance around the dark room.

Omar was a huge man with arms built from years of pounding hot steel into powerful weapons, but was almost puny when compared to Oather. Oather Därbon stood a head taller and his chest was nearly twice as broad as the blacksmith's.

Oather critically examined the sword and found that it was a great piece of work. His eyes intently took in every inch of the weapon, looking at every little detail. He glanced over at Omar questioningly.

"How much?"

"Only one hundred and fifty gold imperials," the blacksmith replied, as though it were a true bargain.

Oather set the blade back down on the counter.

"It's a nice weapon, but that's a little more than I can do."

"But this is one of the best blades I have ever made," the blacksmith retorted, "The steel used in making it was brought from the deepest dwarven mine and is harder than stone."

"That may be true, but it's just more than I can spend."

Omar leaned back against one of the workbenches and thought for a moment. "Maybe we could work out a payment plan?"

Oather considered Omar's offer, and would have really liked to, but he wasn't sure where he'd find the money to pay Omar back and decided he just couldn't do it. "Thank you, but I think I'll just get mine repaired...again."

Oather slowly drew his old sword and handed it to Omar.

"Are you sure, Oather? I know you want it."

"Thank you, but right now I'll just have to make do with what I've got."

"A'ight. Come back later this evening and I'll have your sword ready for you."

Oather thanked Omar again and took his leave of the shop.

## *02. Rude Awakening*

Sunlight streamed through the window and hit Sol directly in the face as he laid in bed. His eyes weren't open, but he could see the sheer brightness of the light through his eyelids, which made his head throb a little. He'd gone to bed late last night after drinking far too much, even by his standards.

A cool morning breeze wafted in through his open bedroom window and he could hear the sounds of people bustling outdoors. Sol let out a short groan and pulled his pillow over his head and gave a sigh of relief as he attempted to fall back asleep. Then, much to his disappointment, Sol heard the unmistakable sound of a cart being pulled close to the building outside.

"Please keep going, please keep going," Sol muttered.

Sol squeezed the pillow tightly and pretended not to hear the sound of the wooden wheels on the street as the cart slowly approached the inn. Despite his efforts, he heard the cart slow down, pull into the alley outside his window and come to a stop. It didn't take long before the scent of brimstone, rotten potatoes and what was probably troll dung drifted in with the breeze. After smelling that, he knew that there was no way he was going to be able to sleep.

"I'll be damned. Oather was right, the gods really do hate me," Sol grumbled into his pillow, which he held tightly to try and filter the awful smell.

Slowly, he came to terms that life just wasn't going to let him sleep any more that day, no matter how much he wanted to.

He moved the pillow and rubbed his eyes hard--partially to help him clear up his blurry vision, and partially to distract himself from how much his brain hurt. Then, he heard the handle on his door rattle and the door slowly creaked open.

Sol quickly turned his head to see a young woman just a few years younger than him, with long curly auburn hair and blue eyes. She wore a light blue dress and white apron.

"Sooollll, it's time to get up."

"Who the hell are you?" Sol asked.

The girl ignored him as she walked in with a tray of fruit and a mug. Slowly, she stepped inside and closed the door with her foot. Holding the tray with one hand, she reached behind her and flicked the latch before strolling over to the bed.

She had a wide smile on her face as she sat the tray down on the small table next to Sol's bed and crawled onto the bed with him, hugging him tightly. As she did, her cheek pressed one of the buttons of his shirt into his skin. He realized for the first time that he was still dressed in the same clothes he'd been wearing the night before. He must have been so drunk that he forgot to change and simply crashed onto his bed.

"I'm Katrina...the new barmaid, remember? I work here and I sat with you last night while we talked about all your adventures."

Sol lifted his right eyebrow, giving her a blank expression as he tried to recall the conversation. His head was still throbbing, so it was hard to think, but he tried his best anyway.

"Won't Gretchen be a little upset with you for being up here?"

Katrina was silent for a brief moment before replying, "Gretchen has gone to the market. You know how she is when she shops, so I don't really expect her to be back until this afternoon. I didn't really think that Tanner would miss me, so I thought I'd bring you some food and see if we could pick up where we left off when you passed out last night."

"Oh, so you're the one that brought me up here?"

"Well, Tanner helped, but after we got you up here you were dead asleep so I just tucked you in and left."

*That explained why he was still dressed in his clothes from yesterday,* Sol thought. The fragments of his memory from last night were slowly coming back together as the girl curled up next to him on the bed.

"You told me you used to work on a ship, and how you were going to own one yourself someday...,"

The girl continued on very enthusiastically, as though she could already imagine herself there with him. It'd never happen, Sol knew, but he didn't want to interrupt her. After all, it was bad luck to have a woman on a ship.

The girl sounded more and more excited as she recited the previous night's conversation, but Sol didn't care as long as he didn't have to think. He wasn't really listening anyway.

As she reminisced, Sol noticed how pretty she was, and how good she smelled. From his vantage point he could see very slightly down the front of her dress.

"Don't you remember?"

She looked at him with her bottom lip sticking out. Sol had barely heard a word she said. His interest in her had shifted and he hadn't noticed that she'd actually stopped talking. She gently ran her soft fingers across his cheek and under his chin, and then slowly tilted his gaze back up to her face, bringing Sol out of his reverie.

"Shhh," Sol whispered.

Without another word, he pulled her up closer to him, closed his eyes and kissed her lips.

## *03. The Lucky Duck*

After leaving the blacksmith's shop, Oather made his way down the street back towards the *Lucky Duck* Inn & Tavern. The inn sign swung gently above two attractive young ladies chatting on the walkway. He didn't know them, but he thought they looked familiar. Perhaps he'd seen them before with Sol. He couldn't make out what they were saying but he assumed they were out doing some early-morning shopping. He gave them a brief nod as he approached. One of the girls gave him an inviting smile as he walked into the inn.

*There sure are some nice people living in this city,* he thought.

As Oather made his way into the tavern, he caught the scent of something that made his stomach growl. He approached the bar just as a short petite woman bustled through the kitchen. She wore her brown hair in a bun with wisps of gray hanging loose on the sides. Her sharp eyes widened as Oather walked towards her.

"Well, good morning, sleepyhead. I figured you would have woken up much earlier. The sun's been up for hours you know."

"You're back already?" Oather asked, "I thought you went to the market to get a few things?"

"Oh, I did, dearie," Gretchen replied, "but they were all out of bread. I was going to get some more wax to make candles but I just didn't feel like doing that this morning, so I came back early."

"Oh, okay. Well, whatever you're making smells delicious."

"I'm glad you think so, since I made it for you and Sol. Here, now eat up," she ordered, setting the plate in front of him as he took a seat at the bar.

"Yes, ma'am," Oather said eagerly, salivating at the smell of her cooking.

Gretchen handed him a fork and he began to dig into the food. Oather had always loved Gretchen's cooking. Over the years she and Tanner had more or less adopted Sol and Oather. They always let them stay at the *Lucky Duck* at no charge. Sol had always promised that he would pay them back someday, but that day just hadn't arrived yet.

"So how late did you boys stay up last night?" asked Gretchen as she picked up the mugs that were lying about the bar and on the floor. "That new barmaid of ours is worthless. Look at these mugs. She was supposed to make sure these were all cleaned last night before she went home."

Oather knew that Gretchen didn't like it when the barmaids got too personal with the customers...or with Sol for that matter. He continued to eat. Oather was not even cutting the sausages, he just ate them whole.

Once the mugs were picked up, Gretchen stopped and stared quizzically at Oather.

Narrowing her eyes, she asked, "What time did Katrina close up the bar and go home last night?" Oather paid more attention to his food and pretended not to hear her.

"Oather," she repeated sternly. "When did she leave last night?"

Oather could just feel her eyes bore into the back of his head.

"I saw her flirting with Sol last night before I turned in. She stayed all night, didn't she, Oather?" Gretchen asked in an interrogating tone. Even though he had heard every word Gretchen said, Oather sat there and shoveled food into his mouth and pretended that he hadn't.

She walked around in front of him. "Well, if you can't talk while you're eating, then I'll just take that plate back." With one quick motion, she snatched the plate from him.

"Hey," Oather cried, feebly clawing for the plate she held at arm's length. Gretchen slapped his hands back and looked him straight in the eyes.

"I don't know what time she left," he said. "When I finally went to my room, she was closing up the bar and still talking to Sol. He was telling her his regular story about being the captain of his own ship and rambling about whatnot," a story which Oather had heard a million times before.

"Is that all, Oather?"

"Yes," he pleaded, "that's all I know. I don't know if she left or not. You'll have to ask Sol. Can I have my plate back now?"

Gretchen held the plate aloft a moment while she thought about what Oather had said.

"Then asking him is what I'll do," she said. She slammed the plate back down in front of Oather and marched towards the stairs that led up to Sol's room.

"Soliere," she wailed, "Wake up, Sol; I want a word with you."

## 04. Katrina's Great Escape

"You do love me, don't you, Sol?" asked Katrina, as Sol gently kissed her neck.

"Of course I do....um...you don't think I do this with just anyone, do you?"

"Tell me again all the places we'll see on your boat, Sol."

"A ship, my dear," Sol corrected her in between kisses. "A boat is a piddly little thing you use to cross a pond, not to explore the world."

"Oh, right, of course," she replied. "Your *ship* then..."

Suddenly, the girl's entire body froze, and Sol didn't understand why. She raised her head as if she was listening for something. When Sol listened as well, he understood.

The sound of footsteps on the wooden stairs leading to the second story of the inn reverberated through the floor of the room. They were faint but grew steadily louder as they reached the top of the stairway.

"Soliere Forrester! Are you up here?"

Sol instantly knew it was Gretchen, as did Katrina.

"Oh no. She must have come back early," Katrina whispered and hastily leapt out of the bed. "She mustn't find me up here, or she'll fire me for sure."

Gretchen reached the top of the staircase and marched down the hall towards Sol's room. Sol heard each determined step as she approached. Katrina turned pale as she anxiously looked around his room.

"Where can I hide?"

Aside from the bed, a small table next to it, and a short bureau where he kept his clothes, there wasn't much else in the room. Sol preferred a simple living space, besides he was typically gone most of the time and hadn't ever been around long enough to collect many things.

Sol got up and pretended to look around for a place to hide the girl. Katrina rushed to the window and looked out.

"Damn," she said. "It's too high and there isn't enough of a ledge to stand on."

Sol followed her to the window. Looking out, he spotted the manure cart parked in the alley below.

"Jump," he said.

"Into the manure cart?" Katrina looked at him as though he just slapped her with a dead fish.

"Are you crazy? That's disgusting."

Katrina took a step up onto the sill to see if she could stand on the ledge. There wasn't enough room, so she backed down.

Gretchen's footsteps had halted right outside Sol's door. There was a brief pause. Then Gretchen pounded on Sol's door.

"Soliere, are you in there? Is Katrina with you?"

"What am I going to do?" Katrina said. "I really need this job."

Sol and Katrina heard the fumbling of keys outside the room. Sol knew that Gretchen had dozens of keys on her key ring and thought that might buy them a few extra moments.

Katrina turned again towards the open window and looked out. Sol heard Gretchen find the right key and insert it into the lock on his door. The latch turned and the door began to slowly open.

Sol quickly weighed the options. He knew the dung cart was outside, so there was a good chance Katrina wouldn't be hurt. She would be furious, but she'd *probably* forgive him. If she didn't, well she most likely wouldn't be working here that much longer anyway, so why should he care? On the other hand, Gretchen wasn't going anywhere and Sol didn't want to have to deal with that.

With his mind made up Sol stepped up behind Katrina and with one quick, well placed push on her back, sent the girl tumbling out of the window. Almost instantly, Sol heard the distinct splatter of Katrina landing in the cart below. He stole a quick glance to see if she was all right, and saw the young woman scrambling to get herself out of the dung cart. The poor girl was absolutely coated in muck, but at least she was okay and almost out of sight.

Sol whipped back around just as Gretchen entered his room. Sol stepped back to cover most of her view of the window and smiled widely at the older woman.

"Well, good morning, Gretchen."

Gretchen squinted at him. There was a moment of silence before she spoke.

"Where's Katrina? Is she up here somewhere with you?"

Sol looked around his barren room, "Nope, she's not here."

Gretchen glanced around quickly to confirm that there really wasn't anyone else in the room. She walked over to Sol and peered into his eyes, smiling as though she was certain she knew what he was up to. She peeked around him and looked out through his window at the ground below. Sol happily stepped out of her way and let her have a good look.

"Soliere Forrester."

Gretchen only used his full name when he was in trouble.

"I know Katrina was in here with you."

"What are you talking about? As you can clearly see, I'm the only one here."

Gretchen searched around the room again. After a few moments, she looked back at Sol.

"Well...I'm sorry, I guess. I just had the feeling that she was here. Not that I'm saying she was to blame. You have a record for corrupting young girls and they don't need to get involved with someone like you."

"Aw Gretchen, I'm hurt. I'm a good guy."

"Yeah, right. You're good, but you do have a tendency for trouble." Gretchen was beginning to calm down. "I just don't want my workers fraternizing with customers. I do not want the inn to get that kind of reputation."

Sol draped his arm over her shoulders comfortingly, "You have nothing to worry about. You run a very respectable establishment."

"Thank you, dear," she said appreciatively. "Why don't you head on downstairs. I'll make up your room and be down in a moment to make you some breakfast."

## 05. Sol and Oather

"What is all that noise going on around here?" Tanner asked as he walked in.

"Gretchen's just trying to catch Sol and the new girl together."

Tanner sat down in a chair beside Oather and laughed.

"Ohhh, that explains a lot. I just ran into Katrina out back and she smelled awful."

Tanner reached over and ripped off a piece of bread from the loaf sitting in front of Oather.

"What are you and Sol's plans now that you're back in town, Oather? Do you know how long you'll be here this time?"

Oather finished off his enormous plate of food and wiped his mouth on his sleeve. "I don't think we'll be around long this time, Tanner."

"Well, where are you off to next? Are you headed back to the capital?"

Oather was slow to answer. He wasn't sure how much Sol would want him to talk about this.

"You aren't clad in royal robes, yet, so I'm assuming things didn't go well with the Duke."

"Well, things were starting to go our way. I think that Sol just about had him convinced to give us the money for the boat, but then Sol met his daughter…then they went downhill from there."

Oather paused for a moment to swallow another bite of food. "I'm just surprised that we lived, actually."

Tanner smiled and shook his head slowly. "So, are you two going far this time?"

"No, we're staying right here in town."

"Oh, really, now…so what are you doing? Because if you're not going anywhere, why won't you be around long? You're trying to confuse me, aren't ya, boy?"

"Oh, no. We have decided that the fastest way to get what we want is to venture down…" Oather began to say before he was interrupted by Sol, who was coming down the stairs.

Sol gave Oather a quick but silencing glare. "What Oather means is that we're going to stick around, but we're going to be doing some work in another part of the town. It's going to keep us pretty busy for a while, but when we get done we'll come back and see you and Gretchen."

"Ohhhhh, finally some steady work?"

Neither Sol nor Oather responded. Oather could tell that Tanner was getting suspicious.

"What kind of work is it?" Tanner asked. "You going back to working on the docks? That was good money, ya know…and it was honest work."

"No, not exactly," Sol replied as he came over to the table and sat down, "but it should pay pretty well."

Tanner raised an eyebrow and looked directly at Sol with his dark brown eyes, "It is legal, isn't it, Sol?"

"Of course it is, it's completely legal. Don't worry; I'm done with trying to get rich by breaking the law."

"That's good. I can't keep covering for you. You know how much Gretchen worries about you boys. You're like sons to her."

"What's that?" Gretchen called from the stairway.

"Oh, nothing, dear," Tanner yelled over his shoulder as she walked towards them. "The boys think they have actually lined up work around here. They might be around a little more than they have been in the past."

"Oh, that's wonderful."

Gretchen wedged herself between Sol and Oather to give them both a hug.

"Well, you can't go out on an empty stomach." she said, moving around them towards the kitchen. "What do you want to eat, Sol?"

"I'll just finish off this bread…and ale."

"It's too early for ale," Gretchen yelled back through the doorway.

Moments later she walked back into the room carrying a tray. "Here, have some cheese and goat's milk to go with the bread. It's better for you than ale."

Oather watched Sol's face scrunch up as she brought the goat's milk to him. Oather knew Sol hated goat's milk, and watching Sol's reaction to it made a smile creep across his face. He watched as Sol drank it anyway and ate the bread. Neither of them said much else until Gretchen and Tanner left the room to get the tavern ready for the day's customers.

Once Tanner and Gretchen were out of earshot, Oather looked over at Sol and asked, "Why didn't you want me to tell them we were going to the ruins?"

"'Cause it would just make them worry. Gretchen worries enough but that would even make Tanner sweat knowing we were going down there. You've heard him rant about how stupid he thinks people that go down there are."

Oather downed half of his mug in one gulp and took great joy in watching Sol wince as he did it.

"We're only going down to the first few levels. Lots of people go there and still manage to find enough treasure to set themselves up for life. That's all we're doing. I don't think they would get too worked up over that," Oather replied.

"Well, you don't know them as well as I do."

"I nearly do."

"I'd really rather not involve them right now, so let's leave it at that. Besides, don't you still have some stuff to get done before we can do this?"

"Yeah, we need a few supplies but we're starting to run short on money, Sol. We still need rope and my sword was ruined, so I'll need to pay for that when I pick it up later…" rambled Oather.

"I get the idea."

"So, where are we going to get the rest of the money we need?"

"You let me worry about that. I've got a plan in mind that should get us the extra money we need."

Oather raised an eyebrow.

"What are you planning, Sol?" Oather asked, almost not wanting to know.

"Just trust me," Sol replied.

Oather rolled his eyes and let out a sigh, "I'll get what things I can with the money we have left then, and we'll get the rest later."

"That's fine."

Sol got up from the table, stretched, and let out a yawn.

"I'll head out in a little bit and work on my plan this evening. We'll have the money we need by tomorrow, but we'll need to be ready to go pretty quickly in the morning," he said as he headed back towards the stairs to his room.

## *06. Jor'Dan Needs Help*

Chancellor Jor'Dan walked down the long corridor that led to the Emperor's throne room. He was head of the Emperor's secret guild of assassins and certainly did not wish to come to his master for help, but he saw no other way.

On either side of the main entrance to the throne room stood two of the Emperor's personal sentinels. They had been recruited above all others to serve as the Royal Guard and were gargantuan compared to other men--each wore blackened armor which blended them into the shadows of the darkened hall.

Their armor was engraved from helmet to boot with interlocking images of skulls and fangs, much like the full body tattoos found on outlanders. Their breastplates, in particular, were subtly carved to show a demonic face baring its fangs. They kept their visors down so that their faces could not be seen. They were truly meant to terrify any opponent who might stand against them.

The guards opened the massive doors in unison and allowed the Chancellor to enter. As he approached them, he felt the "all too familiar" coldness they seemed to radiate. There was something dreadful about them that always made Jor'Dan feel cold, as if the warmth was being siphoned from his body when he was near them. Chancellor Jor'Dan walked swiftly past the two guards and entered the Emperor's private chamber.

The hall was immense and very dim, lit only by a few sconces placed around the outer edges of the room, causing the ceiling to be lost in shadow. There were only two entrances; the main entrance which had a crimson carpet that led to the Emperor's throne, and the doors that led to the Emperor's state room.

The great hall itself was mostly bare, making it feel even larger than it really was. The walls were hung with giant tapestries--red, with the Emperor's insignia upon it in black brocade. The insignia bore a great dragon that sat upon a globe. The dragon's long tail wrapped around the world several times, and the dragon itself had its wings spread as it appeared to roar up to the heavens.

Aside from the tapestries, only a few of the Emperor's favorite trophies adorned the room. A single black arrow mounted to a white marble plaque was fixed to the wall to his far left, and a badly beaten suit of steel armor hung on a wall to his right.

Jor'Dan approached the base of the steps that led to the high-backed golden throne. On the raised pedestal above him sat an old man, Emperor Tor. His eyes were closed, and his chin rested on the tips of his index fingers, above his clasped hands. He sat there quietly as Jor'Dan stopped and knelt before him at the base of the steps.

"Rise," commanded the Emperor

Jor'Dan got to his feet. "Andrea's out of control, Your Majesty!"

"Enough of the melodrama, Jor'Dan. If you want my help, then you are going to have to act according to your position."

"I apologize, my Liege." Jor'Dan stared at the ground, unable to muster the courage to look the emperor in the eyes.

"What has she done that would bring you to me?"

Jor'Dan thought for a moment. He needed to make his case well or risk sounding weak; and the Emperor didn't tolerate weakness within his ranks.

"I believe she is plotting to take over the guild. I have it on good account that she has met with several of the-"

"Why do I care, Jor'Dan?"

There was a long, awkward silence in the room for several moments.

"Jor'Dan," said the Emperor, "how did you get this position?"

"Sire, I, um," Jor'Dan sputtered as his mind raced for a good answer.

"I gave you this position because of your guile and devious nature. When I promoted you to Chancellor I assumed you would be able to handle those within your guild on your own. Is this not the case?"

"Sire, please list-"

"Silence."

Jor'Dan froze. He could feel his heart race and knew he'd angered the Emperor. A grave mistake for sure.

"What makes you think she is plotting anything? From what I have seen of her, she is young and charming but not nearly as ambitious as you make her out to be."

Jor'Dan made certain the emperor was done speaking before he replied.

"Sire, she didn't use to be like that. It's only been since she got that necklace. The last couple of months she has almost completely changed in personality. I've seen her talking in private with the other assassins and I'm sure that-"

"So you're here because of your paranoid delusions?"

Jor'Dan didn't know how to respond, so he remained silent.

"Tell me more about this necklace and perhaps I won't have you executed for wasting my time."

"It…it's magical, and quite powerful."

"What makes you think that?" the emperor asked coldly.

"It radiates a magic like I've never felt before, but any time I attempt to divine any information about it I'm repelled. I even asked one of your court mages to try and he was nearly burned in the process."

The Emperor's fingertips pressed together in front of his face and his gaze seemed to look straight through the Chancellor. Jor'Dan felt a lump form in his throat as he tried to speak, but couldn't.

A stillness settled over the room. Feeling the painful silence overtake him, he began speaking again.

"The necklace is the secret of her power, your Majesty, I am sure of it."

For a short moment neither of them spoke. The emperor seemed to contemplate what the Chancellor had to say.

"She grows more aggressive and insubordinate with each new assignment," Jor'Dan continued. "We must do something about her."

The Emperor slowly leaned forward in his throne; his right hand rubbed his chin.

"I fail to see why I should take an interest in this, Chancellor," The Emperor said unsympathetically. "It is obviously an internal matter within your guild."

Jor'Dan heard the emphasis on the word 'your' and felt his heart suddenly stop beating. He was now unsure if the Emperor would help him after all.

A cold grin spread across the Emperor's face, "Survival of the fittest, as it were?" The Emperor paused momentarily. "Could it be that you are no longer able to control your own people?"

"I'm sorry, Your Majesty, but she is becoming so powerful I do not know if I can take care of this matter alone anymore." The arrogance Jor'Dan had so proudly displayed just moments before was now entirely overshadowed by his cowardice. "I beg you to assist me. I have been a faithful servant and-"

"Silence!"

Jor'Dan felt beads of sweat form on his brow as he looked up pleadingly at his master.

The Emperor sat back in his throne. Jor'Dan's heart raced. He'd never been this nervous when talking to the Emperor, but he knew that his master was not pleased with him. If he could just get some help in eliminating Andrea, he swore to himself that he'd find a way to get back into his Lord's good graces. He just needed more time.

"Sonilauq," the Emperor called aloud. The sound echoed through the large room. A moment later, a tall, broad-shouldered man entered the throne room.

"How may I serve you, my Lord?"

"I want you to assist the Chancellor here with a little problem. Apparently, he has an upstart within his ranks."

"As you wish, your Majesty," Sonilauq replied.

"Thank you, your Ma-"

"You are dismissed, Jor'Dan. Wait for Sonilauq outside. He'll give you your instructions."

Without uttering another word, Jor'Dan stood and exited the throne room.

\*\*\*

The Emperor waited until Jor'Dan was sufficiently away before he continued his conversation with Sonilauq.

"Sonilauq," the Emperor said.

"Yes, sire." Sonilauq replied.

"I want you to work with Jor'Dan and have him bring Andrea to the Commemoration Ball. Capture this woman and bring her to me...alive."

"Yes, Master, but if I may be so bold..."

"Yes, Sonilauq?"

"Why *did* you promote him to Chancellor?"

The Emperor grinned wickedly and replied, "He's a coward and I enjoy scaring the life out of him. However, this game is growing tiresome."

"I see," Sonilauq replied.

"You also wonder why I am going to help that simpleton, Jor'Dan?"

"Yes, my lord. If he cannot handle an effortless situation such as this by himself, then what business does he have running the guild?"

"Ordinarily I'd agree, but the Chancellor's claims intrigue me, and I'm curious about her necklace. I've heard of such items in the past and would like to investigate my suspicions about what it is. In the event this necklace of hers really doesn't have any power, then I will assess her potential and determine if she'd be a suitable replacement for the Chancellor."

"As you wish."

## 07. Halistan's New Job

Halistan stood at the doorway to Father Angelo's office. He was nervous, though, he didn't know why. He'd stood there hundreds of times before.

Today, however, was different. Today was the first day that he was a full-fledged member of the Healing Order. The last couple of weeks had been a blur to him as he finished his schooling. There had been exams and community works that he'd been assigned that needed attending. Life had recently been tumultuous…at least until this morning.

This was the first morning that he wasn't required to get up early for morning worship at the academy, which would have normally been followed by a full day of class and work that he needed to make sure was done. Since he wasn't required to go, he decided to be bad, sleep in and miss the services. Even after waking late, he'd spent most of his day relaxing in his room and re-reading old books.

The absence of a multitude of things to do seemed strange to him. It wasn't bad, in fact it was kind of a relief, but it felt strange nonetheless. Right now, his only duty was to report to Father Angelo in the afternoon and see what work was needed. There was no set meeting time, so Halistan finally managed to pull himself from his books barely before evening worship services.

Halistan had grown up in the church. His parents had gone missing when he was very young, and they had been added to the list that people generally referred to as 'the lost'. In his years at the church he'd been well taken care of, especially by Father Angelo, who had, in a way, adopted him when he first started taking classes.

Taking a deep breath, Halistan knocked firmly on the heavy wooden door that led to the old priest's office. Several moments passed and Halistan couldn't hear any motion on the other side of the door. He raised his fist to knock again, but just as he did, the door swung open.

"Yes?" Father Angelo said as he opened the door, "Oh, Halistan, come in, my boy."

Father Angelo opened the door fully, allowing Halistan to come in.

"Here, please, sit."

Halistan felt obligated now that his old professor had gone through the effort to clear off a place for him, so he sat down.

"So," Halistan said, not knowing what else to say after that.

Angelo was shuffling around the scrolls and books that were piled high upon his desk. He heard Halistan and turned back towards him. Leaning back against the desk, he looked down at Halistan with a smile.

"I bet you're wondering what we're going to be working on, aren't you?"

"Actually, sir, yes. I've been very curious about that."

A week prior, right before his graduation ceremony, Father Angelo pulled him aside from his other classmates and asked him if he would be willing to delay his missionary trip for the church to work on a special project with him instead. The request took Halistan by surprise, but he was happy because he'd always liked working with Angelo, translating forgotten scrolls and church scriptures.

Father Angelo was a very old priest, easily sixty years of age by Halistan's guess, though he'd never have dared to ask the senior priest for certain. Father Angelo had gained some weight in his later years. His hair was all but gone, and his eyesight had become dreadfully poor, forcing him to use spectacles all the time.

Father Angelo's failing sight was what had led Halistan to assist him before. Halistan often helped Angelo read some of the older texts where the lettering was exceptionally small. Halistan, by comparison was very young, the youngest student to ever graduate as a full Healer at only seventeen.

"If there was one job that you could help me with," Father Angelo asked him, "what would it be?"

Halistan thought about it for a moment. He really didn't have a clue as to what he'd like to do if given the chance.

"Um…traveling to the outer edges of the Empire, healing the sick and bringing them the truth of salvation?"

His reply sounded more like a guess than an answer.

"Bah, a textbook answer," Angelo dismissed Halistan's statement entirely, "I know you better than that. I know that while the missionary work you'll someday do is important, in your heart you love research. I've seen how your eyes light up when we cover the scriptural tales of the ancient knights who fought against the legions of demons in the Great War."

Father Angelo was right. Halistan enjoyed his work as a healer, helping those that needed it, but he loved the opportunities he was given to delve into ancient texts. Unraveling the secrets of the past and reading the tales of adventure is what was exciting to him.

"Come, now," Angelo urged him with another clue. "Think. If you could work in *any* room that I've told you about, where would you work?"

Halistan tried again to determine what Father Angelo was talking about, but came up blank, "Uhhh...I really don't know, Father."

Angelo smiled reassuringly down at him, then reached into the collar of his dark brown robe and tugged on a tiny silver chain that hung around his neck. Slowly, he pulled the chain up, grabbed hold of something, and pulled the chain up over his head.

He held his closed fist out towards Halistan and opened it slightly. A small bluish-silver star dropped from his palm and dangled on the chain.

Halistan stared. "The Star of Salus? How...how did you get it?"

Father Angelo offered the star to him. Halistan took it and inspected it carefully.

The Star of Salus was one of the church's most closely guarded holy relics. It was an artifact created by Salus, God's champion, and had been given as a gift to the very first Patriarch of the church. It was created in the shape of a star, which signified IAO: the name of God, who was the first light of the universe.

Halistan didn't wait for Father Angelo to reply. "Does this mean we'll be working in...?"

Father Angelo nodded, and smiled at Halistan, who struggled to contain his excitement. They would indeed be working in the Vault. The Vault was located underneath the cathedral they stood in. It was a closely guarded secret, known to only the highest ranking members in the church and divulged to Halistan very recently by Father Angelo under the strictest confidence. The Vault was where the church kept all its most important documents--first editions of scriptures written by the founders of the church, ancient texts, and other valuable scrolls and documents that the church had accumulated over the years.

It was also one of the most protected rooms in the city. Powerful enchantments had been placed around it and no one could enter it who did not have in their possession one of the few rare holy relics that belonged to the church, one of which was the Star of Salus.

It took a few moments, but Halistan finally was able to pull his eyes away from the star long enough to look back up at Father Angelo, who was grinning from ear to ear, as Halistan held the priceless artifact.

"What will we be doing?" Halistan asked.

"The Council has recently come into possession of some scrolls that need deciphering and cataloguing."

"Why don't they just take them to the Great Library, where all the other new scrolls are kept?"

Angelo didn't answer. For a moment he stood there, and looked to be carefully contemplating his answer.

"These..." Father Angelo began, but paused. "These are 'special' documents."

"Special?"

"Yes, they were all written in Sckrit."

Sckrit was a very old language that pre-dated the church itself. Legend held that some of the church founders had spoken it and used it like a code, since the language had been all but forgotten even then, more than a thousand years ago. Old children's stories said that Salus taught the earliest members of the church to read and speak Sckrit when the church was founded, but those were just fables.

Halistan and Father Angelo were some of the few within the church who knew this ancient language well. Patriarch Altstaat was a firm believer in keeping the church traditional, so decades ago he had mandated that Sckrit be taught as part of the Healer curriculum.

Most thought that learning Sckrit was a useless skill; so they took only the introductory course and immediately moved on to other courses. Halistan, however, had a particular knack for learning Sckrit and took all four levels of the language, becoming nearly as fluent in it as Father Angelo.

"Sckrit," Halistan replied, somewhat baffled as to why that would make the texts so special. "We've seen other texts in Sckrit before. They are rare but hardly important."

That was true. The few other scrolls they'd seen written in Sckrit had merely been records of the Great War. The news that they'd be deciphering more boring logs and journals didn't enthuse Halistan much.

Father Angelo must have noticed how Halistan accepted the news of their new assignment.

"Come, follow me," the old priest told Halistan, sounding as if he had a gift to show him.

The tone of Father Angelo's voice piqued Halistan's curiosity. With the holy relic in hand, Halistan rose and followed the older priest out of his office. They walked down the rear hall of the cathedral to an old stone staircase that led below the church. After a few twists and turns they came to a massive stone door, carved from granite and covered in intricate runes. Halistan had only been back to this area of the church, in the farthest corner of the catacombs, a few times in his life. The dank corridors of this section had never appealed to Halistan anyway, which had further kept him from wandering back into the area.

"Hold the Star out in front of you," Father Angelo instructed.

Halistan did as he was told and held the Star by its chain out in front of him towards the door. With a loud crack, a vertical line formed in the center of the door and the two halves split open, allowing them access.

Halistan stood there in awe, seeing the massive door open for the first time in his life. Father Angelo walked past him and entered the secret chamber.

"Aren't you coming?"

"Oh...oh, yes," Halistan stammered, and quickly followed after his mentor.

As they entered, the candles in several sconces mounted along the wall came to life. Each candle suddenly lit up with flame, taking Halistan by surprise. The secret chamber was a massive room, much larger than Halistan had thought could ever fit below the sanctuary above. Its walls were lined with shelves full of books. Diamond-shaped compartments in the walls were filled with scrolls. Halistan walked in further, following Angelo, and noticed how the entire room smelled like old paper and leather.

Along the wall to his right, Halistan saw a glass cabinet filled with objects. There were holy symbols that Halistan didn't recognize; a ceremonial vestment and a hat.

Father Angelo walked up next to him and pointed at the garments.

"Those are relics that belonged to previous church elders and Patriarchs," Father Angelo said. "The hat belonged to Patriarch Celius, the first Patriarch of our church."

Halistan was astounded that such a garment could have withstood the test of time. The cabinet must be enchanted, he concluded without asking. Angelo motioned for him to follow and they walked deeper into the ancient room.

The Vault was divided into smaller sub-rooms. The chamber they walked into next was set up as a study, with several chairs and a table near some of the bookshelves. In the center of the room was a huge granite table easily twice the size as the marble altar in the cathedral above. Many scrolls laid unrolled upon the giant slab of rock, with lead weights holding them open. Scattered among the scrolls were a few leather-bound journals, an inkwell, and several quills.

"I'd already begun some of the work," Angelo said, "but my eyes just aren't what they used to be and I was forced to give up."

"What did you decipher already?" Halistan asked. He leaned over to look more closely at the scroll Father Angelo had been working on.

Angelo walked around to the opposite side of the table to look at the scroll with him. In a hushed voice, almost a whisper, the old priest asked, "Have you ever heard the story of Alistair Jaeden?"

"Of course. It was one of my favorite stories growing up."

Father Angelo adjusted his spectacles, pushing them back up the bridge of his nose. "I, too, used to enjoy that story. But after reading this, I'm not entirely sure it was a fairytale."

"What?"

"Here, look at my notes."

Father Angelo pushed his journal across the table. Halistan picked up the book and scanned a few pages. The first page contained a translation which spoke of the final days of the war and of the monastery that Alistair had supposedly built after the war was over.

On another page was a scribbled map of sorts that noted several land markers detailed in the text of the scroll. Halistan looked up. On the table next to the journal laid a map of the eastern region of the Empire.

"You don't honestly think this is real, do you?" A hint of skepticism crept into Halistan's voice.

"Yes, I think this might actually be one of the actual lost scrolls of Alistair," Father Angelo replied, with a big grin and a hint of giddiness in his voice.

"Are you certain?" Halistan asked again, unable to shake his tone of disbelief. "We've been fooled before."

"I know, I know," Father Angelo said dismissively, "but this time I had the parchment inspected by some of the Council members themselves. They were able to use their magic to confirm that this scroll dates back to shortly after the Great War."

"This is unbelievable!"

"It's remarkable, isn't it?" Father Angelo asked enthusiastically.

"I'd still like to go over the translations myself," Halistan replied. "I just don't want to get my hopes up too quickly."

"Oh, yes, I understand completely, we mustn't be hasty in this."

Halistan continued to thumb through the notes that Father Angelo had taken already. The older priest stretched his arms out and yawned loudly.

"Oh my, I must be more tired than I thought."

*It was probably past evening service by this time*, Halistan thought. While not late for Halistan, it was later than the Father usually was up. Halistan knew that Father Angelo regularly awoke hours before morning services to prepare for the day.

Halistan held the journal up, "May I take this and look it over tonight? I can review what you've done already and we'll get a fresh start in the morn-"

"Oh, I almost completely forgot," Father Angelo interrupted. "Tomorrow we won't be working on these. We'll begin these later."

"What?"

Halistan was taken aback by this news. Why bring him down here and show him all of this, if they weren't going to start immediately?

"First thing in the morning, I need you to go find Father Lanis."

"Okay…"

"He'll have new formal robes for you. The church, in the persons of Patriarch Altstaat and the Elders, has been invited to a special event being held tomorrow by the Emperor."

Halistan still didn't understand, but he continued to listen.

"I want you to be one of our attendants."

"Really? Me?"

Halistan didn't know what to make of the news. He'd never been to a formal event before and wasn't sure he'd know what to do.

"Yes. You'll be there to assist me and the other Elders while we attend."

"But…but I've never…"

"Don't worry, Halistan, you'll do fine. I'll tell you everything you will need to know on our trip there. We'll be leaving shortly after noon, so don't be late." Father Angelo smiled at him reassuringly which made Halistan feel better. "Now, come. We both need to get our rest. We have a lot to do tomorrow and not much time to get ready."

Halistan took the book and the map that had accompanied it, and walked out of the great room with Father Angelo. As they left, the massive door shut behind them. Halistan held his hand out to Father Angelo, offering him back the Star of Salus.

Angelo placed his hand on Halistan's shoulder and looked him in the eyes. "You hold on to it for me for the night."

"Really? But, won't you get in trouble…,"

"Listen," Father Angelo cut him off. "I've just entrusted you with one of the most closely guarded secrets of the Healing Order, if not the entire church. I trust you with it as easily as I'd trust my life."

"Thank you," Halistan said. He felt his face turn red.

Angelo patted his shoulder again, "Come, we've got an early day ahead of us. The old priest turned and led the way out of the catacombs and back up to the living quarters of the church.

When Halistan got back to his room, he shut the thick wooden door of his room and bolted the latch. He took off his boots and laid down on his bed with Father Angelo's journal in hand. He couldn't wait to read the notes Father Angelo had made already.

He held the book in his left hand and the Star of Salus in his right. The tiny piece of metal almost seemed to glow as he held it in front of him. The Star was made of Neelum. Neelum, which meant 'holy metal' in Sckrit, was an extremely rare and precious metal that looked like silver but had a sparkly bluish tint to it. It was also one of the strongest metals known in the world. The Knights of the church had rings made of it as a designation of their place in the church, but that's the only other time he'd seen the rare metal used.

He thumbed to the start of the recent translation and began to read. He yawned, and as he read his mind kept wandering to everything he'd been told and shown. He had to read each page several times to understand it because he couldn't seem to concentrate.

Halistan continued to read but felt his eyes getting heavy. He decided to close his eyes for just a moment in order to rest them before he continued reading again.

## *08. Andrea Receives a Visitor*

It was a beautiful cool spring day, the kind that Andrea loved the most. The sun was shining bright through the stained glass windows of her bed chamber. It was almost mid-day by the time she had pulled herself from her large, soft, goose-down bed. She had slept later than usual because she hadn't returned home from her last assignment until quite late.

With each mission she accomplished, she grew bolder in her actions, and she loved the exuberance and confidence she felt after each new success.

She was an assassin, mostly. Sometimes she was a spy for the Emperor, and at other times she was simply a liaison-- whatever was needed to get the mission done. She used her looks and charm to get close to her prey, usually high ranking nobles; then dispatched them, seduced them or got them to tell her their dirtiest secrets.

She knew the necklace was changing her, making her more confident and daring. She couldn't explain it, but the changes all started to happen shortly after she'd acquired it. It began when she met a duke from one of the eastern provinces who had become infatuated with her. Before long, he began to grow on her too. There was just something about how he looked at her, a certain sparkle in his eyes, that drew her in like a dragon was drawn to gold.

The Duke attributed his successes in life to a ring he had recently won in a game against another noble. He called it his "good luck" charm. In Andrea's opinion, the silver ring with the black piece of onyx embedded on it was nice, but hardly anything special. But the Duke loved it and talked about it constantly.

Unfortunately, the Duke's new success brought him enemies. One night Andrea received a message from the guild with orders to kill him. She carried out her orders and returned home, but before she left, she took the ring. After returning home, she had the ring fashioned into a necklace. Since then, the necklace seemed to bring her the same kind of luck that it had once brought to the Duke.

Even though it hadn't been that long, it now somehow felt like a lifetime ago. She remembered that she had been quite enraptured with the Duke at the time, but couldn't for the life of her figure out why.

Andrea was brought out of her reverie by one of her servants--a short, older woman in a long-sleeved white dress with a frilly collar--who came into her room.

"Pardon, Mistress," the servant greeted her. "A gentleman is here to see you."

"Tell him I am not taking appointments today and show him out," replied Andrea. She picked up a brush and began brushing her hair.

"It is Chancellor Jor'Dan that is here to see you, Mistress. He asked me to tell you that before you dismissed him."

"Oh. He has never visited here in person," she replied. "Show him to the salon and tell him I will be with him momentarily."

"Yes, Mistress," The servant bowed and left to go attend to their guest.

*The Guild Master is here?* She wondered. *Whatever brought him here must be important. For him to come here in the open like this...during the day, no less...was very strange.*

She dressed quickly in her long boots, pants and favorite shirt--a long-sleeved purple silk shirt that had ruffles around the collar--and pulled back her dark brown hair before heading downstairs to where her guest awaited her.

Andrea entered the salon and saw that he sat on a bench looking out a large arched window at the fields that lay east of her home. She entered the room and bowed before him.

"Good day, Chancellor."

"Good day to you, my prize pupil."

"I'm sorry to keep you waiting. I did not expect you."

"Do not apologize. It is I who came unannounced. I do not normally make such appearances, but your work has certainly warranted it."

Andrea was confused momentarily. She did not know if he meant that she had done an unsatisfactory job on the mission he had sent her on last night, or if he was pleased with her recent accomplishments.

"Is there a place where we might speak more…in private?"

"Oh yes," she replied. "Please, follow me. We can speak more openly in my office." The Chancellor rose and followed Andrea up the stairs.

She opened the door and ushered Jor'Dan into her office. It was ornately decorated, with a huge oak desk and fine dark wooden chairs. The walls around the room were lined with bookshelves, and a large landscape painting hung on the wall behind her desk. Everything was in perfect order, the way she preferred it.

"Please, sit."

She motioned to a leather-backed chair. Jor'Dan took his seat as Andrea rounded the desk and sat down herself.

"What brings you here, Guild Master?"

"Many things bring me here," he said, smiling. "First, I wish to congratulate you on a job well done. Everyone said that Sir Gavin was untouchable."

Andrea simply smiled at the praise from the Guild Master.

"Thank you," she replied.

"How in the name of the gods did you manage to pull it off?"

Andrea started to reply but was cut off.

"It doesn't matter." Jor'Dan smiled again. "Like a good performer, one mustn't give away all their secrets."

"I am happy you are pleased with my work. The praise should be yours, though, for it has been under your guidance that I have flourished."

Her left hand instinctively rubbed the necklace.

"That's true, but you flatter me." Nevertheless, his chest swelled with pride, "It's your exceptional talents that bring me here."

"How so?"

"I have another mission for you. This one is most important to the guild."

"Another mission so soon, Guild Master? I just returned from my last mission. Surely it isn't that important. Perhaps Althea could-"

"No, dear. I am sorry, but I don't trust anyone but you to do this. The very life of our guild is at stake." Jor'Dan's voice took on a serious tone as he spoke.

"How so?" she asked. "We are the most powerful assassin's guild in the five kingdoms. What could possibly threaten us?"

Jor'Dan sat straight up, all signs of pleasantry drained away from his face, "We are under attack by a very powerful opponent, a man by the name of Sonilauq."

"I've never heard of him; he couldn't be that powerful."

"Oh, he's powerful, rest assured. He has had the ear of the Emperor for some time now, and he seeks to destroy me as well as our guild so that his favor with the Emperor will not be opposed."

Andrea said nothing for a moment as silence fell upon the room.

"I fear, my child," he continued, "that he is plotting my demise. If that is in fact the case, then once I am gone, all the members of our guild will be hunted down and killed one by one. He cannot take the chance that one of us might survive and seek retribution. You, being the highest ranking member under myself, will be sought out and killed first. You are his greatest liability."

"How is it this man poses such a threat to us, when I have never heard of him?" Andrea replied, bewildered. "I know every noble of every rank in the Empire."

"He's a very careful individual. He's very powerful and there are rumors that he might even be a sorcerer, but no one seems to know for sure."

Jor'Dan pulled a handkerchief from his pocket and wiped his brow.

"I'm sure you have seen him before, though. He always accompanies the Emperor. The few times the Emperor has attended his own functions, Sonilauq has always been there."

"Yes, I do believe I have seen him. Now that you mention him I do seem to remember him vaguely but, it's very fuzzy…"

"He is more powerful than he lets on," Jor'Dan replied. His voice became a little more than a whisper as he talked about his adversary.

"If he does seek to destroy us, we need to strike him first. I'm assuming that is your plan, Guild Master," she concluded, her determination coming through her voice as she spoke.

"Oh yes, my dear. Undoubtedly so."

"Where can I find him?"

"That information is what brings me to your home so urgently. The Emperor is having a gathering tomorrow night at his Summer Keep, north of the capital city."

"Yes, I know. I have been there several times."

"He is holding a ball for some of his highest ranking court members as well as for other prominent and powerful allies of his from throughout the Empire."

"You wouldn't happen to be on the guest list, would you, Chancellor?" she asked.

He smiled. "Now that you mention it, yes, I am. You will accompany me as my guest. This is a masquerade ball, so you will need a costume. A mask, at the very least, is required."

"That should make things much easier."

"Yes, I know. That is why I suggested it to the Emperor. Just my way of trying to help you out, my dear."

"I assume that Sonilauq will be there?"

"Yes, he will be," Jor'Dan replied.

"It's unusual for the Emperor to attend this kind of function. The ones he does attend are more for business than pleasure."

"This one, too, is business, just masked as a social event. As you know, the Emperor does not have an heir. In such cases, it's been traditional for the Emperor to select an heir from among the children of the court. He would adopt that child, who would become his apprentice and eventually take over the throne."

"I see," replied Andrea, her mind already wandering to ideas about what costume she should wear.

"And during this time, it will be up to you to distract Sonilauq and complete your task. Understood?"

"Yes, Guild Master."

"Good," Jor'Dan replied as he rose from his chair. "I will pick you up tomorrow after dusk and we will make our way to the party. I trust you have something to wear?"

"I'm sure that I can find something that will suffice."

Jor'Dan seemed pleased as he left the office, with Andrea following him. They made their way down the stairs to the front door. Outside, his carriage was waiting for him.

He stopped on the doorstep and turned to look at her face to face. His eyes locked with hers. "This is our one chance. You must be prepared for anything."

"Yes, Guild Master. I already know what I'm going to do."

"Excellent. I will leave the details in your most capable hands."

He entered his coach and motioned for the driver to depart. Andrea watched as he left, then retreated back into her home.

"Clarissa."

Moments later one of her maidens scurried into the town hall.

"Summon Axel. We have a costume to make."

## *09. Unwelcome Home*

"Light," commanded the wizard who stood at the vine-covered entrance to the ruins below. With one single word, a small glowing orb appeared in front of him. As he maneuvered through the narrow opening of the cave, the ball of light followed him and illuminated the darkness ahead.

His name was Zaroth. He was a tall man, who more often than not, wore maroon robes with strange embroidery upon them. Golden glyphs lined the edges of his sleeves and ran along the hem. Despite his advanced age, his features were sharp and distinct. Underneath the hood of his robes were a set of piercing bluish gray eyes and a long sharp nose. His thin lips were ringed by a silvery moustache and a short, graying beard.

"Haven't been back here in a while. Time sure hasn't changed this place very much," the old man mumbled to himself.

The ancient hall was dank and smelled musty. He had to hunch over to allow his tall thin frame to navigate under the low ceiling of rock that stretched out before him. Following the cavern's twists and turns, he came to a larger opening.

The tunnel widened and its ceiling rose as he entered into a town hall. The corridor in front of him extended in a straight line, with no turns, openings, or crisscrossed paths. The walls themselves were made of polished stone bricks, all perfectly flat and unlike those made by any human hand.

He ran his hand along the smoothness of the stone walls and marveled at how little time had diminished them. He remembered how long it had taken to create them when this stronghold was built. Snapping himself out of his reverie, he continued to follow the passage for a short while until he came to a fork.

"Ah, here we go," he mumbled again, as he glanced in both directions. Both passages looked completely identical. Thinking back, he remembered what used to live in these halls to the right. He would go left for now, he decided, just in case it hadn't died yet.

A short way down the passage, the old wizard stopped and pulled back the hood of his robe, exposing his long silver-gray hair. Turning his head sideways, he listened for any noise coming down the hall. He heard nothing, but squinted his eyes as if in anticipation of impending danger. He reached down to his side and quickly freed a small pouch from his belt.

Reaching inside, he retrieved a vial of crushed red gemstones. He uncorked the small vial and knelt down. Carefully, he poured a small amount of red powder onto the ground just in front of him, then corked the small bottle and put it away. He closed his eyes and whispered a small enchantment. With a flash of red light, the powder ignited. All that remained was a small plume of red smoke.

Several steps ahead of the old man, an exact copy of himself came into existence. It faced the same direction as Zaroth and mimicked his movements perfectly. He rose to his feet once more, and he and the doppelganger both began walking forward.

He continued down the corridor, approaching another fork in the way. Both the right and the left passages were shrouded in darkness.

Stopping for a moment, he reached into another pouch and pulled out a palm-sized crystal disk. Holding the disk in his hands, he closed his eyes and began to concentrate. The disk spun for a moment in his hand, then suddenly stopped and sprouted a bright violet flame. The color of the flame showed him the direction he needed to go in order to seek his prize. The colors corresponded to the hues of a rainbow with red pointing left, violet pointing right and the others making up the directions in between.

"This way then," he mumbled. "It won't be long now until I find the fragment…and by Dominia's ghost, I'm going to find this one!"

He had set out on his quest to find this particular onyx fragment months ago. He used every magical detection device in his possession, but the pieces still seemed to elude him. Over the years, the other fragments were rumored to be found by people. Soon after one was found, it would suddenly disappear and become completely lost to any form of detection. It was as if the fragments simply ceased to exist, sometimes taking their owners with them.

Zaroth had heard, for example, of a farmer who had found a fragment and fashioned it into a cloak clasp. The farmer had a bit of a gambling problem, and after he began wearing the onyx clasp, he couldn't help but win. The old man thought that the fragment brought him luck, and would not sell it at any price.

Not more than a fortnight after he had found the fragment, he came up missing. It was rumored that after a long night of gambling and drinking at a local tavern, the farmer was having more of his amazing luck. One of his opponents had lost nearly all of his money, but was so sure that he could win his next hand that, to stay in the game, he offered all his lands as his wager. The farmer took the offer, and when the players laid down their cards, he had once again won the game.

The losing man, however, accused the farmer of cheating. The other townsmen who played and some, who had merely watched the game, also believed this was true. The losing men ganged up against the farmer and attempted to kill him. The farmer fled for his life and quickly ran out of the town. He was pursued into the woods nearby, where he was eventually cornered by the townsmen. Somehow, he managed to get away. Some people said that the farmer had used magic, but regardless of how he got away, no one ever saw him again.

Stories such as this had become quite common for the wizard. It seemed as if every time Zaroth came close to finding a fragment of the orb, the piece would mysteriously disappear. Of the one hundred and fifty individual pieces that he had sought, almost all of them had vanished under mysterious circumstances. The pieces all seemed to fall into the hands of people who, after finding them, prized the little bits of onyx above all their other possessions and kept it with them at all times.

Recently, Zaroth had found out the locations of the very last two pieces. One was rumored to belong to a woman who lived in the capital city. She had the tiny black stone made into a brooch or necklace or some other piece of jewelry. She was, Zaroth had determined, a prominent woman in society. That alone made her a very hard person to approach without arousing suspicion, and Zaroth had decided to wait before attempting to retrieve that piece until he could get more information about her. The last piece, however, was right here in the ruins of Tyric Nor. This was most fortunate for him, since he knew them so well...or at least he used to.

He continued down the passageway, remembering the first time he had walked these ancient corridors. That was a lifetime ago, and some things had changed over time. There were some new passages that he didn't remember and others that had begun to wear away and didn't look anything like they once did.

He looked at the disk again. The flame began to flicker and change colors; first to blue, then to green and finally to red.

"That's odd," the wizard mused. He tapped the disk to see if it was working correctly, but the flame wouldn't change back. As the wizard looked at it, it began to flicker more quickly: the fragment was getting close. Very close.

Putting the disc back into his pouch, the old man stood still and listened. Making himself as still as possible, he fixed his gaze upon the clone which stood equally still in front of him. There was no sound--but despite the quiet, he felt that he was not alone. He drew a sign in the air and muttered an enchantment. Soon he felt a wave of energy envelope him as he became invisible. The clone mimicked his actions but cast no spell, and remained visible. With another command, Zaroth extinguished the ball of light.

He moved cautiously down the corridor behind his doppelganger, waiting for whatever force he sensed to make itself known. He heard a muffled sound of cloth rubbing past rock coming from behind him. He turned quickly, only to find nothing there. Another sound came from behind him, to his left.

Since he was invisible, he decided to stand still and hope to remain unnoticed. Once his pursuers went for the illusion of himself, then he could attack. For several moments nothing happened. No noises at all, from anywhere, could be heard. He waited a few more moments. Still, nothing. He took a few steps forward and waited again.

Another sound, a crack much like a rock hitting the stone floor, echoed from a little further down the corridor. He remained motionless; preparing a massive attack spell to counter what was inevitable. The sound got a little closer. Again it sounded like cloth brushing against stone. He pulled a spell component from his pouch and prepared to unleash the deadly attack.

Then the movement stopped. He heard the muffled sound of a blow dart and felt a sharp prick hit his chest. He unleashed a barrage of magic, bolts of lightning burst from his fingertips. With a tremendous electrifying sizzle, they lit up the passage. Blue and white light streamed down the corridor and bounced off the walls, but hit nothing. His doppelganger disappeared into a puff of smoke as the bolts passed through it.

"Light," Zaroth said, anxious to see what had hit him. The familiar small ball of light appeared above him. He looked down and saw a small dart sticking out of his chest. He ripped the small piece of metal away and threw it to the ground.

"Damn goblins with their night vision and poison da..." Zaroth collapsed to the ground in a heap.

When Zaroth awoke, he was lying on the floor of a cave. Torches on the wall gave off a little light. The stench of goblins overwhelmed him as he awoke. He hated the foul little beasts. They smelled like mildew mixed with dragon dung.

Slowly, his old eyes began to adjust. He could tell he was no longer in the ruins--instead of carefully measured stonework, the walls here were natural rock. Judging by the kind of stone, he guessed that he was now in the caves that lied beyond the original layout of the stronghold, although he wasn't really sure. The cell he found himself in was small, but he was not bound in any way, much to his surprise.

Zaroth's head rang with pain, like massive drums pounding inside his skull. It hurt even worse, if that were possible, when he tried to think. Holding out his hand, he tried to cast another light spell. As soon as he started to mumble the enchantment, his head burst into agony, this time more pain than he could handle.

"The poison they used on you will prevent you from using your magic, wizard."

The voice came from a nearby cell. Zaroth stood up, dusted himself off a little, and looked into the other cell.

Like his own, it was a small alcove, sealed with iron bars and a gate. The prisoner was an elf, short by human standards but probably of average size for his race. The elf wore dark leather clothing. The only things about him that were not dark were his light skin and golden eyes. The poor elf looked haggard; he had chains on his arms, legs and even across his chest. He had bruises on his face, and hung from his shackles as though he didn't have the spirit to live any longer.

"Do you know where we are?" Zaroth asked.

"We are prisoners of the Da'Kar tribe of goblins. Who are you?"

"I am Zaroth. Who are you and how did you get caught here? I thought your kind lived in the great forest of Terrazaz, to the east."

"We do, but my party was betrayed to the goblins by one of our own," hissed the elf as he spat on the ground in anger. "Now my party is dead and I have been captured. They tortured me for information, but they couldn't get what they wanted, so now they will use me as a sacrifice to some demon they worship as a god."

Zaroth was quiet for a moment. Then he said, "That still doesn't explain what you were doing all the way over here."

"We were sent here looking for an enemy of the Elven people, a wretched, decaying monster who calls himself the *Defiler*," explained the elf.

"I see," said Zaroth. "You tracked him all the way here? That's quite a distance from your home."

"We have been following him for many months. I am Khu-Rá, the leader of the King's elite hunters."

"Ah," replied the wizard, as he stroked his silvery beard.

"Enjoy your last few moments of life, human," scoffed the elf, "for they will most likely kill you with me or worse...use you as the ceremonial dinner."

That idea didn't appeal at all to Zaroth. It was time to get out of here.

"Well, enough of this," Zaroth said under his breath. He reached down to his sash and realized that his pouch was gone. The throbbing of his head seemed to be getting worse.

"You don't think they would leave you with anything that you could use, do you?"

"Yes, I suppose you're right."

Zaroth reached into his right sleeve and pulled out a small pouch that had been concealed there. Opening the pouch, he pulled out a small bit of root, placed it in his mouth and started to chew. His mouth flooded with juice from the tiny plant and almost immediately the throbbing in his head began to fade. The plant was quite bitter, but its juice was refreshing as it quelled the pain coursing through his head.

"It's a good thing I always keep a little Benali root on me for emergencies," he said.

He could already feel his head clearing and his strength coming back. Not all at once, but his head felt a little better anyway. Zaroth sat down with his back to the wall of his cell, and tried to rest.

Before long, several goblins walked in. They were slightly shorter than men, about the same height as the elf, but much stockier in appearance. They were a bit large for goblins though, and were more than likely cross-breeds of some kind. Their green skin was covered by crudely made leather and bronze plating that they used as armor. Their eyes were yellow and large fangs protruded from their jaws. Each goblin carried a rusted sword, and Zaroth knew these must be the creatures that had captured him. Behind them walked figure whose face was covered by a cowl.

The goblin guards took their places on either side of the elf's cage. The elf raised his head and looked at the man standing outside his cell.

The cloaked figure knelt so that he and the elf could look at each other eye to eye.

"So, you fell for our little trap," mocked the cloaked figure.

The elf hissed something back at the figure in his native language. Zaroth didn't understand--he knew many languages but had never bothered learning Elven.

"Come now, Khu-Rá," said the voice under the hood. "Turnabout is fair play."

The elf gave him back a look of pure contempt.

"After we kill you and offer your soul to Castor, I'm going to take your head and give it back to your father."

"One day, Marcus, my people will catch you and my father will finish what he started the last time you two met." Khu-Rá replied with a grim smile. "How's the face? Feeling any better?"

The cloaked figure pulled back his hood, revealing his head. His head was little more than a skull atop his shoulders. The skin that used to cover it was burned to the bone and looked decayed. There was no hair left upon the skull or face aside from a few strands that hadn't fallen out yet. His eyes were completely exposed and just sitting in the sockets. There were no eyelids, just rotting flesh upon the bone.

"Your father will pay for this. The curse he has laid upon me has left me somewhere between living and dead...and he will pay. First with the life of his son, then with his own."

"I think it's fitting," retorted the elf, seeing that he had touched a nerve with his captor. "Everything you touch withers and dies. Now your face looks just like your soul."

"Gloat while you can, for soon your soul will be little more than coinage for the gods. Do not worry; I will be sure to tell your father of your demise before I cut his head off, too."

Khu-Rá scowled at the Defiler and jumped up, only to be yanked back by the heavy chains that bound him.

"Now that must have touched a sore spot," the Defiler said.

"You'll never have enough power to defeat my people or my father."

The Defiler reached under his cloak and pulled out a necklace that he was wearing under his garments--a thick silver ring that encircled an onyx ball the size of a human eye, dangling from a leather string. He held it out in front of the elf.

"With this, my power will be strong enough to defeat your people and I will see them groveling at my feet. After that, I'll have the entire forest burned to the ground along with every living creature in it."

Rising back up, the Defiler pulled his hood back over his head and left the room, followed by his goblin guards.

"The fragment," Zaroth mumbled. "So it is here."

Unfortunately, he was still too weak to take it for himself. It was just as well. He would prefer, for the moment, not to have direct contact with the cursed item. The fragments were said to be able to corrupt even the most powerful beings. For now it would be best to bide his time, to wait and regain his strength.

"Well, friend," said Khu-Rá, looking up again, "I don't know what brought you to this cursed place, but this trip will be your last. What brought you here anyway? Was it worth your life?"

The elf seemed to be growing extremely weary and barely able to hold his head up any longer.

"I came here looking for something," replied the wizard.

"It's a shame you'll never find it."

"Oh, I don't know about that. You never know how things are going to turn out." Looking over at the opposite cell, he saw that the elf had passed out and hadn't heard a word he'd said.

"Yes," Zaroth smiled, "one can never tell what fate has planned."

## 10. Sinister Dealings

Oather had left after breakfast to get the rest of the supplies that he and Sol would need before they set off for the ruins underneath Tyric. Sol was drinking ale with Tanner as customers began drifting in for an evening meal and a stiff drink after working all day. The tavern was filling up rapidly and the barmaids were starting to get busy serving food and drinks.

"So, you gonna let poor Oather do all the leg work of getting supplies for wherever it is you two are going?"

"He's got to earn his keep," Sol said, taking another swig from his mug.

Tanner laughed as he set another mug on the tray for Katrina to take to a table. "You mean you just don't feel like walking all over the city. I swear, Sol, you've always been lazy."

Sol pretended to be hurt by Tanner's remark.

"What do you mean by that? I work very hard."

"You only work hard at thinking of ways to swindle people out of their money. Speaking of which, I'm surprised you are still here. By this time of night I thought you would be out doing something."

The door to the inn opened as more people came inside. Sol caught a glimpse of a couple of women who were standing outside talking to one another.

Sol jerked his attention from the girls and back to the conversation at hand.

"Don't worry; I do have plans for tonight. I'm meeting some people. I've actually got to get going," Sol said as he stood and put on his cloak. Moments later he was walking out the door, drawing his hood over his head as he left the building.

Not long after leaving the *Lucky Duck,* Sol arrived at another tavern. When he entered, he saw a large, beefy man sitting at a table along the far right wall. He walked over to the table.

"Good to see you again, Burman." Sol took a seat and pulled his hood back.

"Took you long enough, Sol."

Burman was past middle age and was rather brawny. He had greasy, dark brown hair with wisps of gray.

"Are we ready?"

"Aye, I have everyone ready," Burman replied. He took a swig from his mug.

"So, who do we have with us tonight?"

"I was able to get Laya and Boll."

The barmaid arrived and set down a couple of drinks for them, "Oh yeah," Burman added, "Laya asked me to give you this when I saw you."

Before Sol could react, the big man drew back his arm and punched Soliere square in the face. Sol's seat flipped over and he fell backward onto the floor. When he hit the ground, all the conversation in the bar came to a sudden halt. Silence engulfed the room.

Sol rubbed his jaw where Burman had hit him. He got up and staggered for a moment, then set his chair back up and sat down.

"What the hell was that for?"

"Do I need to hit you again to jog your memory?"

Sol scooted his seat back just out of arms reach. "No, that's quite all right, really."

"I didn't hurt you that bad, you big baby. I do think that Laya was a little hurt by you, though. You know, she's liked you for as long as we can all remember; then to sleep with her best friend? Sol, that's low, even for you."

"A man has needs."

"Do I need to hit you again? That's my niece we're talking about, Sol. Don't forget that."

"I know, Burman, you know I'm kidding…right? Anyway, can we get back to business here? Good thing you didn't spill my grog when you hit me."

"Hey, I was just passing along the message, that's no reason to hurt an innocent drink." Burman straightened himself in his seat. "Now listen up. We're going to be just inside the Southern gates. The city guards don't go down that way much, so we shouldn't have any interruptions."

Sol nodded in agreement as Burman continued explaining the plan.

"Laya will be ready soon. I'll go and meet her and Boll right after I leave here. I don't expect it will take us too long to get to the spot I picked out." Burman took another drink and finished the mug. "I don't even know why you'd want to try this tonight, Sol? It's not like many people will be coming into town. It would be better to wait until-".

"Yes, I know, Burman, but we don't need too many hits to get the extra cash we both need. One or two and we'll both be set."

"We'll be lucky to even get one."

"Well, look for one with a horse. If it's a good horse, then we can get a little more from selling it."

"Aye," replied Burman. "I just don't like horses. They always kick me."

"Don't stand behind them, then. This will work like a charm, it always does. Trust me."

Burman rolled his eyes at Sol. "Well, we should get the others and get over there. You just be waiting and be ready to move in as soon as we signal."

"All right. I'll see you just after dark."

Sol stood and grabbed his cloak. As he prepared to walk away, Burman called him back to the table.

"One more thing, Sol. We're all getting an even split this time. No more of this fifty percent for you and fifty percent for the three of us kind of thing."

Sol looked shocked. "Burman, I would never ever consider short-changing you like that."

"You're such a bad liar, Sol."

Sol took his leave of the tavern. Burman left a few moments later and headed in the opposite direction.

## *11. No Good Deed Goes Unpunished*

It was nearing nightfall and the sun was setting over the ocean. Up ahead, just past the city of Tyric Nor, Serieve could see the last of the day's light shining on the mountains to the north and the snowcapped peaks just beyond the city. The tallest mountain tops were masked by a layer of clouds, but the range as a whole was beautiful to behold. The autumn air, however, was cool and he was stiff from riding from Adessa.

"We're almost there, Pressia," he said, reaching down and patting the chestnut colored horse on her neck. His horse neighed in response as if to say she was glad. He could see the walls of the city off in the distance, still some ways away, but at least the end was in sight.

The tired horse trotted along the stony trail as they reached the point where lit torches began to line the road leading to the city. In the gloom, Serieve could make out the once great gates of Tyric Nor. The walls of the city still towered above their surroundings, but over the millennia had begun to fall apart. Once-massive beams of wood now stood half-rotted and decayed. The wall was dotted with huge holes where the wood had given way and the stone fell.

Approaching the gates, he got a scent of something that didn't agree with him. Mounds of garbage and refuse had been tossed out of the city through the holes in the great wall. Serieve saw broken pots, rusted weapons, shoes and other things that he couldn't make out but could certainly smell.

He could see the gates clearly now. The hinge on one of the enormous doors was rusted and broken, leaving the door open and leaning against the city wall. It would never be closed again.

Upon entering the city, he saw that there were very few people out. As he slowly trotted down the empty street, he saw a man lighting the street lamps. The street was narrow and the stone buildings on either side of him were tall with thatch roofs.

Many of the buildings had been shops at one time. Now most of them were empty and dark, except for a couple of small taverns and a few homes here and there. It was sad how this great city had dwindled and decayed. Now that fewer people came here to scavenge the ruins under the city, there wasn't much of an economy left.

Hundreds of years ago, the city had been booming with adventurous men seeking their fortunes in the depths of Tyric. Serieve had heard stories of the ruins all his life. He had even come to this city once or twice as a child, but the city didn't seem as big to him now as it did back then.

This wasn't his first choice of how to get the money he needed to pursue his dreams of becoming a knight of the Empire. Tough times brought tough decisions; and this was by far the fastest way he could think of to get the gold he needed.

The ruins were rumored to have been created during the time of the Great War by a group of powerful wizards and was once an immense underground stronghold. Some said that the ruins were an ancient dwarven city that had been abandoned before men created Tyric Nor; others said that the gods had created it for some yet unknown reason. No one really knew.

All that had been known since before anyone could remember was that the ruins were full of riches and riddled with monsters whose very descriptions would turn one's hair gray. Many men had ventured down into the ruins and had come back with more riches than one could dream--and many more had gone down and not come back at all. Serieve pondered this as he made his way through the darkened streets.

"It won't be much longer now," Serieve said reassuringly to the horse. "Let's just get out of this part of town. This isn't the kind of place where you want to stop, trust me." He patted the horse on the neck again. The horse neighed with her head down and kept walking. Then, without warning, she stopped and her left ear flickered.

Off to his left he heard a muffled cry. He looked in the direction of the sound, but the street was empty. He heard the cry again.

Serieve dismounted and led the horse by the reins. He listened intently as he walked down the deserted street. Cautiously, he approached an alley that lie between two large abandoned buildings. Again, he heard a woman cry followed by the sound of ripping cloth. Serieve instantly dropped the reins of his horse; he drew his sword and charged into the dark alley.

It took a moment for his eyes to adjust. The only light came from the blood red moon that hung in the night sky. As he got closer, he heard a woman sobbing and again heard the sound of tearing cloth. It didn't take him long to find her. Two large men were holding a struggling young woman. The fatter of the two held her arms and covered her mouth with a large hand to prevent her from screaming. The other man, who was taller but thinner, was ripping off one of her sleeves.

"Quiet, tramp. The more you struggle the more this is going to hurt," the thug said.

"You'd better let her go if you know what's good for you."

Both men looked at Serieve as though he was crazy for interrupting them.

"Ya think you can make us, boy?" snarled the fat man. The woman's pleading eyes stared at Serieve as he moved towards the two men with his drawn blade.

"Let her go!"

The man standing in front of the young woman drew his sword.

"Let's see if you can make us."

The big man lunged with his blade towards Serieve, but he easily dodged out of the way. The man holding the woman tossed her aside and also drew his sword.

Serieve took a defensive stance facing the two advancing men, drawing an additional dagger with his left hand. Again, the taller man lunged at him, followed in turn by the fat man. Serieve deflected the blade of his first attacker and managed to duck the man's wild swing, the force of which spun him around. Serieve countered with a quick swipe of his own blade and cut his attacker's back. He resumed his defensive stance, this time maneuvering himself between the two thugs and the woman so he could protect her.

The tall man cursed as blood trickled from the shallow cut Serieve had inflicted.

"I'm telling you one last time, get out of here and leave the girl alone."

"Yer gonna pay for that, runt."

The taller man, who was standing beside his cohort, quickly nodded his head. Serieve noticed the gesture but didn't understand what he was doing until he heard a voice from behind him.

"Sorry, love," he heard the girl behind him say, just before a hard blunt force struck the back his head.

He staggered and dropped his weapons. His vision blurred and blood poured into his eyes. Serieve grabbed his head with both hands. He fell to his knees, and his head swam before he fell over completely. He saw the girl he'd been defending standing over him, wielding a baton of some kind.

"See how much money he has, Laya."

"I'm gonna gut him for cuttin' me like he did," said another voice... then the darkness overtook him.

Serieve came to and was surprised that he was still alive. He had thought that surely he was going to be killed. It was still very dark and he couldn't see a thing except for a large, dark blur right above him.

"Wake up," said a voice.

He felt a hand pat him on the face.

"Come on, you've got to get up in case they come back with friends."

Before Serieve could understand what was going on, his rescuer helped prop him up so he could sit up against the alley wall. Serieve's hand went to his head again. It throbbed with pain. His vision began to clear up, giving him a better look at the person helping him. He could see he was still in the alleyway but at least his assailants were gone.

"What happened?"

Serieve couldn't make out too many of the other man's features. All he could see was a kneeling figure wearing a dark cloak. The hood was up so his face couldn't be seen.

"You'll be all right," said the man reassuringly. He waved his hand in front of Serieve's face. "Can you see anything yet?"

"Yes, things are starting to come into focus. Thank you."

He paused for a moment.

"Who were those people? How did I manage to stay alive?" He tried to sit up a little more and comfort his aching head.

"Shhh, friend, those were just common low-life thieves. This part of town is full of 'em."

Serieve slowly began to feel a little better. He instinctively reached out to find his sword and dagger. They were still lying next to him.

"My horse, did they take my horse?"

He tried to get to his feet but was still a little woozy so he sat back down.

"Horse?"

"Yes," Serieve answered, "I left my horse on the street while I came to save the girl."

"I'm sorry, I didn't see a horse," the stranger replied as Serieve kept trying to regain his bearings.

"You're actually quite lucky I fended off those bullies. I put myself at great personal danger…Some people might even say that makes me a hero. I'm sure that some people would even go so far as to want to reward me for such heroism…"

Serieve looked up at him with a quizzical look upon his face. The man's voice sounded familiar to him, but he couldn't place it.

"I hear the going rate for having your life saved is worth at least a hundred Gold Imperials."

Serieve pushed back the hood on the man's cloak and saw that he had dark brown hair cut short and blue eyes.

"Soliere?" Serieve asked, unsure if it could possibly be him or not.

"Huh?"

"Soliere. It is you!"

"Ser…Serieve?"

"By hell's gate, what are you doing here in Tyric? Last time I saw you, your brother had started working with your father and you were having delusions of becoming a knight. How is your family anyway?"

Serieve's heart sank at the mention of his father.

"What's wrong? Did I say something?"

"No, Sol, things recently just haven't been going well for my family," he said as he started to stand up. Sol helped him to his feet and the two men left the alley.

"So what's happened? Things not going well back at the 'shire?"

"Let's get going and I'll fill you in."

By now Serieve had regained his composure and was walking pretty much on his own. The two men started walking down the street.

"How long's it been, Sol?"

"Oh, I don't know. Let's see…I was sixteen when I last saw you so that must be a good seven or eight years ago."

"A lot's changed since then," said Serieve, solemnly. "My father passed away about two years ago and my brother Bourne took over the family lands."

"Oh, I'm sorry to hear that. Your father was a good man. So now your brother is running things? That couldn't be good."

"Bourne's not so bad, Sol. You only say those things because you don't like him." Serieve smiled, feeling a little less saddened by things now.

"Well, at least you're smiling again."

"Times have been tough and Bourne really has done everything he can to get things going again, but things take time. He has spent almost all our family's money on rebuilding the shire, but with the taxes that the Empire levies on us, people just aren't able to make ends meet."

"So things back at the shire sound like they have seen better days. That still doesn't explain what you're doing in Tyric."

"Well, before my father passed away, he had been able to secure me a position as a squire for a knight. There were three of us under the knight's tutelage, but as you know, that is very expensive."

"No, I didn't really know that…not that I ever really felt the need to find out what it took to become a knight."

"Well, as squires, we have to pay the knight for our training under him and we are responsible for all our personal expenses, too."

"Wait, you have to pay him for the privilege of working for him and pampering him?"

"That sums it up pretty well, actually."

"That sounds like a great idea. It's no wonder more people aren't doing it. It sounds like you were the one that broke the bank, not your brother."

"Not funny, Sol. You are right though, it was getting terribly expensive. After my father died, I stayed in service with Sir Gavin for as long as I could afford to. Recently, my brother had to cut off my allotment and divert the money to hiring more hands for the fields."

"This is making more sense…you're going down into the ruins, aren't you, Serieve?"

Serieve was quiet for a moment before he spoke.

"Yes. That was my plan. I am a man now, not a full knight by any means, but I think I can hold my own well enough…at least enough to go in and make it out alive."

"Yeah, you really proved that back there," Sol said, laughing.

"That was not an adequate demonstration of my abilities. That harlot struck me from behind while I was trying to save her."

"Hey, settle down, I was just teasing you. Besides, you really have to learn to expect the unexpected, my friend."

The two men turned another corner and soon came to a tavern. Above the entrance hung a large wooden sign, engraved with a smiling duck holding a mug.

"Here, let's get a bite to eat," said Sol. "On you, of course. After all, I did save your life."

The place was busy, packed from end to end with no tables left at all. Tanner looked up from the bar as the men approached.

"'Bout time you got back. Oather's upstairs. He came back with a lot of stuff but wouldn't tell me what it's for. Does this have anything to do with the new job you boys are starting soon?"

"Um, I don't have a clue what he bought. You know those plainsmen, they are crazy…you never know what they are up to."

"I don't think it's the plainsmen that have tricks up their sleeves, Soliere Forrester," Tanner replied.

Serieve knew that Sol hated to be called by this full name and realized Tanner must have known that as well. Sol was about to reply when the barmaid came up behind him. He turned towards her and was greeted with a sharp slap to his face. Sol stood there; slack jawed, with a look of bewilderment on his face for a second as he looked at the girl.

"That was for the window you…you... troll dung trader."

The girl's attack on his friend surprised Serieve. Then, surprisingly as soon as she said it, she wrapped her arms around him and planted a large passionate kiss on his lips.

Smiling now, Sol asked, "So what was that for?"

"I'll show you later," she said, and winked.

From behind Sol, Tanner let out a loud deliberate cough.

"Oh, it's all right, Tanner," the girl told him. "Gretchen's in the back filling more mugs."

Tanner, keeping his mouth shut, looked beyond the girl, who turned to see an older woman standing behind to her.

"What are you doing out here, dilly-dallying around? We have food and drink to serve." Gretchen grabbed Katrina by the arm, digging in her nails as she dragged the young girl back into the kitchen.

After the two were out of sight, Sol leaned onto the bar. "Well, so much for that. She'll be gone tomorrow."

"Yeah, really too bad," sighed Tanner. "I was really starting to like her. It's so hard to find good help these days."

"You're a real gentleman, you know that, Sol?" Serieve replied as he held the bump on his head tightly and winced from the pain.

"Oh, Tanner, this is a really old friend of mine, Serieve. We go waayyy back. Even further back than when I started coming around here."

Tanner stuck out his arm, as did Serieve and they grasped arms in a greeting. "Pleased to meet you."

"Thank you," Serieve replied.

"You don't look like the kind of person Sol would be friends with. You look like a decent person. How'd you meet?"

Tanner poured a couple new mugs and Serieve started to pull out his pouch only to discover that it was empty.

"Damn, they must have robbed me before you came to my rescue."

"Yeah, you can't trust anyone these days," replied Sol.

"Don't worry about it…I'll put these on your tab, Sol," Tanner said as he handed him the drinks.

"My tab? Why my-," Sol began to argue but suddenly stopped when Tanner scowled at him and begrudgingly took the tankard.

"Thank you, sir." Serieve replied and took a drink. He hadn't realized until now how parched his throat was and the ale really helped a lot. Swallowing half the mug in a single gulp, Serieve wiped his mouth and looked up at Tanner again. "Well, believe it or not, I met Sol trying to break into my home some ten years ago or so."

"Don't worry, I believe it ah'right."

"Well, we caught him," continued Serieve. "I saw him and then my brother socked him a good one."

"Yeah, I still remember that," replied Sol.

"Well, after we were done with him we took him to my dad, who had woken up from all the commotion going on. He was going to let the town authorities have him, but he noticed that Sol was extremely thin and he didn't think Sol had eaten in weeks. So he dismissed the guard and insisted that Sol stay with us."

"Yeah, your dad was a good man...not one that I would want to cross, but he had a good heart," Sol said, taking a drink. "Oh, and if I had my strength up there is no way Bourne would have caught me."

"Whatever you say, Sol," Serieve replied.

"At any rate, Sol stayed with us for...hmmm, do you remember how long it was, Sol?"

"Just under a year, I'd guess. It was long enough that your dad made sure he was paid back through all the labor he made me do."

"Stop bellyaching," Serieve scoffed. "It was good for you, it built character."

"I never saw you out there in the fields, you little princess."

"I wasn't a thief, and besides, I did my fair share of work," Serieve said. "So that's how I met Sol. I hadn't seen him since he left our home in search of work on a ship. Not until tonight anyway, when he saved me from a group of thugs by the south gate. They really took me by surprise. Here I thought I was saving this poor girl when she was in on it all along. The nerve of some people," Serieve ranted. "I'm just lucky that Sol came along and fought them off."

Tanner stood on the other side of the bar pouring another drink to fill up a tray for one of the barmaids. He had a skeptical look on his face.

"So let me get this straight. You were going to save a girl from thugs, she turned on you, and it just so happened that Sol was there to rescue you?"

"Come on, Serieve, let's get your head looked at by Gretchen," Sol said.

"Yeah, lucky for me…," grumbled Serieve, but before he could continue his train of thought Gretchen came back out of the kitchen and put some food down for a couple of customers. She made her way to where the boys were standing. She glared at Sol for a moment before she looked at Serieve and saw that he was injured. Her attention immediately shifted to the young man's wound.

"Oh. You poor dear, what happened to ya?" she asked as she came around to Serieve's other side and began examining his head.

"I'm okay, ma'am. I'll be fine."

"Gretchen, this is an old friend of mine, Serieve," Sol explained. "He had a small run in with some locals."

"Here, hon, let's get that looked at and get you some food," Gretchen said as she almost dragged him with her and they disappeared into the kitchen.

\*\*\*

Sol watched his friend get dragged into to the kitchen by Gretchen, and then turned back to Tanner. "Do you guys have another room that Serieve can stay in tonight?"

"Yeah, I think we have one left. He'll get the normal rate, though."

"That's fine," smiled Sol. "He can afford it."

"I'm putting it on your tab," Tanner added as he grinned back at Sol, who had a shocked look on his face. "I think it's only fair, don't you?"

"No. I don't. I'm not going to pay for him."

"Then perhaps we should share with Gretchen a little more about how Serieve was hurt."

"Damn it, fine. Just put it on my tab and we'll leave it at that."

"You want another mug?"

"No, I'm broke enough already. I only got enough off him to pay for his room and I need to get some rest anyway. We have a busy day tomorrow."

"I see. Well, have a good night," Tanner replied as Sol got up and headed upstairs to his room.

Sol entered his room and slowly shut the door behind him. There was an uncommon stillness that told him he was not alone. He quickly jumped onto the bed and pinned the intruder under the sheets.

"I'm glad to see you could make it," he said.

Katrina giggled. "Wouldn't have missed it for the world."

## 12. The More the Merrier

Morning came, much earlier than Serieve had wanted, but
it came nonetheless. He rolled over onto his back, and
instinctively his hand went to the bump on his head again. The
pain had returned. He didn't know what Gretchen had given him
last night to drink, but it really helped with the pain.
Unfortunately, the medicine didn't last as long as he would have
liked.

He groaned and squinted up at the wooden beam that ran
through the middle of the ceiling. As his vision cleared, he
became aware of noise from downstairs. He got up, put on his
clothes, and wondered if perhaps Gretchen might have more of
that elixir that she had given him last night.

Serieve came down the stairs to see both Gretchen and
Tanner sitting at the bar.

"Good morning, Sire and Madame."

Tanner took a drink from the mug he was holding. There
were wisps of steam rising from it and there was a faint scent of
tea in the air.

"Good morning to you, good sir," Gretchen replied with a
smile. "It's been a while since someone with manners stayed at
this inn."

Tanner didn't say anything. The old guy still looked half-
asleep.

"Come, have a seat," Gretchen insisted. "Are ya hungry?"

"Really, ma'am, I'm not all that hungry. Thank you."

"You're fooling yourself if you think I'm going to let you
out of here with an empty stomach, young man."

Gretchen got up and went into the kitchen. Serieve could
hear the sounds of pots and pans being pulled from the
cupboards.

"Actually," Serieve said to Tanner, "if you have any of that
potion that she gave me last night for the pain, that would be
great."

Tanner perked up and looked at him. "That bump still
sore?"

"Yeah," grumbled Serieve. "That girl hit me pretty hard last night."

"Here, let me take a look."

Serieve turned his head for Tanner.

"Hmmmm," Tanner mumbled as he inspected it. "It's looking better, but still has a ways to go."

"It sure hurts bad enough," Serieve said. He caught a whiff of food coming from the back, and heard the sound of meat sizzling on the stove. He stopped thinking about his head and said, "Something smells good."

His stomach started to rumble and he realized that he was a lot hungrier than he had originally thought. Gretchen came out of the kitchen holding a small bottle. As she came through the door, Serieve could smell the cooking food and his stomach growled again.

"Here you go dear. I have a feeling you'll still be needing this." The woman smiled as she handed him the bottle before heading back into the kitchen.

It was a flask-sized glass bottle that had an ornate design around its edges and a cork stopper. It was filled with a bright blue liquid that had the consistency of lamp oil.

"Take a swallow, but not much more than that. Too much will make you feel worse."

Serieve uncorked the bottle and took a swig. The bitter taste made him wince. He had forgotten how bad it tasted last night. Almost immediately, his head stopped pounding and he started to feel a little better.

"What's in this stuff?" Serieve asked.

"You don't want to know. I don't know everything that's in it, but I know enough that I won't drink it," Tanner replied.

Gretchen came back out with a plate of eggs, ham and a few pieces of melon. She sat it down in front of Serieve. "Eat up."

She handed Serieve a fork and he began to eat as she filled him a glass of goat's milk. He loved goat's milk, and took a huge gulp of it as soon as she sat the mug down.

Gretchen sat down upon a stool next to the men after getting herself a hot cup of tea. "Is Oather still out?"

Tanner refilled his mug as well. "Yes, he said that he wanted to go talk to some friends before he and Sol took off today. I don't suspect he'll be gone long."

"That's good. There are a few things I wanted to see if he could do…like help you remove that rafter that fell in the stables after the last storm."

Tanner sat there sipping his tea but didn't appear to be listening to Gretchen.

"It's already going to cost enough in repairs, but it'll be a lot more if we have to hire someone to help fix it," Gretchen continued.

"Speaking of which," Serieve interrupted, "how much do I owe you? I have some extra money in my bags….well, provided the thieves didn't take it."

"Oh don't worry about it, lad, breakfast is on Sol. Trust me, he won't mind."

"No, I can't let you do that," Serieve insisted. "Here, let me just go get my pouch. I need to get my money anyway, so I can get a few things today."

Serieve started to get up, but Tanner reached over and put his hand on the boy's shoulder, pushing Serieve back into his seat. "I mean it, sit down and finish eating before your eggs get cold. I'll get it for you."

The older man left through the side door. Serieve heard Soliere coming down the stairs.

"Good morning, Sol."

Sol ran his hands through his tousled dark brown hair and mumbled something that didn't really sound to Serieve like a greeting. He sat down and grabbed Serieve's mug and took a swig. He quickly slammed down the mug and spat out the drink.

"Yuck! What the devil are you drinking goat's milk for?"

"I like goat's milk, remember?"

Soliere winced. "Oh, yeah. How could I forget?" he replied dryly and grabbed Tanner's mug instead. Gretchen got up and started towards the kitchen door. "What would you like to eat, Sol?"

"I'm okay, Gretchen. I'm going to be leaving in a moment anyway, so I won't have time to eat."

Gretchen ignored his words and continued back to the kitchen for more food.

Serieve set his fork down and looked over at Soliere, "Where are you heading off to?"

"Just to meet with some people. How's your head?"

"Better," Serieve said, smiling, "and thanks for breakfast."

"Huh?"

Serieve could tell by the look on Sol's face that he realized that Tanner was adding more to his tab. "Damn it. You're costing me a fortune. Hurry up and heal, and get the hell out of here before I'm broke. If you keep this up, I won't even be able to pay the fee to enter the ruins."

"Speaking of which, I want to join you and Oather when you go. There is strength in numbers."

Sol sat there for a moment and thought as he looked at his friend. "You don't have any money, so you can't pay the fee, and I'm not paying it for you."

"I still have some money; not a lot, but enough, I think."

"I know you, Serieve," Sol said, glaring at him, "Knowing you, you'll charge head first into a situation without thinking and get us all killed."

"No, I won't."

"I'll talk to Oather about it and we'll let you know. Oather and I work well together. I don't want you throwing us off."

Just as Sol finished his sentence, the large wooden door swung open and Oather walked in.

Seeing his opportunity, Serieve spoke up at once, "Oather, do you mind if I join you and Sol on your trip?"

"Sure, the more the merrier."

"Okay, then," Serieve grinned, "it's settled. I'll get my stuff ready."

"Gah," Sol said. "Fine. I'll be back later. We'll leave at the break of dawn, tomorrow morning. If you're not up, ready, and waiting by the time we are ready, we're leaving without you."

Sol grabbed his cloak and a hat and headed out the door.

Oather made his way up to the bar. "What was that about?" he asked Serieve. "Did I say something wrong?"

"No, just a little disagreement between Sol and me. I'm sure it won't be the last."

Tanner walked back in and handed Serieve his satchel.

"Oather. I'm glad you're here," Tanner said, "Come with me out back. More of those rafters fell and I need your help moving them."

Oather got up and followed Tanner outside as Serieve finished his food. Gretchen reappeared a few moments later to take his plate.

"Thank you ma'am. That was the best meal I have had in a very long time," Serieve said, taking a few coins from the pouch he pulled from his bag. "I know Tanner told me that he would put that on Sol's tab, but I want to give you something. You've been very gracious to me and I want to thank you," he finished as he handed her the money.

Gretchen took the coins with an astonished look on her face. "Thank you, sire. You have been a very pleasant guest. I hope this doesn't mean you will be leaving soon?"

"Quite the opposite actually. I just talked with Sol and Oather and I'll be working with them for a while, so I think you'll see more of me."

"Ohhh, that's fantastic. It's nice to have paying customers around."

Gretchen took his dishes to the back and Serieve got up and prepared to leave. He had a lot to do before he went to make his fortune with Sol and Oather.

## *13. There's a Sucker Born Every Day*

A short time later, after a bath and a change of clothes, Serieve left the inn. He knew that Sol planned to leave first thing in the morning, so he only had a little time left to get the last of the things he needed for his trip and make some much needed repairs to his armor.

Since he was barely more than a squire for the knight that he served, he didn't have a real suit of armor yet, just a shield, a breastplate and a helmet…a helmet that he wished he had been wearing when he got that blow to his head from the girl he'd been trying to save. Still, this was a lot more than many of his peers had. He was fortunate that his family had some stature and money to help him out…or at least used to.

The breastplate and shield both had some dings in them that he wanted to get repaired, and there were some other supplies that he needed to get. If the monsters rumored to inhabit the ruins were as horrific as he had heard, then he wanted to be as ready as possible. Before he left the inn, Tanner had told Serieve about a few good shops where he could buy supplies, and where to find Omar, the blacksmith.

The instructions Tanner had given him were to head north down the street that ran in front of the *Lucky Duck*. When he made it to the downtown bazaar he was to turn left and go west for a few blocks. There would be a store on his left called Matilda's where he could get the rest of the items he was looking for. He needed a lantern, oil, some rope and some food that would last a while and not spoil; such as dried fruits and meat.

He found the bazaar and walked up and down the street no less than a dozen times, but did not find any shop called Matilda's. Serieve was getting frustrated. He decided to go back to the bazaar one more time to check for the store before he headed back to the inn to talk to Tanner.

The bazaar was full of people. There were many tables set up with varied wares and many different types of food one could buy. Each stand had awnings set up to block out the hot rays of the sun. Each stand had different colors. From where he stood, he could see most of the stands in the bazaar, with all the blues, reds, yellows and the various patterns that adorned them. There was a distinct smell of fish coming from most of the shops; it wasn't exactly a bad smell, but it did take some getting used to.

"I'm never going to find this place."

He turned his back to the bazaar and looked down the wide street for the shop that was supposed to be there. The buildings were well built, much better than the buildings he had seen on the south side of town the night before. Most had more than one story, and had many windows that looked upon the street outside, along with prominent signs identifying the shops within.

He could see a book shop with a weathered old sign. There was a clothing and tailor shop not far from the bookstore. He made a mental note of that, because as soon as he struck it rich, he was definitely going to buy some new clothes. He used to always have new clothes, but over the last few years he had to make do with what he already had. There wasn't enough extra money for nicer clothes; which was something he missed very much.

Finally, at the end of the street was an immaculate building with large black marble pillars. The entire structure was adorned with statues of hideous gargoyles in fierce poses to ward away evil. The entrance to the building was a pair of large arched doors made out of oak. Right above the entrance was a large stained-glass window depicting a red dragon. That was their destination tomorrow--the building that housed the entrance to the great ruins of Tyric.

He kept glancing at the beautiful building while looking for the supply shop and bumped into a short, older man and knocked him down.

"Oh, I'm so sorry, sir. Here, let me help you up," Serieve said.

"Oh no, son, it is I who should be sorry," replied the old man as Serieve grabbed his hands and helped him to his feet. The old man was shorter than Serieve, bald, and had a full white beard. He wore a long coat with pants and boots that were a little worn, but were still in good shape.

"I just wasn't paying attention to where I was going and didn't see you coming my way," continued Serieve, helping to dust the man off.

"It's okay, son, we all do it."

"I was looking more at the shops than where I was going. Again, I apologize."

"Like I said, it's okay, my boy. Are you looking for someplace specific?"

"Actually, yes," replied Serieve. "I'm just having a devil of a time finding it."

"Well, perhaps I can help you. What are you looking for? Wait," interrupted the old man before Serieve could reply. "Let me guess."

The man rubbed his chin and squinted his eyes as he sized up Serieve.

"You were looking for a tailor shop?"

"Ummm," Serieve began to reply. He did want a set of new clothes, even though that's not what he was looking for.

"No. I take that back," said the old man as he eyed Serieve up and down again. One brow was raised high while he thought. "Nooo, on second thought…you seem to be more like you are looking for something else."

"Actually I'm-"

"No, don't tell me," interrupted the man again. "You're strong looking…with an air of charisma about you."

Hearing this made Serieve stand straight with pride.

"You aren't from this city, but you aren't a fool. You look wise in the ways of the world."

The older gentleman tilted his head side to side as though he was really trying to get a good look at him.

"You are a nobleman and you are here on business…a quest of some kind, I would bet. Am I right?"

"Well, sort of…"

"I knew it. I always know when I'm in the presence of greatness," he continued. "So tell me, young man, what brings you to our humble city?"

Serieve was staring at the large building at the end of the street. The older man turned to see what had the boy's attention.

"You aren't thinking about going down into those dangerous ruins, are you?"

"Well," Serieve replied, "actually, my companions and I are going there tomorrow."

The old man's face became quite somber, "That's a terrible place. Full of all sorts of horrors."

"I know," replied Serieve assuredly, "but we can handle ourselves."

"Well, sounds like you found what you were looking for. Best of luck to you and your friends, sire."

"No, that's not what I was looking for," added the young man. "I mean it is, but not right at this moment. I was just struck by what a magnificent building it is."

The old man turned to look at the black marble building.

"Aye," he said. "It is something to behold, by far the most spectacular building in the city. It had better be, considering what they charge to give people safe passage down into the ruins and to let them back out."

"Oh, really? Is it expensive?"

"Very much so," scoffed the old man. "They charge to let you enter, and then they turn around and charge you to get back out the same way. It's legalized robbery if you ask me. And if you don't find enough to trade or pay to get back up they will not let you back out. You have to find your own way out. Ohhh, I've heard horrible stories of men such as yourself being hunted down by enormous beasts. The men tried to get out but they didn't have the gold imperials to pay so they were left there to face the monsters."

Serieve listened intently, as the old man talked on.

"You said you were looking for something?" the man said.

"Oh, err, yes," Serieve stammered, "I was looking for a shop called Matilda's. Do you know of it?"

The old man put his hand up and stroked his beard. "Matilda's, you say?" He stood there and thought for a second. "Oh yes. I do remember that store now. It hasn't been on this street for some time though."

"Could you tell me how to find it?"

"Let me think here," the old man said as he appeared to struggle with remembering where the store might have moved to. "It's two streets over and down a bit past the blacksmith."

"Is it easy to find?"

"Um…I would say so…if you know your way around," the man said. "Here, I'm going that general direction anyway. Why don't I walk with you? I want to talk with you more about your trip anyway."

"That would be great," replied Serieve.

"My name is Melic."

The older man stuck his arm out to Serieve in a greeting and Serieve latched arms with him.

"My name is Serieve, squire in the service of Sir Gavin, knight of the realm." Serieve was feeling very proud and gave his full title for Melic.

"I knew you were someone important."

The two started back the direction Serieve had just come from, and the smells of the bazaar once again became noticeable. This time, when reaching the bazaar, the two men made a left and continued down a new road.

"So, what would possess you to go down into those nasty ruins?"

"My friends and I all need the money fast, and there really isn't any other way for us to get it."

"Ahhh, many have done the same over the centuries....most have died in the process."

"My friends and I can handle ourselves. You do not need to worry."

"Aye, I know, lad," replied Melic. "I just cannot help it. Believe it or not, you sort of remind me of myself, back when I was your age."

Serieve smiled after hearing this from the old man. He doubted that he really was anything like his new friend but didn't want to say anything that might hurt the old man's feelings.

"I have gone down into those wretched stone passage ways more times than I can remember," continued the old man as they turned another corner. This last statement caught Serieve's attention.

"Really? You know your way around the ruins?" Serieve asked.

"Aye. I used to act as a guide for those willing to pay me enough to go down there with them." The old man started to reminisce as they walked. "There were many adventures down there. Mind you I never, and I mean never, went too far down. Beasts can get frightful enough to turn your hair gray at their very sight."

"Do you still take people down into the ruins?"

"Oh no, I gave that up a long time ago. I did, however, make maps of the uppermost areas. I made them for several years to sell to those courageous enough to attempt to go without a guide."

Serieve listened to the old man quite intently.

"I made them as detailed as I could and put markers on the map that would show the locations where creatures tended to be found the most. The map also showed some of the traps in the ruins."

"It did?"

"Oh, yes," reassured the old man. "I remember this one trap. It was toward the southern end of the uppermost level. That one was a killer for sure!"

"Tell me about it, please?" Serieve begged like he was a child listening to his own grandfather's stories, which made Melic laugh and give in to the request.

"There is a small area that looks like an altar of some kind. It's very ornate…and very pretty, I might add. In the very center is a round pedestal that has writing on it. I don't know what it says. I don't even know if it's a language that is known to this world anymore. The writing on the very top is inlaid with gold and in the center of the pedestal is a very large diamond."

"I'm surprised that no one has taken it yet."

"Many have tried, my son," laughed the old man. "The thing is, it's not really there."

"It's not?"

"No, not at all. It's an illusion."

"What do you mean?"

"Magic," Melic replied as his hands ballooned out like an explosion. "Yep, see…when you go near it, the large circular area where the pedestal stands is not really there. So you fall through it into a pit of acid below."

"Oh my goodness. That's horrible."

"You're right there, but trust me….that is the least of the traps I have seen there."

The two men kept walking up the street, dodging through the crowd and making their way through the growing number of people in this section of the city.

"Do you still make these maps?"

"I'm sorry, son," Melic replied, "I started getting older and fewer people were going down into the ruins, so I stopped making them."

"Oh, that's too bad."

"However," continued the old man, who stopped walking. He opened one flap of his jacket and pulled out a large piece of parchment, "I do still have the original."

When Serieve saw the parchment, his eyes shot open. He desperately resisted the urge to wrench it from the old man's hands so he could take a look at it. It was folded and he couldn't actually see anything on it. All he could tell was that it was a weathered piece of leather parchment with plenty of nicks and frays along its edges.

"That's your original map?"

"It surely is."

"May I see it?"

"It wouldn't do you much good, since you really don't know your way around down there. It's far too large an area to memorize all the locations I have pointed out on this map. It's the fruit of thirty years of going down into that horrid place. My whole life's work…right here in ink and parchment."

Serieve's eyes never left the tan piece of parchment. He was speechless and wanted nothing more than to have that map. It could make the difference between he, Sol and Oather dying in the crypts and the three of them coming back all rich as kings.

"If I had a few days I might be able to draw out another copy of this, but since I don't…." the old man said as he started to put the map back into his jacket pocket, "I guess the best I can do for you and your friends is wish you the best of luck and hope the gods protect you on your journey."

Melic finished putting away the map and started to walk away.

"Wait," Serieve quickly grabbed Melic's arm. "Sir, I know you don't want to part with it, but I really need that map."

Melic stood there for a moment, pondering the plight of the young man before him. "I'm sorry, my boy. I really can't let it go. It's the last copy that I have."

Serieve grabbed his money pouch. "I'd be happy to pay you for it. I don't have a lot, but just tell me how much you want for it, please?"

Melic stood there looking at him, thinking the proposition over.

"Well….I don't know."

"Please sir, this map could mean the difference between life and death for me and my friends." Serieve could feel the old man's resistance wavering. "Our lives are potentially in your hands and we could really use that map. Just tell me how much you want for it. I have money. I can pay you."

"I don't know, lad. The copies themselves used to sell for one hundred and fifty gold imperials each, and I have sold hundreds of them over the years. This is the original...and the very last map in my possession. It would go, and should go, for ten times that amount."

Hearing the news of how much the map cost, Serieve's heart sank. He only had a little over four hundred gold imperials left to his name, in mixed gold, silver and platinum. He had a lot of stuff to buy, and then he still had to pay his own way into the ruins.

"I could take perhaps..." the old man thought for a moment, scratching his chin, "three hundred gold imperials for it."

"Ouch," Serieve muttered softly. "Would you take one hundred gold imperials for it? I'd offer more but that's really all I can let go of right now."

Melic took the map back out of his jacket and rested it against his chin while he contemplated.

"I like you kid. I might be able to go as low as...let's say, two hundred and fifty gold imperials?"

Serieve mentally recalculated what his expenses were. If he forewent getting the dents taken out of his armor... and cut back on the amount of food he bought.

"I can go as high as two hundred gold imperials." Serieve sighed, knowing that spending that much would significantly reduce the supplies he was going to get.

"Like I told you before, I like you kid, and I would absolutely hate for something to happen to you and your friends. I'll go ahead and accept two hundred for it. You got yourself a deal."

"Fantastic," Serieve replied as he pulled out his pouch and counted out the money to the old man.

"Well, I hate to do this, but I'm starting to run late and need to get to my next appointment. Matilda's is that shop right there down the street. Do you see the wooden sign hanging on that second building?"

Serieve looked down the road and did, in fact, see a big wooden sign that said Matilda's.

"Oh yes, there it is."

The old man handed Serieve the map and grabbed his arm. "Now, you and your friends be careful down there. It's still a very dangerous place, even with as good a map as you have in your hands there."

"Thank you, sir!" he said as sincerely as he could without sounding giddy. "I can't tell you how much I appreciate this. You've done me a big favor and I won't forget it."

"You're very welcome, my boy. I'm glad to be of help, but really, I must be going."

Serieve watched disappear into the growing crowd. It felt like his luck was finally turning around. He couldn't believe that he'd had the good fortune to run into that old man right when he needed him. This map was going to make them rich. Best of all, if they became lost, he could pull out the map and he'd be able to finally show Sol that he wasn't the only one who knew what he was doing.

For the time being, Serieve decided he would keep the map a secret and only reveal it after Sol led them the wrong way. They were all going to be rich now, Serieve just knew it!

## *14. The Big Night*

"There you go, Mistress," Axel said. He stood up and stepped away from Andrea so he could take in the full view of her costume.

Axel was Andrea's best friend, but he wasn't a tailor by trade; he was actually an assassin like Andrea, but had a flair for costumes and the dramatic. He was usually dressed up in a colorful blue, red, yellow and green costume that made him look like a court jester--which was appropriate since he was, in fact, the Emperor's court jester in addition to being a trained killer.

"You look marvelous," Axel said as he stood back and admired his work.

"Thank you, Axel, you did a masterful job."

Andrea looked at her new costume in the full length mirror of her bedroom. For her mission at the Emperor's Masquerade ball tonight, she needed something sleek and seductive, yet unassuming. Axel had suggested an angel, but after some discussion, they came up with another idea.

She wore a full length jet black dress made of strange silky, yet stretchable, material. The sleeves were made of a ghostly white mesh silk which was almost see-through. Running down the length of each arm were long, spindly black tubes covered in black silk which were fashioned to look like the legs of a black widow spider.

Andrea didn't know where Axel managed to find the strange fabric but he did mention that it was made from real spider silk, and assured her that it wasn't cheap, but that the effect was worth it. The material covered her skin but allowed the spider legs on her arms to appear more pronounced.

There were two spider legs connecting below her breasts and another set touching together right below her navel. The final set of spider legs ran down the length of her legs. Half way down her legs, the black material gradually faded from the black into whitish webbing that matched the sleeves of the dress. The back of her dress was open and Axel used some powdered fire-dragons egg to stencil a blood red hour glass shape on her abdomen.

Finally, Axel came back around and tied two straps of webbing from the spider legs on her arms around the back of her hand, then bound the straps together with a small clasp that fit in the middle of her palm.

"What are these for?"

"One moment and you'll see," Axel replied as he finished connecting the straps for her other hand. The clasps were oval in shape, half red and half blue.

"You said that you didn't want to go into this party unarmed, so I thought these would be of use."

"So what are they?"

"Close your fist slowly and as you do so, touch the red part of the clasp."

Andrea didn't know what to expect, but did as he instructed. As soon as she touched the clasp, she could feel it begin to sink in like a button. She pressed a little harder and heard a slight 'click' just before a sharp spike sprang out of the spider leg on her arm.

"Oooo," she gasped, "I like this."

"I thought you might."

"Now, if you touch the blue button, it will retract."

Andrea pressed the blue button to retract the metal spike. Then pressed the buttons back and forth several times for practice.

"There is one other feature of these weapons that you need to know about. When they are extended, if you press the red button a second time, the spike will fire out of the sheath."

Andrea held her arm out straight to try it but Axel quickly threw up his hands to stop her.

"Don't do it now."

"Why not?"

"They are extremely difficult to reload, so just take my word for it."

Andrea sighed. "Fine."

"Here is the final piece." Axel handed her a small black mask covered in the same material as the dress. She took the small mask and put it on. It just covered her eyes but made the entire costume seem much more mysterious. Andrea was very pleased with the final result.

"Excellent job, Axel." Andrea continued to inspect her costume. "I think this will work perfectly."

"There are just a few finishing touches," he said as he held up a ring to her. "This is filled with the venom of a hundred red-fang spiders. Just give it a half twist," he gave the ring a twist and a small needle came out through the center of the gem that adorned the ring, "One little poisonous prick, and he'll be dead in minutes."

Andrea took the ring from the jester, "Thank you, Axel. Nice touch."

"You're welcome, Mistress." Axel bowed dramatically. "I always aim to please."

Andrea paced back and forth in front of the mirror, twirling so she could see all angles. She was satisfied but something still bothered her.

"Axel, you pulled this together awfully quickly. Please tell me you don't have a storeroom full of women's dresses."

"Oh heavens no, I just borrowed a little here and there. That dress was expensive and meant for someone else, but for enough gold and promises, I persuaded a friend of mine to part with it. As for the spikes, I had them made a long time ago for Althea, but she never used them so I had them incorporated into the costume."

"I had a feeling this was going to cost me a lot. Is this mission going to cost me more than I'm going to make off it?"

Axel laughed. "Not at all, I have you covered there, too. The Guild Master made an arrangement with several tradesmen in town to provide him with goods he needs and he pays them later. He'll be charged with them when he pays them."

Andrea laughed so hard she almost snorted. "He is going to kill you. Do you realize that?"

"Oh please, I disguised myself as him when I purchased everything. There's no way he'll ever trace it back to me."

The two laughed about imagining the Guild Master's face when he checked his bill and found an expensive woman's dress on it.

Before long Clarissa, Andrea's favorite handmaiden, entered the room, "Pardon, Mistress, a coach has just shown up at the front door. The driver asked me to send for you."

"Thank you, Clarissa. You're excused." She turned back to Axel. "Well, I'm off. When will you be arriving at the party?"

"I won't be making this event," Axel replied. "I have been given another assignment by the Guild Master."

"Oh, no, I was hoping you'd be there tonight."

"Don't worry, I'll be back soon so you can tell me all about it."

Andrea looked at Axel and held out her hand to him. Axel took her hand and kissed it.

"Good night, Mistress," he replied as he bowed to her. He then took his colorful hat and tossed it up into the air. Andrea watched it almost reach the ceiling then fell to the floor. By the time the hat hit the ground Axel had vanished, and then with a "POOF," the hat disappeared in a puff of purple smoke.

Andrea rolled her eyes. "He's always got to be a show off," she mumbled as she turned and headed down to meet her escort to the Emperor's function.

Moments later she descended the steps and approached the carriage. It was black, accented with silver trim. The driver was holding the door open for her.

"Good evening, Mistress. You look radiant."

"Thank you," She replied and stepped up into the carriage. Inside sat a man dressed in black and wearing a black cloak, with slicked-back black hair and pale white skin.

"What are you supposed to be, Guild Master?"

He smiled widely, baring two sharp fangs, "A vampire. What else, my dear?"

"How interesting," she replied, giving him an approving smile while simultaneously thinking how appropriately dressed he was. Jor'Dan after all, in her opinion, was a blood sucking demon.

"You look amazing, Andrea."

"Why, thank you. Axel helped me."

"That boy. I do not know what to do with him. I do not know if he is a genius or completely insane. Personally, I lean more toward the latter."

"Don't be silly, Guild Master, he's one of my most promising apprentices."

"Well, he should thank the gods for you, then. If it weren't for you, I would have had him killed months ago."

"You just don't like him because he mocks you whenever you're in the room," she replied, looking out the window. She noticed out of the corner of her eye how his gaze lingered on her legs longer than normal.

"Do you like my costume, Guild Master?"

Her sudden confrontation took him by surprise. He tried to respond but nothing coherent came out of his lips. She knew he was on the defensive and she liked it that way.

"From the look on your face, I'm willing to bet you are imagining me more out of it than in it. Am I right, Guild Master?"

"Um, err," he stammered and coughed. "Yes…um…it's very nice."

Andrea smiled and looked back at the passing scenery. After embarrassing the old fool like that, she didn't expect he'd be up for much more idle chit-chat and would leave her alone for the rest of the trip.

It was getting dark outside. Tall pine trees lined the road and she could see the moon, a shining silver disk in the night sky. Andrea lost herself staring at it; her right hand instinctively went to her necklace, her delicate fingers rubbed the small piece of onyx which seemed to calm her nerves slightly. Before she knew it, they were drawing close to the Emperor's Keep.

The carriage passed through the gates guarded by the Emperor's Elite Guard. Each guardsman held a long halberd at his side and stood perfectly at attention.

"The Emperor's royal guard," Andrea stated, breaking the silence, "can you think of a scarier looking group of soldiers? Look at them, they're enormous."

"Yes, quite. There's a rumor that they aren't just men, but half giants," he replied.

The carriage continued past the guards and pulled up to the Keep, where other carriages had already stopped to let out their passengers, who were then escorted up the red carpet to the entrance of the castle.

Finally, it was their turn. Andrea took Jor'Dan's arm as they began to walk up the carpet toward the entrance as distinguished guests. As they reached the grand entrance of the Keep, they were stopped by the Chamberlain. They stood just inside the massive doors while he stepped up and announced them.

"The Honored Grand Chancellor Jor'Dan and his guest, the beautiful Andrea Vinciq," heralded the Chamberlain, after which he bowed and the couple entered.

Inside, the main room was adorned with streamers, and colorful banners decorated the walls. An enormous crystal chandelier hung from the ceiling and covered at least a third of the room. Like a hundred brightly lit stars, it illuminated the entire reception hall in a soft light.

On one side of the room an orchestra played soft but cheerful music, and some of the guests were dancing. On the other side were tables full of food and drink--a stuffed pig, trays of sweetmeats and fruits, bread and cheeses. In the center of the tables was a stone pedestal upon which stood a sculpture made of ice that kept changing shape. When Andrea first glanced at it, it was the form of a great fish leaping out of water. Then it changed to a lunging tiger and then, just before she wandered away, it changed into a large bird enveloped in a flame soaring up into the air.

There were already several hundred guests there, each and every one in costume. There were some that were very elaborate; such as one individual that went so far as to have himself enchanted to look like a dragon. His nostrils emitted smoke whenever he breathed and his long tail kept tripping other guests. Most costumes were more like Jor'Dan's, brightly colored suits with elaborate embroidery and a simple mask that covered their eyes.

At the center of the great room were a pair of long curved staircases that swept away from each other and then back together, coming to a point as they led up to the second floor. Atop the second floor was a landing where the Emperor's throne overlooked the floor below.

The Emperor sat there in a royal purple robe with silver and gold runes sewn around the cuffs. At his side was a wizard's staff and on his other side was a tall, dark-haired man clad in a long white robe. The man's white cloak was trimmed with gold and he wore a tall, arching, white hat with a red stone set in a gold centerpiece. He was obviously dressed as the Patriarch of the Church of Salus. His costume had a red patch on the chest that looked like blood, with a black arrow protruding from it.

Jor'Dan whispered, "Let us greet our host." Andrea nodded and the two ascended the great stairway. When she looked to her left Andrea had a better vantage point from which to see the other guests on the floor below. More people were dancing now and the music had become livelier.

They reached the upper balcony and approached the Emperor. Andrea and Jor'Dan bowed to their host.

"Good evening, Chancellor," welcomed the Emperor. "Who is this pretty little thing that you've brought with you?"

"This is Andrea Vinciq, an associate of mine."

Andrea held out her hand to the Emperor. She could see how much older he appeared up close. He took her hand and kissed it. In contrast to her own, his hand was old and almost frail looking, but when he took her hand it felt much stronger.

"It's a pleasure, your Majesty," she said to him and curtsied. He let go of her gloved hand and gestured to his left. "As you know, Chancellor, my advisor, Sonilauq."

Jor'Dan nodded towards Sonilauq, "A pleasure to see you again."

Sonilauq nodded back with a slight grin on his face. "As always, Chancellor." Andrea held out her hand towards him as well. Sonilauq took it, bowed and placed a kiss on the back of her hand. "A greater pleasure to meet one so beautiful."

"Why, thank you."

"It's good that you could make it, Chancellor," said the Emperor. "Tonight is a very special occasion."

"Yes, my liege, it's a great honor to be at the selection of your new heir," replied Jor'Dan. "How long until the announcement?"

"Not long at all now," the Emperor said, as another young man came forward towards them. He was a younger man with dark brown, shoulder length hair and a handsome face. He wore an old naval captain's hat and overcoat, a dirty pair of seaman's trousers, and a lopsided sword belt that hung low on his left side. Andrea guessed that he must have come to the party as a pirate or a buccaneer. She couldn't tell for certain.

"Bourne," said the Emperor, motioning towards the young man, "come here and meet more of my guests." The man came forward to greet them. He nodded to Jor'Dan and Sonilauq, took Andrea's hand and kissed it. Andrea looked the young man in the eye as he let go of her hand. She liked the twinkle that she saw in his eyes, and knew from his look that he liked what he saw in hers.

"Chancellor, this is Bourne Castille. His father was Duke Castille of the South-Eastern province."

"It's a pleasure." Jor'Dan bowed to the young man.

"He's taken his father's place at court and, considering his young age and the troubles that area has been facing, he has done a remarkable job improving things."

"It's a pleasure to meet you, my lord," Andrea said.

"Likewise, ma'am," he replied. "Your majesty, I am sure that you and Jor'Dan have urgent business to discuss now that he is here, so I thought I might offer my services to the young lady here and show her around."

"Right you are, my child. Please, if you will, show Mistress Vinciq around and introduce her to some of our other guests."

Bourne reached for her hand and escorted her away from the other men, who were now lost in discussion. Andrea looked up and her eyes met with Sonilauq's. She smiled and winked quickly at him before the younger man led her down the stairs.

\*\*\*

"Lovely acquaintance," remarked Sonilauq as he watched her disappear down the staircase. "Hard to believe she's here to kill me." He laughed, amused by the thought.

"Do not underestimate her," said Jor'Dan. "It could be your undoing."

"That necklace she's wearing, is that the one you spoke of, Jor'Dan?" the Emperor asked.

"Yes, my liege," replied Jor'Dan. "I'm sure you could feel the power radiate from it."

"Yes, I could, and you're right: I also could not discern its origin. I could only sense power from it….a dormant power, as if it were sleeping."

"So are we on track with the original plan?" Sonilauq asked.

"Yes, but do heed the good Chancellor's warning," Emperor Tor said, looking towards Sonilauq. "An item like that does not randomly drop into the hands of ordinary people. The fates have marked it for something and it has come into her possession intentionally."

"I will take care of everything, my liege."

"Do whatever needs to be done then, Sonilauq."

## *15. The Reception*

Halistan had never seen a place as beautiful as the Emperor's chateau. It was larger than many of the chapels they had in Valencia and certainly more extravagant. There were many beautiful buildings in Valencia, but few could compare to what he saw at the ball.

The Patriarch led the group of priests into the ball after being announced. They followed the main carpet through the crowd towards the Emperor. Halistan marched slowly behind Father Angelo as he had been instructed, keeping step with the other acolytes. However, his desire to look around kept pulling at Halistan's attention, nearly making him trip up in the formation.

Out of the corner of his eye he saw many of the guests in their strange costumes dancing, and long tables of food and drink, as well as an ice sculpture that he almost thought changed shape. His gaze lingered on the statue for a moment longer, hoping to see if it did indeed change, which almost caused him to bump into Father Angelo as the group began to ascend a long set of stairs.

"Pay attention to what you're doing, Halistan," scolded Janus, the veteran acolyte walking next to him.

Gradually, the procession ascended the steps. At the top, Halistan saw an old man sitting on the throne. Standing next to the throne was a man dressed similarly to the Patriarch. He wore the same vestments, but in an older style--probably several centuries older, at least, going by what Halistan could remember from the historical texts.

There was something different about the man's robe. It had a large patch of burgundy on the front. The procession reached the second floor balcony and the Patriarch greeted the Emperor. As Halistan reached the top step, he could see the man standing next to the Emperor much more clearly. Now he could tell what the burgundy patch was; it was blood with an arrow sticking out. This man was obviously dressed up as Patriarch Raevat, who had been assassinated nearly six hundred years ago.

Halistan was appalled. How could someone want to dress up as the victim of such a horrible tragedy was beyond his comprehension. The other members of the church seemed to take notice of this as well, including Patriarch Altstaat.

"Patriarch Altstaat," the Emperor said. "It's a pleasure to finally have you as my guest."

"It's an honor to be here," the Patriarch replied, bowing to the Emperor. The other priests bowed in unison with the Patriarch. The Patriarch's attention seemed to be focused on the Emperor, as though he was intentionally trying not to look at Sonilauq.

There was a short, uncomfortable silence before the Emperor spoke again.

"You did not wear a costume?"

The Patriarch looked over towards Sonilauq. "On the contrary, it looks as though I have worn the same costume as your other guest. Though I do have to admit, he wears it much better than I."

The group laughed but the tension did not seem to subside any.

"Please," said the Emperor. "Go enjoy yourselves as my most honored guests."

"Thank you, sire," replied the Patriarch. He turned and led the group back down towards the festivities. No one said a word until all the priests reached the base of the steps.

"Well, that was awkward," Halistan whispered to Janus.

"I cannot believe that someone would dare to dishonor Patriarch Raevat that way," Janus replied.

Halistan and Janus followed the elder priests as they greeted many other guests they knew.

"The Patriarch knows more people here than I thought," Janus whispered to Halistan.

"Is this all they do all night, talk to old acquaintances?"

"Yes, the entire evening is usually nothing except discussing pleasantries with various people. It gets pretty boring until the guests start getting drunk."

"People do that here?"

"Absolutely," Janus whispered. "Once I saw a duke or a knight or something drink so much wine that he began singing love songs to a beautiful young lady, professing his undying love for her."

"Ohh, that's actually sweet."

"Yeah, it was real sweet until his wife found out and started beating him with a loaf of bread," Janus said, while trying his best to hold back from laughing. Halistan, too, had to try hard to restrain himself. Their suppressed mirth caught the attention of Father Angelo, who glanced sternly at the two young men. This immediately made them straighten up and stop talking.

As the Patriarch and church Elders made their way through the crowds of people, Halistan tried to alleviate his boredom by looking around. The costumes that the other guests wore were incredible. There were magicians, trolls, a dragon and many knights wearing full suits of armor. Halistan had always been fascinated by knights and wished that he could have been one of those brave men who could stand up for the weak and helpless. Not that he didn't enjoy being a healer, but there was just something about being a knight that seemed more exciting.

## 16. Things Don't Go Exactly as Planned

"And that is Sir Sedric," Bourne pointed to the man who looked like a dragon. "He dresses up as that dragon every year. He was the Emperor's champion and master-of-arms for over two decades, coming to that position after slaying the dragon that he now impersonates."

"How very interesting," replied Andrea, "and who was that up there with the Emperor? I think he said his name was...Sonilauq."

"Oh, he is...um...I know I see him a lot, but now that you mention it, I don't know what he does. I believe he is one of the Emperor's advisors on court matters," Bourne replied as the couple neared the dancing area.

Bourne held out his hand to her, "Would you honor me with a dance?"

She took his hand in her own and they walked further into the crowd of swirling couples. Bourne turned to her, and his right hand went to her waist as he moved her body closer to his. They began to move with the beat of the music. Her face was close to his and she enjoyed looking up into the young man's handsome eyes. If she hadn't been there on business, she could have really enjoyed herself. The couple moved along the dance floor, twirling around other couples until the music started to slow down and their pace slowed accordingly. Out of the corner of her eye, she saw a man approach her. It was Sonilauq.

As he approached, he looked directly into Andrea's eyes, disregarding Bourne entirely. "May I have this dance?"

"Hey," Bourne protested, but Andrea looked at him with a quieting glance, then her look shifted back to Sonilauq.

"I would love to dance with you, Milord."

Sonilauq moved in front of Bourne, who was still standing there in shock, watching as she and Sonilauq melted into the crowd.

"That was very bold of you," she said.

"I can be very persuasive when I want something."

They danced slowly past another couple who were dressed up as elves. Their faces were powdered, and they both wore jet black wigs.

"So many strange costumes here tonight. It's quite a sight."

He pulled her closer, "Many costumes, but none as radiant as yours. You truly look beautiful." Bringing up his hand, he touched her face. Andrea liked the way his hand felt as he brushed her cheek. For a moment, she almost felt like she was floating, before her senses brought her back to reality and she remembered why she was there. They continued to dance for a while longer until the music ceased and a bell rang, signaling an announcement.

"Attention! All guests please come forth!" The portly crier who had made the announcement was standing at the top of the massive set of stairs. He stepped aside and was passed by the Emperor and the Chancellor. They were followed by the herald as they made their way down the steps.

Emperor Tor drew back the hood of his cloak so that his elderly face could be seen. Upon his brow sat a crown of platinum with a large ruby as its centerpiece. Spreading his arms wide, he addressed the crowd.

"Welcome all. It pleases me that so many of my faithful subjects would honor me by attending my little gathering. As you all know, I have ruled this land for many decades, as did my father before me. I, unlike him, did not have the foresight, or rather the good fortune, to find a queen and have children of my own.

"It has long been our tradition that in such a case, the Emperor should choose an heir from one of the highest noble families of his court. Seeing as how you are all the highest families of my court, I have designated tonight as the night that I will choose my heir."

The crowd began to whisper among themselves as they listened to the Emperor. The Emperor held up a hand and a hush settled over the guests.

"Traditionally, it's also been a child that would be selected."

The Emperor paused as the crowd listened intently, "Unfortunately I waited far too long for that, and at my age do not feel I have adequate time to raise a child and teach him my ideals, so instead I have chosen someone older to succeed me."

Again, a low murmur spread through the crowd of nobles. They stopped when the Emperor began to speak again.

"I was faced with trying to find someone who was still young enough that their heart hadn't been jaded by years of political service, but who still had enough experience leading those under him."

The Emperor took a moment to pause and take in the reaction from the crowd before him.

"This year I have made my decision on an heir. This young man comes to us from close by, a small province just outside our fair city. A few years ago, his father passed away. In order to keep his family's stature, he took his father's place in court at an exceptionally young age. In the face of the serious economic problems his province was facing, he has led them into a recovery and demonstrated amazing leadership qualities. I have watched him closely over the years, offering him advice when I could. Now, after seeing him grow so much in such a short period of time, I have discovered there is no one else I could choose who would be a better heir for me.

"Bourne Castille. Could you please come up here?"

A few gasps could be heard from ladies in the crowd, and the entire group began to murmur in surprise. "Bourne, where are you, my lad?" asked the Emperor again as he looked either direction into the crowd.

The crowd parted as Bourne emerged and stepped up in front of the Emperor and kneeled, bowing his head in reverence.

"Your Majesty," Bourne said.

"Rise, my son. Everyone, please congratulate my new heir," the Emperor said as he turned towards Bourne. "That is, of course, if you would be so kind as to accept the offer."

"Ye...yes. It would be my greatest honor, sire."

"Excellent."

Instantly everyone began to clap and cheer for the young man.

"Musicians, if you would, please, this is a celebration."

The orchestra began to play again, this time a very rambunctious tune that livened up the entire hall. Couples began to move back across the dance floor. Andrea took Sonilauq's hand in her own and they walked up to the Emperor and his new protégé. Sonilauq extended his arm to the young man.

"Congratulations, Bourne. You'll make a great leader someday."

"Thank you," replied the young man. He glanced over at Andrea.

She stepped up before him and bowed. "You will make a fine Emperor someday, Bourne. I look forward to serving you."

"Thank you."

Emperor Tor then came up beside Bourne.

"I'm sorry, but we really have some things to discuss, Bourne. It was a pleasure to meet you, Mistress Vinciq."

"The pleasure was all mine, your Highness."

"Yes, it was a pleasure meeting you too. I do hope our paths cross again," Bourne said.

"I'm sure that we will," Andrea replied before the Emperor led him away.

"Well, that was exciting," remarked Sonilauq, stifling a yawn. "You should let me give you a tour of the Chateau. Have you ever been here before?"

"Yes. Once, a long time ago but I didn't get to see much of it." She grinned coyly at him. "Actually, I would rather go someplace a little more private. Do you know a place around here that fits that description?"

"Yes," he whispered as he pulled her close and kissed her. "I think I know just the place." She offered him little resistance as their lips met.

"Some of the guests are not leaving after the party and have their own private rooms here with the Emperor's compliments. Would you care to join me for a drink in mine?" he asked, kissing her once again.

"Mmmm," she moaned softly. "I'd love to."

He took her hand and led her up another staircase and down the hall. Soon, they were in a distant part of the Keep. There were no more guests around, which is exactly what she wanted.

Sonilauq opened the door and escorted her into an elegantly appointed room with one large picture window and a huge bed in the middle of the room. The walls were adorned with elaborate tapestries. The dark wood trim along the window matched the wainscoting on the walls. The other door in the room led to the adjoining suite.

Andrea walked toward the window first and saw another small building not far from the Keep. She walked back a few steps, then turned and looked at her escort. "Now that you have me here, whatever are you going to do with me?"

Sonilauq stepped closer to her and wrapped his arms around her waist. He leaned close, but let her to be the one to kiss him. She could feel how strong he was under his costume. He wore a strange cologne that she'd never smelled before, like chamomile and sumac.

She quickly realized the perfect opportunity was presenting itself to her. She wrapped her arms around his neck and held him tightly as they kissed. With her left hand she gave her ring a little half twist and turned it so that it faced inward. She found a patch of bare skin on his neck and was about to strike when he suddenly grabbed her hair and pulled her back violently.

She was momentarily taken off guard and in that moment he seized her right wrist, "Now, you wouldn't be trying to hurt me, would you?"

He pulled her hand close, revealing the little needle sticking out of her ring.

"Tsk, and I expected more from you. After all the ranting Jor'Dan has been doing about you, I expected something a bit more impressive than simple poison."

Andrea was shocked. She didn't know what was going on. What did he mean about Jor'Dan ranting about her? It didn't take her long to figure out that she'd been set up.

"Where is that pompous bastard?" she demanded. "I'll kill him myself."

"Don't worry about that, my dear. There will plenty of time for that later."

The door to the adjoining room opened, and in came two soldiers followed by the Emperor, and finally by Jor'Dan. The guards took Andrea's arms and forced her to her knees.

"Kneel before your Lord, wench!"

"What is this all about, Jor'Dan?" she screamed at him. Her hair was now in a mess as she thrashed about while she was restrained by the soldiers. "So help me, you had better kill me because if you don't, I'm going to take great pleasure in killing you."

The Emperor walked up to her and knelt down on one knee in front of her. She just glared at him and said, "What do you want with me?"

"Shhhhh, my child," the Emperor said. He reached up to her neck and stopped at her necklace. He examined it for a moment before grasping it lightly between his fingers. He started to chant but as he did a bolt of magic leapt from the piece of onyx to the Emperor's hand, shocking him instantly. He jerked his hand away as he stood up and smacked Andrea hard across the face. The hit stung, but she didn't make a sound. She glared at him menacingly.

"You're correct, Chancellor. That stone is indeed powerful. How powerful I cannot tell, but I do know that it's important."

"Thank you, your Majesty. Now what are we to do with her?"

The Emperor looked down at Andrea. "Guards," the Emperor commanded, "Kill her and bring me the necklace after she is dead. It shouldn't put up any resistance after its owner is destroyed."

Andrea wrenched at the soldier holding her right arm and bit his hand as hard as she could. She caught the guard by surprise and caused him to let go of her wrist. Andrea quickly extended a spike and stabbed the guard. He groaned and hit the ground as blood spilled out onto the floor. The other guard lunged towards her, but as he did she grabbed one of his arms and the needle that was still sticking out of her ring pierced his skin. The guard managed to grab her but only for a second before the fast acting poison took effect. His grip loosened and he slumped to the floor, dead.

She stood up and saw Sonilauq drawing a long serpentine dagger from his robes, while the Emperor and Chancellor turned back towards her to see what had transpired.

"Give up, you've nowhere to go." Sonilauq said.

For just a moment no one in the room moved. Andrea's heart raced, fueled by her anger.

She quickly surveyed the room and knew she had only one option. Sonilauq stepped towards her but before she was within his reach she turned and quickly ran towards the window. Without thinking she jumped and prayed her plan would work.

Glass shattered as she broke through and plummeted from the high window. In one brief moment, Andrea could finally see how high up she was, and she was much higher than she anticipated. She had taken a calculated risk and now she was going to pay the price. She closed her eyes and heard a loud crack as she hit the ground. She knew at once that she'd broken both her legs.

## *17. Lucky Break*

After what felt like forever to Halistan, the Patriarch and Elders seemed to have run out of royals to speak with. Halistan had overheard the Patriarch whispering to Elder DeSpaat that he wanted to speak with Bourne and invite him to visit Valencia. DeSpaat nodded his head in agreement.

Halistan looked at Father Angelo, who was beginning to look quite tired. Halistan couldn't blame him; the Elder was getting old and didn't have the stamina that he'd had when he was younger. Eventually the group split up. Elder DeSpaat and Janus stayed with the Patriarch and found another noble to talk to.

"Halistan, are you hungry?" Father Angelo asked.

"Yes, very."

Father Angelo seemed amused by his answer, but they had been there all evening with nothing to eat and Halistan's stomach had been growling for a while.

"Very well, then. Let's see what we can find."

Most of the people in the crowd were mingling and dancing, now that the Emperor had announced a man named Bourne as his successor. Halistan could see a swarm of royals tightly grouped around Bourne now. So many people surrounded him that Halistan couldn't even see Bourne any more.

Father Angelo and Halistan made their way to the tables covered with food. As soon as one tray would empty, a servant would bring out another. Halistan had never seen that much food at one time before. He had been to some banquets, but nothing this extravagant.

"Here," Halistan heard Father Angelo say to him. He turned towards the Elder to see him offering a small plate that held a pastry and two pieces of beef wrapped with ham and cheese. Halistan took the plate and ate one of the pieces of beef. It was soft, much softer than he expected it to be, and more flavorful than he could have imagined. To his growling stomach, this was heaven. Halistan quickly ate the other piece of beef, and got three more on his plate while Father Angelo was filling his own plate.

Halistan quickly ate the morsels. As he began to fill his plate a third time, he saw Father Angelo looking at the crowd surrounding Bourne.

"I don't envy that boy," Father Angelo said softly.

"Why not? He'll get to live in the castle, have servants…"

"Don't be fooled, Halistan. The life of an Emperor is not an easy one."

Father Angelo took another bite of a pastry and seemed to enjoy it. Halistan didn't want to be disrespectful and try arguing with him that Bourne's life would be harder or easier than anyone else's. Instead, they both quietly ate a few more small platefuls of food and enjoyed watching the costumed guests.

After Father Angelo had eaten his fill, he turned to Halistan, who had just finished stuffing an oversized cream puff into his mouth.

"Halistan," Father Angelo said.

Halistan's mouth was so full that he couldn't reply, so he kept his mouth shut and tried to chew slowly.

"I am going to talk with the Patriarch about how much longer he wants to be here. I fear it will be a while longer. I know he still wants the chance to talk with Bourne himself. In the meantime, I want you to take the Star of Salus and my scepter back to our carriage and lock them in the storage chest."

Halistan gulped down the last of the food and took the holy relics from Father Angelo.

"When you get back, come find me with the Patriarch," Father Angelo said. He smiled. "If I leave him alone with DeSpaat for too long we'll never leave."

Halistan made his way out of the chateau with the help of a few of the Emperor's servants, who pointed him towards a side exit that would take him directly to the stables and carriages. After a few quick turns he was finally outside.

He saw a couple of carriages already re-hitching their horses so they could retrieve the guests who were ready to leave. Most of the guests were still trying to get an audience with Bourne, however, so it was relatively quiet outside as Halistan made his way towards the stable. The party had been so noisy inside that being outside now seemed extraordinarily quiet.

Halistan approached the stables, where he saw dozens of carriages, all neatly arranged in rows and parked so close together that there was barely any room to navigate between them. He walked down the first row but didn't see their carriage. The Patriarch and his party had actually brought two coaches, but Halistan only had the key to the one he and Father Angelo arrived in.

He was starting to check the second row when he heard a loud crash behind him. He jerked around to see what had happened, just in time to see a woman falling from the third floor of the chateau.

Halistan watched in shock as she plummeted to the ground and collapsed in a heap on the ground. Without thinking he bolted towards her. He knew that she was probably dead, but he prayed that she wasn't. If she just had the scantest portion of life left in her, he had a chance to save her.

As he approached her, he slid to a stop next to her and dropped Father Angelo's scepter. Immediately he saw that both of the woman's legs were broken. One was snapped clean in two, so that the bones jutted out through her skin. Halistan looked up at the window she had fallen from and called for help. He could see shadows dancing around on the ceiling of the room, so there must be people up there. A man came to the window and looked out. Halistan saw that it was the man who had been dressed as the Patriarch.

"Help," Halistan cried up to the man. "She's hurt badly."

The man looked down at him and looked furious. Halistan saw the man look back into the room briefly before looking back out the window and pointed down at them.

"She's alive! Down there. Get them!"

Halistan wasn't sure what the man was angry about, but he was bellowing out orders quickly.

"I want her dead," Halistan heard the man yell at someone. He couldn't believe his ears. The man must have pushed her out of the window.

He heard the man shouting again. "I don't care, kill them both!"

Halistan didn't need to hear any more. He knew that he needed to get out of there before the guards caught them. The woman was badly injured, covered in blood. He wasn't sure if he could move her without doing more harm but he didn't have a choice.

He scooped the woman up in his arms. He needed to find a place he could take her while she would be safe long enough for him to heal her. There was hardly anyone back at the stables. Perhaps he could find a place to hide there. He carried her there as quickly as he could. Fortunately, she wasn't heavy and he made it back to the stables quickly. He darted in through a side door into an empty stall.

He gently set her down in the hay and straightened her badly broken body. Her dress covered her injured legs so he ripped it enough that he could clearly see the wounds. They were bad, worse than he'd ever seen. He was an experienced healer but healing bones was difficult at best.

Sweat rolled down his forehead and into his eyes. He tried to wipe it away but found that his hands were covered in blood so wiping didn't help much. He pulled the Star of Salus off from around his neck. Her legs were the worst so he needed to start there.

*She was bleeding from the gash in her leg, so if he could stop that, it might give him more time,* he thought.

He took the star in his hands and placed them on her exposed wound and began to recite his strongest healing incantation. Nothing happened at first, but he continued to repeat the incantation over and over. Slowly the star began to glow, and the light gradually spread first to his hands and from there to her legs.

Halistan kept his eyes closed tight as he chanted. Slowly, the woman's wounds all began to heal. The bones made horrible cracking noise as they pulled back together. Halistan opened his eyes slightly as he continued the incantation. The bones in her leg reformed, and the skin grew back together. In almost no time at all her legs looked like they were back to normal. The glow of the spell spread along her skin and across the rest of her body.

Halistan hoped that she would not awaken at this time. He had healed broken limbs for soldiers, and if they woke up while they were being healed the pain of the wounds was excruciating. As this thought crept through his mind, the woman began to moan. She was slowly waking up.

"Just a little more," Halistan whispered to himself. "Almost there."

It was too late though. The woman's eyes shot open. Her eyes met his. He could tell she was confused and frightened. The pain must have been horrendous. She was silent at first, but that didn't last long before she let out a blood-curling scream that made Halistan think he was going to be deaf.

Instantly the spell was broken and the glow subsided as the scream went on and on. Halistan tried to cover her mouth to muffle the scream, but when he did she tried to bite him. He tightened his grip on the Star of Salus and brought the tiny holy symbol to the woman's forehead.

"Shhhh," he whispered, "sleep."

The star glowed as it pressed against her skin, and the scream died down. Eventually she was quiet. Her body relaxed and loosened. She fell asleep and went completely limp.

Halistan was beginning to resume his spell when he heard shouts from outside. It sounded like armored men running toward the stable and he knew that they had heard the scream.

"Wonderful," Halistan grumbled.

He looked around the stable. There really wasn't any place he could hide. Maybe he could cover himself and the woman with hay, he thought, but he knew that would just delay their capture.

Then he saw some steps leading up to the stable loft. Maybe there would be some place up there that would conceal them until the guards left. He didn't know, but it was worth the chance. He picked up the woman again. She flopped around in his arms, seeming heavier now than she had before, but he managed to carry her up the steps. He heard her moaning a little and knew that she must still be in some pain, but hopefully the sleeping spell would keep her asleep until her body healed enough. That's the best he could wish for.

He heard the men outside approaching the stable. Their armor clinked with every step they took, and from the sound of it, there must have been dozens of them. Halistan frantically looked around but there was nothing that would help to hide them. No crates, no hay, nothing except tools hanging on the walls.

Down below, soldiers began to swarm in and started rummaging through each stall. Horses neighed at them as the men shoved them aside to check to see if anyone was hiding in the hay that lined the stalls. It was only a matter of time before the soldiers came up into the loft. Halistan was afraid to move. If he made a sound they would look up and discover them.

The woman groaned again, this time a little louder than before. He feared that the soldiers would hear her and it made his heart race. He could feel sweat drip down his forehead into his eyes, but he tried to ignore the sting of it. Again he looked around, but there was still no place to go. He decided to crouch down in the hopes it would make them less noticeable.

Then, out of nowhere, a bright line of blue light appeared out of thin air. It expanded up and down until it was the size of a doorway. Halistan had never seen magic like this before and didn't know what it could be. He saw the outline of a figure in the doorway, but couldn't make out what or who it was.

"Come, child."

Halistan heard the voice from the doorway. Suddenly there was a commotion down on the floor of the stable. He heard guards yelling to each other to search the loft, and heard them begin their ascent.

"Come, child," Halistan heard again. "I can save you."

Halistan saw the guards rushing up and didn't know what to do--run through the portal into the unknown or face certain death at the hands of the guards. If he was going to save both the woman and his own life, there was really only one choice. He leapt into the portal with the woman just as the guards reached the loft.

As Halistan emerged from the portal, he was blinded. The stable had been dark and he wasn't used to the light that suddenly surrounded him. He felt someone take the woman away from him, which he was thankful for as she was getting heavy. Then he felt other hands grab him by the arms. His vision began to clear and he saw that he was in a room like a study or a library, surrounded by men in colorful clothes.

Halistan tried to jerk his arms free, but the men held tightly. Another man stepped in front of him and hit him square in the stomach, instantly knocking all the wind out of him. Halistan's knees buckled and he slumped to the ground, until he was held up only by the men holding his arms.

Halistan began to cough and wheeze as he tried to get back his breath. The man that had taken the woman from him laid her down gently. The man looked closely at a necklace that she wore and ripped it off of her.

"This is what I need," he said.

Another man approached and looked closely at the woman's face.

"Is…is this Allisandra?"

"No. It couldn't be," the first man replied. "Although the resemblance is uncanny."

Halistan had almost gotten his breath back and was trying to stand up when the man came back to him. He grabbed Halistan by the hair and jerked his head back to look at his face. The man was tall and slim, with sharp features and eyes that bored right into Halistan and gave him the shivers.

Halistan's mind swam and couldn't make sense as what was going on. He didn't know who these strange people were or what they had planned for them. All he could hope for was that they wouldn't kill him or hurt the girl.

"What should we do with him, Master?" asked one of the men holding Halistan.

"Take him to the dungeon. He's young and will make a nice meal later."

## *18. Time to Go*

"Sol," a voice whispered as a large hand shook his shoulder. "Sol, wake up." Sol stirred a little, turned his head towards the voice and opened his eyes. It was still dark, so he closed them again.

"Wake up, Soliere. We've got to get going," said the voice again. Sol opened his eyes again, and waited for them to adjust. It was Oather.

"What time is it?"

"Just before dawn. It's the perfect time for us to leave."

"Why is that?"

"Because Gretchen has left for the market so we can get out of here without her catching us," Oather replied.

Sol grunted again. "I don't care if she knows anymore," he laid his head back down on the pillow.

"Yes, you do. Otherwise you would have told her upfront where we were going."

Sol turned his head away from Oather. He heard a crinkling under his cheek, and lifted his head to see what it was. He couldn't make it out, so he sat up to get a better look. It was a small piece of paper that was lying next to him. He picked it up and handed it to Oather.

"What is this?" Sol asked.

Oather took the piece of paper from Sol. "You know I can't read, so why are you giving it to me?"

"Oh yeah."

"You really should read that, Sol," Serieve said, from behind Oather.

"Great, the whole gang is here," Sol grumbled into the pillow. He turned aside just enough to uncover his mouth. "If you want to read it so bad, go ahead."

He heard Serieve snatch the note from Oather, "I'd be happy to."

Serieve cleared his throat as though he were about to give a heroic speech to the masses.

"Dearest Sol," he began.

"I am sorry that I had to leave so early this morning but I did not want to take a chance on getting caught by Gretchen again. I know you'll be leaving to make your fortune today and I wanted to let you know that I'll miss you while you are away. Once you return, we'll sail around the world and see all the wonderful things you told me about. Do please keep yourself safe and come back to me soon."

"Love, Katrina," Serieve finished reading the note aloud in a tone that sounded like he was quite pleased with himself.

Sol decided that the two of them were not going to let him get any more sleep so he turned over and sat up and looked at his comrades.

"You wrote that, didn't you, Serieve?"

"What makes you think I'd write that? It's clearly signed by Katrina."

"I know that Katrina can't write that well."

Serieve grinned widely. "I might have helped a little, but the words were all hers. I just helped her...elaborate a bit."

"Stow it."

"I was just trying to help the girl out. She came downstairs a bit ago and really needed my help."

"Fine."

Sol rolled his eyes and wiped his hand across his face. He knew they were right and they needed to get going before it got too late. Across from him was his backpack that Oather had put together for him the day before. Sol got up, stretched, and got dressed. Shortly after, he picked up his gear and let the trio out.

The three made their way downstairs, where they saw Tanner standing behind the bar, holding a rag and cleaning some mugs.

"G'morning, lads. Would you like anything to eat or drink before you boys leave?"

"No, sir, I'm fine," Serieve replied. He set down his pack and sat on one of the barstools.

"Speak for yourself," Oather said, taking a seat at the bar. "I'll take whatever you've got, Tanner."

Serieve set the note down as he sat down at the bar. Tanner picked up the note and looked at it. "What's this?" he asked.

"Nothing important," Sol said, taking the seat next to Oather.

Tanner unfolded the paper and scanned it quickly. "Sounds like the girl is in love. Gretchen will kill you when she finds out."

Serieve shook his head disdainfully, "Sol, you really shouldn't be messing around with this girl. You could make her lose her job here."

"That's not a bad idea," Sol said as he took the note from Tanner.

He walked around the bar, reached down, and pulled a ledger from under the counter. He opened the book and put the note on the page showing the current accounts for the bar. Serieve watched as Sol thumbed through the pages.

"Tanner," Sol said, sounding a bit irritated, "why's my tab so high? I haven't purchased this much."

Tanner grinned widely and looked at Sol, "Remember, Gretchen is still holding you responsible for all of Serieve's lodging and meals."

"Dammit, I forgot about that."

Sol grumbled as he snapped the book shut and handed it to Tanner.

"Do me a favor and make sure Gretchen updates her records today."

Serieve's eyes lit up as he finally understood Sol's intent. "You know Gretchen will fire Katrina as soon as she sees that note, right?"

"I'm counting on it."

"Why would you want to do that? She seems like a nice girl."

"I never said she wasn't nice. I just don't want her here."

Oather leaned towards Serieve, who was clearly not pleased with Sol's answer. "You see," he whispered, "Sol isn't fond of long term attachments, especially ones here where he spends a great deal of his time."

"So that makes it okay to get her fired?"

"I didn't say it was right."

Serieve looked over at Sol again. "I guess you really haven't changed much since we were kids. You're still without honor."

"Amen," Sol replied.

Serieve must have decided it wasn't worth his time arguing with Sol, because he didn't say another word. A few moments passed and Sol finished his drink. Once he was satisfied, he got up and went to the wall where his cloak and hat were hanging. He pulled his hat off, rolled it up and put it in his pack. He then put on his cloak and rejoined his companions.

"Well, are we ready?" Sol asked.

Serieve and Oather both stood up and grabbed their packs and followed Sol towards the door.

"Wait," called Tanner. The three men stopped and looked back at him.

"Sol, you told me before you left on this fool's errand that if I agreed not to tell Gretchen what you had planned, you would clear up your tab before you left. You still owe me seventy-eight imperials."

"Of course I did, but I didn't think you'd actually hold me to it."

Tanner walked out from behind the bar and met Sol half way. As Sol reached the old man, he took a small pouch from his belt and handed it to Tanner. He took the pouch from Sol and opened it up to check how much was in it.

"I'm offended. Don't you trust me?" Sol said.

"I know you, Sol. Of course I don't trust you." Tanner replied as he set the pouch down and hugged the younger man. He let Sol go and looked at Oather and Serieve, "You boys take care of yourselves down there. That's not a place you can just walk in and out of, you know."

Oather's eyes widened, "How'd you kno…"

"It wasn't that hard to figure out, Oather," Tanner replied. "All the secrecy, supplies and skulking about you two have been doing the last few weeks. Do you think you're the first one's I've ever known to try and brave those awful ruins?"

Sol smiled in his characteristic 'I've got everything under control so stop worrying' manner. "You don't have anything to worry about. Just don't tell Gretchen and we'll be back before you know it…trust me."

The men left the tavern and made their way down the street towards the bazaar. The morning air was crisp, clean, and a little cooler than usual. Summer was coming to an end and autumn was approaching.

Oather inhaled deeply to take in the fresh morning air. Sol, on the other hand, felt like he could have used another three or four hours of sleep.

In the bazaar, some shopkeepers had already set up for the day while others were still in the process of getting ready. The men drew closer, making their way past a few patrons getting an early start on the day. Unlike the night before, the smell of rotting fish wasn't present.

"And just where do you think you are going?"

They all stopped immediately and turned to see Gretchen standing behind them, holding a small basket with a few goods in it, her head covered with a shawl. The three men just stood there like they had been caught red-handed in the middle of raiding the pantry. She approached them with a stern look upon her face.

"I know the three of you weren't going to take off without saying good-bye to me first." Oather and Serieve both blushed but couldn't say anything. Soliere tried to speak, but nothing came out.

"Oh, it's okay, boys," she said, letting a smile overtake her previous scowl. "I know you just didn't want to worry me."

"So...so you knew where we were going this whole time?" Serieve asked.

"Of course I did. I'm old, but I'm not stupid," she replied.

Gretchen walked closer to them as they stood there dumbfounded. "Don't worry, I'm not going to try and stop you from going. I learned a long time ago that when young men have their minds set on something, it's nigh impossible to talk them out of it."

"Now, Sol," she began again, "I know how you can be when it comes to money. Do try to err on the side of caution and don't take too large a chance." She reached up and straightened his cloak.

"Oather," she said looking up and pointed her finger at him, "Now you look after these two and make sure they stay out of trouble. You know how Sol can be."

"Yes, ma'am," Oather replied. Sol started to open his mouth in protest. Then he saw Gretchen glance at him and decided to keep quiet.

"And you, Mister Serieve. I have not known you long, but you seem like a very good boy. Do take care of yourself while you are gone and when you get back, please stop at the inn and spend some time with us. Tanner and I have enjoyed your stay."

"Yes, ma'am."

Gretchen stretched her arms out as wide as she could and hugged the three men. When she was done she stepped back and let out a small sniffle.

"Now you boys get on with your silliness and come back when you can pay off your tabs." Sol, Oather, and Serieve smiled back and told her good-bye. Gretchen turned and walked in the direction of the *Lucky Duck*.

Moments later, she was gone. The sun was just starting to rise above the tops of the buildings and more people were drifting out into the bazaar. They turned and gazed down the short but bustling street at their destination, Dragon Hall.

## 19. The Ruins of Tyric Nor

Sol and Oather had seen the building many times over the years, but this was only Serieve's third time seeing it. The first time had been when he and Sir Gavin had passed through this town several years ago, and it impressed him now more than it had then. He remembered some of the horrible and terrifying things Sir Gavin had said that he had encountered when he ventured into the stronghold during his youth.

As they drew closer, Serieve could see the detail of the gargoyles and got a better view of the stained-glass window in the front; and he was captivated by it. The window pictured a dragon fighting several knights. It had one knight in its mouth and two other knights were attacking its flanks.

Sol pointed up at the knight in the dragon's mouth and said with a laugh, "Hey Serieve, look. It's you."

"You think you're funny, don't you, Sol?" Serieve mumbled back, trying not to let on that he might be having second thoughts about this trek after all.

The double doors of Dragon Hall stood wide open. Other than the immense stained glass window above them, the building had no other windows. Inside, there were tables and chairs all around, and a bar to their left. Dragon Hall doubled as a tavern most of the time. People loved to come there and watch adventurers try their luck in the ruins of Tyric Nor. They loved it even more when they were lucky enough to be around when the adventurers actually came back--which happened a lot less frequently.

The bar was empty this morning, other than one old man passed out with his head on a table in the corner. Towards the back, past the table, lattice iron bars reached from the floor to the ceiling, separating that section of the room from the rest of the tavern. In the middle of that area was a pit in the floor, three or four arm-lengths wide. Above the pit hung a large basket, suspended in the air by dozens of ropes.

Serieve studied the contraption, "Is that how we're getting down?"

"Yep," Oather replied.

"I think I might be having second thoughts."

Near a gate with the iron bars stood a table with a large, hairy creature with green skin and the head of a boar standing next to it. The beast stood taller than Oather and held a big axe. Sitting at the table was a dwarf, counting a small pile of coins.

"Ogres," mumbled Oather as they approached the table. "I hate ogres."

The ogre eyed Sol as they approached, then shifted his gaze towards Oather.

"Tidus?" Sol asked.

"Aye," replied the dwarf, not bothering to look at Sol as he continued to count the coins in front of him, taking the ones he counted and putting them in small stacks to the side.

"We'd like to buy passage down into the ruins."

The dwarf stopped counting and looked up at the three men in front of him. He eyed them for a moment. "It'll be six hundred gold Imperials."

"Six hundred?" Sol yelped. "Are ya out of your damn mind?"

The ogre grunted what could only be taken as a warning. Oather's hand went instinctively to the handle of his sword and the dwarf shot Sol an irritated glance.

"It's two hundred for each of ya, and if you don't watch yer tone, boy, it'll be three hundred."

"It's normally one hundred. What's the deal with hiking the price up on us like that?"

The dwarf sat there silently for a moment. "Yer right, it is usually one hundred. One hundred to go down and then one hundred to allow us to let ya back in. I have serious doubts you'll be coming back up, so I want the exit fee up front."

"That's a crock," replied Sol. "If we pay you now, what guarantee do we have that you'll remember us after we've been down in the ruins for who knows how long? You're just trying to scam us, little man, and that's not going to happen."

The dwarf eyed Sol up and down with a look that would have frightened a lesser man, then stood up and went over to the bar. He rummaged around for something in a sack under the counter.

While the dwarf was busy, the three adventurers felt the glare of the ogre holding that enormous axe. Serieve was sure that if either the ogre or Oather made a sudden move the two would start to kill each other.

A moment later the dwarf rose back up, holding three metal disks that were etched to resemble the stained glass window at the entrance. The dwarf dropped them onto the table in front of the men with a grunt.

"Take these. When and if ya come back, give'em ta me and we'll pull ya out."

"Fine," said Sol, who was still none too happy about the arrangement. "Okay, boys, let's ante up."

Sol was starting to undo the drawstrings of his pouch when Serieve grabbed his arm and whispered close to his ear, "Can I speak to you for a moment?"

Sol looked slightly irritated, almost as if he knew what was coming next. The two stepped away.

"Yes?"

"Um…I thought the fee would only be one hundred Imperials, so that's all I have left," Serieve whispered to Sol.

"Damn it, Serieve."

"Well if I hadn't been mugged then I would have it," retorted Serieve. "Come on, spot me the money I need and I'll pay you back with what we make on this trip."

Sol stood there thinking for a moment. "Tell you what, I'll spot you the hundred you need; but, instead of getting an even third, you get twenty percent of the take," Sol said back with a grin. "I'll get the rest of your share."

"Man, you're a bigger crook than the dwarf."

"Take it or leave it, yer choice."

Serieve was silent for a moment, as he weighed his options, of which there were none, before he finally grumbled, "Okay, fine."

Sol stuck out his arm and shook hands with Serieve, sealing the deal.

"Give me the hundred you have."

Serieve handed him a pouch with the money in it. Sol took the pouch and returned to the table. Oather had already taken out his money and had given it to the dwarf while the other two were talking, and now held one of the three disks.

Sol poured the coins from Serieve's pouch onto the table and twenty Imperial Double-Kors spilled out. Sol took out his own pouch and counted out another twenty Double-Kors.

"There is the fee for my friend," he said and pushed the stacks towards the dwarf. He then counted out another forty Double-Kor coins for his own fee. By the time he was finished, his pouch was nearly empty. He had three or four coins left that went back into the pouch.

The dwarf handed Sol the remaining two etched disks and smiled at his new pile of money. "Well, let's get you boys on yer way to fame and fortune."

He got up from behind the table and pulled a ring of brass keys from his belt. He took one key that was bigger than the rest and inserted it into the lock of the iron gate. With a loud click, the gate to the pit chamber opened and he gestured for the three men to follow him inside.

Sol led the way after the dwarf, followed by Oather and then Serieve. As they drew closer, they saw that there were torches on the walls lighting the abyss.

The Ogre that had been standing next to the table followed the men in and took a stance on the other side, near the winch.

"Here's the way down," grunted the dwarf. "I'll offer you one piece of advice. Make camp on the upper-most level here. Most beasts stay away from the well-lit areas."

"Thank you for the advice, sir," replied Serieve.

Sol, who didn't seem to have the least bit of interest in what the dwarf had to say, had already taken out his lamp and used a torch to light it. The three men stepped into the over-sized basket and allowed the ogre to begin lowering them down.

The trip down was long and dark. Serieve lit also lit his lantern but still couldn't tell how deep this shaft went. All he could tell that if you fell down it, you wouldn't live long enough to care how deep it was. Finally, the basket came to rest on the floor of the pit and they were able to get out. In front of them was a passageway that presumably led to the ruins.

On the walls were torches that lit the ruins. Serieve blew out his lamp out and went to take one of the torches off to use instead. He found it was bolted on well and he couldn't remove it.

"How do they change these when they burn out if you can't remove them from the wall?" he asked, looking at Sol and Oather.

Sol ignored him and kept walking.

"The torches were created with the ruins. They can't be removed and they can't be extinguished. They're magic. Everyone knows that," replied Oather.

Serieve looked at the torch again quizzically before catching up to the other two. He'd certainly never heard that before so obviously not everyone knew it he mumbled to himself.

The three came to the end of the tunnel. It opened into an enormous chamber, large enough to be an arena. There were ornately carved columns positioned throughout the chamber. Most of the columns had carvings that resembled snakes slithering up to the ceiling. Others had carvings of warriors brandishing weapons and still others had beasts carved into them.

The three men walked through the giant room. Serieve noticed that there were entryways to both their left and right, each two or three times larger than a normal-sized door.

"Why do you think the passages in this place are so large?" Serieve whispered to Oather.

Oather leaned towards his comrade slightly and whispered back, "For very large monsters." Despite Oather's efforts, Serieve wasn't scared…yet. He was trying to imagine a monster big enough to need a doorway that large; it wasn't something he had thought about before coming on this trip.

Serieve suddenly remembered the map that he had bought and stopped to take it out of his pack. He retrieved it; put his pack back on and caught up to the other two as he unfolded it. He looked it over a moment, trying to find the large passage they were about to pass through. It took him a few moments, but he found it. Beyond the passage it looked like there were several other large rooms similar to this one, of which dozens of smaller passages branched. At the bottom of the map he saw some scribbling that said, "Diamond trap! Beware!" He recalled what the old man had told him about some of the devious traps found in the ruins.

Soliere, still walking in front, glanced back at Serieve.

"Whatcha got there, Serieve?"

"I was keeping this a surprise, but I lucked out and found a man who used to be a guide here in the ruins." Sol's expression grew irritated and he wiped his hand down his face. "How much?"

Serieve didn't say anything.

"How much was the map, Serieve?"

"It was two hundred Imperials."

"Gah! Two-hundred Imperials? I thought you were broke?"

"Well, it's definitely worth it...there are traps down here-"

"Serieve," Sol interrupted, "I know you're not stupid, but come on. Do you really think that map can tell you anything important about these ruins?"

"But I've been following it here and it's completely right." Serieve replied.

"You're an idiot, Serieve. Of course it's right...everyone in the entire empire has been through these main chambers. It's not till we get off the beaten path that it's all made up."

"No, I think you're wrong, Sol. The man who sold it to me was just trying to help me."

"Let me guess, he complimented you a lot to distract you, then sold you his only remaining copy of his map and probably disappeared right after he sold it to you? Am I right?" Sol asked.

"No."

"What was his name?" Sol asked.

"His name was Melic," Serieve replied, "and he did have to leave shortly after we met, but I still believe him."

"Melic? Melic is one of the oldest con-artists in Tyric. Just think of this as a lesson, because I'm still taking a share of your gold for loaning you the money that you gave to that swindler."

"I don't care what you think, Sol. I'm still glad I bought this map and don't worry, you'll get your money back."

Sol rolled his eyes and they started back on their way. Serieve kept referencing the map as they walked through the maze-like catacombs for what seemed like forever. He was surprised, however, that quite a bit of the map was accurate. The main chambers were plotted correctly; it was the smaller passages that seemed to be in the wrong places.

"Any idea how long we've been walking around?"

Sol ignored him. Oather eventually spoke up, just to break the silence.

"Hard to say since we can't see the sun. It does seem like we've searched a good amount of this level. We must have, because it's either that or things are starting to look alike. I think we have passed through this room at least three times."

"Yes, we have," Sol finally said. "I've been keeping track of where we were going and I agree. I think we've been through this way at least once before."

"So, where does that leave us? Are we just going to walk around forever?" Serieve asked.

"It feels like we've been walking all day." Oather said.

"I've been looking for a passage down to the second level, but we haven't come across one yet," grumbled Sol.

"On the bright side, we haven't seen any beasts, either." Serieve said.

"What are you trying to do, jinx us?" Sol replied irritably.

They passed an empty room that Oather said he was certain that he had seen before. Sol stopped and went back to the small room and looked in.

"Ehh," he mumbled. "This will do." His companions looked confused. "Let's make camp," he explained. "We've been walking around for a good while and this looks like an easy place to make camp. We should be able to hear something long before it actually gets here."

"I agree," said Oather. "We should take shifts watching while the others rest."

"That's fine; we can worry about that later. Right now I just want something to drink."

The men entered the room. Each claimed a small section of the floor for his own and set their packs down. Sol took one of the corners. After he had taken off his pack, he leaned back against the wall, immediately popping out his flask and taking a swig from it.

Oather pulled two arm-length rods from his pack and broke them into several pieces. He arranged some broken pieces of stone into a circle on the floor and placed the sticks in the middle. Serieve looked at him questioningly. The sticks weren't anywhere near plentiful enough for a fire. In fact they were little more than small sticks.

"These are lava roots," Oather said, arranging the sticks in a star pattern inside the circle of stones. "They burn for a long time and stay very hot. They're good for making a fire, but the wood itself is weak so it can't be used for very much else."

"I think I've heard of it before but I've never used it." Serieve replied.

"Yeah, I don't remember your dad or brother being the type of person who enjoyed the great outdoors, so I doubt you'd ever see the stuff," Sol said, taking another drink.

Oather poured a little oil onto the roots, and then pulled a piece of flint from his pack and a knife from his boot. Serieve watched Oather as he prepared a campfire. Oather held the piece of flint towards the oil-coated sticks and struck it with the knife. Streams of white sparks showered from the metal. After a few hard strikes the sticks ignited. In moments, the fire spread its warmth across them all and filled the room with heat and light.

"Hmm, I didn't realize how chilly it was down here until I felt the heat of the fire," Sol said.

He dug into a flap of his pack and pulled out a pipe, a small bag of tobacco, and his rolled up hat. He filled the pipe and lit it with the burning end of one of the sticks. After a few puffs, Sol tossed the stick back into the circle with the others and leaned back against his pack, taking another draught from the flask and a puff from the pipe.

Oather and Serieve sat back as well, each pulling food from their packs. Oather chewed on some dried meat that Gretchen had made the previous week, and Serieve began to work on a little bit of cheese and bread that he had set aside.

"Sooo," Serieve said, breaking the silence, "how did you guys meet?"

Sol didn't reply, and Serieve couldn't see his face beneath his wide-brimmed hat. Since Sol didn't seem inclined to talk, Serieve looked toward Oather.

"Soliere rescued me," replied Oather dryly.

"Rescued you? From what?"

Oather didn't respond.

"That's not the Sol that I remember."

Oather stared at the fire, "I was raised on the plains in the southern part of the empire."

"So how did you end up meeting Sol? The lower plains don't sound like a place Sol would normally go."

"No." Oather started again. "One day, soldiers from the empire came to our land and began enslaving the women and children. Many warriors were slaughtered in the battle."

"They couldn't be Imperial soldiers, the empire doesn't keep slaves."

124

"No one ever believes me," Oather said, his voice sounding angry for the first time since Serieve had met the big man, "but I tell you, they were Imperial soldiers."

"How did you survive?"

"I was enslaved along with my mother and younger sister after my father was killed. I was too young to be a warrior and was not much of a threat to the soldiers that attacked us. They separated the youths not yet of fighting age from the women, girls, and babies. Then they took those away as a group while we were taken another way. That's the last time I ever saw my mother or sister."

"That doesn't make sense, though," protested Serieve. "The empire doesn't have slaves. For as long as I can remember, I have never seen a slave anywhere in the land. Are you sure they were Imperial soldiers?"

Oather's expression turned from somber to hateful, "I am positive they were soldiers of the Empire."

"I'm sorry, please go on."

"I was taken away with the other young men of my people. We were marched to a nearby city on the coast. Once we got there I began to tire and could not keep up with the other boys. They began whipping me, but that just made me fall to my knees in pain. I tried to get up but couldn't so they came towards me and were kicking me for fun."

"I'm…truly sorry. Men, especially lesser men, can sometimes be cruel and merciless," Serieve replied solemnly. "Is that when Sol found you?"

"Yes, he saw the guards beating me. He came up and offered to buy me from the guards. Two soldiers carried me to an alley as though they were going to kill me and leave me behind. They met him there and instead of paying them he took them by surprise and killed them both. He was able to smuggle me out of town before the dead soldiers were found and brought me here to Tyric where Gretchen cared for me for many days."

"That's incredible. When I met Sol he was a two-bit thief breaking into my family's home, and here he is saving people's lives. I'm astounded."

"Sol isn't as bad as he wants people to think."

Sol let out a loud snore that interrupted the conversation.

"And on that note, I think you should get some rest. I'll take the first watch and wake up Sol in a while."

Oather unsheathed his sword and took a sharpening stone out of his pack. He began sharpening his blade while he stared into the fire. Serieve laid down and watched the fire burn for a few moments, listening to the crackle of the fire in between the sounds of the stone being run along the edge of Oather's sword. Serieve let out a yawn and sleep overtook him.

## 20. Prisoners

The cell was dark. Even after his eyes adjusted, Halistan could barely see. He knew there were more prisoners--he heard them coughing and moaning in the other cells--but none of them said anything.

After the guards tossed him into the cell like a sack of potatoes, he tried to get a sense of where he was. He was alone in a small hard brick cell. Iron bars sealed him off from the cells next to him. There were other cells across from him, but it was so dark he couldn't tell if anyone was in them.

There was a single window at the end of the block. Outside, it must be nearing daybreak as what little he could see of the sky through the window began to lighten.

He still wasn't entirely certain this wasn't some sort of bad dream. He'd had dreams of rescuing maidens and witnessing incredible magic in the past, but nothing this...real. He went over the nights events in his head again and again. He did find the girl, he did see the portal, and now he was here. A prisoner.

He contemplated what to do next. There must be a way to escape, but all the magic he knew focused on healing and the occasional charm. Both these skills would be as helpful in getting out of a prison as a backscratcher would be in slaying a dragon.

"Pssst," came a voice just off to Halistan's right. The sudden noise startled him and snapped him from his contemplation.

"Ye...yes?" Halistan replied.

There was a scuffling sound from the cell next to him as the prisoner in that cell scooted closer to his.

"Where did ya come from, boy?"

The voice was a man's voice--someone much older than Halistan, by the sound of it--and a little scratchy.

"I..." Halistan began, but he didn't know what to say, really. "I came from the Emperor's ball."

"No, that is not what I meant. Did you come through a portal?"

"Ye...yes, I did."

"Shhhh, the guards will hear you."

Halistan lowered his voice. "Did you come through the portal too?" he asked.

"Yes, nearly a fortnight ago. I've been stuck in this cell ever since."

"What happened? Do you know why you were brought here?"

"From what little I remember of it, I was gambling with a couple of homesteaders who live in the town near my farm. I had been drinking a lot, but thanks to my lucky ring I had done quite well. So well that the other men thought I was cheating."

"Were you cheating?" Halistan asked.

"Not at all, I've never been good at cheating and it just doesn't suit me."

Halistan was surprised to hear that. He had always assumed that anyone who gambled always cheated.

"Anyway, a fight broke out and I was outnumbered. I grabbed what coins I could and ran out the back. The others followed and I came upon this bright doorway of light and heard a voice offering to help me."

"That's what happened to me, too. Um, the portal made of light. I mean. Not the gambling."

The other man tried to laugh, but instead started to cough. Halistan could tell he was sick, very sick. As more daylight gradually filtered in through the window, Halistan saw that there were a half dozen or so cells in the block. The brick wall that separated him from the prisoner next to him prevented him from getting a look at the other man.

"Are there any other prisoners here?" Halistan asked.

"Just one other now. Across from you. His name is Tallmoor. He's a travelling gypsy or mystic or something."

"Have you talked with him much?"

"No, he doesn't have much to say. On the rare occasion when he does talk, he screams about how we're all doomed and such."

"That sounds dreadful," Halistan replied.

"My name is Roland, by the way."

Roland stuck his arm around the wall that separated them. Halistan clasped hands with him in return.

"I'm Halistan."

"Nice to meet you, Halistan," the man replied before starting another coughing fit.

"How long have you been sick?"

"About a week, I'd guess. Although it's hard to gauge time here. Some days I think I've slept through the day and lost track."

Halistan felt for the chain around his neck and pulled out the Star of Salus. He gripped it tightly in his right hand, close to his chest, and reached his left hand out towards Roland.

"I'm a healer in the service of Salus," Halistan said.

Roland began to cough again.

"If you take my hand, I can try and heal your illness."

"Son, I don't know if even a healer can do much against this."

"Please, I'd like to try."

He felt Roland grab his hand. The other man held it loosely, as though he was only appeasing Halistan.

Halistan closed his eyes and began to chant. He said a prayer and then began an incantation. Several moments passed and nothing happened. He felt Roland gently tug on his hand like he was going to pull away, but Halistan gripped the man's hand tighter and recited the incantation over and over.

Soon the star began to glow. A white light emanated from it. The light travelled down Halistan's arm towards Roland, and Halistan heard the other man gasp as the energy flowed into him.

Roland gasped, then wheezed and coughed again. The coughing continued as Halistan chanted, getting worse and worse until Roland jerked his hand away. Halistan heard the noises of the other man throwing up.

Roland coughed a little more before it finally stopped. Both men were silent for several long moments. Eventually Roland broke the silence.

"I…" Roland started. "I feel better."

Halistan breathed a sigh of relief. He was afraid his efforts failed.

"I feel better than I have in years, actually. Thank you."

"Don't thank me yet," Halistan replied. "Your illness is quite severe and you're not through it yet. Rest, and when you awaken, we'll try again."

"Thank you, Halistan. I can't tell you how much I appreciate this."

"You're welcome," Halistan replied, feeling happier now that he felt he'd done some good, "Now get some rest."

## 21. Unfamiliar Surroundings

Andrea rolled over in bed. Her body ached and her legs, in particular, were very sore. She pulled the covers tightly up to her neck and got more comfortable. Her mind was slowly beginning to stir as she awoke.

Her dreams were still fresh in her mind. A costume ball. Her spider dress. An attempt to kill Sonilauq. Jumping from the window right before she awoke.

The room was dark, but she could feel something different about the room. This was not her room. She didn't know where this place was; she only knew it wasn't her chateau. Andrea pulled off the covers, sat up and touched her bare foot to the stone floor. She looked down at herself and saw that she was still wearing her costume.

This sparked her memory and she realized it hadn't been a dream. Her costume was ruined and she had many small cuts all over her body from when she crashed through the window. She reached for her necklace but found that it was missing. She closed her eyes and secretly cursed herself for losing it.

"Where am I?" she mumbled.

She wiped her hands across her face and brushed her hair behind her ears as she took in her surroundings. She heard the sound of rain on a window behind her. There was just enough moonlight through the windows to make out the vague dimensions of the room. The room had a vaulted ceiling and tall windows. She walked around the bed to the windows. They were adorned with very thick and ornate drapes, which were already pulled aside slightly. This was fortunate, as she barely had the strength to move the heavy curtains.

Andrea couldn't tell how high up her room was. The rain was so heavy that she couldn't see much of anything. From the window the only thing that was visible was a stone gargoyle perched on the ledge outside. Its wings were folded in close to its body and its tail rested on the ledge behind it. Then, suddenly, the statue's tail swung around its body. Shocked, she jumped away from the window. A bolt of lightning streaked through the sky, lighting up the room.

"Good evening, my dear," called a voice from behind her. She spun around to see who was there.

A tall man--at least a head taller than Andrea--stood across the bed from her. He looked middle-aged and wore a dark suit with a long coat that reached almost to the floor. The style reminded her of garments that she'd seen her great-grandfather wear, back when she was a little girl. He had black hair streaked with gray at the temples, and piercing steel-colored eyes.

"Wh-Who are you?" she asked.

He bowed before her. "Allow me to introduce myself. I am Nicholas DeVanya, the lord of this castle."

"Where am I?"

"You are in my homeland, Renvara."

"I've never heard of that place. How did I get here?"

The man walked around to her and helped her lie back down upon the bed. She wanted to resist but she didn't know what was going on. Her body ached and she felt so tired. She wanted to fall back to sleep, but she was determined to figure out her situation before anything else.

"I used my magic to bring you here," Nicholas said. "There was no other way to save you. They were almost upon you when I saw you."

"You're a wizard?"

"I used to be, a long time ago."

The pillow felt soft under Andrea's head and she felt her eyes getting heavy. It was becoming difficult to keep them open.

"My legs, I can walk? I fell, I-"

"Shhh, my dear. You are still very weak," he replied. "I healed you. Your injuries were quite severe, but I was able to use my magic to save your life. You are still weak and you need your rest."

She did feel weak, but she needed to find out what was going on. Then she noticed that her necklace was missing.

"When I arrived, I was wearing a necklace."

"I'm sorry, my dear, but I did not see any kind of necklace upon you when you arrived. It may have fallen when you were being chased by the guards."

"The guards?" Andrea strained to remember what had happened to her, but everything was a blur. She remembered Sonilauq and the Emperor's ball but it was all a mish-mash of scattered memories.

"Yes, the guards who were chasing you. When I saved you."

Andrea's head was beginning to spin. She didn't know if she was just still tired or injured or what, but it was becoming hard to think.

He sat down next to her and brushed his hand along her cheek.

"There was a young man," she said, as she strained to put the pieces back together.

"I'm sorry, but I did not see anyone."

Andrea rubbed her forehead as she thought back to last night's events. Andrea struggled to sit up but finally managed to. Things weren't making sense to her.

"Tell me again, how did I get here? Magic...?"

"You are still in need of rest," he said, gently pushing her back. She put up little resistance. He waved his hand in front of her and suddenly her head began to swim and darkness swept over her eyes. "Sleep," was the last thing she heard him say.

## 22. Things that go bump in the night

"Wake up," Sol said as he shook Oather's shoulder. It took a couple of shakes, but then Oather's eyes popped open and his hand went to the hilt of his sword.

"Shhhh," Sol whispered. "I hear something down that way. It was a yell followed by some sort of shriek. Whatever it was, it didn't sound like something we'd want to meet."

Oather was still groggy, but he nodded to show he understood what Sol said.

"Wake Serieve up. I'm going to see if I can hear any more."

Again, Oather nodded to his friend and struggled to sit up.

Soliere walked towards the doorway with his sword drawn. Peeking around the edge, he tried to see if there was any commotion going on outside. Fortunately, the torches that lit most of the enclave allowed him to see far down each of the passages.

He didn't see or hear anything suspicious. Everything was quiet, and Sol wondered if whatever was out there had gone away. Moments later, he heard the awful screeching noise again. It sounded far away, but was still loud enough to hurt his ears.

"Come on," he said, "Get up and get your things. I think we're going to have company soon."

Oather and Serieve quickly readied themselves and joined him at the doorway with their swords drawn. Sol took the lead and the three men left the confines of the room. They moved slowly, attempting to be as quiet as they could. They crept out of the passage until they came to one of the larger chambers. There was another passage leading out of the large room to their right.

"Whatever I heard must have gone that way," Sol said.

"Look." Oather pointed to light tracks and droplets of blood mixed with sand. "Judging by these tracks, it looks like it must have been a man who ran through here and into that passage."

"If it was a man that came this way," asked Serieve, "then what was making that terrible noise? And why aren't there any tracks for it?"

"Maybe it hasn't caught up yet with whoever it's chasing," answered Sol.

"That's a disturbing thought," said Serieve.

"I agree. Let's leave this poor fool to his fate."

Oather shook his head. "We don't have much choice now. We have to find him."

"And why in the nine hells would we want to do that?" Sol asked.

"Because whatever was following him will be here soon, and it's going to either see our tracks or smell us." Oather replied.

"I fail to see why that makes this our problem." Sol replied.

"When that thing is done with him, it's going to come after us next," Oather said in a very 'matter of fact' tone. "And at least if we find him and he's not hurt too badly, he can help us kill it."

Sol knew Oather was right, there was strength in numbers. He let out an irritated grunt and started following the tracks on the floor. The passage led on and on; no rooms branched off. The footsteps became closer together. Sol knew this meant the person was starting to tire and was dragging his feet. It wouldn't be long until they caught up to him.

The corridor started winding to the left as they followed it, and they came to a few rooms to their right. Sol approached the first room slowly and tilted his head to listen for sound coming from the room. He didn't hear anything so he peeked into the room. It was empty, aside from a lit torch bolted to the wall.

He took a quick glance inside the room and caught sight of a figure in the corner, out of direct sight of the doorway. The figure wasn't moving, so he slowly entered the room, followed by Oather and Serieve.

The figure was a man, about their age or a little older, wearing a full set of chain link armor as well as gold chains, talismans, rings and other fine treasures. He had sandy blonde hair and a beard of the same color. His face was dirty and his eyes were closed. He didn't appear to be breathing.

Below the treasures he was wearing, a huge gash in his stomach poured out blood onto the floor.

Sol groaned, disgusted by the sight of the man. "Poor bastard. What the hell happened to him?"

Oather knelt down to examine the man's wounds. He was still trying to determine whether the man was dead or still alive when the man awoke very suddenly, startling all three of them. His eyes bulged in pure fear and he took in a deep gasp of air.

"Monsters!" he cried out. "Hideous...frightful....inhuman! Must get away."

"Shhhh." Oather tried to calm the man. "It's all right, they aren't here now."

Oather went back to looking at the man's wounds. "His wounds are very deep and look like they were made by claws, but I do not know what kind of creature could do something like that."

Sol took a better look. An entire chunk of the man's mid-section was missing. Oather seemed surprised that the man had been able to run away, considering how badly he was injured. Oather looked up at Sol and shook his head, signaling the man's fate.

Sol knelt down closer to the man, hoping that he could get at least a little information from him before he died, "What did this to you?"

The man was losing strength quickly. His breathing had slowed to nearly nothing, but he managed to speak nonetheless, "Beasts...terrible...kill everything."

"Was there more than one?"

Before he could answer, the man gave out, and his head slumped to the side. His eyes, still open, stared up at nothing.

Oather reached over and closed the man's eyes.

"He's gone," Oather said solemnly.

Sol took a bag out of his pack, then quickly started pulling the treasure off the dead man's corpse and shoveled it into the sack.

"What are you doing? He's dead." Serieve blurted.

"You can't desecrate the dead like that!"

Sol didn't bother looking back at Serieve; he was quickly removing rings from the man's fingers.

"You're right, he is dead. So, I don't think he will need them anymore. Besides, he probably took them off some other dead bastard that fell victim to this place, so you can't steal what's already been stolen."

"Your lack of honor offends me," Serieve replied smugly.

"Great, then we don't need to split this with you."

Sol couldn't have cared less what Serieve thought. He continued to pull the treasures off the dead man and stuff them into his sack. Oather seemed perplexed for a moment. Then he must have determined that Sol was right, because he began to help him. Then, suddenly he stopped, stood up and went to the door.

"What?" Serieve asked.

"I hear something."

Serieve also stepped closer to the door and tried listening.

"It sounded like rustling of some kind."

Oather kept listening and held a hand up towards Serieve, motioning him to be quiet. Sol had finished bagging up the treasure; now he joined the other two.

"Whatever is out there is big," Oather said. "I think it may have lost the trail. It sounds like it is searching. Its steps are slow and very heavy."

Sol was listening closely now too. "It sounds like there are several of them."

The three men could hear the creatures moving around through the corridors--slowly, as if trying to determine which way their prey had gone.

"They are going to be here any moment. If we stay here we're going to be found with him," whispered Serieve urgently. Sol moved to the other side of Oather so he could get near the wall and see out the door. He didn't see anything in the passage, which he thought was a good sign. He was fairly certain that the beasts were still a good distance away.

"Okay," Sol said, "let's get out of here. I think if we head the other direction before they start down this way, we may lose them." He pointed to the dead man. "Oather, help me pull him into the hall. They will see him and stop, giving us extra time."

Oather grabbed the man by one leg as Sol grabbed the other. They pulled him out into the corridor, trying not to make any unnecessary noise.

Sol dropped the dead man's leg and motioned for the other two men to follow him. They hadn't gone more than a couple of steps before one of the beasts came around the corner.

Sol looked at the beast with a combination of fear and awe. He'd never seen a anything like it before. It was an immense creature--almost twice the size of a human--with a body like a grizzly bear. It walked upright on its hind legs, while its front paws had been replaced with sharp pincers like those of an insect or a crab. The monster's head was the most grotesque part of its body--large and bald, with four bright red, almost human eyes. It had a long snout full of sharp teeth, with two large fangs rising up from the bottom.

The beast saw the men and charged towards them, swinging its sharp claws to and fro as it closed in on its targets. It made a terrible noise as it ran towards them, less like a growl and more like a high pitched screech which pounded at their ears.

Instantly, they began to run as quickly as they could away from the beast. The sound was so loud Sol thought his ear drums were going to burst. It caused a terrible pain to course through his head. He wanted nothing more than to stop running and cover his ears.

Oather grabbed Sol's arm and dragged him along to help him keep up. Behind them, they heard the sound of the beast tearing into the body of the dead man and ripping it apart, followed by the grotesque crunching noise of bones being snapped in two.

The three came to a large round room that had a single exit on the opposite side. They stopped and tried to catch their breath. Sol held up his hand for the other men to be quiet. He turned his head back in the direction of the monster to listen.

"It sounds like it stopped," he said.

"My goodness," said Serieve. "That thing was huge."

"Aye, it sure was," Oather replied, panting more heavily than Sol had ever seen him do before.

"Shhhh," Sol said. "I hear something else."

All three men froze. They heard more movement from down the corridor. It was slower, but there were more of them. The ground shook from the approaching menace.

"That thing was walking on two feet, right?" Sol asked, looking at Oather.

"Yes."

"That's a lot of steps for one creature."

"That's because it's not just one. It sounds like it has friends…three or four of them by the sound of it."

"Let's get out of here."

The three men turned and skulked silently across the room they had entered. They were halfway across the chamber when a monstrous form emerged from the passage behind them.

"Run!" Sol shouted.

They took off as two more creatures emerged from the halls and joined the first one. The men immediately heard an ear-piercing screech come from the leading beast as the creatures pursued them.

Soliere was in the lead as the three men ran down the passage. They passed several tunnels that branched off from the corridor that they ran through. After they had passed several more, Serieve suddenly stopped. Sol just barely saw his companion come to a halt. Sol and Oather both ran back to see what the hell was wrong with Serieve.

Serieve seemed to be looking at something, so Sol looked at it as well. At the end of the chamber he could see a bright shiny object. He squinted for just a moment to get a better look. All Sol could see was what looked like a white marble pedestal that had something shiny sitting upon it.

"Quick. This way!" Serieve yelled as he darted into the adjacent passageway. It led into another room that had multiple exits leading out of it. Another monstrous screech echoed down the hall towards them. They knew the monsters were approaching quickly.

Sol, followed closely by Oather, and ran after Serieve and caught up to him as he entered the room he stopped. He was looking at a wide, round, white-marble pedestal.

The pedestal was inlaid with beautiful and intricate carvings. Three golden, horn shaped spikes protruded from the top and held a single, flawless diamond that was as large as Sol's head. The entire area was bathed in a white light that shined down on it from a bright disk above.

Sol's eyes bulged at the site of the gem. "That's beautiful," Sol muttered slowly, starting to walk towards it.

"No, you can't go near it."

Sol started to protest, but before he could mutter a single word, the three beasts had caught up to them and Sol's heart sank.

A deathly stillness overtook the room as the horrific creatures stepped into the chamber. They stood there for a moment as the three men looked back at them. The largest of the creatures let out what sounded like a deep growl, then raised its head back, opened its jaws wide and let out a deafening sound that sent shivers down Sol's spine. Oather reached for his sword, but Serieve stopped him.

"When I give the word, run and jump over the pedestal," Serieve whispered to them.

Sol had no idea what Serieve was planning and looked at him like he was crazy, "What in the hell-"

"Now!" Serieve ordered, and ran towards the pedestal. Sol and Oather were both taken by surprise at Serieve's abruptness, and against his better judgment, Sol ran after him.

The monsters bolted after their prey. Their speed was startlingly fast. The leader of the beasts was almost on top of the three men as they reached the edge of the marble flooring that surrounded the pedestal.

"Jump!" Serieve shouted. All three men jumped as far as they could as the beast pursuing them lunged at them.

Sol's eyes went to the massive diamond. He thought about reaching down and trying to grab it, but just then the entire pedestal disappeared. All that remained beneath them as they leapt was a wide pit of glowing green acid.

Serieve hit the ground on the far side of the pit first and fell to the ground, as did Sol. Oather did not jump quite far enough. He slammed into the edge of the pit with a loud thud.

The monster fell right through the illusory pedestal and landed in the pit of acid, screaming in pain as the acid consumed the hair on its body and melted its flesh. It tried desperately to grab onto Oather's dangling legs, but Sol and Serieve jumped up and scrambled to grab Oather before he, too, fell into the pit. They each grabbed one of the big man's arms and pulled him up. Then they turned and dashed through the corridor that left the chamber behind them, their hearts beating furiously as they made their escape.

The two remaining beasts had stopped just short of the pit and did not fall in. Instead, they split up, went around the pit, and continued the chase. All three men were getting tired. Sol felt the sting of the salty sweat drip into his eyes as they ran. They were all panting hard as they tried to outrun the creatures following them.

"These things just don't give up," Sol gasped as they turned and took another passage to their right.

Oather stopped and pointed at a small tunnel at the base of the wall. "Sol, let's go through here. They're too big to fit through."

"You're right," Sol said. "Let's try it."

He knelt down and went through first. The tunnel was barely large enough for him to get through with his pack on. Sol crawled through as quickly as he could, not knowing where it would come out. It was pitch black in the crawlspace, since the lights from the torches that lit the ruins did not reach into the tunnel. The stone tunnel was cold to the touch and as he crawled he kept feeling things that crunched underneath him. He hoped they were just bugs.

Sol heard Serieve enter the tunnel right behind him, and then finally Oather. Soliere heard Serieve groan in disgust as he, too, crushed whatever was on the ground beneath them.

Oather was crawling in to catch up to the other two when the beasts caught up to them. He had been right; the monsters could not fit into the tunnel. Instead, they stuck their sharp, clawed arms into the tunnel and tried to grasp at the men. Oather, fortunately, had already gone further than the monster's long arms could reach.

Sol saw light not far ahead of him. He kept going towards it and saw another opening where the tunnel let out into another corridor. He crawled out and moved aside so that Serieve and Oather could also come through. Once he was out of the way, Sol slumped to the ground to catch his breath.

He leaned his head back and stared at the ceiling as he rested. "What the hell are those things?"

Oather closed his eyes. "I don't know. I've never seen or heard of anything like them before in my life."

Serieve didn't say anything. Instead, he dusted himself off. "Those tunnels are filthy," he said in between deep breaths, as he wiped some of the dirt from his face.

"It's old, Serieve, what did you expect?"

Serieve ignored him and sat down across from Sol, still wiping sweat and dirt from his face.

Sol sat there for another moment, finally starting to catch his breath, and thought about what had just happened. He didn't understand how Serieve had known that the pedestal was just an illusion.

"How did you know about that trap?"

Serieve removed his pack and took out the map he had purchased. He tossed the map to Sol.

"Look at the bottom left corner, where it's circled."

Sol picked up the map and held it so he could read it. On the bottom corner was scribbled, "Diamond Trap – Beware!"

"Hmm," Sol mumbled. "I'll be damned."

"Still think that map was a waste?"

"I still think it's a fake, if that's what you want to know, and our agreement still stands," he replied, tossing the map back to Serieve.

Oather was quiet. When Sol looked over at him, he saw that Oather had a stern look on his face and was starting to stand up slowly. Both Sol and Serieve watched Oather get up, but neither said anything. Oather moved back to the wall where they had emerged from the tunnel and put his ear near the wall.

"Do you hear that?" he asked the other two.

Sol stood up and listened to the wall. He could hear something but didn't know what it was. It sounded like a dozen men breaking rocks with hammers.

"That can't be good," muttered Oather.

"Surely they couldn't still be after us?"

"You bet they can," replied Sol. "Let's get out of here."

Serieve picked up his pack and they quickly followed Sol down the corridor. Just as they turned a bend, the wall behind them began to shake and then crumbled in a crash of dust and rubble. Two gigantic bestial forms emerged from the dust. The creatures' eyes blazed as they scanned the room for their prey. One of them sniffed the air and turned in the direction of the men and began to pursue them once more.

"These things never give up," Sol said as the trio dashed through yet another room.

"How do they know which way we're going?"

"They can probably smell us a league away," answered Oather.

Their pace slowed as fatigue set in. They came across a large room with a tall ceiling and two rows of columns reaching up to the ceiling. There were half a dozen rooms on each wall branching off this main room, but it was otherwise empty.

"Which way now?"

Sol didn't answer. He was concentrating on what they could possibly do to get the creatures off their trail. As he stepped further into the room he heard something. It was faint, but sounded like water running over a waterfall.

He desperately hoped that he was right, and that it wasn't just his imagination playing a cruel trick on him. Sol started to walk towards the rooms that were closest to them. He went to the first one and poked his head in for a moment. Then he came out and went to the next, and then the next. By the time he got to the fourth room he called back over to the other two, "Come on, we don't have much time," and waved for them to follow.

Serieve and Oather followed him into the room that Sol had entered. It was a room about the same size as the common room of the Lucky Duck, but it was completely bare. Sol was already at the rear of the room looking at the ground when they joined him. Not far away, he heard the ear piercing screech of the beasts. They were drawing close again.

When Oather and Serieve joined him, he was looking at an underground stream that flowed through the ruins and came into this room through a trench. The stream flowed along the entire back wall from a tunnel at one end and rushed out through another tunnel at the other end of the room.

"I thought I heard water," Sol told them.

"We've got to get out of here, Sol, they're going to catch up with us any moment," Serieve said urgently. "What are you thinking?"

"This is our way out," Sol replied.

"You are crazy if you think I'm going down that. We have no idea where it will come out….or if it comes out at all. For all we know it may not touch air again for hours and we'll be dead."

"We know they must be following us by scent, Serieve, so we are going to have to lose them in water. This is the only water we have. We are exhausted, and there is no way we can keep running from them. If we try, we are going to just end up like that other poor dead bastard."

Serieve drew his sword. "I'd rather take my chances in a fight than to drown trying to run away."

Sol handed the sack of treasure he was carrying to Serieve. "Here, hold this."

Without thinking, Serieve took the sack from him and with one quick shove; Sol pushed Serieve into the rapidly flowing stream.

Serieve let out a yelp as he hit the gushing water and was quickly pulled along with the current towards the dark tunnel, "I'm going to killlll yyoouuuuuu Ssooooollllllllll…" was all that Sol and Oather heard as Serieve was sucked into the tunnel.

"Your turn, Oather."

Oather looked down at Sol with a look like Sol had gone crazy. "I don't know about this, Sol," he replied. They heard the now familiar footsteps of the beasts enter the room outside.

"They're coming." Sol nudged his friend. "Trust me," he said, and pushed Oather near the edge of the stream.

A moment later the beasts found the entrance to the room. One of the monsters let out a savage howl and charged. Oather leapt into the water and was swept away into the tunnel.

Sol couldn't wait a moment longer. The beast was nearly upon him. Narrowly avoiding the monster's massive claws, Sol dived into the stream.

## *23. Misha*

Andrea rolled over onto her side. She felt the soft down pillow conform to her face. She laid there, wrapped up in the heavy blankets, and slowly opened her eyes. Even though it was dark in the room she could make out some of the room's features.

Her mind raced, recalling what she thought had just been a very odd and horrifying dream. She threw off the blankets that covered her and slid out of bed. Her feet touched the floor and felt the familiar touch of icy cold stone beneath them.

Her heart sank. This wasn't a dream. Andrea eased her foot back down onto the cold floor and felt her way around the bed. Her eyes began to adjust to the lack of light. The room was divided into two parts. On one side was the enormous bed where she had awakened. On the other side were several pieces of furniture and a small round table. On the wall furthest from her, there was a fireplace where a small fire was burning. Andrea heard the soft sounds of the wood crackling as it burned, but little heat emanated from it any longer.

Behind her, the door handle began to turn as someone started to enter. Andrea's mind raced as she looked for something to defend herself with. All she saw was a silver candlestick holder sitting upon the table. She picked it up and held it in her right hand, ready to strike whoever or whatever came through the door.

The door opened and, to her surprise, it was a young girl holding a tea tray. The girl was in her teens by Andrea's guess, but it was very dim in the room and hard to tell for certain. She wore a servant's dress that covered her arms down to the wrist and her lower body down to her shoes.

The girl let out a startled cry and dropped the tray onto the floor with a loud crash. Andrea, seeing how much she'd startled the young girl, quickly set down the candlestick holder.

"Shh, shhh," Andrea said, as she rushed towards the girl. She grabbed the girl's head and held the girl's face close to her own. "It's okay, I'm not going to hurt you," she whispered and held her finger up to the girl's lips to caution the girl to remain quiet. The girl stood there, frozen, as Andrea spoke.

"Do you know where I am?"

The girl nodded her head.

"Good. Do you know how I can escape from here?"

The girl didn't answer.

"Look," continued Andrea, "I need to get out of here and I need you to help me. Do you understand?"

The girl was quiet for a moment longer before speaking.

"I'm sorry, I ca… cannot help you. N…no one can es…escape from here."

"What do you mean?"

"I really can't say anymore, Madame. The Master would not like me talking about it. "

Andrea released the girl, who seemed to have calmed down a little. The girl backed away from Andrea and edged towards the fireplace. She reached into a pocket and removed a piece of paper. She lit it from the remaining embers of the fire and proceeded to light several lamp stands that Andrea now noticed were placed around the room.

"The Master?" Andrea asked.

"Yes, he is waiting for you. I was sent up here to wake you and see to your needs. I brought some tea, as I thought you might like some while you freshen up," the girl said. She came back to take care of the mess on the floor. Andrea stepped out of her way as she knelt down and began picking up the pot, the broken porcelain and the tray, while using part of her skirt to soak up the spilled tea. In the midst of cleaning up the mess, the girl stopped and looked up at Andrea.

"I took the liberty of setting some of your clothes out for you," she said. "There are several to choose from." The girl glanced over at some clothes draped across one of the chairs in the sitting area. "I think the green one would look beautiful on you, like it does in your portrait."

Andrea's attention had turned to the clothes, but when she heard the last statement, she looked back at the girl, who was still busily mopping up the tea.

"Excuse me?"

The girl looked back up at her with a worried look on her face, "You are her, aren't you?" the girl asked apologetically, switching her gaze from Andrea to a painting hanging on the wall above the headboard of the bed.

Andrea walked around to the foot of the bed in order to get a better view of the painting. It was large, at least half the width of her bed and twice as tall. It was a picture of a strikingly beautiful woman with dark auburn hair, a light complexion, and stunning hazel eyes that seemed to radiate light as Andrea looked at them. The woman was indeed wearing a green dress that accentuated her hazel eyes.

Andrea kept staring at the portrait because there was no way to deny it, she was the very image of the woman in the painting.

"How can this be?" she asked.

The servant girl had risen and was standing just a few steps away from her.

"Ma…Madame," the girl stammered, as if she were afraid again, "we…we should get you prepared to see the Master."

"What is your name?"

"Misha," the girl replied weakly.

"Is there a bath nearby?"

"Yes, Mistress. In the chamber across…"

"I think I might just take a bath for now. I still feel sore and disoriented."

"Of course, mistress. I have some medicine that might help you feel better."

"Thank you, I would like that."

Misha reached down into one of her apron pockets. She pulled out a small glass phial and handed it to Andrea.

Andrea inspected it closely. The tiny bottle contained a bright green liquid unlike any she had ever seen before. The bottom half of the bottle was saturated with silver particles. They swished around the inside of the bottle like fine sand in water.

In her business it was never a good idea to eat or drink something given to you by someone else. However, if the girl or her master had wanted her dead, she'd be dead already.

"You'll need to shake it up before you drink it, mistress."

"Thank you, Misha."

Andrea shook the tiny bottle and removed the stopper. Against her better judgment, she tilted her head back and drank the entire contents of the phial. She tried not to taste it, but it was so strong she couldn't help herself. It wasn't entirely unpleasant. It was similar to licorice but burned her throat like a strong spirit. Andrea forced the liquid down and handed the bottle back to Misha.

"Shall I tell the Master that you are still recovering and will not make it to dinner?"

"No, on second thought, I will attend. Just let him know I will take some time," Andrea was finally able to say after swallowing the medicine. "Draw me a bath and then you can tell your master that I will be down when I am finished."

The girl stood there as if she were awaiting more instructions.

"You may go now," Andrea dismissed. Misha bowed and left the room.

Andrea turned back to the painting. The eyes seemed to stare right into her soul.

After some time, she stepped out of the bath chamber, dressed and made herself ready for dinner. That is when she saw Misha waiting for her. The younger woman looked a little anxious at first, but her eyes widened as she caught a glimpse of Andrea.

"Mistress, you....you are beautiful."

"Thank you, Misha."

"Please, the Master does not like waiting. Come this way," Misha said as she quickly started down the hall.

They were at one end of a very long hallway. A wide red carpet swept down the passage. Behind them, the hall ended in a stairwell winding down to another level. Long, woven banners and tapestries adorned most of the hall. In between the banners hung grand portraits of nobles. The second or third one they passed was of a woman holding a child; the brass plaque at the bottom read "*Queen Natalie and Prince Serge 1100-1124 A.W.*"

"Who are these people?" Andrea asked.

"They are the King's ancestors. Queen Natalie would have been the king's grandmother...that is, if she had survived childbirth. She did not, and the king later married the woman who eventually became the Master's actual grandmother."

"Grandmother?" Andrea mumbled to herself. "But that was over a hundred years ago…"

She followed Misha towards the door. To her surprise, it opened by itself at their approach.

With Misha, Andrea entered the room and saw a long, polished cherry wood dining table, large enough to seat a dozen people at a single setting. Atop the table was a banquet of food: a large roasted bird, a stuffed pig, trays of fruits and cheeses, several loaves of bread, elaborate pastries, and cakes of all kinds.

A man stood at one end of the long table. He was dressed like a noble, and Andrea faintly remembered him from the night before. He wore a black dress coat and black pants. His vest was the color of blood and he had a single red rose in his breast pocket.

As she entered, he came to meet her halfway and immediately bowed to her.

"Allisandra, my love," he said as he looked her in the eyes. "I'm overcome with joy that you have returned."

Andrea did not know what to make of the strange man. He was talking to her as if he had known her for years, but she had no idea who he was. Surely he must be the master that Misha spoke of, but she expected him to be older. She held out her hand to him. He kissed it and smiled at her as she forced herself to smile back.

"You must be famished," he said, turning back towards the table. "I did not know what you would like to eat, so I had the kitchen make all of your favorites."

"Thank you. Yes, I am, quite hungry."

She had no idea how long it had been since she had eaten, but all the fragrant food upon the table reminded her that it had been a while.

"Please, sit, my dear," beckoned the gentleman as he led her to the far end of the table.

"I'm sorry, sir, but I think you have me confused with someone else. I do not even know your name."

"You are completely right. You were still stunned last night when you awoke, and you probably have very little memory of our discussion. Where are my manners?" he apologized. "I am King Nicholas DeVanya of the kingdom of Renvara."

"My name is Andrea Vinciq. I am pleased to make your acquaintance," she replied and took her seat. Nicholas bowed to her and returned to his side of the table. When they took their seats, servants emerged from the doors at either end of the room to wait on them. These servants were dressed in the same kind of drab brownish-gray clothing as Misha. They also had Misha's drab brown hair and pale features. One took Andrea's napkin and placed it upon her lap while another poured a glass of wine for her, while another filled her plate with different types of food. In just moments she was prepared to eat, and the women retreated from the room as quickly as shadows from the light.

"Please," Nicholas gestured. "Eat."

Andrea began to eat and started with some of the roast pig. It was the most tender meat that she had ever eaten. The taste was unlike anything she had ever before encountered. She had taken three or four more bites before she noticed that the king was just sitting there, staring at her.

"Aren't you going to eat, your Highness?"

He picked up his fork and took a bite, "The cooks have outdone themselves once again," he said, and smiled back at her as Andrea resumed her meal in silence.

It wasn't long before she noticed him staring again. She stopped eating and looked up at him.

"Is there something wrong, my dear?" he asked.

"You're staring again."

"Oh, I am so terribly sorry, my love. I am just so overcome with joy and disbelief that you are home. I honestly thought I would never see you again."

"You keep saying that, but I really don't think…" a servant entered the room and approached the king. It was a man this time, dressed similarly to the other servants Andrea had seen. The man bent down and whispered something into Nicholas' ear. The king whispered something back. The tone of Nicholas' murmurings was filled with anger.

"Find them….I want…..now," was all she was able to make out. She continued to eat and pretended that she wasn't attempting to overhear anything.

When Nicholas was done, the servant immediately scurried from the room.

"I'm sorry for that…interruption… my love."

"What was it about?"

"Nothing, just a simple court matter that I will attend to after dinner."

Andrea set her fork down. She could tell that something else was going on, but Nicholas wasn't being entirely forthcoming about what it might be.

"Did you enjoy your meal, my dear?"

"Oh very much so. Thank you for being such a gracious host."

"May I give you a tour of our castle?"

"I do not know about a full tour, but I would not mind a short walk," she replied. "I am still a little weary so I'd rather not be out too long."

"But of course, how short-sighted of me. You're still healing. Please, allow me to escort you back to your quarters, so we may talk a little more."

Andrea really had no interest in hearing him dote on her some more, but she saw no way out of it. She could decline, but that would come off as rude and could damage her position with him.

"I would like that very much," she eventually replied.

He stood and offered her his hand. She stood and began to leave when she noticed the door opened at their approach.

"How do they do that?" Andrea asked him as they left the room.

"The doors?"

"Yes, I've never seen doors do that before."

"They are enchanted. I have, in the past, dabbled in the use of magic, and over time I have enchanted most of this castle."

"It must have taken a long time to enchant an entire castle," she said, trying to spur him into revealing more about his abilities and possibly his weaknesses. She wasn't threatened by him, but in her experience it never hurt to get that kind of information for use later, if needed.

He did not reply to the statement. They made it down the hall before he broke the silence that was on the verge of becoming awkward.

"I am sure you have many questions, my dear."

"I do, actually."

"Then please allow me to start with the tale of our tragic story, and more importantly…who you are," he continued.

"Actually," she interrupted him, "I'm more interested in where I am."

Nicholas paused briefly before responding, "All in good time, my dear," he said condescendingly. "We'll get to that soon. There are more important things to discuss first."

Andrea was conflicted inside. His tone irritated her and she wanted to tell him that she didn't care what he had to say unless it got her home. However, she didn't want to anger him and lose any advantage she had from his adoration of her, so she allowed him to continue.

"First, your name is, or rather was, Allisandra Frost," Nicholas began. "Long ago our people left the realm of the Empire and ventured out to find a land of our own. No doubt you are from the Empire and know of the tyranny the people must endure there."

"I am familiar with the Empire," she replied. Andrea could tell by how he started this story that this was going to take a while, which irritated her even more. At least he knew of the Empire, so she couldn't be that far away from it. That was good news, at least.

"Our people did not wish to continue to live under the rule of the Emperor. The taxes levied on us were growing far too great, to the point our people were starving. So we ventured out and eventually settled here."

Andrea made note that Nicholas' people travelled here from the Empire. That meant that she must be somewhat close. Perhaps if she could get a horse she could travel back herself. Surely the king had a horse she could steal if needed. Although, if she played her cards right, she might be able to leave with more than a horse.

"How...interesting," she replied.

"It was my ancestors, the DeVanya clan, who led us to this great land. Our people were happy and I grew up learning how to lead the people. I had a friend....well, an acquaintance, who was the illegitimate son of the high priest of Salus. As a favor to the priest, my father adopted Dominic and allowed him to live here in the castle.

"Dominic became a knight and eventually became the commander or our kingdom's army. All my life, Dominic had been jealous of me. He wished to be king himself, but knew he was no match for me, so he never challenged my birthright.

"When you turned twenty, you were ordained as the new High Priestess for Lila and Dominic met you for the first time and decided that you would be his wife. He tried many times to court you, but you rejected him."

"Pardon me, sire, but if you don't mind me asking. What does Allisandra's rejection of Dominic have to do with anything?"

Nicholas stopped and looked at her as though she slapped him on the face. "It matters, my dear," Nicholas said in a harsh tone again, "because it will give you more perspective."

Andrea knew she was treading into dangerous territory with him. She'd seen arrogant men like Nicholas in the past, who liked nothing more than the sounds of their own voices. She needed to coax him into telling her what she wanted to know. She couldn't do it directly so she had to try another direction.

"I understand that," she began, "but he seems so insignificant. It was your family that had the courage to lead your people here."

"Very true," Nicholas replied. His demeanor changed instantly.

"I'd like to hear about how long it took them to get here. Do you remember?"

Nicholas thought about her question briefly. "Several months, if I remember correctly, but we'll get back to that later. There are more important things to discuss."

This wasn't going to be as easy as Andrea had hoped.

"As High Priestess, you became a prominent member of the Council of Elders and I, too, was smitten by you."

Andrea forced herself to smile at Nicholas' compliment.

"It didn't take long before we were madly in love," he said, as he stopped walking in front of a large window. From the window, they looked down onto what used to be a massive garden. There were no longer any flowers there, but the rows of hedges could still be made out in an intricate pattern, although they were quite overgrown now.

"It was in the center of that garden where I asked you to become my queen and you accepted. Dominic was furious. He despised me for having you. It was the final straw for him and he decided that he would finally take what he wanted; you and my kingdom."

Andrea listened intently as they began to walk again. "What did he do?"

"He managed to convince the Council that I was unfit to be King any longer, and he wanted them to vote to remove me. They did, and instructed him to remove me from the throne. Something he took great pleasure in, I'm sure."

Andrea tried to put the pieces of this together but couldn't seem to. It felt to her like something was missing. "I don't understand how they could 'vote' you out of your kingdom. I thought that was the whole point of being a King?"

"You see," Nicholas replied condescendingly, "as I mentioned before, when our people came here they wanted to be free of the tyranny of an Emperor, so they created the Council. The Council does have the power to remove the King and replace him with another, although up to that point it had never been used."

"I see," she replied. "How did Allisandra vote?"

Nicholas stopped again. His face betrayed his puzzlement as he struggled for an answer.

"You...you, fought bravely for me in front of the Council, of course; but in the end you were outnumbered."

Nicholas straightened himself and pulled his vest taut; and the two continued walking.

"As I was saying, once the Council had made its decision, you rushed back to warn me. You implored me to leave, but I assured you that everything would be all right. Dominic arrived to arrest me, accompanied by the other Council members and a contingent of soldiers."

"That seems a little much, to simply serve you an order from the Council," Andrea replied.

Nicholas suddenly became much more serious than he had seemed before. Andrea could tell he was angered a little by her light-hearted statement.

"Dominic didn't want to just serve an order, my dear. He wanted to humiliate me in front of you. To have you see me in shackles so he could lord over me as if I were a peasant."

Andrea knew she could not let him get too angry, which would prevent her from getting any more useful information from him. "I'm sorry," she said in a soft, innocent tone. "I'm sure it wouldn't have mattered what Dominic tried to do. Allisandra would always see you as the heroic man she loved."

She reached down and gently grabbed his hand. It was cold. Almost like a corpse and she immediately wanted to let it go but she held on, as though she cared. He offered no resistance and smiled at her.

"Yes," Nicholas replied softly, "I suppose you're right."

"So, what happened?"

"I refused to step down."

"I'm sure Dominic didn't take no for an answer."

Nicholas let go of her hand and walked in silence for several steps. Andrea could tell that he was getting angry again, but she felt that the anger wasn't directed at her as much as it was at the memories that stirred inside of him.

"Quite right, my dear. He and his troops attacked and a great battle ensued. When all was said and done, Dominic had been slain, but so had you."

"You mean, Allisandra had been slain, don't you?"

"No, that's what I've been trying to tell you." Nicholas stopped and turned towards her. "I think you are Allisandra, brought back to me after all these years."

"Nicholas," Andrea began slowly, "I'm very flattered that you think that I am Allisandra, but it just couldn't be possible."

"It is possible," he said.

"How? How could that be? Even if Allisandra had been reincarnated immediately after she died, that would have been twenty-six years ago and you would be an old man now."

"There is more to this that you need to know," Nicholas replied solemnly. He turned away from her and looked out another nearby window.

"After I realized that you had been killed. I was angry. Very angry. I gathered my guards and any available men and we counter-attacked the Council members and their soldiers. We defeated them and in an act of rage I had all of them slaughtered."

"Oh, my," Andrea said as she joined him next to the window. "I can understand how furious you must have been, but I don't see how…"

"It matters because the Council members were also the head priests of the gods. Their deaths angered the gods, Lila and Vera in particular."

"How do you know that?"

"I know because they appeared to me. Lila blamed me for allowing your death and as punishment they cursed me and this land."

"Oh," Andrea gasped. She'd never heard of the gods actually interacting with anyone before. She wasn't even sure if they truly even existed.

"They cursed me to live forever with the shame of having not protected you. I can never die and I will never be allowed to leave this land."

"Oh, that's terrible," she consoled him. "I can't imagine how they could be so cruel."

"The gods are like that, my dear."

"When did this happen? How long have you been cursed like this?"

Nicholas turned away. Andrea touched his arm in an attempt to seem more caring.

"The last time I counted it had been several hundred years."

It took a moment for Andrea to grasp what he said. She wasn't sure how much of this crazy story she believed, but to hear that he had been here for that long was incomprehensible.

"Several hundred..." she muttered in disbelief.

This was the moment that Andrea had been waiting for. He was vulnerable. To make her happy he would surely help her get home, but she had to show him that she knew what he was going through. She slowly reached down for his hand and took it in her own. She raised it and brushed it across her cheek and looked up into his eyes.

"You must be so lonely."

"Terribly."

"I understand now why you want me to stay, but if you truly care for me, you need to let me go. I have a family that is worried about me and if you can help me get back to them, I will return. I promise."

Nicholas was silent. He turned towards her and took both her hands in his and looked deep into her eyes.

"I wish I could help you, my love, but no one may ever leave this land. The curse isn't limited to me, but to any and all that come here."

Andrea's eyes widened, "What?"

"It's true," Nicholas replied, "All that enter this land are subject to the curse."

"But...but...how?"

"When the gods cursed me, they summoned great and powerful demons. They inhabit the forests around these lands and any that try to escape are instantly killed."

Andrea jerked her hands away from him and stepped away. At first she thought he was lying. She'd never heard of something like this before but somehow it did make sense. Why else would the servants stay here?

"Surely there must be a way," she pleaded. "You said you had magic. You brought me here with your magic. Can't you send me back the same way?"

"Unfortunately, no. I have tried in the past but it seems the magic only takes people as far as the forest, where those that tried to leave were quickly killed by the demons."

Andrea's mind raced. They were now in the hall just down from where her room was. Her prison.

"So you brought me here knowing that I would never be able to leave?"

"Of course, I couldn't let you die."

"I'd rather be dead than a prisoner!"

The realization of this made her ache inside. She couldn't bear the thought of being imprisoned here. She got a small lump in her throat that kept her from speaking anymore.

"Do not worry, my love," he said. "The gods have returned you to me. That can only be a sign that they have forgiven us. Together we will find a way to release our people from this hell they have been forced to endure."

Hearing the conviction in his voice gave Andrea no hope.

"Until that day, you will live here with me again. This time as my queen, and I will fulfill your every wish." He smiled and tried to step closer to her.

Andrea pushed away from him.

"No, don't touch me."

Nicholas stepped back once again.

"I...I can't even look at you right now," she said furiously.

Nicholas tried to grab her hand, presumably to console her, but she ripped it away from him. She turned away and began walking back to her room.

"No," she said. "I refuse to be held prisoner."

"Until I can devise a method to break the spell, you have no choice."

"We'll see about that!"

Andrea stormed into her room. She expected Nicholas to try to follow her, but he didn't. He simply watched her walk away as she slammed the door shut.

## 24. *Fools Rush In*

There was nothing but darkness as Sol felt his body flow along with the cold water. He couldn't hold his breath anymore and was forced to gasp for air. Instantly, frigid water rushed into his mouth and down his throat.

He could feel his lungs tighten. Then, suddenly, he saw a light. Sol emerged from the dark tunnel. Everything was still a blur as water rushed over his eyes. He frantically reached out for something, anything to grab hold of, but he found nothing. Instead, something grabbed his flailing arms and pulled him out. Instinctively, he spit out the water and inhaled deeply.

It was Oather, and he had never before been so glad to see the large man. Oather jerked him from the flowing underground spring and helped him stand. Sol panted heavily to catch his breath as he got his footing. Almost immediately he saw Serieve standing several paces away, shaking off water and wringing out his clothes.

"Good going, Sol," Sol heard Serieve say sarcastically, as Sol doubled over and retched water onto the stone floor.

"What?" Sol replied when he could finally speak again. "The only way we were going to get rid of those things was to get rid of our scent."

Sol wheezed, barely having the strength to talk at this point. "What else would you want me to do? Let us all die?"

Serieve didn't say anything. He just glared at Sol.

"He's right you know," Oather told Serieve. "Those beasts wouldn't have stopped 'til we were dead, and they were following our scent. There was no other way we could have lost them."

Serieve finished drying off and got his equipment back together. He took the bag of gold that Sol had used to trick him earlier and tied it to his belt.

"You can give that back to me now," Sol managed to say as his breathing steadied.

"I'm sure you'd like that, but you gave this to me and with me it will stay. Just think of it as incentive for you not to try any more crazy stunts with my life."

Oather laughed aloud. "The boy learns quickly, Sol."

Sol, who was in no position to argue, just shrugged, "Fine. It's less weight I have to carry."

"So where are we, anyway?" Serieve asked.

The place where the underground river opened up did not look like the rest of the ruins; it was more cavernous. The stonework was cut like that in the ruins, as well as several of the magical torches, but partly through the room it turned to a natural cavern.

The grotto was an open space where it met the spring. It branched off in several directions, including one passage that looked like it trailed back into the ruins.

Sol looked at the entrance leading back. "Well, I guess we should get back in there and see what else we can find."

Serieve, however, was looking down one of the cave passages. "I want to see what's down here, Sol."

"Why? That's obviously not part of the ruins, so there isn't likely any treasure down there."

"I'm thinking more long term, Sol. If this leads to the surface, and assuming we're not too far from town, then we could open our own entrance to the ruins and make as much as those crooks we had to pay to get in."

Sol thought for a second, "Hmm, you might actually have a point, Serieve. I'm starting to not regret bringing you with us."

Without any further hesitation the three chose one of the caverns' passages and began to explore. They hadn't walked for more than a few moments before they found more torches attached to the cave walls. These were not like the enchanted torches back in the ruins, but were of the typical variety and unlit. Oather doused one with some oil, and using his knife and a piece of flint, managed to light it. He removed the torch from the wall and brought it with him.

"These caves must still be used," he said. "Look at the ground, and you can see some tracks. Goblin tracks, by the look of 'em."

"I hate goblins," grumbled Sol.

The passage wound left and right for quite some time. They had seen some paths that branched off from this main vein, but they decided to explore this path fully before they started branching off. Oather used his knife to make small cuts on the walls at regular intervals to show which way they were going. He made sure to make the marks high on the walls, so they wouldn't be seen by any creatures that might also be wandering through the caverns.

Eventually, the path came to an end. It ended at an escarpment. Not too high above them was a ledge that seemed to continue on.

"You guys up for a climb?" Serieve asked.

"A climb is fine by me," Oather replied.

Sol was exhausted from their encounter with the beasts and the last thing he wanted to do was go for a climb.

"How are you going to climb while you're holding that torch?" Sol asked, hoping to dissuade Oather from following Serieve.

"I can manage," Oather said as he bit the handle of the torch and started to climb up after Serieve. Sol reluctantly gave in and followed up behind them.

The new passage was a little smaller than the tunnel they had just walked down, but it was passable, even by Oather. Serieve took the lead as they made their way through. It did not extend far before it emerged to another open space that overlooked a good portion of the other cave passages.

"Come here. You can see almost everything from up here."

As Sol approached, he could see the other passages. There were large areas that opened into what looked like rooms in a house; all connected together. Many of the passages had light coming from them.

"Down there," Oather said and pointed to an area closer to them and to their right. Sol saw what Oather was looking at and immediately signaled the other two to get down and be quiet. At Sol's direction, Oather extinguished the torch as they looked over the edge. Below them, one of the other cave passages led to a larger chamber.

The room was lined with burning braziers that filled the chamber with an orange light. On one end of the room, eight to ten goblins were kneeling. Their faces were close to the ground as though they were worshipping. They looked like soldiers, and their weapons were laid out in front of them as they knelt. At the far end of the oval room were several other goblins in ornate black and red robes, each wearing a bronze skull cap. Close to the priestly-looking goblins stood two stone altars that had two prisoners chained to them. One of the prisoners was a tall old man, with gray hair and a beard. He wore a wizard's robe and was shouting at one of the goblin priests, but Sol was too far away to make out exactly what was being said. The other prisoner was an elf with black hair, pale skin, and black clothes; he was trying to pull on his chains to get free, but wasn't having much success.

"What do you think they are doing down there?" asked Serieve.

"Probably going to sacrifice them to some god or something," Sol replied.

"What?"

Sol glared at Serieve to keep quiet.

Serieve continued again, this time in a whisper. "We can't let them just die at the hands of those foul little beasts."

"Shhhh, look," Sol interrupted and pointed down at the ceremony. A taller, human-sized, cloaked figure had entered the chamber. The newcomer wore robes similar to those of the goblin priests, but the hood was drawn over his head. The wizard stopped yelling as soon as the figure entered the room. In one hand the newcomer held something that looked like a dagger, and in the other hand he held a black amulet.

The cloaked man walked past the soldiers kneeling on the floor and touched the amulet to the wizard's head. The wizard immediately ceased moving. The elf started to struggle, but one of the priests restrained him while the hooded figure touched the amulet to his head and the elf also stopped moving.

Serieve again looked past Oather to Sol. "We have to do something now. They are going to be killed!"

Sol ignored the comment and kept watching what was unfolding below.

Now that the two captives were incapacitated, a ceremony of some kind began. The cloaked figure stood between the old man and the elf, and the goblins began to chant. The figure raised the amulet into the air with one hand, while with the other he made slashing motions through the air in a repeating X pattern.

The chanting intensified, and then died down to a murmur, and the figure pulled the hood of its robes back to reveal a hideous skull. There was little skin left upon it and it looked like it had been dead for quite some time and was now decaying. Sol felt his stomach churn at the sight of the creature.

"What the hell is that?" Sol asked.

"Serieve do you see….Serieve?" Oather stopped mid-sentence. Sol felt Oather push his shoulder as he continued to watch the scene unfold below them.

"What?"

"Sol, I think we have a problem," replied Oather. "Look."

Oather pointed to the far end of the ledge. Serieve had maneuvered along the edge so that he could get closer to the two prisoners below. Sol and Oather watched their companion make his way closer and closer until he was just above the two captives.

"What is that fool doing?"

"It looks like he's about to start a fight." Oather replied.

"Well, we're not risking our necks to save him this time."

"We have to," Oather replied. "He's going to get himself killed."

No sooner had Oather spoken; Serieve drew his blade, jumped off the ledge and landed on one of the goblin priests. Serieve jumped up and impaled one of the goblins and then turned towards another goblin and struck it down as well.

"Why do we need to go after him? Go ahead, give me one good reason," Sol said as Oather was fixated on the fight going on below.

"He's still carrying the treasure we got off that dead guy," Oather replied.

"Damn it," exclaimed Sol as he rose to his feet. "Well, come on; let's go get his sorry carcass."

Oather followed Sol and the two quickly jumped down. By the time they landed, Serieve had killed the two priests. However, he was quickly being surrounded by goblin soldiers. The grotesque skeletal figure had backed towards the side wall and was shouting orders to the soldiers in their goblin language.

"I'll go left, you go right," yelled Sol. The two men drew their blades and prepared for battle. Soliere struck first, running towards one of the goblin soldiers who was about to attack Serieve. Sol kicked the goblin in the back. The goblin fell to the floor, and then Sol stabbed him in the back. Even after the death of one of their brethren, the other soldiers still hadn't noticed that Sol was behind them. Sol was able to kill another one relatively easily before he got their attention.

Meanwhile, Oather rushed up the right side of the cavern. He struck down a goblin that was turning towards him. The hideous skull-headed creature tried sneaking up behind Oather with a dagger in his hand. Sol saw the skull-headed man lunge at Oather with the dagger, but Oather was expecting the blow. Oather was able to dodge the attack. Oather quickly back-handed the figure and knocked him to the ground.

Shaken by the blow, the skull-headed creature lost its grip on the amulet and dropped it to the ground. Oather quickly snatched the amulet and tucked it into a pouch.

"Let's hurry up and free these guys so we can get out of here," Sol said.

The two men dashed over to the two altars where the old man and the elf were still chained. Both victims seemed to be in a trance. Oather shook the elf.

"Come on, wake up," he muttered. He shook the elf harder. The elf stirred a little and let out a small groan.

"The keys...." The elf pointed to one of the goblin priests lying dead on the floor. "Get the keys."

Oather knelt beside the downed goblin and rummaged through the goblin's robes to find the keys. He did find a small key ring with a single key. He rose and unlocked the chains that bound the elf's wrists. He had started to unlock the old man when more goblin guards entered the room. The skull-headed figure did not stay down for long, and was once again directing the goblins in their attack.

"Here!" Oather handed the key to the elf. "Take care of yourself and the old man."

Sol and Oather readied themselves for another round of fighting. They didn't have to wait long before the next wave of goblins charged at them.

By now the elf had freed himself. He had also freed the old man and was trying to pull him off the sacrificial table. The elf struggled to help the old man up as the old man still seemed incoherent.

"Here, let me help," Serieve said as he put one of the old man's arms around his neck and lifted him off the table while the elf moved the old man's legs off the stone slab and onto the ground. The wizard was just starting to wake up.

"He's heavier than he looks, huh?" Serieve said.

"That he is," replied the elf. "I'll do my best to bring him around. Quickly, go help your friends."

Serieve rose and headed to the middle of the room where Sol and Oather were engaged in fighting half a dozen goblins.

"Damn, how many of these things are there?" yelled Soliere to Oather, who was fighting beside him. Soliere side-stepped to avoid an attack by a goblin on his right. Seeing that the goblin had left itself open after the overextended attack, Sol kicked it in the gut and dropped it to the floor. At the same time as he hit another goblin in the face with the hand guard of his saber.

At the rear of the room, near the entrance, the skull-headed creature was pointing at them. As Sol dispatched yet another goblin soldier, he saw the skull-headed creature pull out a dagger and a vial of black fluid.

Sol was curious about what the skull-headed creature was doing and tried to keep an eye on him while he and Oather fought back the goblin soldiers. Out of the corner of his eye, he saw the creature pour the contents of the vial onto the dagger. The black fluid bubbled and smoked like acid on the blade.

As more goblins came at them Serieve stepped up next to Sol with his sword raised and prepared to fight. Then half dozen new goblin soldiers ran towards them. Sol side-stepped one goblin as Oather kicked another to the floor and stabbed it. Serieve took the lead and fought back two more of the goblins. Sol was beginning to tire. He wasn't sure how many more of these things he could fight off. There seemed to be an infinite number of them trying to get in.

Then Sol remembered the skull-headed creature directing them. Maybe if they could kill it, the goblins would flee. Sol glanced over to where the creature had stood only moments before.

It was still there and the dagger was still in its hand. Sol saw the creature draw back its arm and throw the dagger at Serieve. The world seemed to slow to a snail's pace as Sol watched the blade fly through the air. His first thought was to push Serieve out of the way, but he couldn't seem to react quickly enough. Before Sol could finish turning towards Serieve, the dagger had sunk deep into Serieve's arm.

## 25. Escape from the caverns

Serieve dropped his weapon. He grabbed the handle of the dagger and pulled it out of his arm. Blood gushed from the wound, along with traces of some strange black liquid. Almost at once his arm felt like it was burning. His head started to spin and his knees got wobbly as he fell to the ground.

Serieve tried to get up, but his entire body had become sluggish. It was getting harder and harder to move. Blue and red dots swept across his vision but he could see Sol quickly approaching. The elf that he'd freed from the altar was following close behind.

"Serieve!" Sol snapped at his friend and lightly smacked his jaw. "Don't you pass out on me. Can you hear me?"

Sol looked up at the elf.

"Can you do anything to help him?"

The elf reached over and grabbed the dagger and examined it.

"This poison is from a Tonorian snake, one of the deadliest in the world," he said looking at Sol. "Its venom works fast, but there may be some hope." The elf went back to the altar and retrieved a small satchel. He rummaged through it and pulled out a small glass bottle filled with a thick, bright yellow substance.

The elf uncorked the bottle. He held Serieve's head up, opened his mouth, and poured in the foul-smelling syrup. It tasted like a mixture of alcohol, vinegar and lard. Serieve gagged as he forced himself to swallow.

"What's that?" Sol asked.

"This is sap from the Abraxxis tree; it has some healing properties that can negate many types of poison. Goblins are well-known for their use of poison, so we take this with us on every mission."

Serieve's body trembled as he managed to choke down the medicine, "Good, because…my arms and legs feel…like they are on fire."

"That is the poison, I fear," replied the elf as he held Serieve's head.

"His eyes," Sol muttered, "They're turning white!"

"I can't see," whispered Serieve, followed by a cough.

The elf looked back at Sol, "There is nothing else we can do. I fear it may be too late."

"Oather, can you carry him?" Sol asked.

Oather grunted back.

"Good, then let's get out of here."

"No," Serieve spoke up, "Leave me here. They'll be back and I'll just slow you down."

"I am not leaving you here, Serieve."

Serieve tried to argue, but his eyes rolled back in his head and his body jerked as the elf struggled to hold him. Serieve could no longer feel his arms or legs. It hurt to breath and all he could see was blackness. Finally, even his hearing seemed to begin to fade and all he could make out was the faint rustling of his companions around him.

This is how he would go, in a dungeon. Far from home and unable to tell his brother good-bye. Serieve silently wished he had talked to Bourne one last time before he left to Tyric but he didn't want to disturb his brother so he had just left. Now he regretted that decision. Serieve's body thrashed back and forth several times before he went completely limp on the stone floor.

The elf laid Serieve's head down on the floor and looked up at Sol. "I'm sorry."

Sol said nothing, but Serieve felt Sol laid his hand upon his chest.

Suddenly, Serieve's eyes shot open, and his entire body convulsed. He let out a loud cough; his arms flailed and pushed himself away from the others. He turned over and vomited onto the floor. Shockingly, he was able to see and feel his limbs again. He felt like he had been punched in the stomach by an ogre, but he could at least feel again, which he was glad for.

"By the gods, that stuff tastes terrible," Serieve managed to say as he wiped his mouth.

"Serieve!" Oather bellowed in amazement. The big man nearly trampled the elf kneeling next to Serieve. Oather knelt down and grabbed Serieve's shoulders and hugged him tight. "I thought you were dead."

Serieve wheezed as Oather squeezed the breath out of him before finally releasing him.

Soliere slapped Serieve on the back with a grin. "I told you that you'd do something stupid and almost get us killed."

Serieve managed to crack a smile at Sol. Oather and the elf helped Serieve onto his feet.

The elf went back to the altar and grabbed a bow that was set against the stone, as well as his satchel, a quiver of arrows, and a few pouches. He re-equipped himself and took the pouches to the older man, who was now leaning against the wall for support.

Sol looked back at Oather. "Can you help Serieve walk?" Oather nodded back that he could.

The tall old man was finally walking on his own and joined the others. He pointed at Serieve, "There is no way he can travel in the condition he is in. We should not be taking him with us."

Sol stepped up in front of the old man, face to face, "If he hadn't risked his life to save yours, then he wouldn't be wounded now, would he?"

"He's going to get us all killed," the old man replied.

"Then I'll see you in hell," Sol growled back, staring the old man straight in the eyes. The old man did not say another word; he just glared at Sol, then backed away and mumbled something under his breath.

"Which way do we go, elf?" Sol asked.

The elf pointed to a passage at the end of the room where the altars stood. "That way should lead us out of here, if I remember correctly."

Sol took an unlit torch and held it to one of the braziers to light it, then nodded to the rest of the group to signal that they were leaving.

Oather helped Serieve up and helped him walk as they followed Sol out. The cave here was more like a tunnel than a real cave. It had a low ceiling that Oather would bump his head on every couple of steps. Serieve could hear him grumble each time he bumped the ceiling. The cave passage twisted and turned as they traveled down it. The elf pulled at Sol's arm, making him stop.

"Shhh, listen," the elf whispered.

All the men stopped and perked up to hear anything they could. There was a sound coming down the passage behind them--the sound of soldiers running in their direction.

"Can you run yet, old man?" Sol asked the wizard pointedly.

The older man was wheezing and gasping for air. "The drugs they used on me are still having a strong effect, but I will try."

"Then let's go. They will catch up to us any second." Once more Sol led the way down the passage, this time at a much faster pace.

Sol had gotten a bit of a lead on the others. Oather and Serieve struggled to keep up with Sol and the elf. The tunnel twisted and turned but they were able to keep the elf within sight. The elf went around a corner and Serieve heard the elf gasp. As soon as he and Oather made it around the corner they saw Sol quickly pulling the elf back from nearly falling off a ledge where the tunnel abruptly ended.

"I thank you, sir," the elf said as he recoiled into the tunnel safely.

Sol walked back towards the edge and held up the torch. The chasm was wide, easily twenty to twenty five arm-lengths across--there was no way they could jump it. The passage continued on the other side of the chasm, and it looked like there were the remains of what had once been a rope bridge. Two tall poles stood apart from one another, each with ropes that dangled into the open chasm.

Oather and Serieve joined Sol and they all looked at the vast crevasse.

"If anyone has any ideas, I'd love to hear them," Sol said quietly. However, none of them had the faintest idea of how they could cross to the other side. The chasm was so deep that they couldn't even see the bottom. It just drifted off into darkness and certain doom.

Just then, the old man walked up and joined them. He looked down into the ravine first, then over across to the other side where the remains of the rope bridge dangled.

"I used to know a handy enchantment for rope mending that we could have used on the remnants of that rope bridge…"

Sol turned to the old man, "You are a wizard?"

"Yes."

"Then can you get us across?"

"Normally, it would not be difficult at all…but the poison that was used on me makes it difficult to use my magic," he replied. "However, I will see what I can do. It will take some time."

Sol drew his blade. "Fine. You do what you can and we'll try and buy you some time."

Oather let go of Serieve, who leaned against the cavern wall and drew his own sword. The elf drew his bow and took a defensive position at the edge of the cave tunnel next to Sol and Oather.

Sol stood in the middle, the elf to his left and Oather to his right. Behind them he heard the wizard taking something from one of the pouches that hung from his belt and mumbling incoherent words to himself.

From deep inside the cave passage they could hear the sound of armor clinking, weapons clanking, howls and growls. Sol couldn't see the creatures yet, but he could hear them marching ever closer. The cave echoed with the noise of the approaching horde, making it sound like there was an entire army headed towards them.

"That bridge would be real nice right about now," Sol yelled back at the wizard.

The old man ignored Sol's comments and kept on chanting. Serieve watched the old man close his eyes to focus on what he needed to do. The ropes on the other side of the chasm began to stir. Several of them swayed back and forth till they looked like they were reaching up towards the other ledge. He held his arms up as though he was trying to reach out to the ropes on the other side.

Judging by the sound, Serieve guessed the approaching horde was almost upon them. Serieve wished that that he could help his friends fight against the oncoming goblins, but the thought of moving nearly made him throw up again. He saw the three warriors ready themselves. Sol and Oather gripped the hilt of their swords tight with both hands as they peered into the darkness, awaiting the mass of goblins that were hunting them.

The wizard reached into a pouch and took out a stone, which he held outward towards the swaying ropes. The stone began to glow and the ropes grew faster.

"So how about that bridge?" Sol called back again.

"I'm working on it!" the wizard spat back. Then, suddenly, a white dot appeared in front of the wizard. It expanded into a swirling mass of blue light large enough for them to pass through.

The first of the goblins charged out of the darkness towards the men. They brandished their weapons and bared their fangs in preparation for battle.

"It's about time," shouted Sol over his shoulder at the wizard. "Not exactly what I had in mind, but we'll take it. Let's get out of here!" he said to Oather.

Sol darted towards the wizard and the door.

"NO..." was about all the wizard was able to say before Sol ran past him and leapt into the gateway. In a blur, Oather was right behind Sol and ran towards Serieve. With one quick swoop, Oather grabbed Serieve and the wizard and they all leapt into the portal behind Sol. Finally, the elf ran behind them and he, too, leapt into the portal.

Goblins stormed down the passage as they saw the group disappear into the light. One goblin, who was much bigger than the others and the leader of the assault, tried to reach the elf before he disappeared. The goblin howled loudly and brandished its axe as it neared the portal. It, too, leapt towards the door in an attempt to follow, but just as its feet left the ground the doorway collapsed and disappeared.

The goblin, followed closely by several other soldiers, flew through the air towards the doorway, which was now gone, and continued through the air into the darkness of the chasm, falling to their deaths.

## 26. Strangers in a Strange Land

Sol hit the ground with a thud and a splash. The ground was very cold and wet. He was lying on his back, halfway in a small puddle in a field of tall grass. The glowing portal was above his head. Sol tried to sit up when the wizard fell out of the portal and landed directly on top of him.

"Agh...get off me!"

The wizard struggled for a moment but eventually managed to roll off Sol. Before Sol could get up, first Oather, then Serieve, and finally the elf all fell through the portal on top of him just as the wizard had done. As soon as the elf fell through and landed on the others, the portal flashed brightly and then blinked out of existence.

"Ugh, damn...Oather. I think you broke one of my ribs."

Oather got off Sol and helped Serieve up. Serieve immediately turned away and doubled over as he threw up onto the ground.

"Are you all right?" Oather asked as he helped Serieve steady himself.

"Yeah, I'm fine."

"That is a side effect of the sap I gave you, I'm afraid," said the elf. "It will save you from the poison but make you feel very sick for a while afterwards. It should wear off shortly."

"It could definitely be worse," said Serieve. "Right now, I'm just glad to be alive."

Sol brushed himself off as much as he could and turned to the wizard. "So, where are we?"

"That is what I was trying to say before you dragged me here, you dolt. I don't know! I didn't make this portal. My spell was supposed to recreate the rope bridge that once reached across the chasm, but that spell failed, just before the portal opened."

"What?" Sol asked, a little stunned, as a heavy rain began to fall. "Son of a...damn...hell," he finished, grumbling and shaking his head as the situation sunk in.

They stood next to a poorly made dirt road that was really little more than a wagon trail. Sol looked up at the sky. It was one giant, dark-gray cloud as far as the eye could see. The lands surrounding them were grass-covered plains, with a few rolling hills in the distance. Sol was fairly sure it was daylight, but the sky was so dark that it was hard to tell for sure. Both directions of the trail led off into the grasslands. One way went towards the rolling hills in the distance; the other just wound on until it disappeared into the horizon.

"So, what should we do now?" Sol asked Oather, as the sky opened up into a full downpour. "We have no idea where we are, we're standing on a little dirt road in the middle of absolutely nowhere, and now we're soaking wet."

"It's not that bad. Quit whining, Sol," Oather replied.

"This may be worse than we think," said the elf, as he stepped up to Sol and Oather. "I don't know what it is, but something doesn't feel right about this place."

"You're just imagining things," Sol replied.

"So which way should we go?" Oather asked.

"I'm going that way," Sol said as he pointed down the trail leading to the hills. "You can join me if you want. What's your name, elf?"

The elf bowed his head to Sol. "My name is Khu-Rá."

"What about you, wizard? What's your name?"

The wizard had his back to them, looking off into the distance. He took out a wide-brimmed maroon hat from an inside pocket of his robe and put it on.

"I'm Zaroth," said the wizard, "and who may I ask are you three?"

"I am Soliere, this is my companion Oather, and the one with the green face is Serieve." Serieve started to wave but just got sick again and turned away. "Now that introductions are out of the way we need to decide what to do. Do you have any idea at all where we are…um..err….Zaroth?"

"Hmm, no…I am afraid I have never been to this land before."

He was still looking around at the countryside as he spoke to Sol. The rain was dying down to a slight sprinkle again.

"Well," Sol said, reaching inside his pack pulling out a pipe and a bag of tobacco, "maybe we can at least find a place to get out of the weather before it starts coming down on us again. Any objections to just following this road? All roads eventually lead to cities, right?"

The other men seemed to agree with him, or rather, they didn't disagree, which was more than enough for Sol.

Serieve managed to stop throwing up long enough to rejoin them when Sol looked towards him, "Are you doing okay? Do you think you are up for a walk?"

Serieve nodded his head and they began walking down the road. Sol took a pinch of tobacco and put it in his pipe. He looked left, towards the wizard. "Hey, could you help me out?"

The wizard looked over at Sol and rolled his eyes. He raised his right hand over Sol's pipe and rubbed his fingers together as if he were sprinkling grains of sand. A small green flame sprang forth from Sol's pipe, then died back down, releasing an aromatic smoke that smelled of cherry. Sol took in a long puff on the pipe, holding it from the front to allow him to shield the opening from the rain with his hand.

"Thanks," Sol said as he blew out the puffs of the sweet-scented smoke. The wizard did not respond.

"So…" Sol began speaking to the wizard again, "How did a powerful guy like yourself get caught by those goblins?"

There was a long, awkward silence before Zaroth finally replied. "I was looking for an ancient item when they caught me by surprise."

"That's it? They just snuck up on you? Judging by your age, I thought you were more powerful than that. You know, they say that old mages are the most dangerous," Sol prattled on taking puffs of his pipe.

"You fool. Don't you know anything about magic?" the wizard said. "Magic takes a great toll upon our bodies, so that it ages us quickly and makes us appear older than we really are. Only when mages get to great strength can they begin to use magic to extend their life. If they don't gain mastery of their powers soon enough, then they run the risk of an early death. It all comes with the power we are granted. Therefore, it's nearly impossible to tell how powerful or how old a wizard truly is."

There was a pause where no one said anything for several moments before Zaroth finally spoke again.

"And besides, the goblins carried a type of poison that inhibited my magic. It is a very rare poison and I did not expect to encounter it."

"Ahh," nodded Sol. "So...you were snuck up on and you underestimated your enemy. Not a wise thing for a 'wizard.'"
Zaroth didn't dignify the statement with a response.

"So, how old are you then, old man?"

"Not that old," replied the wizard, sounding a bit annoyed.

"Like...in your teens or something?"

Zaroth sighed as he attempted to ignore Sol.

"Personally I have never trusted magic. I've heard too many stories about it blowing up in your face and not working the way it's supposed to. There's nothing that a good piece of steel can't handle," Sol commented aloud, releasing a long puff of smoke.

"It has always been my experience that it is better to be silent and thought a fool than to open one's mouth and remove all doubt," Zaroth replied with a grin as he waved his right hand between Sol and himself.

Sol started to reply but soon realized that no sound escaped from his lips. He tried and tried but nothing could escape the spell of silence he was under. After a few minutes, he gave up and just walked next to the wizard smoking his pipe and listened to the conversation going on between Oather and their new comrade, Khu-Rá.

"How did you get captured by those goblins back there?" Oather asked the elf.

"I was leading a party to track down the one my people call, 'The Defiler'. He is an evil druid that had plagued my people for too long. We were sent to put an end to him."

"So what happened?" asked Sol, who was taken by surprise that the silence spell had worn off already. "Were you stealthy little elves outsmarted by a group of dumb goblins?"

"We were not!" the elf snapped back but caught himself and calmed down. "We were betrayed by one of our own," the elf went on to say angrily.

"Why is that?"

"We were the best trackers in the land. My team made no more noise than falling feathers. There is no way a group of vile goblins could have caught us so unprepared."

"Oh," muttered Oather.

"It is of no consequence. I will return to my homeland and we will find the Defiler once again. Next time he will not live."

"Hmm," replied Oather, "That is too bad, my friend."

"I do want to thank you men for saving me. I owe you my life."

"Speaking of which," interrupted Sol, "is there any kind of reward for our brave and noble actions?"

"A noble man would not ask such a question," Zaroth replied.

"Even noble men need to make a living," Sol said.

"We don't want anything for rescuing you two," Serieve butted in, "I didn't save you for a reward. I just did it because you didn't look like you deserved that kind of fate."

"Yeah, well, you almost got yourself killed, and you almost took us with you. It was a foolish thing to do," Sol said sternly. Sol knew there was no way he was getting a reward now, so he didn't feel the need to candy-coat the issue.

"It was brave. Don't listen to him, my friend," Khu-Rá said to Serieve.

"You mean stupid," Sol scoffed. "If he had just listened to me then we wouldn't even be in this mess in the first place. We'd be back in Tyric spending our fortunes."

"It is something called courage. Maybe you should look into it sometime," replied the elf.

"Hey, treasure ain't worth anything if you ain't alive to spend it…friend," Sol snapped back. All of a sudden the wizard stopped and raised his arm and pointed off into the distance.

"Hmm," said the old man. "Correct me if I am wrong, but I think that is a tavern."

The party stopped and looked further down the road. Sure enough, there was a building in the distance. It had a thatched roof and smoke rose from its chimney.

"The wizard is correct," Khu-Rá replied in his stiff tone of voice.

"I can finally get out of these wet clothes, and get a bath and…ohhhh, and get some food, and…" Oather rambled.

"Yeah, I think we all could use something to eat," Sol said. "I, personally, just want a drink."

## 27. Dreadful Misunderstanding?

It had been a long evening for Andrea. She had a lot of time to think about being trapped in Renvara. While she was still angry at Nicholas for bringing her here, she did have to admit that he hadn't had much time to debate his actions. She was the one who decided to jump from the window and break her legs, and there was no way of telling what hell she might have been going through if he had not intervened.

She spent much of the night trying to remember more of what had happened. She'd jumped out, hit the ground, blacked out from the pain and awakened here. Still, there were remnants of something else that she couldn't seem to place. Last night she dreamed about the party and there was a blond-haired young man in her dream, but she didn't know where he had come from.

Now Andrea was awake again, but wasn't sure what time of day it was. She could see it was dark outside, but not like night, more like a storm was about to come. She heard a noise outside her room followed by a knock at the door.

"Mistress?" called a voice. "Are you awake?"

Andrea instantly recognized the voice. "Come in, Misha."

The door's latch rattled and the door swung open. Misha walked in, once again carrying a tray with a pot of tea, a cup, some honey, and milk. She set the tray down upon the table in the parlor.

"Good morning, Mistress Allisandra."

Andrea sat up, wrapping the blankets around her body. "Misha, my name is Andrea. Please address me as such."

Misha bowed her head, "I'm sorry, Mistress. I did not mean to offend you. The Master instructed me to address you that way."

"It's fine, you didn't offend me. Just call me by my own name from now on."

"As you wish, Mistress…Andrea. I took the liberty of setting out a robe for you while you were sleeping," the girl continued. A white robe laid draped across the foot of the bed. Misha picked up the robe and held it out in front of her as Andrea slipped from the bed and stepped into it. The robe was soft as silk and fit her nicely.

"Would you care for tea this morning?" Misha asked. Andrea followed her back to the parlor and sat in a chair next to the table as Misha poured her a cup. "Would you like any honey?"

"No, plain will be fine, Misha, thank you," Andrea replied. As she poured, the sleeve of her dress slid up her arm, revealing a dark bruise.

"What happened there?" Andrea asked.

Misha's eyes widened in horror and quickly pulled the sleeve back down.

"It's nothing, Mistress," she replied, trying to not look back at Andrea. "I…I dropped the tea…"

"You didn't get that when you dropped the tray. I was here when you did that, and I didn't see you hurt yourself."

The question made Misha act uneasy, so Andrea decided it was best not to press the issue. As Andrea leaned forward to pick up her cup, she saw that the lower part of Misha's dress had a brown stain, as if it had been used to soak up some dark liquid.

"Is that the same dress you wore yesterday?" Andrea demanded.

Misha looked down at the floor, fidgeting with her hands, "Yes, Mistress. It…It's the only dress the Master has given me."

"I see," Andrea said. "Misha, where are the rest of my clothes kept?"

Misha, still looking at the floor, pointed to the corner of the room, near Andrea's bed. "There, in the bureau, Madame," the girl replied in a soft voice.

Andrea walked over to her dresser. She opened the cabinet doors to see several dozen beautiful dresses hanging within. On the back side of the doors were little slots where shoes were kept. Andrea rifled through the assortment of clothes and came across a blue dress with white trim that was a little smaller than the others in length.

"This will do nicely, I think," Andrea said. She took the dress over to Misha. "You're not that much smaller than I am and I think this would fit you well. Here, try it on."

Misha looked up at Andrea with a face that Andrea wasn't sure was expressing horror, or just surprise.

"I...I ca...can't, Mistress. The Master..." the girl replied weakly.

"Do not worry, Misha," Andrea consoled the girl. "You have been given explicit orders to do anything I ask, have you not?"

Misha nodded her head yes, slowly.

"Well then, I am asking you to please try this on."

Misha reluctantly took the dress from Andrea and set it upon the bed. She began to take off her old, drab clothes until she stood there in just her undergarments. She slid the dress on and Andrea helped her lace it up in the back. It fit almost perfectly. The long sleeves of the dress were a little loose but nothing that was really noticeable.

Andrea led Misha over to the mirror and let the young girl see what she looked like. The bright blue of the dress made the young girls eyes sparkle as she saw her reflection.

"Oh my," Misha gasped. "It's so beautiful."

Andrea smiled at the girl through the reflection. "It looks stunning on you, Misha. You may keep it as a gift from me."

Misha's face went from awe to sudden fear and she pulled away from Andrea.

"What's wrong?"

"Oh no, Mistress," Misha shook her head. "If the Master saw me with this he would be furious."

Misha instantly reached back behind her to begin unlacing the dress but Andrea grabbed the girl's hands to keep her from removing the dress. She stood directly in front of the girl and looked her in the eyes.

"He will not say anything, Misha, I promise. I want you to have this dress. He will not be upset with you, I give you my word."

Misha stood there for a moment, her hands fidgeting again, looking back at Andrea. Then suddenly her eyes began to water and a tear fell down her cheek.

"I do not know what to say, Mistress."

"'Thank you' will suffice."

"Thank you, Mistress. No one has ever done anything like this for me before. I love it."

Andrea went back to the bureau and found a pair of shoes that matched the dress. Misha, meanwhile, was looking at herself in the mirror again, completely entranced at her appearance.

"Here, try these on," Andrea offered. Misha did so gladly, and the shoes fit perfectly.

"Thank you again, Mistress," Misha said. She walked back and forth in front of the mirror in her new shoes and dress, her face beaming as she did so. Misha stared at herself in the mirror for several moments before she suddenly came back to reality.

"Oh," Misha exclaimed. "I almost forgot, I've drawn a bath for you. I was going to let you know before, but in all the excitement it…it slipped my mind."

"That's fine. I enjoyed our little time together but I guess I should prepare for the day."

"I'll stay here and tidy your room, Mistress." Misha politely bowed to Andrea.

"Take your time. I shouldn't be long," Andrea replied as she left the room.

*** 

Misha watched Andrea leave the room and took one more quick glance at herself in the mirror, smiling brightly into the reflection. She loved the way the dress looked on her. It was the nicest thing she had ever been given.

She looked over at the bed and saw that it needed to be made. She walked back over to it and began to strip the bedding. Then there was a knock at the door. She turned back towards the door and saw it swing open. In walked her master, King Nicholas.

"Andr…" he began saying as he entered. The look upon his face transformed from curiosity to fury instantly as he sprang upon her.

"Thief!" he yelled at her. Misha was frozen in terror as he charged at her. He grabbed her by the throat and lifted her high into the air as he squeezed her neck tightly. Her hands grabbed hold of his powerful arms as she attempted to free herself from his stranglehold.

"Pl..ple..ase." She desperately tried to beg for her life, but he squeezed harder as she tried to talk. Misha began to see spots sweep across her eyes.

"Nicholas!"

Nicholas let go of Misha and she dropped to the floor, holding her throat, desperately gasping for air. He turned to see Andrea standing behind him.

"What do you think you are doing?"

Nicholas regained his composure and adjusted his shirt, which had come loose during the encounter.

"I caught this scamp stealing your things," he replied.

Andrea darted past him and knelt down next to Misha. "She wasn't stealing anything. I gave her that dress to wear."

Nicholas was quiet for several moments before finally speaking.

"In the future, you would do well to inform me of such…gifts."

"I wasn't aware that I needed permission to give away my things," Andrea snapped back at him.

"I suppose you're right," Nicholas conceded. "I apologize for the misunderstanding then."

Andrea helped Misha stand and walk over to the nearest chair. Nicholas walked past them to the window where he peered out towards the castle grounds. Misha's head pounded and her ears rang as she massaged her throat to make it feel better.

"It's a fine day. I would like you to go riding through my kingdom with me."

"Why do you think I'd want to do anything with you right now?"

"Well," Nicholas said as he walked slowly around the room, "I was thinking about how upset you were last night about being imprisoned here with me, and I think I might have come up with a solution."

"I'm listening."

"Go riding with me and I'll show you a few things. I can explain it then."

Misha could tell Andrea was hesitant to go. Misha opened her eyes and looked at Andrea. "Go, Mistress. If he can help you, then you must."

"Why don't you just tell me now?"

Nicholas took a few more steps closer to the fireplace and turned back towards Andrea and Misha. "I think it would be easier to explain after I show you."

Andrea quietly contemplated her decision before finally looking to Misha.

"Will you be all right?" Andrea asked.

"I'll be fine, Mistress. I was just scared."

Andrea relented. "Fine. Leave us, Nicholas, and I will prepare myself."

"Very well then. I will meet you at the stables as soon as you are ready," Nicholas said and left the room, closing the door behind him.

"Are you really all right?"

Misha sat on the chair, holding her bruised throat, trying to calm down.

"Thank you for saving me, Mistress. I owe you my life," Misha replied in between sobs.

"I'm so sorry, Misha," Andrea said as she pulled Misha close to her. "Do not worry, that will never happen again."

## 28. Escape Attempt

Halistan sat in his cell. It had been quiet for hours. Well, quiet except for the snoring coming from Roland. Roland was sleeping, as he was still recovering from his sickness. Halistan had tried healing him three times so far and he was pretty sure the older man was nearly healed completely. He had all but stopped coughing, which was a good sign.

Halistan had the Star of Salus held out in front of him, hanging by its chain. It was a beautiful, albeit small, holy symbol. Legend said that it had been forged by Salus himself and given to the first Patriarch of the church. Now, Halistan held it in his hands by a random twist of fate. There was very little light in his cell, but even in the dark the Star seemed to glimmer.

Halistan wondered if Father Angelo knew what had happened to him. How was he ever going to get out and get back home? Some of the other elders, such as Elder Despaat, probably thought that he had run off and stolen the Star for himself. Halistan wondered what Father Angelo would think. Would he assume something bad had happened to him or would he think that he was a thief?

Attempts to steal the Star and other holy relics had occurred in the past. The Star was generally under heavy lock and key except when needed by an elder. So it'd be easy to see how someone could think Halistan had stolen it, even though he hadn't. At least not intentionally. Thinking about the possibilities made Halistan's stomach ache.

"Hey, boy," Halistan heard from across from him. This was the first time he'd heard Tallmoor speak.

"Yes, Tallmoor?"

"I saw how you helped Roland with his sickness. That was very kind of you."

"I'm just trying to help him. I'd do the same for anyone."

"I believe you. That's why I think we need to get you both out of here, before…"

"Before what?"

Tallmoor was silent, as though he were contemplating exactly what he should, or should not say.

"Before...the guards come for you."

"Come for me for what?"

Tallmoor wouldn't say any more. Halistan heard Roland shuffle around like he was beginning to wake again.

"What are you two talking about?" Roland asked, sounding as though he were still half asleep.

"We need to get you two out of here."

Roland shifted around again and Halistan heard him grab the bars of his cell.

"It's about time you came to your senses. What's finally changed your mind?"

Tallmoor stood up and walked to his bars so that he could speak to them more clearly.

"Over the years that I have been here, I've seen many people fall prey to Nicholas. Some of them I felt no pity for. They were selfish, evil people that got what they deserved. Others were kind and good but met their fate in the most horrible manner I can imagine and they definitely didn't deserve it."

"So, what has finally changed your mind?" Halistan asked.

"I don't know. My wife and I used to fight about this a lot. She thought we should rebel against Nicholas and I was always too afraid to. That's how I ended up here. She tried to defy him and he took me. If she doesn't do as he wants then he'll kill me. I'm tired of being used as his bargaining chip. If we can escape then maybe we'd have a chance...I don't know."

"Escape is certainly better than the alternative," Roland replied.

"What alternative?" Halistan asked but was ignored by the other two men.

"What did you have in mind, Tallmoor?"

Tallmoor thought for a moment.

"Orman, the guard, will be coming to give us our ration of food soon. I've known him for a long time, even before I was brought here. He's not a bad man but he, like all of us, must do as Nicholas demands."

"So, what are you saying?"

"I'll lure him in here and get us out."

"Just how are you going to do that?"

"Don't worry about that. Just know that when I do we'll need to get out of here as quickly as we can. We'll need to be extremely quiet. The walls have ears in this cursed place."

"I don't think that will be a problem."

Before Roland and Tallmoor could continue, heavy footsteps came clunking down the steps to the lower level of the dungeon. The heavy wooden door flew open to admit a middle-aged man carrying three bowls of gruel. It was Orman coming to give them their dinner.

Orman was what the priests back in Valencia referred to as 'stunted', by which they meant that his mind didn't work right and he wasn't as smart as normal people. There were several stunted people that worked in Valencia whom Halistan had seen over the years, but they were never priests; they just helped to tend the gardens and do menial jobs. Father Angelo used to tell Halistan that it was their job as healers to shepherd the stunted and help them however they could.

At hearing the sound of Orman coming, the three men quickly moved to the back of their cells, quit talking, and pretended like nothing was going on. Orman carefully carried bowls of food to the prison cells, trying not to spill them. First he set one bowl down on the ground outside Roland's cell, then shoved it toward Roland with his foot before walking to Halistan and doing the same. As he approached Tallmoor's cell though, he stopped right outside the cell. Tallmoor was lying on his side at the rear of his cell. As Orman approached, Tallmoor let out a painful-sounding moan.

"You okay, Tallmoor?"

Tallmoor moaned again and rolled over towards Orman.

"I...I think I hurt my shoulder again, Orman. It's terribly painful. Could you help me pop it back into place one more time...please?"

Orman set down the last bowl, grabbed his keys from his belt and opened Tallmoor's cell. As Orman approached the old man, Tallmoor turned and used both legs to kick Orman in the stomach.

Orman staggered back and hit the bars of the cell, stunned. Tallmoor got up and hit Orman several times in the face. Halistan could hear the punches--they sounded awful as Orman grunted after each blow.

"I'm sorry Orman," Tallmoor said, "but this is for your own good."

Tallmoor hit Orman a few more times and the other man's body slumped to the floor. Tallmoor grabbed the keys from his hand, then exited his cell and locked Orman inside. Then he rushed over to Halistan's cell and unlocked it. From there, he went over to Roland's.

"Did you...kill him?" Halistan asked.

"No, but he won't feel very good when he wakes up."

"Okay," Roland asked. "So what now?"

"Follow me."

Tallmoor, with keys in hand, led them through the door that led to the guards' quarters on the upper level of the dungeons. There, Halistan saw racks of beds along the walls and storage areas for weapons. However, most of the beds looked unused.

"There haven't been any real soldiers in the castle for a hundred years. Now there's only a few gypsies or townsfolk that Nicholas forces to act as servants," Tallmoor explained as they made their way through the castle. He took them down a corridor that led to a circular stairwell.

"That leads up to the rooms that were used by the guests of the royal family. Now they are all empty, but servants still clean them occasionally. It'd be best if we avoided them so that we don't run into anyone who would call Lucian."

"Lucian?" Halistan asked, as they continued past the stairwell and down another corridor.

"Yes, he is Nicholas' lackey. Very nasty fellow. Pray you don't meet him."

"How much further until we can get to the exit?" Roland asked.

"If we keep going this way, we'll come to another set of steps that lead out on the east side of the castle. From there, with luck we can sneak off the castle grounds and make it back to town. I have friends there that might hide us."

"It's as good a plan as any," said Roland.

The men got to the end of the corridor and Halistan saw the steps that led outside. His heart raced. He was glad to finally get out of this place. The last few days had been like living a nightmare. Once he got back to town, he might be able to find a way to get back home.

As they approached the steps, the door at the top opened and an older man walked in, accompanied by two of the biggest dogs Halistan had ever seen. The larger one had two heads. Both of them were black and had evil red eyes. Standing on all fours, they were nearly as tall as the man they were with. As soon as the beasts saw the escaped prisoners, they began to growl. Fire spewed from their jaws and burning spittle dripped like lava onto the floor.

The man with them had long graying brown hair, a long face with a sharp nose, and piercing eyes that made Halistan's blood run cold. He stopped in the doorway as soon as he saw them. He looked directly at Tallmoor, and the two locked eyes.

"Lucian," Tallmoor muttered.

Halistan could see Tallmoor was shaken. His body began to tremble as he tried to turn away and run.

"RUN," Tallmoor called as he bolted back down the passage they'd come from.

The monstrous dogs leapt from the steps at them. Like Halistan, Roland didn't have much time to react as Tallmoor ran past them. Roland tried to turn and run after Tallmoor, but didn't make it far before the larger, two-headed, beast was upon him.

Halistan, frozen with fear, just stood there as the hellhound collided with Roland and knocked him to the ground. Then he turned back to Lucian in time to see the old man draw his blade and rush at him. Lucian knocked him to the ground and pummeled him repeatedly. After the third or fourth hit Halistan was too weak to try and fight back. His vision blurred and his head fell to the side, where he saw the massive two-headed dog mauling Roland. He saw his new friend's face and knew that the beast had already done its job. Roland was dead.

## 29. *Pushing Boundaries*

Once Nicholas left, Andrea managed to find a pair of riding pants, a pleated off-white long-sleeved shirt, and some brown leather riding boots in her bureau. Andrea left the castle through the lower, eastern door that led to the stables. Even though she was sure it was mid-day, the sky outside was so dim that she could barely tell it was daytime at all. As she approached the stables, Nicholas emerged, riding a black stallion. He held the reins of an identical horse that was already saddled for her.

"You look ravishing."

Andrea ignored his compliment and mounted her steed. Her teeth clenched as she tried to control her anger towards him. Just looking at him made her wish she had a dagger to plunge into his heart. She could tell that he was a man who didn't like to be snubbed, which brought her a certain amount of satisfaction.

Nicholas glowered at her momentarily before galloping off towards the main gate of the castle. She quickly readied herself and galloped after him, catching up to him just as they began their descent down the mountain. In the distance, she could see plumes of smoke from the chimney stacks of a far off town.

The road sloped downhill gradually, twisting back and forth until it finally reached the base of the mountain. The road continued around the mountain to her left, but Nicholas diverged from the road. She followed him as he ventured into the forest ahead of them.

Nicholas picked up his pace and darted into the forest. His steed seemed to know the path; it dodged in and out of the way of oncoming trees. Andrea struggled to keep up. Just as she was ready to give up and stop, she caught up to him.

She looked around the strange forest. There was an unnerving feel to the place. She couldn't put her finger on it, but something was wrong here. She felt as though a thousand eyes were peering at her from the shadows. The great trees that made up the woods spread out wide enough to almost block out the sky, and made the forest more dark than the dismal land already was.

Nicholas went silent as they finally emerged from the forest into a grassy field that stretched out towards the rolling hills. In the distance, Andrea saw some people come into view on one of the hills. She rode towards them, wanting the opportunity to meet them. As she rode closer she saw that they were an elderly man, a middle-aged woman, and two little children; a boy and a girl.

At first they didn't seem to take any notice of her as she approached them. The little girl was holding the old man's hand and seemed to be pulling him behind her towards the older woman, while the little boy was playing in the field.

Andrea stopped a hundred paces from where the family congregated, close enough that she could hear the little boy yell "Gran Papa, watch this," before he did a tumble part way down the hill.

The old man looked over at Andrea as she began to wave to them. Nicholas, who had been riding behind her, came to a stop next to her as she waved back to the family.

The little girl pointed at Andrea and tugged at the old man's hand. At first their faces were blank. Then, without warning, the old man picked up the girl that held his hand. The middle-aged woman quickly ran over and snatched the little boy up in her arms, and they turned and ran away from Andrea and Nicholas.

Andrea sat there and watched them flee as if their very lives were in peril.

"Do you have this effect on everyone in your kingdom?" she asked Nicholas as they watched the family flee down the side of the hill.

"A true leader cannot always be popular, my dear."

"Unpopular is one thing; terrifying is another."

"My people respect my power and authority. That is all I need from them."

"Apparently."

Nicholas turned to her and moved his horse closer to hers. She turned to look at him. His hand rose slowly and brushed her cheek before he suddenly grabbed her by the jaw and looked her straight in the eyes. She tried to pull away, but his hand was far too strong for her, so she stopped jerking and just scowled back at him.

"Do not test my patience," he said.

They both sat there for several moments longer, staring each other in the eyes before he released her. As soon as his grip released, she pulled away from him. He was strong, stronger than any man she'd met before. She had felt the strength in his hands when he grabbed her. Her jaw ached awfully where he had gripped it, but she didn't want to give him the satisfaction of knowing that he had hurt her. She refused to show any sign of weakness.

Nicholas looked forward again, taking in the view of his land. He drew a deep breath and let out a loud, contented sigh. Andrea sat glaring at him.

He turned his head just enough that he could look over his shoulder at her.

"You seem quiet, my dear."

"I don't have anything to say."

Actually, she had plenty she wanted to say, but for now she thought it was best to keep her thoughts to herself. Both were silent for several moments before Nicholas finally spoke up again.

"You have to understand that such displays are sometimes necessary to keep them in line."

"I see."

The two began to ride again. The silence built up between them like a dam that was about to break.

"I believe you had something you wanted to show me." Andrea said.

Nicholas rode next to her as their horses walked slowly through the fields outside the wood line of the forest.

"See those trees?" Nicholas pointed. "Those mark the edge of my territory and are the home of the horrible beasts that imprison us here."

"Go on," Andrea replied. It was good to know where the boundary was. If she could get through that forest she'd be free from him and he wouldn't be able to follow her. "Do they ever venture from the forest?"

"Sometimes, but not often. In the past, if they ever did, we were able to fight them off."

"Have you ever tried to lead the people against them, to wipe them out so that you can finally be free?"

"Once, a long time ago," Nicholas replied, "but they overwhelmed us and we were forced out of the woods. The beasts did not follow us and seem content to keep us imprisoned."

"So what was it that you needed to explain? If you can't defeat the demons that keep us here, how do you plan to help me escape?"

"I was doing some research some time back and found some texts that talk about ways to control the creatures. With the right ingredients, I could use my magic to make them ignore you as you traversed the forest, and then you'd be free."

For the first time since she'd arrived she felt a glimmer of hope that she might be able to get back home. She didn't want to let on to Nicholas that she was happy to hear this news, but she hoped that what he said was true.

"How long would it take to do this?" she asked.

"Some of the ingredients I'd need are quite difficult to get. And some of the plants needed are quite rare, but I could grow them I think. For instance, the Full-Moon Hibiscus must be watered under the light of one hundred full moons before it even blooms a single time."

Andrea could feel the anger building up inside of her. She did her best to breathe and calm herself. She wasn't sure what he was talking about and didn't care to know. She just wanted to know how long Nicholas' magic would take but she was beginning to surmise that it wouldn't be quickly.

"How long would it take to get the materials needed for the spell?"

Nicholas took a moment and thought about her question before finally responding, "If all went well, I could probably have it ready in eight…maybe nine years."

"What?" Andrea wailed in disbelief. "Is there no other way?"

Andrea tried to hide her anger but she knew deep down inside that Nicholas wouldn't be able to help her. He'd known before telling her that any chance of helping her would take so long that it wouldn't matter, and he had concealed it from her. She felt her heart pounding in her chest and she wanted to take off and never look at him again.

Andrea didn't wait for a response. She pulled hard on the reins to the right and spurred her horse to a full gallop and rushed toward the forest. Whatever charm and hospitality Nicholas had shown her upon her arrival, she was certain now that he was a liar. It had all been an act to gain her favor. She was certain that his story about the forest being filled with demons was also a lie too, and she was determined to leave this place forever.

The plains faded away behind her as she rode towards the forest. She charged into the woods at a full gallop, narrowly avoiding the low-hanging branches. What little light there had been before was now gone. She wanted to look behind her to see if Nicholas gave chase, but the woods were so dark that she couldn't see. Her horse was quite agile for its size. It weaved in and out through the trees at an amazing pace without any guidance from her.

The forest went on and on. It wasn't long before she could feel the steed begin to tire from its sprint. She pulled on the reins and allowed it to slow to a walk. Only scant streams of light were able to penetrate the thick canopy of the trees. Andrea looked around, trying to determine which would be the best way to go. She had absolutely no idea where she was, but if the forest surrounded Nicholas' realm, then if she ventured further into it, eventually she should come out on the other side.

The forest was quiet. Eerily quiet. There were no birds, insects or any other animals at all. The only sound to be heard was the sound of the twigs and branches snapping under the weight of her horse. Behind her, to the right she heard a rustling sound. She whipped around to see what it was. Her horse whinnied and began shaking its head back and forth.

"Shhh," Andrea cooed, trying to calm the horse. It didn't have much effect, and the horse's coarse mane swished back and forth across her face. Andrea heard the sound again, this time on both sides.

She tried to see what the source of the noise could be, but it was hard to make out much in the dim light. The horse was becoming spooked and increasingly hard to control. Andrea held the reins tightly to try and get the horse to stop flailing, but she was losing the struggle.

A branch snapped behind her. Before she could look, the horse bolted into a gallop again. The sudden burst of speed took Andrea by surprise and it was all she could do to keep hold and stay mounted. Andrea ducked down close to the horse's neck as it raced through the forest. She could hear something behind her--lots of things, actually, and it sounded like they were catching up to her.

The horse turned sharply, but she didn't know why. Andrea held on tightly as her hair came loose and got in her face. She did her best to get it out of her eyes and mouth. When she did, she saw why the horse had changed direction. There was a steep ravine to her left and the horse was running along the edge of it.

Several creatures stepped out of the shadows in front of her. They were huge and looked like they were on fire. Upon seeing them, her horse let out an awful sounding shriek and skidded to a stop, almost throwing Andrea. Thankfully, she was able to hold on.

The horse turned left and descended into the ravine. At the base of the ravine it began running again at full speed. Andrea held on but was getting shaken left and right. She wasn't sure how much more she could take before she'd lose her grip.

The ravine twisted right, then sharply to the left. The horse followed it as quickly as it could. Just as they got to the left turn, she saw another beast directly in front of her. It raised a massive claw and struck at the horse.

Andrea's horse reared up and threw her off. She landed on the hard ground. She rolled over and tried to get her hair out of her face and stand up. Just as she got to her feet, several large creatures jumped down from the ravine ledge and landed in front of her.

They were like dogs, but giant in size, nearly the size of a mule and unlike any dogs Andrea had ever had the misfortune of seeing. They had glowing red eyes, reddish brown bodies, and flames that danced along their teeth.

Now three of the monsters were in front of her. They bared
their fangs and growled menacingly. Andrea looked around for
anything she could use for a weapon, but her options were
limited. Next to her was a broken limb, which she grabbed
quickly and wielded in front of her like a club.

Her horse stood next to her. She saw that it had one of its
rear legs primed and ready to kick as the beasts began to encircle
them. Above her, Andrea heard galloping hoof beats and a
mounted figure came to a stop at the top of the ravine. It was
Nicholas. For the first time, she was glad to see him.

"Help!" Andrea called to him. She hoped that he'd rush
down and help her, but he didn't. He sat there and did nothing
but watch while the beasts growled at her. Andrea saw the look
of satisfaction upon his face as he watched her prepare herself to
fight for her life.

One of the monsters snapped at her horse while another
circled around. The movement startled her steed but did not
distract it enough from the third monster behind it. The horse
jerked violently as it kicked hard into the air, hitting one of the
monsters directly in the jaw.

She heard the monster yelp and retreat from its attack on
the horse, while the third leapt at her. Andrea swung wildly and
hit the monster, but the blow had little effect and the monster
knocked her to the ground. Her horse turned just in time and let
loose another kick that hit her attacker in its mid-section and
wounded it badly. The monster let out a horrible cry as it was
knocked away from her. It got up, and while the horse was
preparing another kick all three beasts turned and fled.

Andrea started to push herself to get back on her feet when
she saw Nicholas ride down the slope of the ravine. He reached
her just as she regained her footing, and quickly dismounted.

"Are you all right, my love?" he asked, almost sounding
sarcastic. He reached out to her, but she slapped his hand away
which had little effect, except to make her hand sting.

"Why didn't you help me, you…you troll?" she spat.

Nicholas' demeanor went from satisfaction to rage as he
instantly back-handed her. The blow struck her across the face
and felt like she had been kicked by her horse. Andrea spun
around from the force and fell to the ground, landing on her
hands and knees.

She was disoriented for a moment, but before she could
recover she felt Nicholas grab her arm and yanked her back up.

"You stupid wench!" he yelled at her. Andrea's head rang from the blow so much that her vision blurred, but it slowly came back to normal.

"This is what happens to those who do not heed my warnings. Did you think you could escape? Is that what you were trying to do?"

Andrea's arm hurt from him squeezing it so tightly. She tried to push away from him but she had very little strength. His anger burned like fire as he looked at her and he finally threw her back to the ground.

"Get up, we're going back to the castle," he hissed.

Andrea could feel her eye swelling from the blow but managed to get back up and re-mount her horse. She looked at her shirt. The cloth was shredded where Nicholas had grabbed her. She looked closer and saw that she was bleeding a little from claw-like cuts on her arm. She pressed the torn cloth to the wounds tightly to stop the bleeding and rode to catch up to Nicholas before she encountered any more of the demons.

The trip back seemed to take ages longer than when they were first riding away from the castle. Neither Andrea nor Nicholas spoke all the way back to the castle.

Upon their arrival, several servants were there awaiting them. Andrea dismounted, as did Nicholas, and the servants took care of the horses as they left. They entered through the same side entrance that Andrea had used earlier, but Nicholas began walking towards the dining hall while Andrea started towards one of the stairways leading to her room.

Nicholas saw her and quickly snapped in her direction. "Where are you going, my dear? Dinner is this way." He motioned to his left.

"I'm not hungry. I'm going to my room."

Nicholas walked over to her. There was a sinister look upon his face and she dared not challenge him again right now. She was hurt and did not think she could withstand another hit like before.

"Then the least I can do as a host is escort you there."

The two of them walked silently up the stairs and down the hall. She looked at each door they passed, wishing it was hers.

Finally they arrived at the end of the hall where her room was. She quickly opened the door and entered, trying to close it quickly so Nicholas could not follow her; but as she tried to seal the door Nicholas stopped it and held it open.

"I wish to be left alone, Nicholas," Andrea said as she turned to him. Slowly, Nicholas stepped closer to her until they were a breath apart. She glared up at him as he looked at her. He raised his hand and gently brushed hair away from her bruised eye and cheek. Even though he was careful, the light touch still hurt. Andrea made certain not to wince, no matter how much she wanted to.

"Why do you test me?" he asked.

Andrea held her tongue. She wanted to tell him all the reasons why she despised him, but she knew better. Nicholas grabbed her chin with his left hand and forced her to tilt her head so that he could look at her eye more closely.

"I have tried to help you, tried to reason with you, and most of all tried to show you my love, but you reject me at every turn."

He let go of Andrea's face and began to trace a finger along her jaw. Andrea closed her eyes and secretly wished she had something to stab him with. Nicholas inhaled a deep breath, as though he were trying to breath in her essence.

"I can smell your fear," he said with a baleful grin, "and even if you do not realize it now, you will give in to me. You are my servant now and you will either learn to do what you are told or suffer the consequences."

Anger swelled up inside Andrea to the point she couldn't take it any longer. Instinctively she kicked Nicholas as hard as she could in the groin. Her foot found its mark and Nicholas howled in pain. Andrea grabbed his hand and bit into it as hard as she could. His skin was as thick as leather but she did her best to break through it.

Nicholas started to sink slightly from her kick and desperately tried to wrench his hand from her. He pushed and pulled with incredible might but Andrea fought to hold on as she sank her teeth into him. Eventually he used his full strength to throw her to the ground and she was forced to let go.

Andrea's eyes met his and she could see his furious anger shine through them like those of a madman.

"I will never give in to you. I will die first," Andrea spat.

"So be it," Nicholas replied with a flash in his eyes, "Until then, you will remain here, alone."

Nicholas stormed out of the room and slammed the door shut. Andrea picked herself up and ran to the door. She could hear Nicholas chanting on the other side. The door began to glow and then it subsided. Andrea tried to open it, but it was stuck. She pulled harder on the door, then kicked it and pounded her fist against it.

"Nicholas, let me out of here right now," she commanded, but got no response. She heard steps walking away from her chambers and knew that Nicholas was leaving. Andrea sunk to the floor and rested against its sturdy frame, actually relieved that he was gone.

She waited until she could no longer hear Nicholas' steps and got up to go to her bed. As she neared it she saw that her costume had been draped across the bed and had been stitched up. It almost looked like it was new. She picked up one of the sleeves and looked to see if the button was still there that went on her palm, and it was. She pressed the red button twice and watched as the hidden spike from the spider leg sprung forth and stuck into the headboard of her bed. The polished metal shined brightly. Next time she met Nicholas, she'd be ready.

Andrea pulled the spike free and reloaded it into its sheath. She remembered how difficult Axel had said that it was to reload, and for once he wasn't joking, but eventually she managed to do it. She ripped both sleeves from the costume and fashioned them into gloves.

She could tell the room had been cleaned while they were gone. She found a tray with a pot of tea, fruit, and pastries, as well as another vial of the green healing medicine that Misha had given her before. Misha must have left these for her, Andrea surmised.

She reached for the medicine and drank it. With any luck it would help with the throbbing she felt in her face and would make her ears stop ringing. It tasted slightly different than she remembered from the first time she took it. It still had the same licorice taste, but there was something different about it.

In almost no time, she started to feel groggy. Her eyes suddenly got very heavy and it became difficult to keep standing. Andrea cursed herself for being such a fool and staggered towards her bed. She barely made it before darkness swept over her eyes.

## *30. Revelations*

Lucian opened Halistan's cell and threw him into it. He pushed Halistan so hard that he slammed into the rear wall of the cell and collapsed to the floor. He was beaten badly and could barely keep himself conscious.

As he laid there, he heard Lucian walk out of the dungeon, followed by one of his monsters. Lucian returned moments later, dragging the body of Tallmoor behind him. Orman was still in Tallmoor's cell, so Lucian dragged Tallmoor to the cell that Roland had occupied.

Halistan blinked several times to clear up his vision and was mildly successful. He could now see well enough to make out Lucian standing in front of Tallmoor's old cell with Orman inside it.

"P..p..please, Sire," Orman sobbed. Orman was on his knees in the cell, gripping the bars of his cage and pressing his body into them as if there was a way he could squeeze through them to get free.

Lucian kicked Orman in the face through the bars of the cell, and knocked him back.

"I've no use for a fool who lets prisoners escape!"

Orman crawled back to the bars on his hands and knees. "Please, don' gimme to him. I'm sorry. I'll be more careful next time. Please!"

Lucian watched the man beg. His eyes were so cold that Halistan dared not look directly at them. Slowly Lucian reached through the bars and snatched Orman by his hair. He pulled Orman's head hard against the bars and looked him in the eyes.

"You cost the Master a meal."

Tears streamed down Orman's face, making him look like a child being scolded by a parent.

"That was your responsibility and you failed our Master."

Orman began sobbing again, this time harder than before.

"For that failure, you will take his place and serve as an example to the rest of the clan of the price of failure."

Lucian jerked Orman's head back and released him. Orman fell backwards as Lucian stormed out of the dungeon. Orman bawled at the top of his lungs and kicked the bars of his cell, but they didn't budge.

The man cried for some time. The sobbing grew fainter and fainter until it got to where Halistan could barely hear it anymore.

Halistan laid there, trying not to move because his body hurt when he did. He slowly gripped the Star of Salus and chanted a healing incantation. He felt warmth emanate from the star and flow into his hands. It spread up his arms and through his entire body. Slowly, he began to hurt less until finally he felt restored.

He must have been hurt more than he thought because the spell drained him of most of his energy. Still, he was glad to not be in pain any longer. He let himself rest a little longer before he got up. He heard Tallmoor stirring in the cell next to him. He thought that there was a good chance Tallmoor might be dead, too, but it seemed that he wasn't.

"Tallmoor? Are you okay?"

Halistan heard Tallmoor moving around a bit more on the prison floor.

"Tallmoor, can you hear me?"

There was more scuffling. It sounded like Tallmoor was scooting closer to the wall that separated his cell from Halistan's.

"Yes," Tallmoor replied. His voice was ragged and he wheezed a little as he spoke.

"I was afraid you were dead."

"Nicholas wouldn't kill me. I'm worth more to him alive than dead."

"So what are we going to do now?" Halistan asked.

Tallmoor was silent for a moment before he let out a long sigh.

"We need to get you and Orman out of here."

"But how?" Halistan asked.

Orman's sobbing was getting louder again. He must have been listening to them talk.

"I don't know yet," Tallmoor said, "but it's my fault that Orman is in here. I never dreamed that Lucian would be so cruel. I shouldn't have taken advantage of my friendship with him."

"There's no way you could have known," Halistan replied.

"I should have known. Lucian is as much a monster as the beasts he surrounds himself with. Orman is from my clan and I should have watched out for him, but I didn't. Instead he'll now be a meal for Nicholas."

"Meal? What do you mean meal?"

Halistan was sure that Tallmoor couldn't really mean that Nicholas was going to eat them. That was just impossible. Who would do that?

"Haven't you been listening to anything, boy?"

Halistan heard Tallmoor stand up in his cell and grip the bars tightly. "Nicholas...Nicholas is a monster."

"Yes, but surely that's an exag-"

"No!" Tallmoor shook the bars of his cell violently. "Nicholas is a demon. Cursed by the gods and doomed to live here for eternity."

"A...a what?"

"You heard right. He's a spawn of the Abyss and feasts on the souls of the living."

Halistan wasn't sure if Tallmoor was being melodramatic or not. He was certainly worked up but there was no way it could be true. It just couldn't be. Halistan turned and sat with his back against the wall as he thought about what Tallmoor said.

"How could a demon become a king?"

Tallmoor released his grip on the cell bars and sat down in his cell.

"It...it happened a long time ago; before I was even born."

Halistan noticed that Orman's sobbing had all but ceased as he listened to Tallmoor.

"Nicholas' family, the DeVanya's, had ruled this land for several hundred years. The DeVanya's led the people away from the tyranny of the Empire and created a new kingdom here in Renvara. His family ruled alongside the great council, which was comprised of the head priests of the gods the people worshiped: Venastus, Lila, Vera and a few others that I forget."

"Do you know if they worshipped Salus here or not?" Halistan asked.

"Actually, I believe they did," Tallmoor replied in an unsure voice, "It's so hard to remember the stories of my grandfather--but if I remember correctly, then yes."

"What was the council for?" Halistan asked, intrigued by Tallmoor's story.

"The people never wanted to be ruled by a single individual again. They created a council that together could overrule the King if the people so chose."

"So, they could oppose the King?"

"If the need ever arose, then yes, but more often they served as advisors to the Kings. This worked for many generations…well, at least until Nicholas ascended to the throne. Nicholas, from what I've heard, ruled for many years. He never took a queen but was enchanted by a young woman named Allisandra. She was very beautiful, and the youngest priestess ever to be appointed as Matriarch of the goddess, Lila."

Halistan saw Orman shift around so that he could watch as Tallmoor told the story. He had stopped sobbing, thankfully, and was listening like a child at bedtime.

"Nicholas tried for years to get Allisandra to marry him and become his queen, but she only had eyes for a man named Dominic. He was a good man and a holy knight for the church of Salus. I had forgotten that until you mentioned Salus, but if I remember right he was the only one of the male gods to be worshipped here."

"I'm glad to hear that," Halistan replied. "I'm a priest in the service of Salus. I'm a healer."

"That explains a lot," Tallmoor replied. "I've never seen anyone else with healing magic like yours, but it would make sense if you were a priest of Salus. It used to be said that Dominic had the power to heal too, but I thought those were only old wives tales."

"He must have been a priest of some kind then. Only the priests have healing magic."

"It's possible, but the story, as it was told to me, was that Dominic was simply a knight."

Halistan thought for a moment then had a revelation, "If he were a paladin, then he might have been able to. The strongest of holy knights did have some healing magic."

"A pala…what?"

Halistan was taken aback momentarily as he'd never had to explain what a paladin was before, and wasn't quite sure how to go about it.

"A paladin is a holy knight."

"Well that's what I said, but you said they didn't have magic."

"No, a paladin is a special kind of holy knight. It's said that they are selected by Salus as his champions because of their indomitable spirits."

Tallmoor listened intently to Halistan and seemed to get lost in thought as he reflected on the stories he'd heard. "Hmm," Tallmoor finally responded. "That would make a certain amount of sense. My grandfather used to tell me that Dominic was a powerful warrior and one of the few people who would stand up to Nicholas. It was well known that Nicholas hated and resented Dominic terribly."

"If Nicholas is a demon, I could see why he would hate Dominic. Paladins are very powerful and demons flee from them like roaches flee from light. Some paladins were rumored to be so powerful that they could control lesser demons, just like the priests of my order," Halistan replied.

"Oh," Tallmoor said, "but, this was before Nicholas was cursed."

"It was?"

"Yes. I'll get to that in a moment, but did you say that Paladins and those of your order can control demons?"

"Yes, my order is often called upon to banish demons from villages. Why?"

"Do you know that kind of magic?" Tallmoor asked slowly.

Halistan didn't understand why Tallmoor was suddenly so curious about this. He thought it was common knowledge that priests could banish demons.

"I...I have been taught the basics," Halistan stammered in response, "but I've never seen a demon and have never been able to practice those arts."

"You're wrong," Tallmoor replied, "The beasts that Lucian keeps as pets are demons. Demons that Nicholas has summoned as servants and guardians of his domain."

Halistan thought about it for a moment and felt stupid for not realizing it before. Of course they were demons. What kind of dog has glowing red eyes and fiery breath?

"I see where you're going with this," Halistan said.

"Good. Do you think your magic could work?"

"I don't know. I've never tried it, but even if I could control the beasts, what good would it do with us unable to get out of here?"

"The beasts are smart. Maybe they could get the keys for us."

"Keys," Orman interrupted. "Yes, get keys."

Halistan thought about it some more. He did remember back to his schooling, and he tried to recollect the incantations needed. That sort of magic was quite different from the healing spells that he was accustomed to casting.

Halistan looked up to see Orman staring at him, anticipation written all over his face. "I could try it," Halistan conceded. "How do we get one of the beasts to come? I'll need to be able to see it before I can cast a spell."

"Leave that to me," Tallmoor replied.

## 31. The Tavern

Sol, Oather, Serieve, the elf and the wizard arrived at the tavern. The hike to get there felt longer than it looked, but Sol was glad they'd finally found someplace to rest. A single story building, made of stone, sat at the far edge of the village. In the distance, on the other side of the tavern, was another building with a wide open front gate, which looked to Sol like it must have been a stable. The sky was getting very dark by this point; and it was still very damp and misty. The wind started to pick up. There was a strong chill in the air.

A wooden sign swung over the entrance, *The Drunken Fool.* The party walked into the tavern with Sol in the lead. The main room was full of men, as several women entertained the patrons. There was only one empty table, which was all the way across the room.

As they entered, the talking came to a sudden halt. They walked across the room to the empty table and everyone stared at them as they sat down.

Sol glanced around at the villagers, but as he did they looked away from him. Almost everyone in the room had very pale, pasty colored skin, and dull brown hair that looked as bland as the countryside. Even the fairer-haired women seemed a little dull.

Once seated Serieve leaned towards Sol and whispered, "Nice crowd, huh?"

"Yeah, real pleasant people," Sol replied.

Sol whistled very loudly to the barmaid as the room remained deathly quiet, "Five ales."

A moment later a girl arrived at their table with several mugs and then quickly scurried back to the kitchen.

"Not even so much as a hello," remarked Oather. He took a drink and winced as he forced himself to swallow. Sol took a drink and also wanted to gag. It tasted like old bath water, but he kept his composure.

"This is terrible," he whispered to Oather, "but let's try and not draw any more attention to ourselves."

Oather nodded in agreement and took another, albeit small, sip of the ale. Oather smiled wide and most of the other bar patrons went back to their own conversations. Some people continued to look at the group, but only for a brief moment at a time. Sol had the feeling that they were now the topic of nearly every conversation in the room.

"These people sure do make you feel welcome, don't they?" whispered Soliere.

Zaroth did not sit at the table with them, but instead remained standing. "I'm going to inquire about a room," he said as he made his way past the chairs of the other patrons towards the barkeep, who was serving more drinks at the bar.

Oather untied his belt pouch and took out the onyx amulet that he had taken from the dead goblin priest.

"What's that?" Sol asked.

"I found it back in the cavern. It doesn't look like it's worth much, but I might be able to get something for it."

"Are you joking? No one would want that. Onyx isn't rare or anything. It's only used for accenting real gems."

"It doesn't matter, I like it. It's a good memento of our journey," Oather smiled as he played with it.

He tried to wear it but the cord on the amulet was too short to fit over his large head. Instead, Oather pulled some twine from his pouch and replaced the original piece to make it long enough for him to actually wear. He looked at it for several moments then tucked it under his tunic and left it.

"Ehh, whatever," replied Sol, who'd been watching his friend play with his new toy, "How much money do you have left, Oather?"

"Let me check."

Oather pulled out his pouch and took out a gold coin and a small handful of silver ones.

"That will barely pay for the drinks we ordered," Sol replied.

"Well, don't you have some money left, Sol?" Serieve asked.

"Some, but that is our reserve money, and this isn't enough of an emergency."

"I would certainly call this an emergency," Oather replied.

"Actually," Khu-Rá interrupted as he pulled out a small pouch and poured its contents onto the table. Several small and medium sized gems, one of which was a diamond the size of Oather's thumb, fell from the bag. "This may at least get us a place to stay for the night."

Sol grinned. He couldn't take his eyes away from the small fortune. "You bet it will. It's enough to stay and possibly even buy some horses to help get us the hell out of this town."

Sol hastily called the barmaid back over to their table. She wore the same kind of clothes that everyone else in the tavern wore--in her case, a drab brownish-gray dress that reached her ankles. She had brown hair done up in a bun and dull brown eyes.

"Wha'cani do fer ya m'lord?" She had a very strong eastern accent that Sol could barely understand. It was spoken so fast that all the words sounded smashed together.

Sol held one of the smaller sapphires up to her, "We'd like to order another round of drinks and some food...what do you have?"

"W've 'nley got sop t'day. Wouldjalike some?" she asked with a smile, taking the gem from Sol's fingers.

"Um," Sol started to reply, but needed a moment to understand what she said. "Yes, we'll all take a bowl."

The maid turned and headed back to the kitchen. She hadn't gotten far before Sol called her back again.

"Do you know where we might be able to buy some horses?"

She stopped and her eyes widened but she didn't say anything. The room got quiet again.

"Perhaps in the village?" Sol asked. "Or someone here that could part with...um."

She stood there quietly for just a moment longer before answering.

"I'm...I'm sorrah bu' there aren anay fer sale heya," she stammered before running off back to the kitchen.

"Well, that was weird," Sol said to his companions in a hushed tone. The others nodded in agreement.

\*\*\*

206

While the other men sat down together at a table, Zaroth made his way to the bar and found an empty stool. A heavyset man stood behind the bar cleaning glasses with a dirty rag.

"Ca' I getcha adrink?"

Zaroth declined.

"Do you have any rooms available?"

The barkeep stood there for a moment, as if he wasn't quite sure he wanted to rent a room to Zaroth.

"Ya, we gotta room ferya, but-cher gonna haveta pay upfront," he finally replied, holding his hand out.

"Fine."

Zaroth held out his hand and gold coins began magically dropping from his hand onto the barkeeps outstretched palm. A good dozen or so large gold coins fell and overflowed onto the counter.

"Is that enough?" asked the wizard. The barkeep was beaming as he nodded in acceptance.

"Upstairs," said the barkeep. "Youca' ha da firs rum on da righ'."

"That'll do. I'll head up there in a bit. Can I get something to eat first?"

Upon hearing his request, the barkeep immediately turned and headed into the kitchen.

\*\*\*

The barmaid returned moments later with four bowls. She set a bowl down in front of each of the men. Sol looked at his portion. It appeared to be nothing more than some cut potatoes in boiling hot water. He glanced up at the girl.

"Is this it?"

"Wha're ya expectin? Thas ah dat grows heya," she replied, scowling at Sol as if he'd personally insulted her.

"It'll be fine, thank you," Serieve interjected before Sol could answer. The barmaid trailed away after setting down some spoons for the men.

Sol took a spoon and tried the makeshift stew. It tasted like what it looked like--unseasoned water with potatoes in it. "There's not even any salt in it," Sol grumbled, just loud enough for his companions to hear, but they all ate it anyway.

Sol finished eating his 'meal' and pushed the bowl away. Oather was starting a second bowl while Serieve and the elf were still working on their first. Neither of them were really showing much interest in the food.

"Now we just need to get out of here," Sol said.

"I guess we could head out and see if there's anyone willing to sell us some horses in the village," replied Serieve.

Sol rose from his seat and leaned towards Oather and whispered, "I have a better idea. I'll be right back," and walked out. Sol could tell Oather knew what he was up to and began to quickly eat the rest of his stew so he'd be ready when Sol was done.

When Sol emerged from the tavern, the sky was dark. The weather was still misty and drizzly, but Sol was starting to get used to it. He remembered that the stable was just around the other side of the tavern. Sol looked around to make sure no one was watching, and then he walked around the corner towards the stable.

He approached the stable slowly, trying to determine if anyone was around. He couldn't hear anything, so he entered and was greeted by the smell of damp hay. His eyes quickly adjusted to the dimly lit stable and he could see there were five stalls on each side. The first two were empty, aside from bits of hay, but towards the back, there were three horses penned up in their stalls.

*Jackpot*! Sol thought, *now if Oather can just get the guys outside and ready in time.*

He opened the door of the first stall. There was a saddle on the ground beside the horse, a beautiful black mare with gray spots on her legs and a blanket on her back. Sol took the saddle and began to dress the horse. The horse whinnied when he started to put the saddle on her. Sol stopped and petted the mare's nose.

"Settle down, girl, it's okay," he said in a comforting voice. The horse shook her head, but didn't offer any more resistance as he finished saddling and bridling her.

He started towards the second horse when out of the corner of his eye he saw a boy standing at the entrance of the stable. The boy's mouth was open in awe and his eyes were lit up. He couldn't have been more than nine or ten years old and he wore the same drab clothing that the other villagers wore.

The boy turned and dashed back towards the tavern. Sol knew he had to catch the kid before he could alert anyone inside. He bolted past the gate of the stable in time to see the boy round the corner of the tavern, heading for the front of the building. Sol was right behind the boy. He was just about to catch him when the kid pushed open the door of the tavern.

"TIEF! TIEF!" the boy cried as he bolted into the tavern. The kid kept running until he was halfway to the bar at the back of the room. Sol was so close to the kid that he too burst through the main door. He, unlike the kid, came to an abrupt halt as soon as he entered. He stood there a second as everyone in the room suddenly was staring at him.

"Hees stelin' de 'orses," exclaimed the boy in the same unintelligible dialect that all the locals spoke. Sol almost didn't understand what the kid said, but he figured it out quickly as some of the men jumped up out of their chairs at him. One man took a swing at him. Sol dodged the first swing, but another caught him square in the gut.

A man, close to the bar, picked up a mug and looked like he was going to throw it at Sol. Oather leapt up from his seat, picked up the chair he was sitting in and threw it at the man. It was dead on target and the man fell to the ground.

Sol recovered from the blow and slugged the man who had hit him. Out of the corner of his eye, Sol saw Oather getting jumped by several other men.

Zaroth remained seated at the bar. He had his soup in front of him now and was trying to eat it, hardly paying any attention to what was going on in the room. Serieve and the elf, on the other hand, rose to their feet. Serieve stepped up onto his chair, then onto their table. He leapt from the table to tackle the man who had just hit Sol in the stomach. Both Serieve and the attacker fell to the floor, but Serieve was able to recover first. Serieve quickly got up and hit the man again.

Sol was surprised by Serieve's help, but thankful. Sol still had another attacker in front of him, but this one had been distracted by Serieve hitting his friend. Sol waited just a split second for the man to turn his attention back toward him and then let loose a tremendous and calculated blow to the man's nose, breaking it on contact.

The barkeep came out from around the bar wielding a large wooden club. He edged around the group of men fighting until he was behind Oather.

"Look out, Oather!" Sol yelled.

Oather spun around and caught the overweight man with a right hook. The barkeep dropped the club and staggered back helplessly and crashed into Zaroth who was still sitting at the bar and ignoring the fight. As the barkeep collided with Zaroth, Zaroth was pushed face first into his bowl. The wizard quickly pulled back from the hot soup and cried out in pain as it burned his skin.

Then everything seemed to stop.

All the fighting froze for a moment as Zaroth stood up. The hot stew dripped from his face and beard. His skin was bright red and a vein popped out on the side his forehead. The wizard gritted his teeth and his eyes were filled with anger. Then his robes began to ruffle stiffly like they were being blown in a fierce storm.

"What the h…?" Sol muttered. He barely realized that Khu-Rá was tugging at his arm. "We must leave, now!" Khu-Rá said.

Sol nodded his head slightly in agreement, still bewildered by what he was seeing. He grabbed Oather and bolted towards the door. First Sol heard a loud noise. Then he saw flames racing around him and then everything was as bright as the sun. The next thing he knew he was thrown through the air and out the door. His arms waved as he flew away from the tavern and landed some ten or fifteen paces away from the entrance of the tavern. Oather landed an arm's length away to his right and slid forward before coming to a stop on the grass.

His vision was blurred and his ears were ringing loud, but he saw Serieve lying on the ground near his right foot. Sol tried to lift his head off the ground but didn't have the strength.

"You all right?" Sol asked Oather, but he realized then that he couldn't hear his own words.

Oather's arm moved, so Sol knew that his friend was at least still alive. He tried to push himself up enough that he could turn around and see what had happened. It took a lot of effort but he was able to do it. He propped himself up with his right arm and looked back.

The tavern was now engulfed in flames. It didn't have a roof any longer and most of the front wall was gone. The whole place was a giant inferno. He then saw a dark figure in the flames. It was Zaroth. The wizard walked through where the main entrance of the tavern had been just a few moments before. His eyes glowed red like hot coals, as did his hands as he walked, untouched, through the flames.

Sol let the fatigue overtake him, and he slumped back down onto the wet ground. Zaroth walked towards him, knelt down and looked into Sol's eyes. He snapped his fingers a few times in front of Sol's face, trying to get a reaction. Sol couldn't seem to answer. His head was swimming. Zaroth grabbed Sol by the sides of his head. Sol saw the wizard's mouth moving as if he was yelling at him, but he couldn't hear a thing.

Zaroth let Sol's head go and took something out of his sleeve. Sol closed his eyes. Seconds later, he could hear again.

"Sol!" shouted the wizard. "Can you hear me yet?" Sol weakly nodded his head yes.

"Here, eat this, it will make you feel better," Zaroth said. He pushed something that tasted like an orange slice into Sol's mouth.

Sol did his best to chew it but he was incredibly tired. Whatever it was that the wizard had given him, he noticed, tasted pretty good. It was sort of like a spongy orange-spice cake. This made Sol try a little harder to eat it. Sol used what little strength he had left to motion Zaroth closer. Zaroth leaned closer to Sol.

"Horses…where are the horses?" he managed to ask.

Zaroth looked at Sol for a moment, then answered, "They got away and ran back towards the town." Sol closed his eyes and cursed under his breath.

Zaroth rose and attended to Oather, Serieve and Khu-Rá as well. It took a minute but Sol started to feel marginally better. He laid there for a few more moments before the wizard came back to him.

"Come on, Sol, we have to get out of here," said the wizard. "I don't think the people who live in that village will be very happy with us."

With Zaroth's help, Sol sat up. Khu-Rá was already starting to recover and was on his feet. Oather was just lying there, as was Serieve.

"What the hell was that?" asked Serieve as the elf tried to help him to sit up.

"Yeah," Sol jumped in. "I thought you didn't have very much of your magic, old man."

"The poison must have worn off more quickly than I expected. I exerted more power than I normally would have because I thought I was still weakened," Zaroth attempted to explain but Sol just didn't care anymore.

"Damn," was all Sol could say as he tried to stand on his own.

"Come," urged the wizard. "We really must leave this area before more locals arrive."

Khu-Rá did what he could to assist the three men as the group started hobbling away from the flaming building. He helped Serieve to his feet as Sol and Oather stepped over the charred remains of some of the villagers who hadn't been lucky enough to get out. Soon, they were heading back the direction from which they had originally come.

## 32. *Speak of the Devil*

"Slow down, old man," Sol tried to yell between deep, laborious breaths as he was pulled along by Oather, who was in somewhat better shape after the explosion.

The men made their way back down the road at as fast a pace as they could manage. Zaroth kept a good lead on the other men, who all panted heavily as they tried to keep up.

"We don't have time," replied the wizard. "We've got to keep going."

Sol stopped, and pulled Oather to a stop with him. Serieve and Khu-Rá followed suit. Zaroth kept moving, but he soon noticed that the others weren't behind him any longer and stopped to look back.

"What are you fools doing?"

Sol glared at the old man. "Look, we didn't blow up that tavern, you did!"

"Yes, but you are the thief who started the mess in the first place. You are just as guilty as I am. Besides, do you really want to take the chance that they won't hang you out of association? We're all strangers to this land, and we all came here together; so I doubt they will make any distinction between you and me."

Sol clenched his teeth. He knew the wizard was right.

"Well," said Serieve, "it's apparent that you have the use of your magic back. Can't you just make another one of those portal things and take us back to Tyric?"

"I told you, I didn't make that portal, and I've already thought of that. Something is blocking me and I can't leave."

"You were just going to leave us here, weren't you?" Sol snapped.

Zaroth didn't reply, but Sol could almost feel the wizard grin at him inside as he deduced the wizard's plan.

"Let's at least get off this main road," Sol said. "We can go at a slower pace and not be spotted as easily." Sol pointed to the woods. "We can go that way."

It was starting to get colder. The men could see their breath turn to small wisps of fog every time they exhaled. As they made their way through the woods, their pace slowed. It was nearly impossible to see as they made their way through. Sol kept getting poked in the head with many sharp, thin tree branches.

"Ow," grumbled Sol, as another tree branch swung back at him after the wizard passed by.

"Here," called the elf, "follow me. My people have a much easier time seeing in the dark than humans."

Khu-Rá took point and led them through.

"Watch that…" Khu-Rá started to say when Serieve got snagged on a root sticking out of the ground and tripped and fell. Oather helped his friend back up and they continued on.

"Never mind," the elf said.

They worked their way further and further into the forest. Sol had lost track of which direction they were going shortly after they left the road.

"Do you know where you are going, elf?"

"No," replied Khu-Rá. Sol didn't like the answer he got but really couldn't do anything about it.

"Do you have any clue how to get back to civilization?" Sol asked, attempting to get any glimmer of good news.

"No," the elf replied again, pushing another tree branch out of his way.

"Do you at least know how to get us back to the road if we don't find anything else?"

The elf stopped in his tracks. "Maybe."

"Gah! I knew I shouldn't have let you lead."

"Why?" Khu-Rá asked, "Do you think you could do any better?"

"Maybe."

"Look, human, in case you haven't noticed, we are actually on a trail."

Sol looked around but couldn't make out a trail but lied anyway, "Of course we are."

"Trails are made by people trying to go somewhere, so once I saw this trail, we started following it. Eventually, we will find something. More than likely a village," Khu-Rá replied smugly and started walking again.

"Carry on then," Sol said, gesturing as though he was motioning the elf back onto the trek, a little embarrassed to discover the elf actually did have a plan in mind.

Khu-Rá didn't walk more than ten steps before he halted and put his hand towards them, signaling for the others to stop.

"What is it?"

"Shh," replied the elf as he turned an ear to the direction they were walking. "I hear something."

Sol listened as well.

"You're right, I hear something too."

"What is it?" asked Zaroth. The men looked off in the direction of the sound. They saw a pinpoint of light that flickered in the distance.

"Let's find out," Sol replied.

The elf led the men just a little further before the woods opened into a wide, grass clearing. In the center was a large campfire encircled by a half dozen or so wagons. The men emerged from the woods and crouched down to inspect the caravan.

"I think...it looks like a camp of some sort. Probably traders," Sol whispered. "They have a fire going at least."

"And they have a good sized fire," added Oather enthusiastically as he rubbed his arms to warm them.

They could make out several larger men leaning against felled logs in front of the fire. Sol could hear them talking and laughing but couldn't make out their exact words.

To his left he heard the distinct sound of a horse neighing. He glanced left looking for the sound and saw a group of horses grazing beside the wagons.

"Here's our chance," Sol whispered eagerly to the others. "We'll sneak around-"

"No," hissed the wizard. "I'm tired of your foolishness. We aren't doing that again. We are going to try to be diplomatic. With any luck we can find out where we are and how to get back home."

"Sorry, Sol, I'm with the wizard on this one," Serieve chimed in.

"Fine," Sol replied. "You all stay here and I'll go talk to them. We'll seem less threatening if we approach them one at a time."

Oather gave Sol a puzzled look, silently telling Sol that he wasn't sure about this plan.

"Trust me," Sol said with a smile. "They are just travelers like ourselves, they aren't looking for a fight."

Sol straightened his shirt and walked towards the group.

## 33. The Mystics

The wagons looked old, and were decorated in different colored fabrics, which in Sol's experience usually meant they were either a traveling show or merchants. The wagons were boxy in shape and most of them had windows on the rear compartment, leaving only the front bench exposed to the elements.

Sol walked in between two of the wagons. The one to his right had the rear door open. Sol tried to look inside as he passed but it was so dark that he couldn't see anything. As he stepped closer, he saw three men sitting around the fire, drinking and talking with each other. They were dressed in common clothing; very loose shirts and pants with worn leather boots.

A small pot rested next to the fire. From the aroma that filled the air, it was full of stew. It smelled immensely better than the potato-filled water they tried to pass off as soup back at the tavern. Sol's stomach grumbled and he couldn't remember when food had ever smelled so good.

The men jumped to their feet at Sol's approach. They were all very large and gruff looking. The one closest to Sol, and the largest of the three, had brown eyes and dark brown curly hair and a beard. These men certainly weren't like the townsfolk they had met earlier. Instead, their clothing was brightly colored and new.

A woman, whom he had not noticed before, sat near the pot eating. Two other women stood behind her, talking to each other and shrouded in the shadows. They were dressed similarly to the men, but in much more form fitting clothes.

"Whoa!" Sol said, as he stopped and threw his hands up in front of him. "I mean you no harm."

The men said nothing.

"Allow me to introduce myself," Sol said in a playful, entertainer sort of tone. "My name is Soliere, but you may call me Sol, for short. All my friends do, and we're all friends here, right?" he said stepping closer to the three men.

The men continued staring at Sol. The women retreated to one of the wagons.

*Oh great, I've already managed to insult them*, Sol thought.

"What is it you want here, stranger?" asked one of the men, in a very deep voice. Sol eyed the man up and down. The man must have been at least as big as Oather, but older and overweight. He could very well have had an entire keg of ale under his shirt by the look of his belly. His two companions were younger and more fit.

Sol smiled and stepped closer.

"We just wish to share your fire and talk. My friends and I are lost and are trying to find our way home," Sol said, grinning. He was now just a few steps away from the largest man, who stood there eyeing him suspiciously.

\*\*\*

Outside the range of the campfire the others waited for Sol. Serieve, leaned towards Oather and whispered, "I don't think he trusts us. He's probably met Sol before."

Oather tried hard not to laugh. "Wise man," he whispered back.

\*\*\*

Sol turned and looked back at his companions.

"That," Sol said pointing, "is Oather. That is Serieve. The elf next to him is Khu-Rá, and the old man in the back is Zaroth."

Sol turned back towards the new men. "See, now we're all friends."

The largest man stood there quietly for a moment.

"You are new to this land, aren't you stranger?"

"Yes, I am. Is it that obvious?"

The large man smiled and said, "Yes, it is, my small friend."

The man stuck out his arm to greet Sol.

Sol sighed in relief and took the man's arm in greeting. "At first I thought I might have interrupted the wrong kind of people."

"Come my friend…join The Damned," yelled the man as he pulled Sol towards his two companions and their warm fire.

Sol looked back to the darkness from which he had come and waved to the others to come closer. Oather, Zaroth, Serieve, and Khu-Rá all came out of the darkness towards the fire.

"I am Vego," said the large bearded man. "These are my cousins Mîkel, and Jasen."

Mîkel and Jasen grunted and sat back down with their mugs. Sol understood them not saying much, since they both seemed slightly drunk.

"Welcome, friends!" announced Vego as Oather and the others sat down to join them.

"Chera," he called to one of the younger females. She was standing close to a bright red wagon decorated with silver stars and moon shapes.

"Get some more bowls for our companions. I am sure they are hungry from their travels." The girl turned and headed to a wagon covered in blue fabric.

"You bet we are," Serieve grinned. "The stuff we ate earlier I think made me feel worse." Oather nodded his head in agreement.

Sol took out his pipe and filled it with tobacco. He picked up a dry twig lying close to the campfire, set it aflame, and used it to light his pipe.

"What brings you strangers to this land?" asked Mîkel, who sat closest to Khu-Rá.

"We don't know," answered Serieve "We-"

"We are just passing through," interrupted Zaroth. We have been traveling a long time in search of new lands."

"You aren't walking your whole journey, are you? Where are your horses?"

"We lost them. We are looking for new ones if you happen to know where we can buy some," replied Sol.

"That is most unfortunate for you," replied Vego.

The young girl returned with five bowls and spoons for the strangers. Another, older gypsy woman who was carrying fives mugs of ale followed her. The girl filled the bowls and handed one to each of the strange men, while the older woman handed them each a drink.

Oather took the bowl from her and began eating immediately. Serieve managed to at least thank her before beginning. The girl approached Zaroth and began to hand him the final bowl and spoon.

"Be careful not to spill it on him," Sol said to the girl sarcastically. She looked at him quizzically. Zaroth shot Sol a hateful glare before thanking the girl and taking the bowl.

No one else said anything; they just started eating their food. Oather took a bite and after a quick evaluation began scarfing the food down as quickly as the tiny spoon would allow.

Sol took a bite and was quite surprised at how good it tasted. It had potatoes like the stew at the tavern, but there was more to go with it now. Carrots, onions, celery, a couple of vegetables he'd never seen before and, most importantly, beef. Before Sol had taken a few bites, Oather had finished off his bowl and Chera had filled it again.

After the men had been taken care of, the women returned to the wagons and left the men to eat. Vego and his cousins didn't say much. They just sat and sipped their drinks and stared at the fire while their guests ate. Jasen's head drooped as he let out a snore.

Setting his pipe aside, Sol gulped down another two large mouthfuls of stew and chased them with a swig of his ale.

"So, could you point us to the nearest town where we can get some more horses and head back home?" Sol asked.

Vego rolled his head sideways to face Sol. Vego was obviously drunk. His face was all red and sagged as if he were about to pass out.

"No, my friend, you will not be able to buy any horses here."

"Why's that?"

"This is a hard land and it is not likely that you'll find anyone willing to part with theirs."

"Can you tell us which way we need to go to get out of this land?" Khu-Rá asked.

Vego let out a small chuckle, "That, you will have to ask Yaeva."

"Where are we, by the way?"

"Vego!" a voice interrupted the big man as he was about to speak. The big man's head whipped around to the blue wagon behind him.

An old woman peeked around the door of the wagon. She wore a blue silk wrap around her head and was clad in brightly colored clothing. Her dress was a deep blue color embroidered with streaks of yellow, red, and purple.

The woman stretched out her hand towards the men at the fire and curled her fingers, beckoning for the men to come closer.

"Come here, strangers. Let me have a look at you."

Sol looked at Oather, unsure as to whether they should go or not. Oather shrugged his shoulders in response, knowing what his friend was thinking. Sol decided an old woman couldn't pose much danger and got up. He set his empty bowl down and picked up his pipe and took a puff as he walked towards the wagon.

He looked back and Oather was just starting to stand but Serieve, Khu-Rá and Zaroth remained seated.

"Well, come on. I'm not the only stranger here."

The others, including Zaroth, rose and followed Sol to the wagon.

The old woman ducked back into the carriage. Sol could hear her jewelry clinking as she made her way back in. As he neared the wagon he could see faint candlelight emanate from within. He stepped up onto the steps and crouched over so that he could get inside.

Once he stepped in, Sol found that the wagon was bigger on the inside than it was on the outside. Sol stuck his head back outside the wagon and looked at it, then back inside--and inside, it really was bigger. He wasn't sure what to say, so he just went in as the old woman had instructed. He was sure that all of them wouldn't fit, especially Oather, but now it seemed there was plenty of room for them all.

Sol noticed first that the room smelled strongly of cedar and jasmine, blended with a scent that Sol could only describe as burnt dirt. The shelves were cluttered with jars and trinkets. The wall to his right was covered in hanging clothes and other fabrics. A hat was hung at the top which had a bright red and blue feather that dwarfed the hat itself and looked like it was going to fall onto the floor.

The ceiling was painted black and covered with white specks like stars in the sky. On the floor to Sol's left was a purple trunk with a lock on it.

"There is nothing in there that would interest you, Soliere," the old woman said as she walked around to the other side of a small table in the middle of the cabin.

She pulled out a chair and took a seat at the desk. It wasn't until now that Sol noticed how small she was, even for an old woman she was small and plump. She gestured for the men to sit. They all sat, cross-legged, upon the bare floor in front of the old lady. Even though she was sitting on a chair, she was still eye level with most of them, though she was still a little shorter than Oather.

The room was lit by a dozen or so candles and the brightest candle sat upon the table in front of the old woman's face. The shadows it cast across her skin, which only served to deepen her wrinkles and make her look even older than Sol first thought. For the first time, he managed to look her in the eyes.

She had two pupils in each eye. They were side by side and overlapped in the middle. Sol wondered if she could actually see or if she was blind.

"How did you know my name?" he asked, intrigued by her right from the start.

"I know many things, stranger," she smiled back at him. "Most importantly, I know how to listen. You introduced yourself as you entered our camp."

Sol rolled his eyes as he knew she had pulled one over on him. He heard Serieve snicker behind him.

"Are you Yaeva?" Sol asked, and the woman nodded her head yes. "Vego told us that you can help us find our way back home."

The old woman sat there, her weird eyes staring at him. She squinted as though she were peering through him rather than at him. Silence enveloped the room.

"In due time, my child. First, I must see what the fates have in store for you," she said. She pulled out a deck of cards that were about twice as long as her small, frail looking hands.

Zaroth groaned, "We really don't have time for this drivel. You can no more see the future than I can. You people are just charlatans who wouldn't know true magic if it flew out of the heavens and landed right on your camp."

Yaeva placed the deck of cards upon the tabletop and leaned towards Zaroth, who was sitting there glaring at her.

"You believe that, don't you?" she asked, peering directly into the old wizard's eyes. "Why don't you let me give you a demonstration, and allow me to guess your true age, wizard?"

Zaroth rolled his eyes again.

"If you think you are all knowing, then be my guest."

This got Sol's attention, "Okay, now we're talking. I would like to know that myself."

Yaeva glanced at Sol and winked her right eye as she leaned further across the table and motioned for the wizard to come closer. Zaroth leaned towards her, and she cupped her hand around her mouth next to his ear. Sol could hear her whisper something to the old man. Zaroth's eyes bulged, momentarily, before resuming his normal stoic look. She pulled away from him and he did not say anything else.

"Don't we get to hear?" griped Sol.

"You'll learn in time."

"I won't listen to this hogwash." Zaroth stood up and walked out of the wagon. Oather moved aside as the old man exited and slammed the door behind him.

"Wizards tend to disregard any form of magic they themselves do not understand," Yaeva said.

"Give me your hand," she said to Serieve.

Serieve looked to the others reluctantly before finally giving her his hand. She stretched out her hand and took his, pulling him closer to her. She uncurled his fingers and held them out straight as she closely examined his palm. Serieve didn't say anything; he just sat there bewildered.

"First, I shall look at your past. Once you know I can see the past, there will be little room for you to doubt that I too, can also see your future," she said, looking at the four men before looking down to Serieve's palm.

"Hmmm," she began.

"What? What is it?"

"Very interesting," she replied.

"You recently were injured in an encounter that you jumped into without thinking, didn't you?"

"Ye…yes, how did you know?"

"Many things can be learned from the palm. This particular event was written by the fates. It was to be your last," she continued. She extended a finger, the exceptionally long fingernail of which was painted red from the cuticle to the end of the finger, then gold up to the end of the nail itself, and used it to trace several of the lines on Serieve's hand.

"You see this line?" she asked. Serieve looked closer at his own hand.

"I don't see anything."

Yaeva pointed to a wrinkle that ran the length of his hand, across his palm. "You see all the intersections of these lines? This is your life line and until yesterday it was shorter. Now you have new lines that stretch the rest of the way across."

"I...I think I see it now," Serieve replied.

"Something happened..." she paused, "and the fates rewrote your destiny. You have a place in this world yet." She let go of his hand and he sat back looking intently at his palm.

"Do not jeopardize it by leaping into situations before you know what you are getting into."

"That's what I keep telling him," Sol said. "See," he kidded Serieve, "you should listen to me."

"You are one to talk, young man," she snapped at Sol. "Your aura speaks volumes of the trouble you have gotten yourself into."

Sol didn't reply. He just shrugged innocently, as if he had no idea what she was talking about.

"Here, now let me see your palm," she said to Sol. He stretched out his hand to her and she grabbed it and pulled him closer. Sol watched and she seemed to have trouble making things out. She leaned over and grabbed the candle that sat just off to her right. She held the candle closer to Sol's hand to get more light to shine on his palm.

"Hmmmmmm," she said.

"What?"

"It's very difficult to make out." She set the candle back to its base and traced several of the lines on his hand.

"I see that you yearn to have a ship and sail the seas. I see a lot of turmoil in your life but nothing specific about your past. Your future is also just as hard to read. I see ships, and war, and treachery. You will someday turn on an ally. Only after the deed is done will you realize the mistake you made."

"So I'll get my ship then?" Sol asked, ignoring the rest of what she said.

"Oh yes, you'll get your ship," she replied. "Several, if you play your cards right. The better question is, will you be able to keep them?"

She let go of his hand and Sol sat back. Oather shot his hand to her, outstretched so that she could see it clearly.

"Look at mine," Oather said, his voice laced with eagerness.

Yaeva looked it over once and let go of the big man's hand.

"Do you see anything?"

She looked up at him. "You're a good boy," she smiled. "You're going to do just fine in this world. One piece of advice though…"

"Oh yeah? What's that?"

"Stay away from cliffs that overlook the ocean."

As Oather pulled his hand back, Yaeva's attention went to the deck of cards on the table.

"What about him?" Sol asked about Khu-Rá.

Yaeva looked at the elf, "I'm sorry dear, you were so quiet that I almost forgot you were there. Come closer so that I might do a reading for you."

Khu-Rá was hesitant to move but eventually scooted towards her and gave her his hand.

"This will be the first time I have ever done this on one of your race, but I should be able to tell you something," she said as she rubbed his flattened hand between hers.

Khu-Rá's hands were not much larger than her own, but his were much thinner and the fingers were longer and more dexterous.

"You are filled with a hate for someone. It's almost overwhelming. He used to be a friend of yours, didn't he child?" she asked, looking up at Khu-Rá's face. He seemed stunned at her words. His mouth opened slightly in disbelief as he nodded his head, yes.

"In time, you will have to learn to not let this hate consume you. The fate of your friends, as well as all you hold dear, may depend on it," she said, releasing his hand. Khu-Rá withdrew his hand and slid back to where he had sat before.

Yaeva's attention went back to the deck of cards. She took them in her stubby little hands and began to shuffle them. Sol wondered how she could possibly manipulate the cards as skillfully as she did with her short fingers and long fingernails.

After a moment of shuffling she stopped and held the deck out to Sol.

"Tap the cards so they may attune themselves to you," she told him. Sol reached out and tapped the deck once. She then held it out for Serieve, Oather and Khu-Rá to do the same. One by one they each touched the deck. Then she shuffled it some more.

When she stopped she held the deck in her hands and closed her eyes tightly. She whispered something the others did not understand, then opened her strange looking eyes again.

"This is the Deck of Fortune," she said as she looked at each of the men staring at her. "It cannot tell you exactly how your life will go, but it can give you hints of things to come."

She placed the deck onto the table and drew the top four cards. She laid them face down in a row, left to right next to the deck. She then flipped the first card over and revealed a picture of a black sun.

"Ohh," the old lady muttered.

"What is it?" Serieve asked.

"This is the black sun card. It's typically a sign of trouble ahead. But it really depends on the other cards revealed with it. Let's see what we have next."

She turned over the next card and it revealed a picture of several people standing in a circle.

"Well, this is a good sign," she told the men, looking up from the cards to Serieve.

"What's it mean?"

"This is the sign of friendship. You are going to meet new companions shortly."

"That's not much of a fortune," Sol scoffed, "We've already met them. The wizard and the elf here aren't part of our group."

"Perhaps," she replied, "but the cards never lie. If they say you will meet new people, you will meet new people."

The anticipation in the room, and especially on Serieve and Oather's faces, heightened considerably as she moved to the third card and flipped it over slowly.

This one had a man wearing a devil mask and holding a knife. The old woman looked down at the card with a serious expression.

Serieve started to say something but she cut him off.

"This is a very ill omen."

"What does it mean?" Serieve asked anxiously.

"Calm yourself, child, all is not lost. There is still one last card."

Serieve didn't talk anymore, but his face told how desperate he was to see the fourth card. His eyes were glued to it as the old woman moved her hand across the table. She slid her thumbnail underneath the edge of the card and lifted it up so only she could see its face.

Her eyes bulged and she gasped before laying the card down so the men could see it. This card was completely black.

"What does this mean? Please, we have to know," Serieve asked desperately.

"Oh this is most grave, my child. This is the card of death."

"In the near future," she began saying, but paused momentarily, "one of you will die."

She closed her eyes as though she was concentrating, then opened them and sighed deeply.

"Who will it be?" Oather asked. "Do you know what will happen?"

"No, my child, the cards only give hints and no more." She pushed herself up from the table. "I can tell you no more."

"Well, it's been nice knowing you, Serieve." Sol smiled as he slapped his friend on the back.

"Shut up, Sol."

Sol feigned a hurt glance. "Sorry, my friend, but life's just that way sometimes. Better luck next time."

Sol stood up and stretched. "So, can you tell us now how to get out of this land?"

Yaeva picked up the dealt cards and placed them back into the deck, which she slowly picked up and began to shuffle again. She did not look at the men, only down at the cards moving between her hands.

"Well?" asked Sol, a little more emphasis in his voice.

Yaeva sat there, looking down as she shuffled the cards.

"You, like everyone else here in this cursed land, cannot leave," she replied in a somber tone.

"What do you mean?" Serieve asked. All the men had confused looks upon their faces.

"This land was cursed and terrible magic prevents anyone from leaving. If you try, then you die, simple as that. Even then, your soul will still remain trapped here."

"Surely there must be a way out," Sol replied. He eyed the old woman suspiciously. "You know of a way out, I can tell it by your voice. You do not have the same accent as the villagers and your clothes are newer than theirs."

"You have amazing insight...for a man. Perhaps I've underestimated you," she replied looking up at Sol. "There are some ways out of this land but we cannot take you. We do not have the power to do so."

"Then who... who can help us escape?"

"King Nicholas rules this realm. He alone can set you free."

"Can you take us to him, please?" asked Serieve.

Yaeva looked up at the young man and smiled.

"I will do as you ask. Sometimes he shows mercy and helps those who enter his land accidentally. If he likes you, that is."

"That's great! How could he possibly not like us?" Sol said, with a wide grin. "When can we go?"

"Go, wait out by the fire and I will ready my clan."

Sol led the way out, followed by Oather, then the others. As he stepped down to the ground he stretched his arms out and cracked his neck.

"I hate sitting like that for too long a time. Makes me all stiff."

Finally, Serieve stepped down to the ground and looked to Oather. "So what do you think? Do you believe in all that stuff?"

Oather's face was blank.

"Oh, don't tell me you believe any of that dung," Sol said mockingly.

"Shh," Oather said, coming out of his reverie. "She might hear you."

"Oh, please," Sol scoffed as he and the others walked back towards the fire.

"I don't know, how did she know I was wounded?"

"Anyone could tell that. I mean you still look a bit green to me too."

The men walked back towards the fire where Zaroth was standing alone.

"Are you fools done playing with these side show con artists yet?" Zaroth asked.

"I think she really knows some things. How else could she have been so right about us?" Serieve replied.

"I don't see how any of you could believe such nonsense. What did she say? The future holds nothing but uncertainty mixed with some supposed ominous event followed by saying someone will die someday, somewhere, somehow…or something equally ambiguous?"

They were all quiet a moment, then a smirk spread across Sol's face as he looked at the wizard.

"Was she right?"

"Right about what?"

"Was she right about your age?" Sol replied.

"No," Zaroth mumbled as he looked at the ground, averting his eyes from Sol, "she was off by three years."

"Three years isn't too bad. Especially for an old man like yourself."

Zaroth dismissed Sol's statement altogether. He turned his back to the men and looked at the fire.

"Personally, I think you are just jealous that she has an astounding skill that you just aren't good enough to master." Sol said, once again pulling his pipe from his bag. "It's okay though, we understand that you're not that good a wizard. Perhaps Yaeva would tutor you…"

Vego approached from one of the other wagons. "We'll be ready to go in a moment," he said, cutting off Sol's tirade. "Yaeva has requested that we take you to the castle, to see the King."

"Yes, thank you. We would appreciate that," Serieve replied.

"Come, then. We will get you loaded and we will be off."

Vego led the men to one of the far wagons and motioned for them to enter. Zaroth entered first, followed by the elf and the cavalier. Sol motioned for Oather to go in next but the big man just stood there.

Lightning flashed through the sky again, followed closely by another clap of thunder.

"Get in, you big lug," Sol yelled over the sound of the thunder.

29

Oather shook his head, no, and looked to Vego.

"Can I ride on the front bench with the driver?"

"Do you know how to handle one of these?" he asked Oather. Oather nodded his head, yes.

"Then you may drive it if you like. I don't think Chera wanted to drive anyway," Vego said. He pointed to the front bench, and Oather stepped up to the seat as Vego went to get the horses.

"Fine," Sol said dismissively, and waved his arm at Oather as he entered the wagon.

Within moments the gypsy men had the horses harnessed and they began to break the camp circle. Vego in the lead cart, followed by Yaeva's wagon, then Oather's, and then the last two wagons.

# 34. Unpleasant Surprises

Andrea's eyes opened slowly. She had slept as soundly as she ever had before and her eyelids felt as though they were made of lead. The lamps in her room were lit, which helped since almost no light came in through the windows, despite having the drapes drawn.

When she lifted her head, she could make out a figure in her room, but her vision was little more than a light blur.

"Misha?"

The figure moved closer to her and knelt down beside her bed.

"No, my dear," Nicholas whispered back to her.

At the sound of his voice, Andrea's eyes quickly shot open. She pulled back the sheets of her bed and sat upright.

"Nicholas," she growled, "what do you want?"

He stood up and looked down at her.

"Poor Misha sat here for you all night and most of the day, just waiting for you to wake up. I guess you were simply exhausted, because you never did," he said. Andrea could hear a wicked tone in his voice.

Her vision began to clear, and she could see him walk towards the parlor.

"What are you talking about, Nicholas?" Andrea had an unpleasant suspicion about where this was going.

Nicholas stepped aside and turned the parlor reading chair towards her bed as if it were a prize. Andrea squinted to make out what was in it. At first it was a blue blur that covered most of the chair, but as her vision cleared up she could see it was a person dressed in blue clothes, sitting in the chair.

"No," Andrea whispered. "Nicholas, what did you do?"

Her eyes came more into focus as she drew closer to the figure.

Misha sat there, still wearing the pretty blue and lace dress that Andrea had given her yesterday, but what Andrea saw was not Misha, but an ancient corpse. Its skin was wrinkled; its hair and nails were long, cracked and yellowed. The corpse's eyes were wide open, as was its mouth, displaying the most frightful expression Andrea had ever seen. From the corpse's features, Andrea knew it was Misha--the likeness was vague but true.

Andrea reached out and touched the corpse, hoping that what she saw was a lie, but knew it wasn't even before her hands felt the coldness of the once-young girl's dead body. She closed her eyes in an attempt to quell the anger that welled up inside of her.

"The poor thing really could have lived a long life," Nicholas said nonchalantly as he looked down at Andrea in front of the chair. "She put up quite a struggle before I finally drank deeply from her soul. I must have imbibed seventy or eighty years' worth of life from her before she-"

He was cut off as Andrea turned and attacked him.

Her swift move nearly took him by surprise, but he was still too fast for her and caught her by her right arm and her neck. He pulled her close and looked deep into her eyes.

"You monster!" she screamed and struggled to free herself from his grasp.

"Why did you do that? She did nothing but serve you loyally!" she howled at him.

Nicholas held her tightly by the throat, his surprisingly strong hand tightening its grip, making it harder for her to breathe.

"You left me no choice."

"I had nothing to do with you killing her," Andrea spat back at him with what little breath she had left.

"You are wrong, my dear. Misha fulfilled her purpose in life by quenching my thirst and serving as an example for you."

Andrea stopped jerking and trying to escape his grasp.

"What you will come to understand, my love, is that you will give yourself to me willingly, or your fate shall be a thousand times worse than this little wench's was." He smiled menacingly as he relaxed his grip on her ever so slightly.

"That is still better than spending even one more day with you."

While Nicholas had been gloating, she managed to get her left arm inside of his grasp. She was able to angle it up, so that her spike was right underneath his neck and he didn't even realize it. With the last of her energy, she shot the spike up into his skull.

The hit couldn't have been better. But instead of dying instantly as Andrea expected, Nicholas let go of her, stepped back and desperately tried to pull out the spike. Wailing, he staggered around the room, knocking over furniture.

Andrea couldn't believe he was still alive. She aimed her other spike at him as he thrashed about the room. As soon as she had a good shot, she unleashed the second. He happened to turn towards her just as she triggered the spike and it caught him square in the chest.

He let out another muffled cry as the second spike hit him, but he still didn't go down. Finally, he stopped and got a good grip on the spike jutting up into his head. In one quick pull he jerked it out and threw it to the floor. The metal spike bounced off the floor and rolled under the bed.

Nicholas glared at her with pure hatred as black blood dripped from the wound onto his clothing. Slowly he reached for the second spike and pulled it out of his chest as well. Nicholas tossed that spike to the floor as well and looked down at the hole in his chest.

Miraculously, the wound began to seal up, as did the one on his neck. Andrea couldn't believe what she was seeing. By all accounts, he should be dead, but he wasn't.

"What are you?" she muttered.

"I…told…you," Nicholas said in a gravelly voice, "You…cannot…defeat me."

Andrea was shocked. Nicholas rushed at her and she knew she should move, but she couldn't. With a speed she couldn't comprehend, he rushed at her and slammed into her. She flew across the room, hit the wall and fell to the floor.

Andrea tried to get up, but she couldn't. The blow had knocked the wind out of her and all she could do was gasp for air. It felt like her chest was crushed. Nicholas stood over her. Andrea closed her eyes and tried to breathe deeply. She couldn't see Nicholas but she could feel him above her. She could almost feel his satisfaction in thinking he had broken her.

She reopened her eyes, turned and looked up at him.

"I will never give in to you," she said through clenched teeth.

"Yes, you will."

Nicholas turned and left her room, shutting the massive door behind him. Andrea could hear that someone else had joined Nicholas outside the door.

"Shall I do anything with her, master?"

"No, Lucian, leave her for now."

"As you wish, sire."

"I'm going to feed. If Yaeva gets here before I return, make sure my guests are welcome."

## 35. The Castle

The trek to the castle had been slow. They had ridden all night and most of the day and now it was nearing nightfall again. Sol was nearly ready to get out and walk and just wait for them at the top, but laziness won out over impatience, so he sat on the bench next to Oather until the horses managed to finally pull the wagons to the top.

The King's castle sat atop the tallest mountain in the realm, overlooking a town below. It was an enormous structure of black stone with spires that seemed to touch the clouds. The mountain it sat upon was split in two by a massive ravine that separated the castle grounds from the trail down the mountainside. The two parts of the mountain were connected via a stone bridge.

The bridge itself was wide enough that three of the wagons could have crossed it side by side. It was made of a gray stone that was beginning to crumble, though it still looked sturdy enough.

They made their way across the bridge to the gates of the keep itself. The walls were several stories tall, as were the ominous iron gates. The gates were open and very rusty. Sol didn't think they could even be shut anymore, if they had ever been shut at all.

On either side of the gate was a statue of a menacing gargoyle. Oather watched the statues, seemingly fascinated by them, as the wagons crept their way past them.

"Oh, this looks nice," Sol quipped, "the sort of place that just welcomes you in and makes you feel all warm and fuzzy inside."

Oather simply let out a worrisome grunt in reply.

"Is this where we are going?" Sol and Oather heard a voice to their right. Serieve had exited the back of the wagon and was walking next to them as the wagon entered the castle gate.

"Woke up, did ya?" Sol asked.

"Yes, the incline of that road toppled us over onto Zaroth. He wasn't too happy about that, so I decided to leave him alone."

The wagons continued into the courtyard of the keep and drew up near the main entrance to the castle. The large wooden doors were twice Oather's height and at least four times as wide. On each side was an alcove where guards could stand watch, but they were empty. The entire castle looked abandoned and dark, as if no one had lived there for quite some time.

The caravan came to a halt directly in front of the castle's main doors. Vego dismounted from his wagon and approached the entrance, but before he got near them though, they opened with a loud creak.

Vego stopped where he was and waited. The door on the right slowly opened just wide enough for a person to slip through, and out stepped an older man with a patch over his left eye, carrying a lantern. He was dressed much differently than the people of the village. His clothes, while not new, looked formal compared to the dingy scraps that the village people wore.

The man approached Vego and they exchanged a few words. Sol could see Vego's arms moving while he talked to the one eyed man, and every once in a while he would point back to the wagons.

After a moment or two, Vego turned and came back to Sol and Oather's wagon.

"It seems that the master is out, but his servant, Lucian, has agreed to take you in for the night until the master has returned. You will most likely be able to return home tomorrow."

"That's fantastic!" Serieve exclaimed.

Sol and Oather stepped down from the wagon, Serieve joined them as the wizard and elf emerged from the back of the wagon.

Lucian stepped forward towards the men.

"As you are aware, the Master is not in, but I will be happy to attend to your needs until such a time that he returns."

"Thank you," Serieve replied graciously.

"Now," Lucian said, "I will show you to where you can get some rest."

The older man turned and re-entered the castle through the main door. Sol and the others followed him in.

They passed through an entry hall, then into the main foyer of the castle. It was so dark inside that Sol couldn't make out anything more than a few paces away from Lucian's lantern.

Two more turns brought them to a wide, cylindrical staircase that led up and down. Lucian took the steps that led down. Sol quickened his pace until he was side by side with the old man.

"I notice that this castle is pretty bare. How many people live here?" Sol asked.

"It's nightfall. Most of the servants have already gone to bed."

"That may be true, but I haven't seen any guards."

"There isn't a standing army in this land, and very little need of guards here."

"That's very interesting," Sol said as he rubbed his chin in thought.

The group passed through another hall. No one said much of anything until Sol finally spoke up again.

"Sooo, what time do you expect the King to return?"

"Most likely in the morning," Lucian said. "He had urgent business to take care of in the village."

He led the group down another long hall with two doors at the end. Lucian stopped just before they reached the doors and turned to face the men.

"Here are your rooms. At one time, these were the barracks for the castle guards, but they are now empty. There are three beds in each room so you may divide the rooms as you like amongst yourselves."

Lucian stepped back and opened each of the doors for the men, taking a moment to light a torch near the doorway in each room. Sol, Oather and Serieve stepped into the room on the left. Zaroth watched which one Sol took, and then went into the other.

"A servant will attend to you in the morning when it is time for the morning meal. I trust you will not be requiring anything else until then?" he asked pointedly, looking directly at Sol.

"No, I think we will be fine. Thank you," Sol replied.

Lucian bade them good night and left by the way they had come. Sol watched Lucian until he was out of sight.

"Well, it looks like Oather and I will bunk with Serieve. Elf, I guess you get to bunk with Mister Sunshine in there," Sol said as he pointed to the room Zaroth had just entered.

Khu-Rá nodded and entered the room, closing the door behind him. Sol went into his room, followed by Oather. Serieve had already claimed the bed furthest from the door. The room itself was sparse, just three beds, each with a footlocker at the end.

Sol claimed the bed closest to the door and plopped down, letting out a loud sigh of exhaustion as he did so. Oather was left with the middle bed, but he didn't seem to care as he looked extremely tired. Sol hadn't noticed how worn out Oather looked until he saw Oather lie down on the bed and almost instantly fall asleep.

"Damn, I guess he was more tired than he let on," Sol said as he stretched out on his own bunk. He didn't hear a response from Serieve, so he lifted his head up to look over at the far bunk. Serieve had also fallen asleep.

"Well, I guess it's just me," Sol said to himself. He reached up and removed the torch from its holder. He was about to douse it in the bucket of sand which sat below the torch when he suddenly stopped.

*Hmm*, he thought, *I might need this later.*

He reached back up and replaced the torch in the wall holder. Turning over onto his side, he fluffed the pillow under his head and closed his eyes, letting sleep overtake him.

## 36. A New Plan

Halistan heard Tallmoor stand up in his cell. From the noises he made, he was rummaging around for something, and seemed to find it. Whatever he found, he used it to start raking across the bars of his cell, making a terrible racket.

After several moments, Tallmoor stopped and they all listened. Nothing could be heard, so Tallmoor started doing it again. This time he yelled loudly in addition to raking the bars.

Again, Tallmoor stopped to listen, but nothing was heard. He had just started to rake the bars a third time when Halistan heard the clicking of claws on the stone floor of the dungeon. The smaller of the two hellish hounds walked in, and it looked angry. The beast stalked towards Tallmoor's cell, growling menacingly. Wisps of flame escaped its ferocious jaws.

Halistan gripped the Star of Salus in his hand, closed his eyes, and concentrated. In his classes, his professor had stressed that in dealing with demons, willpower was everything. Even the most powerful priest would be helpless if he didn't have a strong conviction in his heart as he cast the spells.

Halistan steeled his emotions and began chanting the control spell. He could feel his will reaching out across the room to the beast. The hellhound stopped walking towards Tallmoor and glared menacingly at Halistan. It growled again, this time much more deeply. It made a guttural noise that sounded like personified hatred towards him.

Halistan breathed deeply and pushed from inside as hard as he could, but he could feel the monster pushing back. It didn't want to be controlled and fought him as hard as it could. The beast began to walk towards him, growling louder and louder as it approached. It stopped just in front of the cell. It shook its head violently to fight back against Halistan, but Halistan could feel the beast beginning to waiver.

Then, the monster looked up at him, hatred burning in its eyes, and leapt towards Halistan, slamming hard into the bars of the cell. Its snout and front paws reached between the bars in an attempt to get at Halistan, who jumped backwards just in time to keep from getting slashed by the monster's sharp claws.

Without thinking, Halistan made a fist while gripping the Star of Salus, raised it high, and smashed his fist down hard on the massive snout of the beast. The hellhound yelped loudly and jerked back from the cell. The fight was over.

The hellhound stopped growling and laid down at the base of Halistan's cell, now as calm and docile as any pet that Halistan had ever seen.

"Well, I'll be," Tallmoor said in an exasperated tone. "I've never seen anything like that before."

Halistan sat down in his cell, feeling like he had just run a hundred miles. Beads of sweat dropped down his forehead and ran into his eyes as he rested. He wiped them away and panted heavily.

"Can you make him do what you want now?"

"Yes, I believe so." Halistan looked into the beast's eyes, "Go. Bring us the keys to our cell."

The hellhound rose up on its front paws and looked at Halistan.

"Go on, I said."

The beast stood up and trotted away from them. The sound of its claws clicking and clacking echoed through the dungeon for a moment, then faded away.

"I've seen one of those monsters rip a man limb from limb," Tallmoor said, still sounding astounded by what he had seen.

"I wasn't sure if that would work, to be honest," Halistan replied.

Halistan looked at Orman who was finally smiling. It was the first time Halistan had seen the man smile. He grinned widely like a child watching a magic show, which made Halistan feel good inside.

Halistan scooted back against the wall, tilted his head up and shut his eyes. That spell was so draining that he needed to rest his eyes for a quick moment.

His rest was short-lived, though. As soon as Halistan was finally able to relax, he heard the clicking of the hellhound's claws against the stone floor as it headed back towards them.

The beast came straight to Halistan's cell and dropped a large key ring at the base of the bars.

"Quick, get the keys and unlock us," Tallmoor said.

Halistan jumped up and picked up the keys from the floor. The hellhound stood there watching him inquisitively. If it weren't for the evil-looking eyes, fiery breath, and overall fearsomeness of the beast, Halistan thought it would make a good pet.

Halistan steadied himself, because he had to focus. He took the keys and began trying to unlock his cell. Finally, on the fourth key, he was able to unlock his cell. The door swung open and Halistan cautiously stepped out, fearful that the beast might turn on him and attack him now that he wasn't protected by the bars. The beast just stood there, obediently watching him walk out. Once Halistan was convinced the beast would not harm him, he went to Tallmoor's cell. After freeing Tallmoor, they released Orman, who was so grateful to get out that he began to squeal. Tallmoor had to cover Orman's mouth to get him to be quiet.

"What do we do now?" Halistan asked.

Tallmoor thought for a moment. It was obvious to Halistan that the older man hadn't thought this far ahead--probably because he didn't really think they would get out.

"Well," Tallmoor started to say slowly, "normally, I'd head out the eastern door, but we saw how well that worked last time. It's still the fastest way out and the least likely to encounter Nicholas."

"I'm not as worried about Nicholas as I am Lucian," Halistan replied. "You said Nicholas is a demon so my magic might work on him too."

Tallmoor's eyes widened in shock. "I don't know, boy. Let's just hope that we don't have to find out, but you're right. That would be the easiest way to get out. Let's try it again."

The three men edged themselves towards the exit of their cell block. Halistan noticed that the hellhound continued to sit there, just watching them.

"What do we do with him?" Halistan asked, pointing to the hellhound.

"We could see if he wants to follow us. Maybe he'll be helpful again."

Halistan quietly called to the beast, who instantly came to his side and took his place next to Halistan.

Tallmoor listened but didn't seem to hear anything. "I think we're clear to go."

The three men made their way through the catacombs. None of them spoke a word as they walked. Each made an extra effort to be quiet, but ironically, what made the most noise was the hellhound's claws as it walked on the stone. The clacking sound seemed to echo in all directions and made Halistan nervous.

The first turn they came to, Tallmoor motioned that they would go left. After a few more turns, Tallmoor stopped and motioned for Halistan to come closer to him. Halistan leaned in and Tallmoor whispered, "Do you know how to ride a horse?"

Halistan nodded yes.

"Good. Just ahead and down the hall is the east exit again, and that will lead towards the stables. Once we get out, we'll run there as fast as we can and ride out. Can you do that?"

Halistan nodded again, and Tallmoor motioned for them to follow him. They had taken all of two steps when the hellhound began to growl. They all instantly stopped and Halistan's heart sank as he wondered if the spell was wearing off. Then, from around the corner they were just about to pass, they heard another set of clacking and the two-headed hellhound came around the corner to block their way.

The beast was bigger than Halistan remembered, and far larger than the one he'd enchanted. The two-headed beast growled at them and Halistan saw the two beasts staring intently at each other.

Halistan grabbed at the Star of Salus in an attempt to cast another spell at the two-headed beast, but before he could do so, Tallmoor grabbed his shoulder and shouted for them to run.

Instantly Tallmoor and Orman retreated back down the hall. The hellhound that Halistan had charmed leapt at the two-headed beast and the pair of them began a terrible fight. Halistan knew that the smaller beast would quickly be outmatched, so he, too, began to run after Tallmoor and Orman. They had a good head start on him but he thought he saw which way they went. He turned a corner and found a corridor that split in two different directions, and also connected with a stairwell leading to the upper levels of the castle. The noise coming from the hellhounds fighting behind him was horrendous. He heard a yelp and knew that the smaller hellhound had probably been injured.

Tallmoor and Orman were nowhere to be seen and Halistan couldn't tell which direction they had gone. Suddenly another, louder, cry came from one of the hellhounds and then there was silence. Halistan knew that the two-headed beast had slain the other and would now be coming after them.

Tallmoor and Orman were probably out of the castle by now. His only hope to get away was to lose the beast. Halistan thought there was a chance that the beast might be trained to stay in the catacombs as a guard and wouldn't venture into the upper levels.

He thought it was worth a chance so Halistan headed up the circular stone stairwell, hoping that he was right.

## 37. Roaming the Castle

"Psssstt," Sol whispered as he shook Oather's arm. Oather didn't stir. The barbarian had his pillow balled up under his head. He was asleep on his side and snoring lightly.

"Wake up," Sol said again, this time shaking his friend a little harder.

"Ugghhh," Oather groaned, finally rolling over to face Soliere kneeling beside his bed. The thief had a glimmer in his eye, which Oather knew wasn't a good sign.

He rubbed his eyes and looked at his friend, "What do you want? It's not time for breakfast already, is it?" His tone perked up as he said this. He realized that was a distinct possibility and hoped that it was true.

"No," Sol whispered. "Get up. I want to look around this place."

"Ugh," Oather groaned again, now fully aware why Sol was bothering him so early. "I don't want to go." Yawning and turning away from Sol, he buried his face into the pillow and tried to go back to sleep.

"Come on, you lug, get up," Sol whispered, still trying to keep his voice down, and prodded him again. Oather tried to pretend that Sol didn't exist.

"Ok, fine," Oather heard Sol say, which made Oather secretly hope that Sol was finally giving up. Then he heard Sol stand up and go back towards his own bed. There was the sound of some rustling, which only lasted a moment before he heard Sol coming back. Sol was apparently not going to give up so easily.

Oather tried thinking about being back at the Lucky Duck, back in his soft bed that Gretchen always had made for him when he came back tired after helping Sol with whatever "plan" they had been working on. He buried his face further into the pillow, trying anything to take his mind off where he was now and what Sol was doing.

Then Oather heard the sound of liquid in a small flask being shaken. He heard the distinct sound of a cap being unscrewed.

"You wouldn't dare," Oather said with his eyes closed.

"Depends on if you are going to get up." Oather could almost feel Sol grinning as he said it.

"I know you wouldn't waste any grog just to get me up."

"I am counting on being able to refill it while I'm here, so I won't be without for too long."

Oather squeezed his eyes tight, hoping that Sol was bluffing. A single drop landed on the side of his face. The cold liquid made him flinch. Oather turned over and glared up at Sol, who stood above him, grinning from ear to ear.

"Come on, Oather," Sol said, kneeling back down so that he was almost eye level with Oather. Oather clenched his teeth, looked at Sol and attempted to think of a good reason why he couldn't go, why he shouldn't go, but his exhaustion fogged his mind. He looked at Sol, his knuckles whitening under the pillow.

"This guy is a king, and kings have coffers which they use to pay servants. Soooo..." Sol let the words hang there as he grabbed Oather's arm and feebly tried to pull him out of bed.

"Okay, okay. I get the point," Oather grumbled, jerking his arm away. "Give me a moment to wake up." He rolled back over and closed his eyes again.

"Oh, no you don't, Oather," Sol snapped sternly, shoving Oather hard with his foot; nearly hard enough to make him roll off the bed onto the floor. Oather caught himself and shot Sol an irritated glance. Sol smiled back at his friend, holding the flask over Oather's head.

Oather sat up in the bed and swung his big feet off and onto the floor with a thud.

"Shhh," Sol whispered. "Try and be quiet. We don't want to wake the princess over there. The last thing we need is another lecture."

"I wouldn't lecture you if you weren't doing something wrong," Serieve replied, taking Sol and Oather both by surprise. Sol looked over to see the cavalier propping himself up on his elbows.

"Oh," Sol said. "You are awake then."

"Yes, I'm awake. Just what do you think you are doing?" Serieve asked, obviously not in the best of moods.

"Just looking around. Don't get your codpiece in a bind."

Serieve looked at Sol, who was grabbing the torch from the wall, and Oather, who was straightening his clothes and putting on his boots.

"I'll just go with you to make sure you don't get into too much trouble."

Sol stood there for a moment, the smile washing from his face. He definitely didn't seem thrilled about the idea of Serieve joining them.

"Fine, just try and be quiet. Can you handle that?"

Serieve stood up and began to re-equip himself, starting with his breastplate.

"Leave that," Sol said to Serieve, "It'll make too much noise."

"No, I don't want to take a chance of losing it."

"We'll be back. I promise."

Serieve thought about it for a moment before giving into Sol and leaving the breastplate behind. He wasn't happy about the notion, but laid it on the bed with his helmet.

"I have your word, right?" Serieve questioned dubiously, looking at his armor lying uselessly on the bed.

"Trust me."

Serieve did not seem convinced, but left the armor behind anyway. Sol was opening the door leading into the hall when he saw the elf coming out of the opposing room. Sol quickly closed the door behind him. It was still slightly ajar, but it did prevent Oather and Serieve from following him through.

The elf shut his own door and seemed to be surprised to see Sol.

"What are you doing?" the elf asked.

"I was about to ask you the same thing," Sol replied.

The two stood in front of each other, the light from Sol's torch dimly illuminating the passage.

"The wizard has left. I was going to look for him. I am afraid that he will do something that will anger the king, which could jeopardize our chances of getting home. I have decided to find him and make sure that he doesn't."

"My thoughts exactly," Sol replied. "I woke up and thought I heard something moving out here. I was going to check and make sure the two of you were all right. Imagine my surprise finding that you had the exact same idea."

Through the narrow opening of the door, Oather could see Khu-Rá eyeing Sol suspiciously.

"Here," Sol said, "why don't you let me help you look for Zaroth. With both of us, it is more likely that we will find him and be able to bring him back. Agreed?"

"Agreed."

Just then, Oather yanked hard on the door, pulling the handle from Sol's grip and opening it. He walked out and nearly bumped into Sol.

Sol turned around in mock surprise. "Oather, what are you doing awake?"

Oather started to reply but Sol cut him off.

"You must have been awakened by all the commotion. Good thing, too. The elf needs our help. Zaroth has apparently snuck out. In the middle of the night no less and we need to find him before he does something the king doesn't like."

Oather looked at Sol with a confused stare but said nothing.

Sol turned back to face Khu-Rá.

"Well, Oather and I will go this way," he said, pointing in the direction that Lucian had brought them down earlier that evening. "Khu-Rá, why don't you go that way?" he said, pointing the other way.

Khu-Rá nodded and began to walk away.

"If you find him before I do, come right back here. I will return periodically to see if you have found him," Khu-Rá said to them, looking back over his shoulder, as he vanished into the shadows.

Sol stood there next to Oather until the elf was out of sight. He then pulled Oather into the hall, followed by Serieve.

"What was that all about?" Serieve asked as he closed the door behind him.

"Nothing important, the wizard is gone. Forget it, we have more lucrative things to attend to," replied Sol as he started down the hall followed by his companions.

## 38. Damsel in Distress

Halistan ran up the steps leading out of the dungeon. He stumbled on the last one and fell down.

"Light," he said, and the star began emitting a beacon of light.

He scrambled to his feet and fumbled to hold up his holy symbol and keep the light steady so that he could see where he was going. The light shone down the dungeon passageway. Alcoves lined the walls, each filled with a different statue.

The staircase spiraled up to the main floor of the castle, and to another level beyond. Halistan kept on climbing past the main level to the next floor, hoping that either the beast would stay in the dungeons, or think that he had remained on the main floor.

He kept running, trying hard not to stumble as he climbed the stairs, until he finally reached the top level. He stopped running when he reached the summit. He was breathing heavily and wiped the sweat from his eyes. He tried to slow his breathing so he could listen for the beast following him, but nothing could be heard. Internally he thanked God that the beast had given up on him. He sat down on the top step of the staircase and rested.

It took several moments for him to catch his breath he and took the chance to look around. This part of the castle was kept up very nicely. It wasn't dusty like the dungeon. The carpets were clean, and the suits of armor that decorated the hall were nicely polished. A stark contrast to what he had seen in the castle so far.

Then he heard a loud thud several doors down the hall. At first, his heart jumped as he thought the devil-dog might have found which way he had gone and was after him again, but it didn't sound like the massive beast. Instead it sounded like someone hitting a door. Then he heard it again, and this time it sounded like someone kicking a door.

"Let me out of here, Nicholas. When I get out I'm going to kill you!"

Halistan slowly tip-toed down the hall closer to the door that the sound was coming from. There was more screaming from the other side of the door. It sounded like a woman's voice. She was cursing Nicholas over and over, using curses that Halistan had never heard before, which made him blush.

"Goodness, she's mad," Halistan said under his breath as he approached the door.

"Um...hello, miss?"

The kicking and hitting stopped.

"Who is this? Can you get me out of here?"

"My name is Halistan."

"That's great, but can you get me out of here?"

Halistan grabbed the handle of the door and tried to push it open but it wouldn't budge. It didn't seem like it was locked, it just wouldn't open. More like it was stuck than locked. Halistan stepped back and rammed into the door as hard as he could. Instantly he was knocked backwards. He could tell that he had bruised his arm and shoulder, but the door hadn't even shuddered.

"It's stuck pretty good, mistress."

"Can you find something to use as a battering ram?" she replied.

Halistan looked around but other than a few empty suits of armor he didn't see much that would help. He took another step back and inspected the door. It looked like a normal door but something wasn't right about it. Halistan again pulled out the Star of Salas and held it out in his hand. He closed his eyes and whispered a small incantation. The star began to glow and he could feel a magical aura surrounding the door.

"What are you doing?" Halistan heard the woman ask through the door. He could tell by her tone that she was irritated.

"I'm just checking if the door is magically sealed, and it is."

"Then how do I get out of here?"

Halistan thought for a moment. In his teachings as a healer they were taught how to undo curses and enchantments. Perhaps he could dis-enchant the door and set the woman free.

"Stand back. Let me try something."

He heard the woman step away from the other side of the door. Halistan took the star into his right hand and placed it on the door. He closed his eyes and softly chanted. At first, nothing happened. He concentrated more on the door itself but the enchantment was strong. He could feel the power of the door pushing back at him.

Halistan continued to chant, clenching his eyes shut as he concentrated as hard as he could. The star began to glow, then flickered, then glowed brighter as Halistan pushed with all of his will into the incantation. Slowly the light from the star began to spread to the door. It expanded further and further, and the door pushed back harder and harder.

Halistan felt his brow begin to sweat and his hand shook as he pressed it against the door. The glow from his spell grew even further and eventually spread across the entire door. The glow intensified until it burst into a shower of sparks, destroying the spell cast upon the door.

He bent over and took a deep breath, panting as though he had just sprinted a league. The door swung open and inside he could see a beautiful bedroom with a grand painting above the bed. Halistan stepped inside and saw a woman standing near a fireplace.

To his surprise it was the same woman whom he had healed a few nights before.

"Thank you so much," she said as he walked in.

In his rush to save her the other night, he hadn't realized how pretty she was. Her long auburn hair contrasted her hazel eyes and red lips. He found it difficult not to stare.

She looked at him intently. "You," she said.

"Y-yes," Halistan replied.

"You were in my dream the other night."

"I was?"

"Yes, you saved me."

"That wasn't a dream. I did save you. You jumped out of a window and were hurt. There were guards that were coming with orders to ki…" Halistan was interrupted by the woman. She walked up towards him as he was talking, grabbed him by the head and pulled him down to kiss him on the lips.

Halistan was stunned. This was the last thing he had ever expected her to do. It felt wonderful, but he just didn't know how to react. Slowly she pulled her lips away from his and looked him in the eyes.

"Thank you," she whispered.

"You...you're welcome," Halistan replied. He could feel the warmth in his cheeks and knew he was blushing but he couldn't help that.

"We need to get out of here before that megalomaniac returns."

"That's what I was trying to do when I came across your room. Do you know how to get out?"

"Yes, I can get us out and we can take a couple of the horses from the stable. Just let me grab a couple of things and we'll get out of here."

He saw the woman turn and grab a few small items from her bureau. After collecting her things she turned towards him. Her eyes widened and the color ran from her face as her gaze went to the door.

Halistan didn't understand what was wrong with her until he heard a growl come from behind him. He turned and watched as the two-headed beast that had been chasing him entered the room.

## 39. *Saved by an Elf*

Andrea let out an ear piercing screech. Halistan stood there frozen as he looked in terror at the ferocious monster. Its wide jaws dripped fire as it entered. The beast saw Halistan and leapt at him. Halistan dodged to the right and the monster narrowly missed him as it flew by and crashed into the bed. The beast landed and turned back towards them. Halistan looked for Andrea and saw that she had managed to get out of the beast's way as well.

The two of them stood on either side of the monster, while the monster's two heads growled at them. The monster took a step forward, seeming unsure about which of its prey to go after first. It didn't take long for it to decide that Halistan would be its first choice, and both heads focused on him.

The monster shifted its stance towards Halistan. It was about to leap again when Andrea raised her arm and shot some sort of spike at the monster. The spike hit its mark squarely on the beast's flank.

Both heads looked upwards and howled in pain as streams of fire shot out of the creature's mouths. The monster's right head twisted hard to the right to try and reach the spike that was stuck in its flank, but couldn't reach it. The creature spun around several times in desperation, knocking over and scattering all the furniture in the room.

Andrea backed against her dresser in an attempt to stay out of the beast's way. Halistan was almost up against the fireplace as he watched the beast writhe in pain. The distraction was short-lived, as the hellhound quickly gave up on getting the spike out and turned its attention towards Andrea.

It stopped and glared at her ferociously, baring its fangs and emitting a terrifying, guttural growl. The beast took one step forward, and both heads snapped at her. Andrea found a silver candlestick holder that she wielded like a club, ready to strike the beast if it attacked her.

Halistan looked around for something he could use as a weapon but there was nothing around for him to use. His mind raced frantically. Any moment now the beast would attack her and there was no way that she'd be able to fend it off with a little candlestick holder.

His mind raced but only one solution came to mind, although he wasn't sure if it would work. Time was running out and he had no other options. Halistan pulled the Star of Salus off from around his neck and held it out in front of him towards the beast. He closed his eyes and concentrated on the control spell that he'd used earlier. He began to chant the words and he could feel heat start to emanate from the star in his hand.

He opened his eyes as the monster took a swipe at Andrea with its massive paw. She managed to avoid being struck by it and ran to the other side of the bed, using it as a blockade between her and the hellhound. Halistan continued to chant, this time louder. One of the beast's heads shook as though it was disoriented. The beast's right head stared at Andrea and it swiped at her across the wide bed, but she was too far away for the beast to reach her.

Halistan felt his heart beating frantically as he continued to force his will upon the beast. He chanted louder and louder, but the beast fought back. He could feel its will pushing back against his own. The monster's left head drooped and the entire left side of its body seemed sluggish, but the right head remained fixated on Andrea.

The beast swiped at her again but realized that she was too far away. It tried to jump up onto the bed, but only its right legs were able to move. The monster seemed bewildered and its left head shook again. Then it turned back towards Halistan.

Beads of sweat rolled down Halistan's forehead as he focused all his energy on the spell. It seemed to be having an effect on the beast, so Halistan concentrated harder. He felt his will enveloping the beast. The beast had a strong will and didn't want to give in easily, but Halistan pushed harder.

Then, suddenly, the beast's free head looked up towards the ceiling and let out the most horrendous howl Halistan had ever heard. It was loud and guttural and caused an unnatural fear to swell up from inside him. The fear was uncontrollable and the spell instantly dropped.

Halistan dropped to his knees in exhaustion, staring at the beast that had just beaten him in a battle of wills. Sweat dropped off the end of his nose as he watched the monster turn back around towards him. Both its heads and all four eyes looked down at him. There was a sense of malicious satisfaction in them that made Halistan's heart stop. They looked as though the beast knew it had won, and now it was going to take its time and slowly rip him asunder.

Halistan wanted to get up. He wanted to flee. He wanted to be anywhere but here so the monster couldn't get him, but he couldn't. The spell had drained him of nearly all his energy and now there was nothing he could do about it.

The beast licked its lips and crouched down, preparing to launch itself at its prey. Its eyes were intent upon Halistan. He closed his eyes and prepared for the worst. He heard the beast spring at him, then hit the floor with a thud. The monster howled in pain. Halistan jerked his eyes open and saw an arrow sticking out of the side of one of its heads.

The hellhound quickly got back onto its feet and spat a cone of flame towards the doorway that caught one of the chairs on fire. It looked like it was about to charge at the door when two more arrows flew at it, impaling it in the neck and chest. It turned as though it wanted to flee, but there was nowhere to go. The door was the only way in or out of the room.

Just as Andrea reached Halistan, a man came in through the door. He was short for a human and had another arrow locked and ready. The hellhound looked at the man with such an intense anger that Halistan thought the beast might explode.

Another arrow caught the beast in one of its eyes, causing it to howl again in pain. It sprayed another, larger, stream of flame around the room. Halistan could feel the heat as if someone had set a bonfire in the middle of the room.

The hellhound leapt at the man with the bow, only to get two more arrows in the chest and fall to the ground, dead.

Halistan laid there, stunned at what he had just been through. His heart felt like it was going to burst out of his chest.

"Are you okay?"

She looked him straight in the eyes as he looked up at her.

"Yes, I'm fine. Wh...who saved us?"

"I don't know," she replied.

"Who are you?"

Their rescuer slung his bow over his back as he approached them. "I am Khu-Rá, and captain of the Elven King's royal hunters."

"Th…thank you," she replied trying to catch her breath.

Halistan sat up. Andrea helped him to his feet and he saw that his savior was indeed an elf. Halistan had never met an elf in person, as they were rarely seen in Valencia.

"Thank you, sire, we owe you our lives," Halistan said.

"I am glad that I got here in time to help. If I had been any later then I fear this would not be such a happy introduction."

"How did you find us?" Andrea asked.

"I heard you scream while I was searching for my companions. Who are you? Do you live in this castle?"

"No," Andrea replied. "My name is Andrea, and I am a prisoner of the demented ruler of this land."

"It seems then my companions and I are not the only prisoners here. And you, boy?" he asked looking up at Halistan.

"I'm…I'm Halistan. A healer from Valencia."

"Are you well enough to travel?" Khu-Rá asked them both. Halistan and Andrea both nodded yes.

"Good, because I feel we should get away from this place as quickly as possible. I fear dreadful things are transpiring here."

Andrea and Halistan both agreed with him. Khu-Rá stepped back to the doorway and peeked out, looking for any other would-be attackers. Andrea took one of the lamps that remained in the room and handed it to Halistan.

"We'll need this, unless you can see in the dark like the elf," she said as Halistan took the lamp from her.

"Come, we must find my companions and leave this place," Khu-Rá said to them. Andrea's riding clothes were still lying upon the floor next to the bed. She picked them up and immediately began to undress. Her actions shocked Halistan. His eyes widened and he froze in place, his jaw dropping in disbelief.

She didn't bother saying anything as she slid her night dress off her shoulders. As it hit the ground she looked over at him and coughed, getting his attention. He realized he was staring. Awkwardly, yet quickly, he turned away from the woman and took a stance with his back to her at the doorway with the elf.

"Not very modest, is she?" he asked the elf, attempting to make small talk.

"We are short on time; modesty is a luxury that we cannot afford. She realizes this," was all the elf said in response. When Andrea was ready the three left together, following Khu-Rá down the hall with his bow in hand.

## 40. Curious Wizard

Zaroth made his way through the dim hall of the keep to a stairwell. A small, glowing ball of light hovered above his right hand. The tiny ball of light lit his path just enough for him to see, but hopefully not enough to attract too much attention. He had managed to find his way into the main chamber of the castle and now was walking up the long straight staircase that led to one of the upper levels. The fortress was vast. He had been walking for some time, his ears pricked to hear any sound in the vicinity.

The entire castle was pitch black, and, so far, he had not seen any evidence of any other inhabitants of the castle, of Lucian or of anyone else. It almost seemed to be deserted, although he was ready to extinguish the light spell at the first sign of any life.

At the top of the stairs he could go either left or right. To the left there looked to be a set of doors leading to another room; to the right was yet another hallway.

Zaroth decided to try the room to the left. He approached two ornately carved double doors. He reached out his left arm to push them open when they opened by themselves. This surprised him for a moment.

Hmmm, enchanted doors, he thought. That's a good idea. I'll have to do that when I get home.

The wizard stepped through the open doorway into the largest personal library he had ever seen. In his travels he had seen many libraries, some belonging to great empires, and others to the prominent Wizards; but, of all the personal libraries he had seen, this was the largest. His old mentor, Sasha, had possessed a sizable library, but it was nowhere near the size of this one.

He walked farther into the chamber. The light from the hovering sphere allowed him to see the far reaches of the covered walls. The bookcases were several stories high, with rolling ladders attached to them so that the books could be reached. Zaroth was tempted to see what kinds of books the King had in his possession. Then he saw a table that had several books lying on it, along with a large piece of unrolled parchment that looked large enough to be a map.

As he approached the table, the sphere floated nearby and lit up the tabletop, allowing Zaroth a better view. He grabbed the small ball of light, placed it in the air directly above the table, and let it go.

"Stay," the wizard commanded under his breath. The ball obediently remained where it had been placed.

There were several ancient-looking books lying open above the map. Zaroth lifted one corner of the closest book to get a glimpse of its title, but it didn't have one. It was simply a black hardcover book with pages that were yellowed and brittle to the touch. He made sure to be very careful as he turned the pages. The book and the map had been placed on this table recently, for although the text was old, there was no dust on the book cover, nor on the map, nor on the table itself.

Zaroth's attention moved on to the next book. It was a smaller book, about the size of a travel log, with a soft leather jacket. It had been opened to a page of text on one side and a full-page illustration on the other: a demonic figure, holding out his hand with a black sphere hovering above it. The sphere radiated dark light, and the artwork took up the entire page. Although the book was hand-written, the text was crisp and legible. Zaroth recognized it immediately. He quickly snatched up the book and began to read.

> **Description:** The Orb of Chaos, or so it has been named by those unfortunate enough to have encountered the foul artifact, is the creation of Castor, the god of Chaos and ruler of the Void, the realm of lost souls. It is not known why Castor created the orb originally. All that is certain is that its first known appearance was roughly a millennium before the Great War. It was thought to have been destroyed but pieces of it continue to be found in the strangest of places.

UPDATE 05.213AW – When it was destroyed, it was allegedly broken into one hundred and fifty pieces. However, I have uncovered many texts that estimate the number of pieces of the orb to actually number in the hundreds. More investigation into this matter is warranted.

UPDATE 01.328 AW – During my pursuit of the orb, I have managed to accumulate over a hundred pieces but barely had enough to make a fraction of the sphere, so there must be more.

The text on that page ended on that line. Reading the text brought back memories for Zaroth and had to read more. The room was silent, and the only sound to be heard was the crinkle of the pages as he continued.

**Powers:** As with any item created by the gods, the Orb gives its controller remarkable powers, although most have not been validated. Its primary function seems to be as a conduit from our reality to others.

In all noted references to the object, it seems focused on the Void and other realms of the dead, and appears to be able to funnel that energy into our realm to be used in various ways by the controller.

Theoretically, the orb could be used as a gateway to reanimate the dead, or legions of the dead. With the orb giving them an infinite amount of energy to pull from, the undead could never be destroyed.

This is the only confirmed function of the orb. It is for this reason the council of elder wizards has decided to collect the pieces of the orb and reassemble them here in the vault. We fear it is the only force that might be able to stand against the Host of Devils sweeping across the land in this terrible war.

I, and my apprentice Alazzaar, have been
tasked with collecting these pieces but the
search has been difficult. If we cannot recreate
the orb soon, I fear that even this underground
fortress will not be able to protect us from the
evil that promises to envelope the world.

"Alazzaar," the old wizard mused. "It's been quite some
time since I have been called that. Sasha was so full of herself
back then. So melodramatic."

The text about the sphere ended and the next page listed
another artifact: the Star of Salus. He closed the journal, no
longer interested in reminiscing. This was his old teacher's
journal, but he had no idea how it could have gotten here. To his
knowledge, only one other copy had been made of the journal,
and that was by another wizard of the council, Gabrel, an old
friend of Zaroth's who had disappeared some time ago. This
copy, however, looked to be the original; it was in Sasha's hand-
writing.

Zaroth pocketed the book and turned his attention to the
map, which appeared to be one of the Empire. It showed the
capital city, which was circled, as was the mountain range next
to the city of Tyric. There were many locations that were circled,
with short hand-written notes crossed out next to them.

Sitting on top of the map, directly over the part of the map
showing the location of Tyric, was a thick, palm-sized disk of
glass. He could feel magic radiate from it. Zaroth easily
recognized the glass for what it was, a scrying device, used by
some wizards to view people or places from a remote location.
Such devices were very rare and typically expensive, so he was
somewhat surprised to find one lying about unguarded.

"Intriguing," Zaroth mumbled aloud, tucking the glass
into the pocket of his robe next to the journal. Several scrolls
laid next to the map. One was a long list of people and places,
most of which were marked out. There must have been hundreds
of entries on the list. Zaroth unrolled the scroll to the bottom of
the list to see how it ended.

> ~~Gryphon Keep, in the possession of Duke Aaron~~
> ~~Ogre Shaman King of the Marshland Forrest~~
> ~~Great Eastern Wall~~
> ~~Kirkindal Mountains, in the lair of a dragon~~

~~Monte Crissia, in the possession of Earl Flembert~~
~~(no longer in possession, was given away, see below)~~
~~Capital City, possessed by the consort of the~~
~~previous Earl~~
Ruins of Tyric – undead druid lich

Zaroth compared the list to markings on the map. Each line item seemed to correspond to location marked on the map and as they were crossed out on the list, they were struck through on the map. All but one.

"Oh no," Zaroth muttered as he looked up from the map. *This can't be...* he thought as he pieced together the clues.

"It's impossible...he couldn't have..."

The wizard's mouth fell open in disbelief as he came to the revelation of what was really happening.

He fumbled through the pockets of his cloak and removed one of his pouches. Frantically, he searched through it until he found what he was looking for, a small crystal disk. He took the disk from the pouch and held it in his hand.

He closed his eyes and spoke the command, "Trace."

The disk began to glow. Then a flame erupted on its surface--first red, then orange, then yellow.

"It's moving?" The wizard was baffled. "Perhaps there is still time."

"Follow," Zaroth commanded the ball of light. He rushed out of the room, using the disk to guide him.

## 41. The Study

"Damn, Serieve," grumbled Sol. "Could you try and be a little louder? I don't think we've managed to wake up everyone in the castle yet."

"Sorry, but it's hard to see where we are going, and you're holding the only torch."

The trio had emerged from the spiral staircase that led down to their rooms and were now near the castle foyer.

"Let's try that way," Sol pointed off to their right.

"Why that way?" Serieve questioned.

"Just a hunch."

Serieve really couldn't argue with that, so he followed as Sol turned and started down another seemingly random passage.

Sol had managed to find a hall that took them deeper into the castle. The floor had a long rug that covered the cold stone floor. As they walked, Serieve noticed paintings hanging on the walls. He stopped to look at one. It was a picture of a woman holding a newborn child. He noticed that there was a brass plate at the bottom with some writing on it. He started to read the writing on the plate but Sol had stepped too far ahead and the light was stripped away.

"Hey!" Serieve exclaimed. "I wanted to read that."

"You can read it later. Right now, we're busy."

"Fine," Serieve said, but he was clearly unhappy with Sol.

From what little Serieve could see, the castle was very nicely decorated. Empty suits of armor were placed every so often through the hall in niches where there wasn't a painting. Admittedly, some of the armor looked like it had seen better days. Serieve noticed that most of the suits of armor were lightly battered but occasionally one would have a hole in it which looked like it had been pierced by an arrow. He wasn't able to look long before the light began to fade once more and he had to catch up to his companions.

"Where do you think most of the good stuff would be kept, Oather?" Sol asked quietly.

"How should I know? There is a staircase, let's go up. There doesn't seem to be much down here."

"Agreed," Sol replied.

They ascended the long straight staircase. The upper level led to another set of halls lined with doors. The hall directly in front of them had six pairs of doors running down the corridor.

"I wonder if these quarters belong to the servants or to the guests?" Sol asked.

Oather shrugged his shoulders, "I've no idea."

"It's doubtful servants would be quartered up so high in the keep," Serieve replied. "Back home, servants are quartered in separate wings or in the lower levels. Upper levels are generally restricted to the butlers and the ladies-in-waiting, and guests; set apart from the specified staff. However, in this place-"

"I'm tempted to check it out," Sol said, looking at the brass doorknob of the first door, "but we shouldn't take a chance, just in case any people are actually here."

Oather nodded in agreement.

"Psst," Serieve whispered to get Sol's attention. "What about that door down there?" He pointed to their right. There was one hall that was perpendicular to the staircase they had ascended and there was only one door visible in that direction.

Sol squinted to look. "How did you see down that far? I can barely see it."

"I don't drink as much as you do," Serieve replied, which made Oather snicker.

The three crept their way down the hall, attempting to be as quiet as possible. The room at the end of the hall appeared to be isolated from the rest. As they approached, Sol could see that the door was slightly ajar. A faint light emanated from inside the room.

Sol leaned his head near the opening of the door to listen, but didn't hear anything. He pressed a finger to the door and slowly pushed it open. The door opened with a loud creak.

It opened into a study. As he entered, Sol saw several plush and comfortable-looking reading chairs placed around a small round table in front of a fireplace that had a weak fire going in it. Sol could tell it had been burning for several hours and was now close to dying.

Sol saw several lamps in the room. He looked at the torch he carried, which was also starting to die down, and used it to light the lamps, then threw the remainder into the fireplace.

"Shut the door so no one sees us in here," Sol ordered Serieve as he entered behind them.

Serieve stepped in and looked around with the others. A large soft rug covered most of the floor in this room, stopping several paces from the fireplace. In the furthest corner of the room was a fine oak desk and a leather-covered chair. The wall behind the desk was a wooden bookshelf lined with texts.

Sol glanced at some of the covers: *Gods and Holy Artifacts, The History of the Ruins of Tyric, The Book of Pell, Torture and its Application to Justice, Anatomy of Griffins*. Sol looked at those books with disinterest, and completely skipped over the rest as nothing of importance. Then his attention was grabbed by the cabinet lining the wall to his left.

It was an ornately carved, dark-stained wood cabinet with glass doors and silver knobs on the front. Inside, Sol saw what looked like fine crystal drinking glasses sitting next to several short, round bottles with long necks.

"Now this is what I'm looking for," Sol said, smiling, as he opened the cabinet and grabbed one of the glasses.

He looked back over his shoulder at Oather. "Check that desk and see if there's anything good in the drawers. I'm sure there is some good stuff in here, I can feel it."

Sol picked up one of the bottles filled with an amber-colored liqueur. The label was so old that it could no longer be read. Sol's eyes narrowed and a grin spread across his lips. He uncorked the bottle and poured himself a glass. Setting the bottle down, he picked up the glass and took a sip.

It went down smooth. He felt the burn flow slowly down his throat and into his chest. He let out a contented sigh, and then took a larger gulp. He was right, it was some of the best he had ever had. Far better than the stuff that Tanner had locked in his cellar and which he *had* been saving for a special occasion.

Sol walked around the room, with his drink in hand. Above the fireplace was a painting of a middle-aged man with black hair, wearing a very fine suit and draped in a purple cloak. There was a placard below it that read, "*King Nicholas DeVanya*"

Sol stood for several moments looking at the painting, wondering how much a painting could be worth....then shrugged off the idea, as the painting would be too cumbersome to deal with. Then he noticed the mantle above the fireplace. At each end of the mantle was a silver candlestick holder. Sol grabbed one and could tell by the feel that it was solid silver, unlike most that were usually cheap and hollow.

"Hey," he called to Oather. "Carry this; it could be worth a coin or two." He tossed the candlestick holder to Oather, who caught it in mid-air. Sol grabbed the other holder and tossed it to Oather as well.

"Are you sure you don't want me to hold those, Sol?" Serieve asked with a wide grin on his face.

"No!" Sol quickly snapped, "You're too prone to acts of insanity to carry anything else of mine."

In the middle of the mantle was a dagger. It was a silver ceremonial dagger with a decoratively carved pommel, but the blade was covered in dried blood. Sol finished his drink and set it atop the mantle. He picked up the dagger, looked at it for a moment, and slid it into his boot.

"Well, there doesn't seem to be much more use in staying here," he said as he picked up his empty glass. Returning to the liquor cabinet he decided to fill it once more before they left. Sol looked around the shelf, sliding some bottles aside attempting to find another bottle of what he just drank but there wasn't one and the bottle he had been drinking from was empty.

*Damn*, he thought, wishing that there had been enough for just one more glass.

Seeing nothing on the main shelf that struck him as appealing, he looked up. As luck would have it, there was another bottle of the same kind of liqueur up on the top shelf. He reached for it, but it wouldn't move. He pulled again, this time harder, and was surprised when it tilted forward. He was more surprised by the deep rumbling sound that came from behind him. He jerked around to see Serieve and Oather staring at the fireplace as it began to shake and move. It swung out and revealed a doorway to a larger chamber.

\*\*\*

Zaroth turned a corner to his right. The disk was indicating that the piece of the orb that it was attuned to had stopped moving.

*By the gods, please let those fools stop running around so I can find them*, he thought. He followed another hall to a dead end and realized that he had to find another way to get there. He remembered a staircase back a ways, perhaps if he went down, he could make it further that direction on another level. It was worth a shot he decided.

He was starting back down the hall he had just traversed when the disk changed. The direction of the piece didn't change, but the flame changed from blue to a bright red that flickered wildly.

*Oh hell*, he thought. Zaroth took off with renewed fervor to find them as quickly as he could. He knew it wouldn't be long now until disaster struck.

## 42. *Interesting Find*

Sol stood there in amazement as the fireplace swung out before him, revealing a hidden room behind it. Serieve jumped up from his seat with a bewildered look upon his face. Oather stood there quietly as Sol slowly approached the opening.

He crept towards the fireplace, attempting to determine if any sort of threat lay in the room. Reaching the hearth, he looked around the edge and saw nothing but a dark room. Nothing could be heard inside either.

He glanced down into the fire to see if his torch was still there, and it was. The handle hadn't been burned and was sticking just outside the fire, so Sol grabbed it. He flinched and swore under his breath because the handle was hotter than he'd expected, but it didn't burn him too badly.

Oather stepped up behind him as he held the torch into the dark room. Light spilled into the space, illuminating the room with a golden glow. Oather's jaw dropped as he walked in and beheld a scene unlike any he had ever seen before.

Along the walls were massive chests of gold, silver, platinum, and jewels. The wall to his right was adorned with weapons, all of which were accented with beautiful gems. Ceremonial suits of armor laced with gold stood at attention against the walls, all surrounded by more piles of gold and platinum coins and jewelry.

Oather saw more torches along the wall. He took the torch from Sol and began to light them one at a time. As he did so, the light increased, reflecting off all the gold and jewels in the room.

Regaining some of his composure, Sol whipped off his satchel and dashed to one of the chests and began filling it with pieces of platinum. He looked back over his shoulder to see Oather digging through a pile and pulling out all the gems he could find.

"Forget these little bags, Oather, come help me. We're taking this entire chest!" he said, smiling.

"We can't do that, Sol," Serieve said as he watched the two.

Sol stopped and looked over at the cavalier as if he couldn't believe the words that he'd just heard coming from Serieve's mouth.

"And why the hell not? I'm certainly not waiting for another chance like this to fall into my lap," he replied and returned to looking around the edges of the chest for a way to carry it.

"Just how are you going to get it out? Do you think the king will just say, 'Sure, go ahead and loot me. Make yourselves at home. Don't worry, I'll still help you leave this hell hole?'"

Sol stood there quietly for a moment. He looked at Oather, who in turn was looking back at Sol, his expression disheartened because he knew that Serieve was right. Soliere let out a sigh and sunk to his knees in front of the open chest full of gold and jewelry. He laid his face down upon the cold coins and closed his eyes as he felt the cool metal press against his skin, a wide grin stretching across his face, nestling against the coins as if they were the bosom of a large breasted woman.

Oather retrieved his small pouch and started picking some gems from the pile Sol was resting upon. Sol grabbed the big man's arm, making Oather stop. With his eyes still closed, Sol turned his face towards Oather, his cheek still pressed against the immense wealth of coins.

"Let me enjoy this for just a moment," he sighed. Oather nodded and rose to find another pile to plunder. As he did he saw Serieve admiring the weapons upon the wall.

"They are probably just ceremonial and not worth a damn in a fight," Oather told him.

"You may be right, but there are a couple here that have some potential," replied Serieve. He pointed to a large sword to the far right. "Look at that sword there," he said.

The sword was almost as big as the one Oather carried. It had a wide, polished blade and a finely honed edge. Sol watched Oather take a closer look before removing it from the wall. Oather swung the blade through the air once or twice to get a feel for it.

Oather unsheathed his own blade and compared the two. This made the new blade look even more magnificent. He tossed the old sword away without a second thought and sheathed his new toy, which fit the sheath like a hand in a glove. Next to Oather, Serieve had also found a new weapon. He was wielding a long-sword, first using it one-handed, and then gripping it with both as he cut through the air.

"Find one you like too?" Oather asked. Serieve smiled and nodded as he too exchanged the new blade with his old sword.

"With any luck the King won't notice until after we're gone," Oather whispered.

Oather eyed the rest of the weapons hanging upon the wall. In the center was a mace. It was a finely crafted weapon, perfectly symmetrical, with eight thick outward-facing blunt edges topped with a marble-sized polished steel ball. He took it and tied it to the scabbard on his back.

Sol decided it was time to get up. As much as he wanted to stay there, it was far too dangerous. He sat up and began pulling out the choicest gems and stuffing them into his pouch, which he had emptied of the coins it had contained.

Serieve had taken to looking more around the room instead of filling his purse with treasure like his companions. Sol looked up as he was trying to fit one more large ruby.

"Aren't you going to load up, Serieve?"

"No, I'll take part of what you get."

"Like hell you will," Sol replied, seemingly shocked that Serieve would even dare suggest such a horrible thing. Serieve laughed and scooped up a couple of gems that laid atop a pile of gold coins in a chest next to him and dropped them into his pouch. As he pulled the strings of the pouch closed, he noticed a dark area towards the back of the room.

"What's that?" he asked.

Serieve walked towards the back of the room, where there were no torches and the light seemed to dim as if it were being sucked from the room. He found a dark gray granite pedestal standing about waist high. Upon the pedestal sat a large onyx sphere about as wide as his arm was long and formed into a perfectly round orb. He moved closer for a better look, but the closer he got, the more the light around the area seemed to darken.

Sol stood up and walked towards Serieve, who was now also getting Oather's attention.

"What is that thing?" Sol asked as he and Oather joined Serieve.

Serieve did not answer. He just stared at the orb, almost in a daze. Sol was now close enough that he could almost make out his reflection in the glossy surface. There were minuscule lines on the surface of the sphere which made it look like a puzzle where each piece intricately fit with the others. At the top of the orb, there was a round, empty hole.

Sol nudged Serieve and broke the cavalier's concentration, bringing the young man back to reality.

"Uh…I don't know," Serieve replied softly, still partially enraptured by the artifact.

"It looks nice, but there's no way we'd be able to sneak it out and I doubt we'd get much for it anyway," Sol said, pulling Serieve away by the arm. Serieve slowly turned away and followed Sol back towards the piles of gold.

"Shhhh," Oather suddenly spoke in little more than a whisper, holding his finger to his lips. "I hear something."

The three slowly drew their weapons and crept to the opening of the room. They all heard the latch on the door to the study turn and the door open. Sol motioned for the others to halt as he took up an ambush stance near the entrance of the room. He steadied his breathing, keeping it slow and inaudible. He heard the study door slowly open as someone entered the room. Then he heard a voice whispering.

"What is this place?" said a young man's voice.

"I don't know," replied a softer sounding woman's voice. "It looks like a study."

Sol readied his blade and pressed his back to the back of the fireplace entrance, prepared to strike. He was about to step out into the open and confront those who had entered, but as he took his first step out he was greeted with a drawn bow and a razor sharp arrow pointing at his face.

His eyes followed the shaft down to its possessor and saw it was held by an elf.

"Khu-Rá!" Sol exclaimed in relief as he lowered his weapon, followed in turn by Oather and Serieve.

"Quick," Sol said to the elf. "Come see what we found, it's amazing!"

Khu-Rá began to reply, but as he lowered his bow, he was grabbed by Sol and dragged into the room.

Sol turned back to the elf, stopping in the middle of the gold-filled room.

"Isn't this one of the most beautiful things you've ever seen?"

As he presented the discovery to Khu-Rá, Sol noticed several new people enter the room. One was a boy who must have been in his late teens or early twenties, with blonde hair, and next to him walked a goddess with hazel eyes and long auburn hair.

"We must find the wizard and..." the elf started speaking again, but was interrupted by Sol gently pushing him aside and walking past him.

"I stand corrected, this is the most beautiful thing I've ever seen," Sol said as he walked up to the woman. "And who, my dear, are you?" His eyes locked on hers, a dashing smile spreading across his lips.

The woman looked back at him, and then rolled her eyes.

"Is this who we came to find?" she asked, looking around Sol to Khu-Rá. The elf nodded to her.

"I am Soliere, World Class Adventurer and Captain," Sol stated proudly and bowed to her.

"Listen, you oaf, save it. We don't have time for this," she said. "We need to get out of here." Andrea pushed Sol out of her way as she approached Khu-Rá.

A confused look swept across Sol's face, as if he simply couldn't believe that a woman had just said that to him, especially after he had told her his self-appointed title. He turned to face her as she walked by, and started to say something when he noticed that Serieve had wandered back to the sphere again.

"Serieve, what are you...?" Sol was unable to complete his sentence before a loud and terrible voice interrupted him.

"Get away from that, now!"

## 43. The Enemy of My Enemy

"Nicholas," Andrea breathed, almost inaudibly, as she turned to see the King enter the room. He looked determined and furious. He did not even look at her as he marched past her. His sudden appearance made Andrea freeze, even to the point of almost not breathing.

The Dark Lord of the Realm walked past her as though he was on a mission. All she could do was watch him as he went by, but as he did so she saw him glance at her and his eyes burned with fury. The quick look kept her frozen and sent chills down her spine.

Serieve seemed to be in a trance-like state as he stood near the orb, staring at it. Nicholas was rapidly approaching him when Sol intercepted him and pulled on the King's arm. Nicholas abruptly stopped and looked at the younger man.

Sol donned his brightest, most sincere smile.

"You're Majesty," he exclaimed. "Look at what we, your newest and most humble servants, have found for you," Sol smiled widely and spread his arms, proudly displaying his gift to the lord.

Nicholas' eyes burned with hatred as he looked at Sol.

"No need to thank us," Sol began as he turned around; showing off the room as if he single-handedly had saved the kingdom from abject poverty.

"Do you take me for a fool?"

The look on Sol's face changed from pride to disgrace as he bowed, "You wound me, my lord," he replied, lowering his arms and feigning a hurt look.

"Thief," Nicholas growled.

With a speed that Andrea had never seen before, Nicholas attacked and grabbed Sol by the throat. Sol reacted quickly, but not quickly enough to evade Nicholas. He tried to free himself from Nicholas' grasp, but the grip was too tight.

Khu-Rá drew his bow back again and prepared an arrow. Nicholas raised his other hand and an invisible wave of force knocked the elf to the ground. The arrow that he had started to nock fell harmlessly to the floor.

Oather, it seemed, had also been taken by surprise by the speed of the King, but quickly drew his new sword. The sound of the blade being unsheathed echoed through the chamber.

Nicholas released his grip from Sol, who fell to the ground, landing on his hands and knees. He coughed horribly as he tried to breathe. Oather raised his sword in what would certainly have been a tremendous blow, but as his blade arced towards its target his right wrist was grabbed and squeezed so hard that he instantly dropped his weapon to the ground with a loud clank.

Before Oather could react, Nicholas grabbed him by the throat, too, and began to squeeze the life from him. Andrea wanted to help, but she was shocked as Nicholas choked the man in front of him, who looked twice his size.

Andrea watched as Nicholas stared intently at Oather. She could see Nicholas' eyes begin to cloud, then swirl from a bluish gray color to a hideous yellow-green. The pupils began to flatten and became a slit, like a snake's eyes.

She had never seen anything like this before, not even in her nightmares. His arms grew, ripping through his fine royal clothes. His legs also lengthened and cracked as they bent backwards, like an animal's hind legs. Nicholas lifted Oather up into the air as the other man gasped for air, unable to break free from the choke hold of the massive clawed hand that held him by the throat.

Nicholas reared back, still holding Oather in the air. Horns emerged from his forehead and bat's wings sprouted from his back. The clasp holding his cape broke and the garment fell onto the ground.

Nicholas' eyes burned as if lit by an unholy green fire. Oather frantically tried to free himself from the demon's grasp, but his strength was fading. He furiously hit the demons arm, which had little to no effect.

As Oather struggled to free himself from Nicholas' grasp, Nicholas reached up with his other clawed hand and took hold of a tiny onyx pendant that Oather wore.

"This belongs to me," Nicholas growled in an inhuman tone.

Andrea stood there, not believing what she was witnessing. Oather's legs dangled limply in the air as he lost consciousness. She looked for a weapon and saw the sword that Oather had dropped.

She lunged for it, but her quick action caught Nicholas' attention. He effortlessly tossed the huge man down on top of her, effectively pinning her underneath Oather's bulk. The barbarian's weight was more than she could have possibly imagined and her tiny frame crumpled beneath it. Her head hit the stone floor and blackness swept over her eyes.

## 44. Facing One's Demons

In the rear of the room, Halistan had backed away and was now standing next to the hypnotized Serieve. His heart pounded and he could feel his body shaking at the horror going on before him. His eyes were glued to the demon that had single handedly dispatched one of the biggest men Halistan had ever seen--and now it was turning towards him.

He fumbled for his holy symbol, finally becoming frustrated and ripping it out from under his shirt and off the chain on which he kept it. Magic was his only chance at survival. Over the last day, he had found that his magic did work on demons, as demonstrated by controlling the hellhound; but he had failed to control the two-headed beast. Now an even more menacing demon stood before him, but his magic was his only defense. He had to try or he'd surely die.

Halistan gripped the holy symbol in his left hand and held it out to the beast that now was looking directly at him. The demon took a step forward. Halistan could feel the floor shake with each step the monster took towards him. He held his ground and began to pray. The star began to glow in the palm of his hand.

"Through the darkness, flee before the light of Salus, Demon," he yelled, holding the star outwards toward the creature, but the beast took yet another step towards him.

Halistan was drawn to the hate-filled, yellowish eyes of the demon. He could feel them weighing down upon him without a trace of opposition. Halistan tried again to dispatch the demon, but again nothing happened. He tried again and again, each time growing louder, until he was out of breath as the monster continued to stand defiantly in front of him.

They were now just an arm's length apart, close enough that the monster could almost be touched by Halistan's outstretched hand. He could feel the power of the monster, like the heat from a raging fire. Halistan chanted with renewed zeal, forcefully presenting his holy symbol towards the demon. The star glowed brighter than white hot metal being drawn from a forge, but the beast did not waiver. Then Halistan heard an ominous sound.

The monster chuckled and bent over towards him. Halistan's heart beat rapidly and he had a terrible sinking feeling in his stomach. The demon raised its massive, clawed hand up slowly and placed it in front of Halistan. The monster's hand, with its reddish maroon skin and long claws, was easily two or three times larger than Halistan's. When the monster enclosed its hand around his own, Halistan was frozen with fear.

He stood there mesmerized, not knowing what was going to happen. He heard the monster say something he didn't understand--it was both in a language he did not know and in such a deep tone that he did not know if he even heard the words correctly. Before he could ponder it much longer, his hand began to burn intensely, smoke suddenly rose from the two clasped hands.

He tried to rip his hand away from the beast--which let loose a full-bodied laugh as their hands erupted in red flames. A small inferno enveloped their hands, and Halistan screamed in agony.

Halistan jerked wildly as he tried to free himself, but the monster's grip was too strong. The smell of charred human flesh filled the room as the monster clenched his clawed hand around Halistan's. Then finally, after what seemed like an eternity of burning torture, the beast released his hand. Halistan quickly jerked his charred appendage away and fell to his knees, holding his arm and staring at his hand in disbelief.

The demon pushed Halistan aside and stepped over him, on his way towards Serieve who still stood there, captivated by the sphere. Nicholas grabbed him and with one hard push, shoved him out of the way. Serieve hit the wall and fell down. The sudden impact roused him from his hypnotic state.

\*\*\*

At first, Serieve just laid there confused for a moment. He didn't know what was going on. All he could see was his companions lying about the floor, with smoke drifting up from the priest who knelt on the ground closest to him. Oather was sprawled out on the floor beyond, and he couldn't tell where Sol was.

Directly in front of him was a monster of unspeakable horror. Serieve's first instinct was to get up and draw his weapon, but he soon realized that he could not move. He was frozen in fear as he watched the beast take Oather's necklace he'd made with that piece of onyx.

The demon outstretched a massive clawed hand over the black orb and chanted something incomprehensible. Serieve could feel wind starting to swirl around him. Even though they were in an enclosed room with no windows, the wind came. As the demon spoke the wind picked up until Serieve felt that he was in the middle of a massive gale.

He knew he had to get up, but it was hard. Almost like an invisible hand was pushing him down. He watched the monster as it took the tiny piece of onyx and placed it into the small open hole in the orb. The winds grew stronger. Serieve was able to finally stand on his own, but he was afraid the wind would knock him over again.

Suddenly the sphere rose up off its pedestal and began to spin slowly. Serieve couldn't help but stare at it. It began to emit a blackness that seemed to suck the light of the room into it. A blackish blue light poured from the cracks in the orb. Then the cracks began to slowly vanish, until the surface of the orb was solid, smooth and jet black.

He forced himself to take a step, then another, and another. He was getting some of his strength back and could take larger steps. He managed to reach the young priest. He reached down and grabbed the young man by his shirt and dragged him away from the monster looming over the sphere. The beast paid them no attention as it chanted.

Serieve tugged hard on the younger man and reached Sol, Oather and Andrea. He let go of the boy and sunk to his knees between Sol and Oather. Sol laid there coughing and holding his throat, so Serieve turned his attention to Oather, who laid motionless in a heap on the floor.

The cavalier pushed with all his might and was able to roll Oather off the young woman he was lying on. He shook Oather by the face to get a reaction, but got nothing. Taking more drastic measures, he slapped Oather hard, harder than he actually intended, but it made Oather stir--which at least indicated that he was alive.

"Oather, get up! We need to get out of here," Serieve yelled over the howling winds coursing through the room.

Oather's head rolled from side to side. Finally, his eyes opened and he looked at Serieve.

"Come on you big lug, we need to get out of here," Serieve yelled again. Oather nodded his head in agreement and sat up. The woman next to him was unconscious so Serieve picked her up, while Oather hoisted the young priest over his shoulder.

Sol, by this time, had also risen and was stumbling through the wind towards the door. Several steps away, the elf had managed to get to his knees and was also attempting to stand. Sol grabbed him as he passed and pulled the elf with him towards the door of the treasure room.

## 45. Zaroth Cuts In

Zaroth looked down at his tracker. The flame was now bright green and flickered frantically. *It must be close now,* he thought, and turned another corner. Directly in front of him was a hall with a single door at the end. He heard a strange commotion from that direction and strange flashes of light came through the door's opening.

*What have those fools done now?* Zaroth wondered. He sped towards the door. As he entered the room, he saw another door opening to reveal a secret passage that led to a room behind the fireplace. Strong winds blew throughout the room, making his robes flutter and his long gray hair blow around his face. He put his arm up to block the wind from hitting him and marched into the secret room.

There he came face to face with Sol, who was stumbling around, attempting to help the elf get up.

"Leave this place....now!" Zaroth yelled. Sol barely seemed to recognize that the wizard had spoken to him, but nonetheless he managed to get out of Zaroth's way. Serieve and Oather quickly followed behind Sol, carrying two others with them. Zaroth disregarded all of them and looked into the room.

To his astonishment, at the back of the room hovered a black sphere--the object he'd been searching for all these long years. It momentarily stunned him to see it already assembled. The sphere gave off a magnificent glow of black light, more enchanting than he could have possibly imagined.

Next to the artifact stood a monster,--a demon the likes of which Zaroth had never encountered in person, but which he had read about in ancient tombs. Procuring the sphere would be more difficult than he'd hoped, but he was certain that this beast would not be able to stand in his way for long.

Once Zaroth knew the others were out of the way and couldn't interfere with his plans any longer, he raised a hand to the secret entrance of the treasure room, then clenched his hand into a fist. The secret door closed behind them, sealing the wizard in with his foe, and his prize.

Zaroth pulled his wand from a pocket in his left sleeve. It was an ancient-looking wand made of a red wood that had faded slightly over the years. The tip was scorched black and it radiated with power in his hand.

"I'm taking the orb," Zaroth yelled over the thunderous noise of the gale force winds. This got the demon's attention. It stopped chanting and turned away from the sphere towards him.

Surprisingly, the beast spoke back to him. Its voice was guttural and vile sounding, but Zaroth could understand what it said.

"You cannot stop me, wizard. Even now the power of the sphere fills me, and as its power grows, all the dead of this land will rise once again and be mine to command."

"We'll see about that."

Zaroth pointed his wand at the demon. An explosion of fire and light erupted from the tip, creating a tornado of fire in the center of the room.

The tornado began moving toward Nicholas. The demon crossed its arms and braced for the blast. Soon the creature was enveloped in fire. Zaroth watched to see what effect the spell would have on it. The beast stuck one arm out from the fire and growled. Almost instantly the flames dissipated.

The monster looked down and saw a large two-handed mace sticking out of a pile of gold a few steps away from him. It turned and ripped the mace out with a single hand, sending coins scattering across the room. Zaroth knew what his opponent intended to do with that evil weapon, and did not want to give the monster the chance.

Zaroth waved his wand towards the monster again, unleashing volley after volley of lightning bolts. The first couple of bolts hit the monster as intended, but with a wave of its hand, the demon sent the other blasts flying into the walls of the treasure room causing stone and dust to be thrown everywhere.

The beast gripped the mace tightly in his hands and stepped towards Zaroth. A sinister grin spread across its demonic face as it approached.

"Entangle!" Zaroth commanded, hoping to stop the beast from getting close to him. Vines sprang from the cracks of the floor and grew up and around the demon's body. They quickly spread around his monstrous goat-like legs, then around his torso, and finally up around its massive arms.

The spell seemed to work. Even though the monster tried to take another step forward, the vines held tight. Zaroth outstretched his left hand toward his opponent and clenched his fist tightly in mid-air. The vines began to constrict around their prey. Zaroth could hear them pull tight against the monsters body. A smile of satisfaction swept across the wizard's face as he prepared his finishing attack.

Then, surprisingly, the demon grabbed one of the vines, pulled it in front of his face and hissed loudly. The vine began to change from green to gray just before it disintegrated in the monster's hand. The vine withered, and as it did so the withering spread throughout the rest of the vines. Almost instantly they fell off the monster's arms, then off its mid-section, and finally dropped harmlessly off its legs.

Again the monster laughed at the wizard and stomped its foot down in triumph. The impact made the floor shake, and almost made the wizard loose his footing. Fortunately, Zaroth was able to keep standing, but the shaking did manage to disrupt the spell he was preparing to cast.

Zaroth prepared a quick defensive spell in his mind. "Wall!" he shouted and waved his wand in front of him. Gray light poured from the tip of the wand and erected a semi-transparent wall of grayish white light between him and the beast. Zaroth let out a sigh of relief that the spell had worked as quickly as it did, for the demon was almost within striking distance.

The monster stopped just short of the barrier, reared back and let loose a ferocious howl. Zaroth stood firm and readied another attack spell. The demon clenched the mace tightly in both of its clawed hands and struck the force barrier with an incredible blow. After a single hit the wall began to waver, flickering slightly before reforming.

The sight of his shield spell almost faltering caused a lump to grow in Zaroth's throat. In the past, he had seen that spell stand firm against three club-wielding giants without so much as a challenge. At this rate, he knew the barrier wouldn't last long.

He needed help before the monster could break through. He quickly rummaged through one of his pouches with his left hand and pulled out two small emeralds. He placed them upon the ground at his feet. The monster drew back and hit the force field again, this time very nearly destroying it.

Once the emeralds were in place, Zaroth stomped down on them as hard as he could with his boot, crushing the gems in the process. He looked at the area of the room where he wished for the spell to take effect and concentrated. Two plumes of green smoke began to rise from the cracks in the floor behind the demon.

The demon saw the smoke and turned to investigate. Soon, two nasty swamp trolls took form. The trolls rose to their full height, each a head taller than the demon. They were muscular, with green scaly skin. Their faces were horrid to behold, with long, jagged yellowish-green teeth, and they drooled a green slime that burned the stone with a sizzle as each drop hit the floor.

The two grotesque creatures attacked the demon with their claws. The demon managed to block the first but was cut deeply in the arm by the second. Immediately the wound began to fester as brown-colored pus dripped from the gashes.

The demon howled in rage. Zaroth smiled again and prepared another spell. The demon dodged another attack from one of the trolls, and then brought the mace down upon the head of the troll that had just wounded it.

The troll dropped to the floor, dead. The demon was drawing back to take a swing at the other troll when Zaroth unleashed another powerful lightning attack which hit the demon in the back. It howled in pain, and dropped the mace it was wielding as the lightning scarred its flesh.

Zaroth, quite satisfied by the successful attack, raised his wand to cast another lightning spell. Just before he let loose the spell, the demon grabbed the other troll and spun around. Zaroth cast the devastating spell, sending it flashing through the air, but the demon used the troll as a shield to block the blast. The troll cried out in pain. Wisps of smoke rose from the huge hole that had been burned right through its body, but it was astonishingly still alive.

The demon grabbed the troll by the head and violently twisted the beast's head, ripping it from its body. The remains of the troll dropped to the floor in a lifeless heap.

Zaroth was amazed and stunned by the maneuver he had witnessed but quickly regained his composure. He tried to prepare another spell, but it was too late. The demon picked the mace back up off the ground and with one last amazing blow, it destroyed the force field that had protected the wizard.

The demon stepped forward, past where the shield had been erected, and let out a cruel and ominous laugh as he back-handed the wizard. Zaroth's concentration was destroyed as he hit the ground. His vision blurred and he could taste blood in his mouth. It was laborious to breathe and he couldn't move his body. He was forced to watch as the demon stepped forward to gloat over him.

Zaroth tried to look up but as he did, he felt what seemed like a tree trunk kick him in the stomach. The force of the kick knocked out what little air he had in his lungs and waves of spots swept across his vision. He could feel the wand still in his hand and considered a spell but he knew he would never cast it in time. Instead he reached into his pouch with his free hand and found a short piece of crystal, about as thin as his wand but only half as long. He gripped it in his hand and used what little strength he had left to break it in half.

The demon raised his foot and prepared to crush the wizard's head like an egg. In a flash of light, the wizard disappeared.

## 46. Exodus

In the study, Sol stopped and watched Serieve carry the woman out of the secret passage. Oather and the boy followed Serieve, and the entrance to the treasure room closed behind them.

"Is she alive?" Sol demanded. "If not, dump her. We don't need the dead weight."

"I think she's alive, Sol," Serieve replied. He set the young woman down in one of the plush chairs of the study. As he released her, the woman's head rolled around to face him. Her eyes opened slightly and she let out a groan as her hand went to her head.

"How about you, boy? Can you walk?" Sol snapped at Halistan, who looked up at him and nodded yes.

"Good, let's get out of here. We'll find another way home."

Sol was heading towards the door when he heard the woman call out, "Wait."

"What?" Sol asked, looking back from the door of the study.

"The nearest town is hours away by foot. We'll need horses. I can take us to the stables," she managed to say, still holding her head as if in terrible pain.

"There are horses here?" Sol asked. "Now there is a plan. How far are we from there?"

"Not far," she replied. "The stables are on the west side of the castle, I can lead you there."

"Oather, you want to carry her?" Sol asked.

"I can walk," she said. "But I may need someone to help steady me."

Sol turned from the doorway and helped Andrea up to her feet. He took her arm and put it over his shoulder so he could help her walk. Then a tremendous boom came from the treasure room and seemed to shake the entire castle.

"Okay, people," Sol said, "we need to leave, now!"

Out in the hall the castle seemed to have taken on a whole new life. Morning was coming, for there was some light in the halls, at least enough for Sol to make his way without a torch. There was no sound in the castle, but he was beginning to get an ominous sinking feeling. He felt like he was in a mausoleum instead of a sleeping castle. He couldn't put his finger on it, but something was very wrong here. The feeling intensified his desire to leave.

He looked down at Andrea, "Which way from here?"

She pointed to a hall ahead of them which turned left. Together they led the party down the hall, making turns here and there, down halls Sol had not seen yet. They came to a hall larger than the previous one, which was adorned with a brilliant red rug that stretched the entire length of the passage.

As they started down the hall, Sol caught a glimpse of something at the far end. It passed so fast that he couldn't see it clearly, just that it was big and seemed to dart across the hall. He motioned to the group to stop, waiting to see if it would move past again.

"What is it?" Khu-Rá asked.

"I thought I saw something."

"Something like what?" the elf asked in a cautious tone.

"I don't know. It was big but I couldn't see anything, it was too quick."

"There must be more of them," whispered Khu-Rá, sounding more worried than usual.

"More of what?" Sol asked, not entirely certain he really wanted an answer.

"Beasts," Andrea replied. "We were attacked by one earlier."

"So what? We'll just kill them--what's important is for us to get to the stables as quickly as possible."

"No, my friend," said Khu-Rá. "It would be best for us to avoid these. If there are more of them, they would quickly over-take us."

"Is there a way to go around?" Sol asked, looking down at Andrea. Andrea closed her eyes in thought.

"There are other ways, but I do not know them as well. I'm only familiar with this route."

"Well, I haven't seen anything more, so maybe it was just passing by....where do we need to go?"

"If we head this way, there is a hall to the right that will take us to a staircase that leads to the west entrance, near the stables."

"We can make that. If we keep quiet we can make it to the other hall and out."

Khu-Rá and Andrea both nodded in agreement and the party made its way toward the other passage at a slower and much more silent pace. Sol and Andrea took the lead, followed by Khu-Rá, then by Oather, and finally by Serieve, who was still helping Halistan.

Suddenly, another, much louder, boom echoed down the hall. It seemed to shake the walls, and several suits of armor fell over with a loud crash.

"So much for being quiet," Sol grumbled, but they kept going. They had reached the passageway to the right and were about to turn into it when they heard something running towards them from the far end of the hall.

From around the corner at the far end of the hall behind them stepped out a huge, reddish-brown beast. It had two ghastly heads, and its eyes were lit up like flames. Fire dripped from is long fangs.

"Go! I will try and buy us some time," Khu-Rá ordered as he nocked an arrow into his bow. Sol ushered Andrea quickly down the hall, followed closely by Oather, Serieve and Halistan.

Khu-Rá drew back his bow and quickly lined up his shot. This monster was unlike the other hellhound they had encountered. As it approached, he saw that its eyes actually glowed with a bright, yellowish-orange light. He released the arrow, then another and another, but the beast kept coming towards him. As each arrow hit it, the beast would slow for a split second before speeding back up. As it drew closer Khu-Rá could see that it actually had seven or eight arrows in it. It wasn't a new hellhound--it was the one he had killed before, somehow brought back to life. Khu-Rá lowered his bow and dashed down the hall after the others.

He ran as quickly as he could and caught up to them as they neared the stairwell.

"It's the same hellhound!" he cried, running up behind Sol and grabbing his shoulder. "It's the same!"

"How can that be?" asked Andrea. "I saw you kill it with my own eyes."

"I do not know, but it's coming, and I know that it's the same one."

The party picked up their pace and were almost running down the stairs as Khu-Rá made his report to Sol.

"It must be that sphere," Halistan called out from behind Sol.

Sol glanced back over his shoulder at the young man as they made their way down the steps. "What do you know of it, kid?"

They heard a loud howl and the menacing tapping sound of the beast's claws on stone as it ran after them.

"Not much, but at the church I did research on artifacts," Halistan replied, panting heavily as they kept on running. "I remember hearing of a cursed item, a sphere created by the demi-god, Castor, that was said to bring creatures back to life," he finished; trying to catch his breath some more as Serieve almost dragged him to the end of the stairwell.

"That's great, kid, but that doesn't help us any. Do you know how to stop something brought to life by that thing?"

They rushed down the passage at the base of the steps. Behind them the tapping continued, and was almost upon them.

"I have an idea." Halistan stopped running, almost tripping Serieve in the process.

"What are you doing?" yelled Serieve.

"Go on without me, I'll catch up."

Serieve looked at the young man for a split moment like he was crazy, before doing what he was told and running to catch up with Sol and the rest of the group. They had reached the doorway leading out to the stables and were filing out as quickly as possible.

## 47. The Hellhound

Halistan watched the others leave, and then heard the sound of the hellhound running towards him. Its pace had slowed, presumably because of its injuries, but it was still coming at him. Halistan pulled his wounded hand away from his chest and looked at it. Most of his hand was blackened, as if he had stuck his hand into a pile of ash but it wasn't, itself, burned. He managed to open his clenched fist and looked at it for the first time since it had been burned by the demon.

His fingers opened to reveal his palm, which wasn't burned like the rest of his hand. Instead, the skin was as white as ever, but in the middle of his palm was the star of Salus. The holy relic was literally burned into his skin; it felt like it was attached to the bones. He tried to open his fingers fully, but as soon as he tried, sharp streaks of pain shot up his arm. He instinctively clenched his fist closed again.

He opened his hand enough to look at the wound. All around the star the skin had been burned away. The area was surrounded by green pus that bubbled between the star and his skin. Just looking at it made it hurt worse and almost made him nauseous.

The hellhound bounded towards him down the long hall. Its eyes emanated pure evil as it growled and spit flames. Halistan stole another quick glance at his hand before he knelt down on one knee. He opened his hand as wide as his charred fingers would allow and placed it flat upon the ground, touching the star to the stone floor.

Doing his best to calm his frantic nerves, he closed his eyes and whispered a prayer. His hand began to burn again. The burn started slowly but soon felt like his hand was on fire again, hurting almost as badly as when it had been burned before. He winced and held his breath in an attempt not to cry out in pain. His eyes burst open and he could see light spreading out across the floor from underneath his palm as the beast lunged at him.

Suddenly the light beneath his palm shot out to either edge of the passage, then up along the wall. The spell was complete. The hellhound leapt at him but hit an invisible barrier. With a bright flash of light, the monster was thrown backwards down the hall. It immediately jumped back up to its feet and lunged again, and again got thrown backwards by the invisible field Halistan had created.

Halistan rose to his feet and looked at his hand again. The infection seemed to have grown and his palm throbbed terribly. His hand felt like he had grabbed a hot iron from the fire. He clenched his fist again and held it close to him.

The hellhound struck at the invisible barrier again and again but could not penetrate it. Halistan heard it growl in frustration and saw it bare its fangs at him in rage. He turned away and ran to catch up with the others.

## 48. Getting Out

Oather exited behind Sol and Andrea. It was indeed morning, although he still could not see the sun through the thick clouds.

"That's the stable." Andrea pointed at a smaller building directly in front of them. They headed towards it when Sol saw Oather stop and draw his sword.

Sol stopped to see what Oather was doing.

"Get the horses, Sol!" Oather yelled. To their right a dozen or so skeletons were digging their way out of the ground. Several had already broken up through the ground and were heading toward him.

The skeletons were covered in dirt and wearing rusted helmets and chain-mail armor, and their eyes glowed the same yellowish-orange as those of the hellhounds. They had no weapons, but reached out to him with their boney fingers.

Khu-Rá launched several arrows at the closest ones but the arrows just got stuck in the ribcages of the skeletons and didn't seem to affect them at all.

"Go!" Oather yelled. "I will handle them." Khu-Rá reluctantly conceded and ran after Sol into the stables.

As the first skeletal soldier approached, Oather swung his blade and cut right through the creature's upper body, snapping bones and cleaving armor and immediately dropping it to the ground.

Turning, he cut another skeleton across the mid-section, severing it in two. With the first two skeletons fallen, he prepared for the next ones to reach him. The skeletons on the ground were still moving, clawing their way to the severed parts of their bodies. As soon as the bones neared each other, they rejoined and the skeleton rose back to its feet, right next to Oather. Oather's attention had been on the next few coming at him, not on the ones he had already dispatched, so he was caught unaware when the beast jumped onto his back and began to strangle him.

He grabbed at the creature's boney arm and pulled it away, but by then the other skeleton had also risen again and grabbed his arm. The two skeletons were trying to pull him to the ground. He managed to kick the second one off of him and turned to run towards the stable, carrying the first skeleton with him. The skeleton was still grappling him, and tried to bite him on the neck before he was able to get hold of it and throw it off of him. But it wasn't long before the skeleton stood up and charged after him again.

Sol, Andrea, Serieve and Khu-Rá burst through the stable gate on their steeds, with two horses in tow. As they rode past Oather, he grabbed one of the free horses and leapt upon its back. It was not saddled like the others but Oather didn't care.

## 49. Narrow Escape

Halistan ran through the castle doorway and into the thick of the skeleton soldiers that were chasing his companions. Halistan ran past the skeletons around him and towards the group. At once, the skeletal minions began to chase after him instead.

He saw the group was riding away from him at a full gallop upon their horses. His heart sank as he saw their distance from him increasing rapidly. He knew that he could not catch them on foot and the skeletons were quickly catching up to him.

Immediately, the young man stopped and faced his aggressors. He pulled his wounded arm away from his chest and raised his hand to the sky. He closed his eyes tightly to block out the pain surging through his burned hand.

"Back!"

Even though his fist was clenched shut, streams of white light erupted from between his fingers and from his palm. The area all around him was suddenly bathed in white, holy light. The skeletons paid no heed to Halistan and ran headlong into the circle of light. The first skeleton to approach him shattered into sparks of white flame as its bones flew in all directions.

A moment later, several more skeletons met the same fate. They, too, were shattered and thrown back away from him. Halistan held his hand high, holding the remaining skeletons at bay as they surrounded the edge of the priest's spell, clawing at the barrier with their sharp boney hands.

\*\*\*

Khu-Rá saw a bright light next to the castle exit, and he could see Halistan standing in the middle of it. Khu-Rá at once turned and galloped towards the growing legion of undead. With the last horse in tow, he sped towards them and soon fell upon the circle of undead warriors.

His horse reared back and came down upon two of the undead, crushing them into broken shards of bone upon the ground. He broke through their line and into the area covered by the protection spell.

"Quickly, we must leave!"

Halistan jumped upon the horse but did not manage to get on completely. Instead he laid on his stomach across the horse's back, frantically attempting to kick one leg up onto the horse. Khu-Rá slapped the rear of the horse hard and caused it to burst into a gallop through the oncoming undead. Halistan had managed to grab a handful of the horse's mane by then, and held on for dear life as the steed galloped away. Khu-Rá kicked one more skeletal soldier's skull off its shoulders and charged through the rest.

He caught up to the young man, who was still struggling to cling to his horse. They had managed to put some distance between themselves and the undead creatures following them. The elf stopped the young man's horse and helped him up onto his steed before trying to catch up to the group.

Up ahead Sol and the others had stopped to wait for their companions at the castle gate. Khu-Rá looked back and saw undead rising from all parts of the castle grounds. Above the castle, a black cloud was forming. Unlike the rest of the clouds that covered this land, this one was almost completely black. It formed a perfect circle above the castle, and there was a thin funnel cloud reaching up from the rear of the castle to the center of the cloud, feeding it.

As the cloud grew, more and more dead rose from the ground. They were everywhere, their numbers growing by the dozens. Each one that dug its way from the ground was followed by three more. In moments, the castle grounds were filled with undead, all of which seemed to be heading towards them.

"What in the name of the gods…" Sol began to say, but his words drifted into silence as he stared in awe.

"I don't know and I don't want to," Oather replied. He was also staring at the growing black cloud and the growing horde of undead.

Sol looked back towards the main gate of the keep and spurred his horse onward. He was followed closely by his other companions as they made their way down the steep, winding road that led away from the infernal castle.

## 50. Unexpected Find

The air was charged with energy and thunder bellowed through the clouds. Lightning danced through the sky as Sol and the others made their way to the base of the mountain. The sky was darkening, even more than Sol had seen before, as the cloud above the castle grew.

Before him the thin dirt road led away from the castle and forked in the distance. It was surrounded on each side by dense woods. He knew the path to the left eventually led back towards the mystic's camp, and for the time being that sounded as good a place as any.

"Go that way," he heard the young woman say as she pointed to the right.

"Why?" he yelled back over his shoulder, but didn't change his direction.

"There is a town that direction," she replied back to him. "Maybe we can get help there."

"I doubt it."

Andrea reached around his waist and pulled hard on the reins, causing the horse to halt. The others followed suit and also came to a stop.

Sol whipped his head around and saw the woman glare at him stubbornly.

"What do you think you're doing?"

"We need help and…" Andrea started to say. She was interrupted by the ground shaking, accompanied by what could only be described as the sound of thousands of drums beating.

Serieve looked back up towards the Keep. "It's an army," he muttered, awestruck.

"That's impossible," Sol replied.

The undead had assembled in ranks and were marching in lines out of the castle. Each step reverberated through the stone of the mountain. The cloud stretched out above them as they watched the massive army march down the twisted mountain road like a giant snake made out of bone.

Thunder resounded through the sky and a bolt of black lightning struck the highest spire at the rear of the castle. Then another struck, and another; sending sparks flying off the castle's gray walls.

The booming steps of the army grew louder and louder with each footfall.

"We need to get to the village, they can help us fight them," Andrea said.

"No, we don't, let them fend for themselves," Sol retorted, snatching the reins from Andrea's hands.

"We need to at least warn them, Sol," Serieve said. Sol looked at his friend as if he couldn't believe the words that were coming from Serieve's lips.

"And why the hell do we need to do that?"

"They deserve a fighting chance!" Serieve argued as his horse whinnied at the sound of the army of undead slowly creeping ever closer to them.

Sol thought seriously about their situation, but warning the townspeople would take time and they had precious little of that. He sat upon his horse and looked up at the undead horde while grinding his teeth. Andrea tried to grab the reins again, but Sol jerked out of her reach.

"It is the noble thing to do," Khu-Rá stated, drawing nearer to the others.

"We cannot leave this land anyway," Andrea said.

Sol looked at Andrea questioningly.

"It's true. This land was cursed, and if you try to leave, then you will most certainly die. Our only chance is to see if we can enlist the help of the villagers," she continued.

"We know that already, but I'm not willing to bet that those people can help us," Sol snapped back. "Have you seen them? They can't even help themselves!"

"No one deserves to die helplessly, and if I can give them a chance to fight for their lives, then I am going to do it!" Serieve stated boldly, as if he no longer cared what Sol wanted.

The sound of the marching army echoed louder and louder all around them. Another blast of lightning leapt from the sky to the castle. Serieve pulled on the reins of his steed, circling around towards the path to the right and started galloping away.

He was followed quickly by Oather, Khu-Rá and Halistan.

"Well?" Andrea demanded. "Are we going, or are we going to wait for that army to get here?"

Sol let out a frustrated groan and rode after his companions.

In moments, Sol and Andrea had taken the lead again and Andrea was directing Sol which way they needed to go. They rode for quite some time and as the cloud grew, it blocked out more light, making it harder for them to tell where they were going.

"That way." Andrea pointed down to where the hills sloped into a grassy ravine that looked more like a dried creek bed. It led off into the distance and around the hills. Sol spurred his horse on, though he could tell that it was tiring. Its neck was sweaty and they had been running hard since they left the castle, but this was no time to stop. They galloped on.

"How much further to the town?" Sol growled at Andrea.

"I don't know. I didn't actually get to see it."

Sol stopped the horse and twisted around so he could see her. His eyes showed he was angry but she didn't back down from him.

"Then how do you know there is a town there?"

"I saw villagers run in that direction, you dolt, when Nicholas and I were riding here. Where else would they be going?"

"Oh, I don't know…their home!"

"Look," the group heard Khu-Rá say, interrupting the tiff between Sol and Andrea. "There's something in the grass up ahead."

It looked like a dark pile of laundry dumped out in the middle of the creek bed. Khu-Rá rode towards it slowly, trying to assess if it was a danger before he got too close. He was followed by the others, though not too closely.

As they approached, Sol could tell that the pile of rags were maroon robes. When he drew closer, he saw that they were wrapped around an elderly man with a beard.

"Zaroth?" the elf said. He dismounted from his steed and knelt next to the crumpled old man.

The old wizard laid there like an old bag thrown upon the ground. Khu-Rá lifted his face and leant an ear close to his mouth to listen for breath.

"He is alive, though just barely."

Halistan dismounted and assisted Khu-Rá. Clutching his wounded arm to his chest, he tried to examine the wizard.

"He is wounded very badly," Halistan said, looking at the elf.

"Can you help him?"

"I can, but right now my power is drained."

Zaroth momentarily awakened and coughed, spitting out blood as he did so. Halistan wiped it away with his shirt as Khu-Rá held the old man. Oather dismounted and joined the three on the ground.

"If we get him to the town, we might be able to get help from them," Halistan said, looking up at Sol.

"Fine," Sol said, rolling his eyes. "Oather, do you mind him riding with you?"

Oather did not say anything, but simply knelt down and picked up the old man's limp body as if it were a rag doll. The barbarian eased the unconscious wizard onto his horse and leapt up onto the horse himself, taking seat behind Zaroth to help steady the unconscious old man.

With a little help from Khu-Rá, Halistan was able to remount his own horse. Sol looked back. Far in the distance, the castle sat like an evil watchdog looming over its prey. The cloud above the castle was still growing. It now enveloped the entire mountain upon which the castle sat and judging by the rate it was growing, it wouldn't be long until it grew to encompass the entire realm.

"Now, which way is the town?"

Khu-Rá pointed up and over the hills that sat to their right. "There is smoke in that direction."

Sol looked, and sure enough, he could make out thin wisps of smoke trailing up into the gray sky.

"It's as good a way as any, I guess," Sol said as he turned in the direction of the smoke and spurred his horse on.

Their horses climbed the small hill. Once they reached the top they had a much better vantage than Sol had thought they would. He, of course, halted the steed and looked back in the direction of the castle.

"What are you doing?" Andrea asked. She relaxed her grip around Sol's waist.

He reached down to his left boot and pulled out a rolled piece of leather and a small cloth. He unwrapped the cloth and took out two small pieces of glass. Each was round but one was larger than the other. He unrolled the leather and placed the two pieces of glass inside, one at each end in small grooves cut into the leather, then rolled the leather around them.

"What are you doing?" Andrea asked, sounding slightly annoyed that he was ignoring her.

"Just lookin'," he replied indignantly. He put the leather tube up to his right eye and looked towards the castle.

He saw the castle, but it was different now. It was darker and almost seemed to absorb the light. Bolts of lightning continuously rained down upon it. He could vaguely make out the castle grounds--they were teeming with movement flooding out of the main gate of the keep.

Legions and legions of undead marched down the main road from the castle. There were more soldiers there than he had ever seen at one time. There must have been thousands of them; all lined up in perfect rows, marching down the mountain.

"Great mother of…" His speech trailed off.

"What?" Serieve asked. "Let me see."

Sol didn't move. He just sat there for a moment. Eventually, he handed the device over. Serieve put it to his eye and looked.

"What is it?" Andrea asked. Very irritated by now, she grabbed the device from Serieve and looked for herself.

"Oh my…" was all she got out before she lowered the looking glass.

"Did you see the road? It was filled with them," said Serieve.

Sol nodded yes. "Did you notice that along the road, even more undead creatures rose up from the ground and joined the ranks? I've never seen anything like it in my life."

"Where could they all be coming from?" Serieve asked. "There couldn't possibly be that many dead buried on that mountain."

"I don't know."

Sol grabbed the reigns of his horse forcefully and kicked his horse into a full gallop, followed closely by the rest of his companions.

## *51. The Town*

Sol rode hard, pushing his steed to its limits. Sol kept checking on the group as they rode. He saw Oather struggle a few times to keep the wizard upright due to their speed, but Sol knew they had to keep going.

They kept up the pace and finally saw a settlement in the distance. The sky darkened as though night was approaching. They had been riding a while, but certainly not for the whole day, but it was getting dark regardless. The black cloud continued to spread across the land and Sol wondered if that could be the cause.

Sol kept riding until they were almost upon the closest buildings of the town. Once he reached them he allowed his steed to slow down to a trot. The town reminded him of the southern side of Tyric. Most of the buildings were two-story, very dingy and old looking. They had thatch roofs, and in general looked like the same craftsmanship as the inn they had found shortly after they had arrived in this strange land.

Sol expected to see more people. Even if it was getting dark, there would surely be some people out. Up in the distance he finally saw a man walking down the street. He carried a torch, and was lighting one of the lanterns that lined the road. He was dressed in gray pants and a filthy shirt. He had a long face and at least three days' growth of beard. After lighting the first lantern he walked towards the next, which was closer to them. With any luck, Sol thought, he wouldn't recognize them.

Once Sol was near enough, he stopped his horse and looked down at the man.

"Where is your Burgher?"

The older man looked up at him after he lit the street lamp. He didn't say anything; he just gave Sol a strange look.

With a bit of annoyance in his voice, Sol tried again.

"Where is your leader? The one that oversees this town?" Sol asked.

The man stood there for a moment longer. Then his eyes burst wide open and a look of terror swept across his face. He dropped his torch and ran down the street to a building just past the second street lamp.

"What do you think is his problem?" Andrea asked.

Sol shrugged his shoulders, "I don't know. Everyone we've met here has been crazy. I should be getting used to it, but I'm not."

Khu-Rá rode up next to Sol. "I do not like the feel of this place. We should warn them and then be on our way."

"Agreed," replied Sol as they began trotting down the street again.

***

They reached the building that the lamplighter had run into. It appeared to be an office of some kind. As they stopped, a man came out. Fat, balding, and middle-aged. He somehow looked familiar to Sol. His right arm was in a sling and he had a patch covering his left eye.

"Whah de ye wan', stranja?"

Serieve jumped in immediately, "Sir, you and your people must leave town, an army of-"

The man began to laugh aloud in the middle of Serieve's warning. Serieve stopped speaking at the older man's interruption. Sol saw several doors of the other buildings open and some of the townsfolk came out.

"Sir, I implore you, please have your people get their things and leave before the army of undead-" Serieve was interrupted, again, this time by Sol grabbing his arm, signaling him to stop.

Serieve, in his urgency to warn the Burgher of the approaching danger, had not noticed several dozen armed men surround them. Oather's horse whinnied as the townsmen began to flank them. Sol looked side to side and took a mental count of them. Most of the men carried loaded crossbows, others had swords drawn and several others merely carried pitchforks.

Sol looked to the man in front of them and put on his best smile.

"As we can see, your fair town seems to be in good hands and certainly doesn't need our help. We thank you for your time but we really must be going-"

"Stop!" yelled the Burgher, his menacing laugh changed to a sinister growl.

Oather gripped the reigns of his horse, wondering if they could charge through the town militia, but one knowing glance from the Burgher told him that even if they did manage to get through the men, their backs would be filled with arrows as they sped from the town.

"We have no quarrel with you," Sol said. The man was silent and just stared into Sol's eyes.

"Just let us go and you'll never hear from us again."

"Ah canno' do tha'," the Burgher replied. The soldiers drew closer and were now just a few paces from them, completely encircling the group, their weapons raised and ready.

"We're harmless." Sol smiled down at the man. "What could you possibly want with us?"

"Harmless?" the Burgher yelled, his face becoming a deep shade of red.

"Ye call' destroyin' a buildin' 'armless?"

Andrea leaned forward, whispering into Sol's ear, "What is he talking about?"

"Do ye' ca' killin' a dozen of me people in an attem' to steal, 'armless?" the Burgher finished, fury resounding in his voice.

"What did you do, Sol?" she asked, quietly demanding an answer.

Out of the corner of his eye, Sol saw Oather place his hand upon the hilt of his sword. Sol knew Oather was prepared to draw his sword if Sol so gave the word. Khu-Rá's bow was on his back; he knew he could not ready it before the militia killed him, so he sat still, waiting for whatever was to happen next, to happen.

Sol sat upon his horse, eyes locked with the Burgher.

"You, you're the tavern owner, aren't you?"

The fat, balding man nodded yes.

"Then you know how powerful we are," Sol said sternly. "We do not wish to harm you or your people, we just wish to warn you and be on our way. So, if you do not wish to incur our wrath again-"

"Lia'! You 'ave no such powa," the Burgher yelled. "Tha' was done by yer wiza'd, and by th' looks of eht, he is'n no shape to do it ag'in."

Sol's bluff had been called--Zaroth couldn't even sit up straight on the horse without Oather holding him.

"Get off yeh 'orses!"

Sol looked over at Oather, who cocked an eye back at Sol's questioning glance. Sol tapped Andrea's leg.

"Get down," he said to her. She hesitated momentarily, which made Sol wonder if she was going to do as he ordered.

Slowly, Andrea dismounted, stepping down into the muddy road that ran through the tiny town. Sol dismounted after her, as did each of their companions. Oather stepped down and hoisted the unconscious wizard onto his shoulder.

Halistan clutched his arm to his chest as he tried to get off. This disrupted his balance, causing him to fall into the mud. Khu-Rá stepped forward to help the young man, but was met with a pitchfork pointed at his face. Instead, one of the soldiers grabbed the young man by the shirt and jerked him roughly to his feet.

"Wait," Andrea protested as the soldiers began to disarm them and place them all in shackles. "I'm not with these men. I was captured and was trying to escape."

The Burgher stepped in front of her and grabbed her face with his stubby fingers. "Ye' are the mos' wretched in thi' lot." Small droplets of spittle landed on her face as the fat man spoke to her.

"Ye' are de mis'ress of the dark lor', Nicholas. Yer p'nance, an those tha' serve ye, shall be great indeed," the obese man sneered at her.

He pushed her by her face away from him as he turned around.

Sol, seeing a golden opportunity tried to catch the Burgher's attention.

"Like she said," Sol attempted to say as the man walked away, "we're not with her. This is all one big mistake…" Sol's plea trailed off as the man hobbled back into the building. The words fell on deaf ears.

Andrea glared at Sol as he watched the man walk away. Sol looked back at her and smiled widely. Andrea then kicked Sol as hard as she could in the leg. It wasn't what she was aiming for but seemed to satisfy her nonetheless.

"Ouch. That was uncalled for," he said to her as the guards grabbed them all. Soon they were all shackled, and the townsfolk began to shove them towards the building.

Inside, they were marched down a hall to an open room. Several hard wood benches curved around the front of a desk that sat much higher than the surrounding pews. The Burgher took a seat behind the desk as the guards herded the prisoners into the room.

Sol's manacles dug into his wrists as they entered. He started towards one of the pews to take a seat, just like the many other times he had been through trials in the past, but a soldier kicked the bench away. Then he kicked the back of Sol's right leg, forcing Sol quickly down upon his knees.

"Hey," Sol started to protest, but the soldiers paid him no attention. They dropped the others to their knees as well. Zaroth was carried in by one of the larger guards, who simply threw the unconscious wizard down upon the floor next to the others. He let out a slight groan as the soldier dropped him but remained unconscious.

Sol looked up at the Burgher. "What is this? A trial?"

The Burgher looked back down at him, hatred filling his eyes, "Why? Do ye' wish ta plea' gilty?"

"No, we had nothing to do with the deaths of your people. That was all his fault," Sol argued, pointing at Zaroth with his nose.

"Tha's too bad. Dis is yer sentencin'...yor alreaday been foun' gilty," smiled the Burgher wickedly.

"What?"

"That's not fair!" Andrea exclaimed, which made the Burgher laugh out loud again.

"Life i' not fair, geet used te it."

The town Burgher straightened himself on his bench and began to speak.

"Fer yer crimes agan' this town, ye'll all sha'll sacrificed to de demo's. At firs light ye sha' ah beh tak'n an' trown inte de fed'n pits."

The Burgher balled his left fist and pounded upon the desk and yelled at the guards.

"No' tak'em to da cells 'til sun-up."

Two guards grabbed Sol by the arms and, one on either side, began dragging him through an open door to their left and down a stone stairwell. Sol struggled to get free but the guards held him tight.

Oather jumped to his feet and attempted to break the hold of the guards, but was met with a swift kick to the stomach. Then a guard hit him across the back of the head with the stock of a crossbow and the big man fell to the floor. It took six guards to carry him to the cell down below.

## 52. *All Dressed Up and Nowhere to go*

Sol was shoved hard into the cold, dark cell, followed shortly by his elven companion, the boy, the woman, and Serieve. One guard tossed Zaroth's limp body onto the middle of the cell floor. The wizard was probably dead from all the abuse he'd taken while he'd been unconscious, but Sol didn't care enough to find out.

Looking around, he saw that the jail was lit by a single lamp that hung from the wall near the only door. The room was sectioned off into four cells formed from iron latticework and the stone walls of the building itself. Along the wall of their cell was a wooden bench wide enough for four or five men to sit on at one time, but barely deep enough for one to sleep on. Sol took a seat on the bench and waited for the guards to leave.

The guards struggled to drag Oather inside the cell. Several of the guards were fat and definitely out of shape, and he heard them grunt as they lugged Oather in. Their condition made sense to Sol--being so cut off from the world, they probably didn't see much action and instead spent most of their lives drinking ale and making up 'big fish' stories to pass the time. Finally they managed to get Oather far enough inside the cell to shut the iron gate. Panting heavily, the head guard shut and locked the door and followed the others back up the stairs.

"Well, isn't this just great," Sol grumbled as he looked at Serieve, who had taken a seat on the bench next to him.

"Okay, I'll admit, this didn't turn out exactly how I thought it would," Serieve said apologetically. "I just didn't think about-"

"You never think! You're lucky my hands aren't free or I'd…" Sol didn't finish the sentence. A devilish grin swept across his face as Serieve looked at him. Sol slung his head forward, smashing his forehead into Serieve's nose.

Serieve's head flew back from the blow, which made him also hit the back of his head against the stone wall of the cell. Once he regained his composure, his face scrunched up in anger and he awkwardly attempted to hit Sol back. His bound arms made it difficult but he tried anyway, and missed.

"Stop it!" Andrea commanded. She stood looking down at the two men. "Just stop it. This is getting us nowhere."

Serieve stopped and glanced at her. He looked back at Sol and scooted away to the far edge of the bench. A small trickle of blood ran down his nose and past his upper lip.

"You had that coming," sneered Sol. Serieve didn't say anything. Instead, he glared at Sol in silence.

Sol let out a sigh and slumped over slightly as he sat on the bench. His cloak was all bunched up underneath him and made it hard to move around, but he finally got comfortable. Once he did, he kept fidgeting with the inside lining of his cloak, not paying much attention to anyone else.

Khu-Rá took a seat in between Sol and Serieve, who was now trying to wipe the blood from his nose off onto the shoulder of his tunic.

"Is he okay?" the elf asked, nodding towards Oather who laid still on the cold stone floor of the cell. Andrea knelt down next to him. It was difficult, with the irons holding her wrists behind her back, but she managed to get her face close to his, looking for any sign of life.

"I think he is breathing. I'm sure he will be fine."

"He's fine, I've seen the big lug take harder hits than that," replied Sol, as he continued to feel along the inside edge of his cloak.

"What are you doing?" Serieve asked.

"Looking for something..." Sol replied, "Ah, there it is."

He slid a tiny curved piece of metal out of the stitching of the cloak and held it with his fingertips for Serieve to see.

"I hope you've gotten better at that since we were kids," Serieve said.

Andrea looked at Serieve questioningly.

"Sol used to always try and pick the lock on some shackles that my father had at our home, but Sol was really lousy at it.

"Shut up, Serieve," Sol said. "I got it sometimes."

"You could barely do it when you weren't wearing them and never when you were. Admit it; you're nowhere near the lock pick you think you are."

Sol looked up at his friend and smiled as they all heard a click, then a clank as the shackles dropped onto the wooden bench.

"You were saying?" Sol said as he stretched his arms out in front of him, thoroughly enjoying having his hands free.
"When you've been in as many stinking Imperial jails as I have, you get a lot of practice. You know what they say... necessity is the mother of invention."

"Me next," called Andrea. She jolted over to Sol and knelt down with her back facing him so he could get to her shackles.

"Gladly, my dear," Sol said. He unlocked them in almost no time at all.

Sol stood and looked at the elf. "Would you like me to free you too?" The elf nodded and turned his back to Sol so he could get to the lock. Serieve stood up next and offered his chains to Sol.

"What do you want?" Sol asked.

"Get these off me, Sol."

"No, unbeliever, you get to stay locked up. That way we can make sure your noble sentiments don't get us into trouble anymore." Serieve's face turned a slight shade of red as he looked back at Sol. Sol could almost feel Serieve's blood starting to boil as the other man glowered at him, which of course made Sol smile wider.

Sol looked at the priest who had taken a seat on the floor. He walked over to the boy, "Turn around and I'll get those off you as well." Halistan rose and gladly turned so Sol could take off the chains. As the manacles fell from Halistan's wrists Sol got a look at the boy's hand. The priest's holy symbol was burned right into his flesh. All around the symbol was blood and oozing green pus that trickled down the boy's hands and dripped off his charred finger tips.

"That looks painful," Sol said, as the young man brought his arms back to the front and clenched his hand back close to his chest, wiping the pus onto his shirt. The boy's shirt was stained with the mixture of the blood and pus that leaked from his wound.

Halistan ignored Sol's remark and stepped around the barbarian so he could examine Oather for himself.

Sol joined him and quickly undid Oather's shackles. He and Halistan turned Oather over onto his back. It wasn't easy, as Oather was out cold and his dead weight didn't want to move. Sol looked at Oather's head and saw a nasty cut coated in blood.

"Can you help him at all?"

Halistan took a closer look at the wound, "I think so. I'm still pretty exhausted but I might be able to do something."

He reached out his right hand and placed it upon Oather's head. Halistan closed his eyes and began to chant quietly. Sol couldn't make out what the priest was saying but the boy's hand began to glow as it touched Oather. The glow didn't last long before it subsided and Oather opened his eyes.

## 53. Resuscitation

"Welcome back to the land of the living."

Oather sat up and looked around. He blinked several times as his eyes adjusted to the darkness. Next to him Oather saw the wizard lying unconscious upon the ground.

"Is he still alive?" Oather asked.

Halistan rose and walked around Oather to get a better look at the broken old wizard. Zaroth laid motionless on his back as Halistan knelt close to him.

"Put him up on the bench, please," Halistan said.

Oather picked the wizard up and set him gently down upon the wooden bench that ran along the prison wall. The wizard's right arm dangled off the edge of the bench.

Halistan laid his head upon the old man's chest.

"He's alive, but barely, I think," Halistan said as the others gathered behind him.

"What do you think happened to him?" asked Serieve.

"The same thing that happened to us, you idiot," replied Sol. "Or did you forget our little encounter with the King?"

"Yes, I know that, Sol," Serieve shot back. "What I meant is how he got away in the condition he's in."

"I don't know," Sol replied, looking down at Zaroth, "but after witnessing firsthand how powerful this wizard is, then seeing him beaten to a pulp like this makes me wonder how powerful that man...demon...thing, whatever he is, really is."

"He's a man cursed by the Gods," Halistan said, looking up over his right shoulder at Sol. "Well...at least according to the other men I met in the dungeons."

"Sounds like a real nice guy," Sol said sarcastically. "But it doesn't really matter right now. What matters now is getting out of here before sunrise."

"What do you have in mind?"

"I don't know. Even if we do get out, we'll still be trapped in this land, just like everyone else here, so we're still prisoners whether we get out or not."

Oather let out an unhappy sigh.

"This must be what it feels like to be sent to Traboschon," Sol said to Oather.

"Aye."

Overhearing the two men talk got the elf's attention. "What is that place, Traboschon?" he asked.

"It's a prison--a horrible place. An invisible island just off the coast of the southern desert, where the Empire sends those that it wants to forget about. Once you go there, you never come back."

Khu-Rá leaned closer, enthralled by Oather's description.

"Are you sure there isn't anything you can do for the wizard, kid?" Sol asked, interrupting Oather's grim explanation.

"Not right now," replied Halistan. "I am completely drained of strength."

Sol stroked his chin and tried to think of other options, but he came up blank.

"Even if I were rested," Halistan said, "I do not know how serious his injuries are. I still may not have the power to heal him enough to make a difference."

Sol bit his upper lip while he thought. He looked over at the iron gate of the cell.

"I could try and pick it," he said, "but these little picks I have aren't designed for a lock that big. More than likely they would snap in two if I tried."

Sol looked back down at the priest. Halistan was picking up the wizard's arm that hung off the edge of the bench and rested it upon the wizard's chest.

"Do you have any other magic you can use?" Sol asked. "Anything that takes less energy than healing spells?"

The priest sat there quietly for a moment before answering. "I can conjure food and drink."

Sol looked down at the boy in utter disbelief.

"Great! At least we won't die hungry," Sol quipped. "Too bad we'll still be dead."

Halistan shrugged his shoulders but remained quiet.

"Anything else?"

"No, not really, even the simplest spell would be difficult for me right now."

"How long do you need to rest to get back enough energy to help the old man, kid?"

Halistan thought for a moment then finally spoke, "Probably a few hours," he replied.

"Yes, I think a few hours would be enough."

There were no windows in the room they were in but it was just reaching nightfall when they were captured from what Sol remembered.

"Night seems to last forever here," he said, "so I'm sure we at least have that long until sunrise. Here is what I propose....actually, Hal, go ahead and get us some food."

Halistan knelt down and closed his eyes. With a wave of his left hand, several loaves of bread, some fruit and a pitcher of water appeared on the ground next to him. Oather snatched up a loaf, ripped it in half and began to eat as he tossed the other half to Sol.

Sol took a bite and said, "I'm going to go ahead and try to pick the cell lock. If I can do that, we're going to probably have to fight our way out."

Sol swallowed another mouthful of bread and tapped Halistan on the shoulder, "Kid, you rest and do whatever you need to do. Then do your best to help the old man. If we can heal him, perhaps he can get us out of here without having to go up against all those guards, unarmed."

Halistan nodded in agreement and stood up with the others. He turned towards Andrea.

"Miss, would you mind assisting me? It'll be hard for me to hold my book while I read my prayers."

"Yes, I'll help you," Andrea replied.

The two of them moved to a corner of the cell away from the rest of the group.

Sol approached the cell door and stuck his arms through the bars. His hands felt around the front of the lock until he got an idea of the kind of lock he was dealing with. Serieve walked up next to Sol.

Serieve cleared his throat loudly. "Ahem."

"Can I help you?"

"Come on, Sol. You've had your fun, now take these off me."

Sol turned to look at Serieve.

"No."

"Why not?"

"It's your punishment for getting us into this mess. You never listen to me and now this is the second time you've put our lives in danger. For all I care, you can keep those chains on until we get all the way back home. We'd all probably be safer with you under lock and key anyway."

Khu-Rá and Oather joined them near the cell gate.

"Nobility always has a price, my friend," Khu-Rá said to Sol.

"Well, it's not worth the cost if you ask me."

"It is often that we cannot immediately see the value in noble pursuits, but I have never in my hundred and fifty years not seen it become worth tenfold the price that was paid …you must give it time."

Sol looked at Khu-Rá with a mixture of disbelief and bewilderment…as if the elf had just spoken in a foreign language. Sol blew him off and went back to examining the lock.

"I for one, congratulate you, my friend. I feel this world would be a better place if there were more men like you in it," Khu-Rá said to Serieve as he bowed his head to the cavalier.

"Thank you."

"You know, Sol, if you can get the gate open I am almost certain that we'll face at least a few guards. Serieve will be of no use to us if he is cuffed."

Sol pretended like he didn't hear Oather and kept working.

"It would be far better to release him now than to try and do it when we have a dozen guards charging at us," Oather continued.

Sol thought about it for a moment, and then looked over at Serieve, "All right, I'll set you free. If nothing else it will get you people to leave me alone so I can work."

Serieve smiled wide, relieved that he would finally get the uncomfortable iron shackles off his wrists.

Sol raised his finger and pointed at Serieve's face. "Before I take these off, though, you have to swear to me, on your father's grave, that from now until we get back to Tyric you will do exactly as *I* say and stop being such a damned fool."

Serieve's jaw dropped as he listened to Sol.

"Swear it," Sol growled.

Serieve stood there for a moment before he finally sighed and lowered his head, "I swear."

A contented smile spread across Sol's face. "Deal."

Serieve spun around slowly and Sol went to work on releasing him from his irons. In moments they fell off the cavalier's wrist. Serieve stretched his arms out and rubbed his wrists, thankful to finally have the manacles off.

## 54. *Little Talks*

In the far corner, Andrea knelt next to the priest. She took his holy book out of his pack and set it down in front of him as he had asked.

"Please turn it to page three hundred and ninety four," he said. Halistan used his left hand to steady himself, as he had a hard time staying upright.

"May I see?" she asked, which took Halistan by surprise.

She slowly reached for his right arm. He reluctantly let go of his tunic and let her see the wound. He opened his hand slowly. With each finger he extended she could see more of the blood and pus. She got a whiff of the wound, which made her almost retch and jerk her head away.

It smelled like week-old rotting flesh. She thought she was going to be sick, but she stifled the reaction and turned back to look at the wound again. This time she was more prepared for it. The young man's holy symbol was intact--a bluish-silver star that seemed to be burned right into the palm of his hand.

Andrea looked back up at the young man's face. "That must hurt terribly."

"Yes," he replied. "To be honest, it's all I can do to keep from screaming in pain whenever I have to touch something, but I'd prefer not to show that kind of weakness to these other men. I'm sure I'm on the verge of being left behind by them as it is, and I don't need to give them any more reason to do so."

"Don't worry about them," Andrea replied. "They are more bark than bite, especially that blow-hard, Sol. I'm not sure why we're even following him anyway. I doubt he could lead ants to a picnic, much less come up with a way out of here."

Her statement made Halistan smile.

"I think you're right, but I don't really have any better ideas, so I just go along with everyone else."

"You and me both," Andrea winked at him. "Let's at least get that wrapped up for you."

Andrea looked around, but there wasn't much in the cell that would have been any use. The other men, except for Zaroth, were all crowded around Sol as he picked the lock. She thought briefly about ripping off one of her sleeves to dress Halistan's wounds but another thought came to mind instead.

Andrea got up and walked over to the men. Sol was still working on the lock, but the bottom of his cloak was bunched up on the floor as he knelt in front of the gate. She picked up the end, but none of the men paid any attention to her. She bit the end of the cloak to make a tear, and then proceeded to rip a long swath of it off.

Sol whipped around just as he heard her rip his cloak, "Hey, what do you think you're...?"

Andrea stuck her finger into his face and glared at him. "This is your idea and if you want us to follow it, you need to give a little."

Sol looked at her in disbelief. Finally he shook his head and went back to working on the lock.

Andrea walked back and knelt down next to Halistan. She took his hand, trying hard to be gentle, but could tell she was hurting him some as she began to work. Halistan was quiet while she wiped away some of the blood and foul smelling green pus and wrapped his hand in the material.

"May I ask you a question?" he asked her.

Andrea wasn't sure what to say at first.

"Sure..." she replied in a cautious tone.

"Are you from this land?"

Andrea was shocked by the question. It took her a moment to stop shaking her head no. "Of course not. Why would you think that?"

"Well, there was a painting of you in the room where I found you, so I thought this might be where you were from. Were you the one who opened the portal that brought us here?"

"No, that wasn't me. I think that was Nicholas."

"Oh," Halistan replied. He was obviously confused. "But-"

Andrea put her finger to his lips and he immediately quit speaking.

"I am not from here. Nicholas tricked you into bringing me here, because he thought I was that woman reincarnated. The woman in the painting was someone named Allisandra who lived a long time ago, but she is definitely not me."

"Oh," Halistan said again.

Andrea was quiet as she finished tying the knot in the bandage. She looked up so she could see the younger man's eyes, "No, I'm not her, but Nicholas and the rest of the servants in the castle seemed to think that I was."

"I've heard stories of people who had unfinished business when they died," Halistan said, "and the powers sent them back to finish whatever it is they needed to do before moving on to heaven....or hell."

Andrea sat next to Halistan, pondering his words. She couldn't believe she was even listening to him.

"Powers?" she asked.

"Well, most people call them gods, but they aren't gods. They were created by IAO as caretakers of the world."

Andrea's eyes glossed over as he began talking about the gods. She had no interest in gods or anything that would tie her to this awful land. She had finished dressing his wounded hand, so she released it and he pulled it back.

"Thank you," he said. Returning to his earlier thought, he continued, "I wonder if something like that happened to you and they sent you back to come here."

Andrea felt her temper rising. She could feel anger swell up inside her but she didn't want to take it out on Halistan. He had saved her life but she didn't feel like talking about this any further.

She leaned close to him, looked him deep in the eyes and whispered, "The only purpose I have at this point in time is getting out of here. Then I'm going to find a way to kill that bastard, Nicholas, and that is the last I want to hear of this. Do I make myself clear?"

Halistan's eyes bulged and he slowly nodded yes.

## 55. *Fool's Bargain*

"Damn it," Sol cursed as he threw the last of his small metal lock picks to the ground after it snapped in half. He was exhausted and frustrated and had begun to feel the tension of the situation bearing down on him. He didn't know what time it was, but he knew it was late, and he was sure that it couldn't be too much longer until dawn, and their certain doom.

Sol walked over to the bench where the unconscious wizard rested. Oather had taken a seat next to the old man. Oather was tired, too, but the bench was too shallow for him to sleep on, so he sat there with his head resting on his palms as he drifted in and out of an uncomfortable rest.

Across from the bench, sitting on the ground near the bars of their cell, Serieve and the elf had taken a spot where they sat with their backs to each other for support as they slept. Serieve's head had fallen back and was resting on the elf's shoulder.

"So, what do we do now?" Oather asked Sol in a voice so low it could have been a whisper.

"I don't know," Sol replied, wiping his hands over his face to fight off some of the weariness he was feeling. "I'm still thinking about that…needless to say, whatever we come up with, we're going to have to do it soon."

Sol looked down. To his left he saw the boy lying on the ground upon his back, with his hand tucked near his chest as he slept. Andrea sat near him, leaning against the stone wall that made one side of their cell. Her eyes were closed but Sol couldn't tell if she was actually asleep or not. For the first time since they had fled the castle, he noticed that she was actually a very beautiful woman. The realization made him wonder what her role in this whole affair was, but he shrugged off the thought. Instead, his mind wandered back to the situation at hand.

"How long has he been asleep?" Sol whispered back to Oather.

"I don't know. A good while now….since about the time that you broke the second or third pick."

Sol got off the bench and went to the boy. Sol knelt over him and he tried to wake the young man. "Hal," he whispered as he shook him, but the young man didn't stir.

"Hal, wake up," he said again, this time slapping him lightly on the cheek, but that still didn't have any effect. Sol let out a sigh and looked around the rest of the cell. Everyone seemed dead to the world, so Sol looked back at the kid.

Reaching up slowly, Sol placed his hand over Halistan's bandaged wound and squeezed it tightly.

Instantly, Halistan jerked awake and let out a horrific yelp as he pulled his hand from Sol's grasp. He saw Sol kneeling over him and darted away, scooting as far as he could before running into Andrea.

"What…what did you do that for?"

"I couldn't wake you, so I had to do something."

Serieve and Khu-Rá began to stir on the other side of the cell, "Well, it seems I got everyone up."

"Mmmnnnnggggg," moaned the wizard. The sound immediately got Sol's attention, and he went to the old man to get a closer look. Zaroth was still unconscious but at least Sol was sure he was alive now.

"Hey, kid, can you do anything for him?" Sol asked Halistan, who was trying to stand up but was obviously still very exhausted. The young man stumbled towards Sol, using his left hand to steady himself as he neared them.

Halistan pushed Sol out of the way and looked at the wizard. He opened one of Zaroth's eyes, which was rolled back so Halistan couldn't see it very well. He laid his good hand on the wizard's head and looked back at Sol.

"There might be something I can do…"

"Well, then, get to it."

"I know some spells that might work, but they are very advanced and I've never attempted them without the help of an elder. They may not work."

Sol knelt down on one knee next to the boy. He pulled the younger man closer until they were face to face, and whispered softly so that only the boy could hear him.

"You have to at least try. I've already failed at picking the lock and any time now the guards are going to come in and march us all to our deaths. This man might be our only hope of getting out of here."

Halistan peered into Sol's eyes as he spoke. Sol could tell the boy was scared and that he was putting a lot of pressure on him, but at this point they didn't have many other options.

"I know this might be hard, but we have to try. For your sake, and the sake of us all, we cannot be here in the morning when the guards come back down."

"I don't know, Sol. If the spell isn't done right it could actually kill him instead of healing him," Halistan said, as dread crept into his voice. Sol put his hand on the younger man's shoulder.

"I know you can do this. Our lives are in your hands."

Sol let go of him and Halistan looked back at the old wizard. Then Halistan looked around the room, and finally up at Andrea, who now stood behind Sol. Her eyes met his, and with a nod of her head she told him to do it. He looked down at the hand that she had bandaged just a short while before, and started undoing the bandaging.

Taking a few quick breaths to ready himself for the pain, he pulled the wrapping off the wound.

"Just breathe and relax. You can do this, just like you have before," Andrea said. As Halistan removed the covering, Sol's hand clenched. This was the first time Sol had seen the wound up close, and it looked agonizing. He didn't know how the kid could stand it.

Halistan looked at the face of the old man. Very slowly, he lowered his hand to the wizard's skin until it finally made contact. Touching his wounded hand to the wizard must have hurt, because Sol saw Halistan flinch and start to pull his hand away, but the boy quickly stopped himself. Halistan closed his eyes and chanted--under his breath at first, with the spell becoming louder as he repeated it.

Sol couldn't understand what the boy was saying. It was slightly melodic and the words were in no language Sol had ever heard before. Halistan repeated the chant over and over until he was loud enough to be heard by the others. There was no reaction at first, but he kept chanting. Then Halistan's hand began to glow.

Slowly the glow grew into a white light and spread over the old, fallen wizard--across Zaroth's face, down to his shoulders, then down the old man's body until it reached his feet and he was completely enveloped. Then it subsided, almost as if it had been absorbed into the man's body.

Halistan slowly removed his hand from the wizard's head.

"I've done all I can, now we'll just have to…" Halistan began to say, but before he could finish, Zaroth's eyes shot open and the wizard breathed in deeply.

"…wait," Halistan finished with a surprised look.

Zaroth's eyes closed again slowly as he exhaled and his body relaxed.

"Gale, is that you?" Zaroth asked weakly. "Thank the gods, the spell worked in time…I wasn't sure if it would."

Halistan began to re-wrap his wounded hand with the bandage cloth.

"Bring me some Mizeen tea, would you please, Gale?" Zaroth said. "Make it extra hot, my head is killing me."

"How are you feeling?" Halistan asked slowly.

"F…fine, I guess…who…?" Zaroth replied.

"We don't have time for many questions," Sol interrupted.

Zaroth's eyes shot open again as he looked over and saw Sol above him.

"What are you doing in my…" the wizard's voice trailed off.

"Listen, we're in jail and we need to get out."

"What…why are…" the wizard began again, sounding utterly confused.

"We're here because you blew up the inn, and now at dawn--which should be any time now--we're all going to be executed."

Zaroth sat up and rubbed his face, seeming to become more coherent as he looked at Sol.

"I'm not supposed to be here," Zaroth argued. "I am supposed to be back to my tower."

"Well, guess what, it didn't work. We found you lying in a pool of mud just outside of town. Now, can you help us get out?" Sol asked with more urgency.

"Yes, I can get us out-"

"Great!"

"Don't blame this on me, though, Sol. If you hadn't tried to steal…"

"There's no time to cloud the issues with the facts, old man," Sol said as he ushered the others back, giving Zaroth more room. "Now, let's see what you can do."

Zaroth peered up at Sol with a look that distinctly said that this was why he disliked Sol so much.

The wizard looked around the room, then held up his hand and said, "Light." A ball of light appeared. Zaroth placed it above him so that he could get a better look at their surroundings. Sol, and all the others shielded their eyes as they adjusted to the light.

The wizard was silent in thought for a moment.

"Where's my wand?"

Sol stood there, blank faced. "I don't know...we didn't see it when we found you."

"Blast," Zaroth muttered. "It's of no matter; I still have a few ideas."

Zaroth parted the group so he could make his way to the stone wall. He took his right hand and put it up his left sleeve. He seemed to dig around for something, feeling around, deep into the sleeve. Eventually, he found what he was looking for and brought out a stick of what looked like purple chalk.

Sol gave Oather a bewildered glance. Leaning over, he whispered, "Okay, now I know the old man has lost his mind. Maybe the kid's spell didn't work right, you think?"

Oather shrugged as he continued to watch the old man, "Makeshift wand, maybe?"

Zaroth stepped closer to the stone and knelt down. With a sweeping motion he drew a line up the wall, then drew an arch, then continued down the other side, making an outline the size of a large door. He then drew a circle in the middle of the wall and a triangle inside that, with a strange symbol at each point of the triangle.

The wizard then closed his eyes and began to mumble. It sounded like a combination of whispering and growling but beyond that it sounded like gibberish.

Suddenly, the chalk at the base of the wall seemed to catch on fire and bright blue and red sparks spilled off it onto the ground. To Sol, it resembled firesalt, the white grainy substance used to fire cannons on ships, after it had been ignited. The sparks trailed up both lines until they met at the top. As they neared the top the sparks began to grow brighter and brighter.

Just before the two sparkling balls reached each other, Sol saw Zaroth quickly turn his back to the wall and covered his head. Sol knew this wasn't a good sign and tried to brace himself but it was too late. Once the balls touched they erupted into a small explosion of fire, sparks and smoke, with a force that shook the building and knocked Sol to the floor.

## 56. *Making a Run for it*

When the smoke cleared, the wall was gone. Sol tried to ask what that was, but his ears were ringing loudly and he was furious. Oather managed to get up first and helped Sol to his feet.

"Do you even know how to be subtle?" Sol growled at Zaroth.

"I was under the assumption that time was of the essence," the wizard replied indignantly.

"Yes, but we don't want to alert-" Sol started to argue, when they all heard the sound of troops clamoring down the stairwell to the lower level.

"Too late. Quick, everyone out!" Sol ordered as he pushed the wizard through the hole. Zaroth was soon followed by Andrea, Oather and the others, with Sol being the last one out.

It was hard to climb up out of the hole that the blast had created. The ground was soggy and squished underneath them. Halistan in particular had a hard time, since he could only use one arm. Oather finally grabbed Halistan and tossed him up.

Sol, was the last one up. When he reached the outside, he saw that it was still night, but nearing dawn. It was the darkest kind of night, a night when neither of the moons were out and all the stars were covered by overcast clouds. This was a blessing to Sol as Oather pulled him up and out of the hole.

Perhaps they'd be able to take advantage of this and slip away quickly, Sol thought. Behind him, he heard metal clanking as their pursuers frantically worked their keys to open the cell door.

"This way," Sol called to the others in a hushed tone, waving them in his direction. They were behind the town hall, which seemed to be the biggest building in this tiny little village, and they were concealed by its shadow, as the town lamps were only hung on the main street on the other side of the building.

Soliere went to the corner of the building and peeked around the edge to see if anyone else was outside. Unfortunately, several guards had just run out from the front and into the street, yelling that there had been a breakout. The soldier, accompanied by two others, began running down the street, banging on doors and calling the alarm. Within moments men began pouring out of the other buildings, some only half dressed but with weapons in hand, following the other guards.

"Well, so much for slipping out undetected," Sol sneered at the wizard. He looked out into the darkness which surrounded the town, attempting to make out what lay beyond the town street lights and hoping that the forest was close by.

"Khu-Rá, can you see what's out there?"

The elf looked back for a moment and turned back to Sol.

"It is not good. The land extends out, and then begins to slope downward to where it meets a lake. A very large lake, I cannot see the other side of it."

"Damn, that doesn't help us any. The water would be too cold to swim and we don't know how far we'd have to go," Sol assessed the situation under his breath. He looked back around the corner again. Even more of the townsfolk were arriving.

Sol looked back at the group. "Let's try and sneak around these buildings to the other side. If we can make it to the edge of the woods, I think we'll be able to elude them and get away."

The others didn't seem very comforted by the plan, but none of them spoke up with anything better so Sol took that as a sign of agreement.

"Zaroth, do you have any magic that could help us?"

"No, I'm still weary from my fight with that beast. I will need time to recover before I'd be of any real help."

Sol wasn't happy to hear that, but there was nothing he could do. He led them around to the other side of the main building; where there was another building close by that they could dart to.

One by one, they dashed across the space between the city hall and the next building. Sol crept behind it slowly when he heard a commotion coming from behind the city hall. Several soldiers climbed their way up out the hole they used to escape. Sol saw their torches light the area as four or five guards climbed out.

"So much for a discreet getaway," Sol said.

"There they are," Sol heard one of the guards shout. "Get them!"

Sol broke into a full sprint towards the forest, but glanced behind him to make sure the others were following him. They were, but the guards also began to chase them. Several more men joined the chase on horseback. Sol knew that they wouldn't be able to outrun them unless they made it into the forest, so he pushed himself harder to run faster. His heart was beating hard and he was taking in huge breaths of the cold night air, which made his lungs ache, but he kept going.

Sol looked ahead to see how much further they had until they met the edge of the forest when he was almost run into by a soldier on horseback. The horse reared up in front of Sol, just barely missing him with its hooves. Sol dodged to his right to get away but was met by another mounted soldier. This one was wielding a sword and before Sol knew it, the blade was pointed down at his chest, so of course he quit running.

In no time at all, they were surrounded by soldiers on horseback, and then shortly by the foot soldiers. The captain of the guard looked down at Sol, with his blade pointing at Sol's neck.

"Thaw ye coul' get 'way, didge ye?"

"I just wouldn't be me if I didn't try." The comment was quickly met with a kick in the jaw by the soldier, knocking Sol to the ground.

Oather jerked another soldier off the horse to his left and threw him to the ground, ripping an axe from the soldier's grip. Oather drew back the weapon and was about to plant it into the soldier's chest when he heard a loud voice behind him.

"Stop!" the Burgher called out.

The Burgher had arrived, and at his one loud command everyone ceased all movement. He pulled soldiers back roughly until he was standing in front of the group. The obese man marched up and helped Sol to his feet and ordered the soldier that kicked Sol to go back to town.

Sol rubbed his jaw for a moment. He had halfway been expecting to get hit, and was able to brace himself just before it happened, which prevented any real damage from being dealt...aside from a little damage to his ego.

"Eht sems ye have may' some p'werful frien's heya," said the Burgher. "Com wit meh," he commanded as he turned and began walking back towards the town. The foot soldiers surrounded the party. They took the weapon from Oather, which he gave up very reluctantly.

The group was led back towards the town. Sol's feet were getting cold, as his boots were now thoroughly soaked from the moist ground. The wind had picked up and it began to drizzle again. It seemed to Sol that cold, wet weather was all this land ever saw. It was becoming clearer to him why everyone here was always in such a terrible mood.

Andrea started walking next to him, "Who do you think it is?" she asked. "How could we have friends here...we don't know anyone."

Sol shrugged his shoulders, "I dunno...but I am a little curious myself. I was beginning to think everyone here hated us."

"Well, I could understand them hating you," Andrea quipped back, "but I haven't done a thing here except get brought here against my will."

"You weren't the only one," Serieve chimed in. "Do you think we chose to come here? Trust me, this is the last place any of us wanted to come."

It wasn't long before they were back in the little town. As they walked down the main street, Sol saw at the far end of the main road there were some brightly covered wagons; a bright red one and a bright blue one.

"The mystics," Sol grumbled, just loud enough for Serieve to hear him.

"Great," Serieve whispered back, enthusiastically. "Maybe they can help get us out." He was interrupted by Sol elbowing him in the ribs.

"Don't you get it?" Sol whispered back. "They set us up. They knew what the king was and intentionally took us there knowing that we'd be killed. All he wanted was that thing that Oather had, and they served us to him on a platter."

"Oh..." Serieve replied, sounding a little disheartened, "So, what are we going to do?"

"I don't know, but I don't have a good feeling about this."

## 57. *Short Lived Victory*

The Burgher led the way as they approached the big blue wagon. The door was opened and the short steps were lowered for them to enter the wagon. Sol recognized Yaeva's wagon and saw that the man that opened the door was Vego. The rain was starting to pour down, so Sol was more than happy to go inside.

At the far end, Yaeva sat at her table next to an old man. The Burgher went and stood next to her. His arms were crossed and Sol could tell that the Burgher was angry. Yaeva motioned them inside and beckoned them to come closer to her at the table. The room still smelled heavily of incense, so much so that it made Sol's nose itch a little as he breathed it in. It wasn't a bad smell, just a little overpowering.

"Come, please sit," she said to them as they approached her.

"No thanks, we'll stand," Sol insisted.

"Have it your way."

Vego and two soldiers entered the wagon and remained at the back after closing the door. The rain picked up to a full downpour which sounded like nails hitting the top of the wagon.

"Tallmoor?" Halistan asked as he pushed his way to the front.

"Halistan!" Tallmoor replied as he got up from the table. He hugged the young man as Halistan warned him to watch out for his injured arm.

"You know this man?" Sol asked.

"Yes, Tallmoor was one of the men in the dungeon with me," Halistan replied excitedly, "I wasn't sure if you were able to get out. Did Orman make it too?"

"Yes, yes. He's actually sleeping in the other wagon. We managed to escape and we met back up with Yaeva and the others. She told me about all of you and about what Nicholas is doing."

"So, what is this all about?" Sol asked bluntly.

326

"A great deal of things," she replied as she looked down at some cards that she had on her table in front of her. "The truth, forgiveness, evil and even salvation...though I do not know which, if any, will actually happen."

"Dis is eh grea' wase a time," growled the Burgher. "Dees peeple canno' hep us."

"Don't judge by appearances, Cornwall."

"What's he babbling about?"

"He...I...we wish to make you a proposition," Yaeva replied.

"What kind of proposition?" Sol asked, leery of the answer he would receive.

"Dees peeple should bea pu' to death an ley us ge' ba' to da ma'ers et han'."

Yaeva pointed up at the old man. "Shut up, Cornwall. Do not make me tell you again." The old man's face turned bright red with anger, but he didn't say another word.

"Okay, someone better start explaining what's going on here, or else."

"Or else what? What makes you think you are in any position to make demands, young man," Yaeva said, with a malicious tone to her voice.

"Well, for starters we're still alive. The Burgher over there is all in a panic over something, and the fact that this whole charade is going on leads me to believe that you want our help, or you want something from us. Am I right?"

"I knew it was unwise to underestimate you."

"So what is it that you want? Does he think we can do something against that undead army coming this way?"

"No, he thinks you are useless and simply wants to kill you. I, on the other hand, think that you can help us stop it."

"And just why do you think that?"

"It is in the cards," she turned over two more cards from her deck. The first card had a series of skeletons drawn on it, and the other had a bright, shining four-pointed star.

"This is ridiculous," Andrea replied as she stepped out from behind Sol. "We're running out of time. We must all leave, now."

Yaeva looked at Andrea and her jaw dropped wide open. "This can't be." Yaeva stood up. Even though she was only four feet tall, she still stood so she could get a better look at Andrea.

"The rumors are true then," she said quietly. "You really have returned."

"What is she talking about?" Sol asked.

Andrea's head sank and she let out a short sigh. "We don't have time for this nonsense. I am not who you think I am."

"Who does she-"

"Just forget it," Andrea cut him off.

"My dear, you know we cannot dismiss this so easily. Your return is part of this."

"You're from here?" Sol asked, now very confused.

"No."

"Then what is she rambling on about?"

"Everyone here thinks I'm some girl that died a long time ago."

"No," Yaeva replied. "We think you're the reincarnation of Allisandra."

"Whatever. What difference does it make? I'm not her."

Yaeva let out a sigh of exhaustion and sat back down. "Dear, may I ask your name?"

"I'm Andrea."

Yaeva looked deep into Andrea's eyes and held her hands out. Andrea took them. "Andrea. I don't pretend to know how the gods work. I don't know why they do the things they do, but I do know that all this horror started when Allisandra was killed by that monster, Nicholas. Your arrival here now must surely be the gods' way of telling us that a reckoning has come."

"It doesn't matter. We have to get back to the task at hand."

"Dear child," Yaeva replied, "it matters very much. I'm certain that your return has something to do with everything that is going on now."

Everyone watched Yaeva intently as she spoke. Inside the room it was so quiet that Sol could hear his own heart beating like the sound of a drum. Even the rain hitting the roof outside seemed to die down as the old woman held Andrea's hands.

"So does someone want to explain what in the nine hells is going on around here?" Sol interrupted.

Yaeva broke her gaze with Andrea and looked at him and said, "Very well. A long time ago, back in the early days of Nicholas' reign, there was a woman named Allisandra. She was the high priestess of Lila, the goddess of love and nature. As the high priestess, she was a member of the council of elders, who acted as advisors for the King. The council represented the people in front of the King, and this had worked for hundreds of years."

Sol tried listening, but he could feel his eyes start to glaze over and he wasn't sure how long this story might get. "I'm sure this is a very intriguing story, but can we get to the part about the cursing, please?"

Yaeva stopped and raised an eyebrow at Sol, "A wise man knows when he should be patient and listen."

"But a wise man also knows when he doesn't have long until an undead army will start marching into town and killing people."

"Point taken, just bear with me," Yaeva replied.

Sol nodded and allowed her to continue.

"Nicholas got to know Allisandra through the council, and eventually fell in love with her. He was unmarried and needed offspring to continue his family's bloodline. If he continued to rule without an heir, then eventually the council would be forced to pick an heir for him or replace him as king all together. Nicholas was a tyrant even back then and his relationship with the council was strained. He often worried that they would replace him.

He tried many times to woo Allisandra, but she only had eyes for one of his knights, Dominic Ensteele. Dominic was a champion of the kingdom and was loved by all. People would come from all the surrounding villages to watch him in tournaments.

This worried Nicholas, as he heard rumors that if he didn't provide an heir soon, the council would be in favor of replacing him with Dominic. Things grew more desperate for him when he learned that Dominic had asked Allisandra to marry him. Since Allisandra was a member of the council, her marriage to Dominic would definitely cause the council to replace him as king. This caused Nicholas to go mad, and he plotted day and night, searching for ways to retain his power.

Eventually, he came up with a plan. In a rare gesture of kindness, he offered to host the wedding for the young couple. The entire kingdom became enthralled by the marriage of Dominic and Allisandra.

The day of the wedding came. People from all over the kingdom came to watch. All of Allisandra's family was there, as were all of Dominic's, and the entire council of elders. That was when Nicholas launched his plan. While preparations were being made for the wedding, Nicholas had been putting together a secret army of 'enforcers', mercenaries from outside the kingdom led by an evil man named Lucian.

On the day of the wedding, the enforcers quickly dispatched all the council guards as well as all the members of the council. Nicholas led the assault and attacked Dominic. Dominic was a powerful warrior but he was outnumbered by Nicholas and his enforcers and was eventually killed.

With Dominic dead, Nicholas planned to take Allisandra as his wife and force her to give him an heir, but she fled. He chased her as she tried to escape up the ramparts of the castle walls, but when she found that she couldn't escape, she leapt from the wall and fell to her death."

"Okay, so what does any of this have to do with the curse?" Sol said with a yawn.

"I'm getting to that," Yaeva replied. "The terrible events that unfolded that day angered the gods. Lila, in particular, was furious with Nicholas. That night, after everything was done, Lila and Vera appeared to Nicholas. They condemned him for his wickedness and punished him. They twisted and mangled his body, transforming him into a grotesque demon. That way his outward appearance would mirror his horrific soul.

"After that, they cursed him to live that way forever and bound him to this land so that he could never leave."

"Why did they feel the need to keep everyone else here?" Andrea asked. "Because of them, no one can leave this land."

Yaeva stopped and looked at Andrea, apparently confused by her question.

"You know, the demons they created to keep others here too," Andrea explained.

"Those were not summoned by the gods. Those were created by Nicholas himself. After being cursed, he had to live off the souls of the living. For this reason, he did not want his 'cattle' to escape. He summoned the hellhounds to prevent anyone from leaving...except those that have his permission."

Sol saw Andrea close her eyes and take a deep breath as though she was trying to keep herself from choking someone. "That son of a swamp witch!" she growled. "That makes much more sense."

"What's that?" Sol asked.

Andrea's face turned red as she began to speak, "I tried to escape and was attacked by the demons in the forest. Nicholas showed up and allowed them to attack me for some time before he came to help. They ran away upon seeing him. At first I thought they were afraid of him, but he simply dismissed them after he thought I learned my lesson."

Sol became frustrated by the conversation going on. All Yaeva had done so far was tell them the history, but she hadn't seemed to offer any solutions. The things she said so far made sense up to a certain point, but there were still things that didn't seem to connect. He glanced over at the Burgher, who looked bored by the entire conversation and yawned deeply. The man wore the same plain brown clothing as everyone else in the city--clothes that looked like they had been handed down for generations and were void of any color they might have once had. Nobody here wore new clothing or bright colors--except the mystics.

"You...you have permission from the King to leave this land, don't you?" Sol asked, interrupting Andrea's rant. "Neither you or any of the other mystics you travel with dress like the locals, and you certainly don't have the same accent. You actually sound like you're from the empire. Now why is that?"

"Very astute of you, Sol," Yaeva replied. "We...did...have the ability to leave unharmed through the forest. However, after we dropped you off, we attempted to leave again but were unable to. We lost two men and one of our carriages trying to get out of the forest."

"So, why did you come here?"

"We didn't know where else to go. By that time, an ominous cloud had begun to grow above the castle. I could feel there was something evil coming from it, so we didn't want to go there. As fortune would have it, just before we made it to town Tallmoor found us and told us what was going on."

"And what would that be?"

Yaeva began to answer but Tallmoor spoke first. "I was the one who learned what Nicholas is doing. He's got the pieces of that…that thing he's been building, and he plans on using it to destroy the gods."

"Oh, poppycock," Zaroth blurted out. He had been in the back and earlier Sol thought he had seen the old man dozing off from boredom, but he must have snapped out of it because he sounded angry.

"The orb cannot be used that way," Zaroth scoffed at the old woman's explanation. "The orb will not make him strong enough to defeat a god. While it is true that it will make him a little more powerful and allow him to create an army of undead, it won't make him strong enough to break the curse of a god."

"Oh no…" Halistan muttered. Everyone turned to see the horrified look upon the young man's face.

"What?" Sol asked.

"Zaroth is wrong," Halistan stated. "He can use it to destroy the gods."

"Oh, really, how?" Zaroth replied.

"Think about it. The gods derive their power from their worshippers. Well, the twelve false gods do anyway," Halistan corrected himself.

"Skip the religious drivel and get on with it," Zaroth demanded.

"Yes, well, the more worshippers the gods have the more power they wield. That is why they continually have their priests evangelize to others, to bring in more followers. If there is no one alive to worship them, their power wanes severely."

"Damn," cursed Zaroth. "That makes sense. He can't wage a war against the gods directly, so he is going to start a war of attrition. Why didn't I see it before?"

"So," Serieve jumped in, "his plan is to just kill…everything?"

"Simple, but effective, I guess," Sol replied.

"Even we, his faithful servants are not safe," Yaeva replied. "With the power of the orb he no longer has to feed so we are of no use to him. Any of us," she said quietly.

"So what do we do?" Sol asked. "We're all trapped in this damn place and it's only a matter of time before the undead army gets here."

"Dat is why I thin' dis is a wase a' time!" spat the Burgher. "We nee' ta p'pair ta dafen' oursel's."

Yaeva looked up at the Burgher, "Just how long do you think you can hold off an army," she snapped. "Eventually, this town will fall. Our only chance is destroy Nicholas." As she spoke the words her voice became solemn, almost as if she couldn't bear the weight of what she was saying.

"And I take it that you want us to do that?" Sol asked sarcastically.

Yaeva did not reply.

"You can't be serious? And just what do we get out of this deal?"

"We are prepared to pardon your crimes and help you get home," Yaeva replied stiffly, suddenly taking a very businesslike tone.

"Ha! Have you lost your damn mind? We barely got out of there with our lives. There is no way we are going back. I'd rather take my chances with the demons."

"Stopping him is the only way any of us are going to live," Yaeva replied, almost pleading with the younger man.

"I tole ye the'd be a no use ta us," grumbled the Burgher.

"Come on, Oather. Let's get out of here. We'll find our own way out," Sol said as he turned and grabbed Oather by the arm, but Oather pulled back and stood his ground.

"You aren't really considering this, are you?" Sol asked, shocked by Oather's actions.

Oather looked at the Burgher, "Are your people willing to fight for their homes?"

The Burgher nodded, "Aye, dey are. Is dee onley thin dey have in dis worl'"

"Did you not hear her? It'll be you against an entire army!" Sol argued.

"And you will completely pardon our crimes and let us go if we help defend your town?" Oather asked and the Burgher nodded back his confirmation that they would.

"Oather, don't be crazy, this is suicide."

"I know what I'm doing, Sol. I know we cannot defeat Nicholas, but there may be a chance that we can save this town…and…and if I am going to die, I would rather die fighting than die running," Oather finished, looking away from Sol.

Sol looked at each of the others. A deathly stillness had settled upon everyone. The grave situation had everyone at a loss for words.

"So, whether to die fighting an undead army, or die fighting an undefeatable monster. Some choice," Sol spat. "You can all do what you like, but I'm going to find my own way out," he growled as he turned and stormed out of the wagon.

"For once, I actually agree with him," Andrea said.

"As do I," muttered the wizard. They both turned and followed Sol back out into the cold, rainy night.

"All is lost, I fear," muttered Yaeva, lowering her head. As she watched, the cards on the table were blown off by the wind.

## 58. *Tough Decisions*

"They're all fools," Sol muttered under his breath, but loud enough for Andrea to hear as she walked next to him. The rain was pouring down on them hard now. Sol and Andrea walked briskly towards a larger building that looked like it might be an inn. Zaroth followed several paces behind them.

Andrea didn't reply, she just walked silently with Sol as he ranted.

"What kind of choice is that anyway? Fight and die, or fight and die."

Sol wiped the drops running into his eyes away and swept his dark hair aside so he could see. The door to the building was open. Sol walked in first and began shaking the water off him as he looked around for an innkeeper or anyone who might be around. The short hall he stood in opened into a larger reception area to the left, where an elderly man sat upon a stool behind a booth. Next to him stood an elderly woman, dressed in the same drab brownish-gray clothes that seemed to be common in this town. Both had shocked looks upon their faces as they watched the three enter.

At once, the woman turned and exited through a door to their left.

"Ca...ca' I hep ye, sires?" the old man asked.

"Yes, we need rooms."

"O..o', 'C..course."

The old woman that had disappeared a moment before returned through the door carrying dry linens. She went to Andrea first and draped one around her. Andrea thanked her as she shivered from the cold. The woman handed another one to Sol, who used it to wipe his face and dry his hair as best he could. She turned to hand one to Zaroth but stopped suddenly as she realized he was not wet at all. He grinned at her and she slowly stepped away from him, apparently not knowing what to make of him, but not saying anything. She returned to the old man's side as he spoke with Sol.

"We dat be jus' one room, or willja be need'en moe?"

"Three rooms," replied Sol.

"Tha'll be tree bit's."

Sol pulled out his pouch, which was now filled with some of the gold he had taken from the treasure room. It was stuffed with large gold coins, but Sol didn't know how many constituted a bit. He took out one and saw the man's eyes widen, so he went with that.

"That should cover it."

"Y...ye', sire...tha's 'nuff fo ah tree," the old man managed to speak, as he snatched the coin quickly from Sol.

"Hey, wait...I was only wanting to pay for...ah, forget it," Sol tried to argue but was too tired to care. The old man quickly tucked the gold coin away.

"Aneese, plea go an git tree rums redy," the innkeeper asked the woman as she scurried back through the door once again.

"Don't I get any change...?" Sol began to ask, when he heard the large wooden door of the inn open again. Sol turned to see who it was, only to find Serieve, Oather, the elf and the priest trudging into the inn from the rain. They staggered into the reception hall, dripping wet.

"What are you doing here?" Sol asked. "Shouldn't you be preparing to die?"

Oather shot an irritated glare at Sol but held his tongue. Instead, he just stood there dripping water all over the floor.

"No," snapped Serieve, "we came here to get some rest. The army will be here by tomorrow night, and we're going to need our energy to help defend this town."

Serieve approached the old man in the booth. "Cornwall asked us to tell you to give us some rooms."

The old man nodded and pointed back towards the entry hall. "Ple's, go way in the parla' whi' weh p'pare dem for ya," and he left through the doorway.

All of them--Sol, Serieve, and the others--made their way back to the hall, where they saw another open area further down the hall. This was a much bigger room, with several large padded chairs sitting around a wide open stone fire pit in the middle of the room. A good-sized fire burned in the waist-high stone hearth and Sol felt the warmth as soon as he entered.

Approaching the ring of chairs, he saw that they were definitely old and that the padding was very worn. They were wide, with padded arm rests, and sat lower to the ground than most chairs, but as tired as he was, he didn't care how they looked, as long as they were comfortable.

Sol plopped down into the closest one and propped his boots up onto the stone fire pit. He was soon joined by Serieve, Oather, the elf, and the wizard. Sol saw Andrea and the priest enter and come to stand on the other side of the fire from him, even though there were still unused chairs. They seemed to prefer just standing next to the fire instead of sitting.

Andrea stood with her eyes closed, feeling the warmth of the fire. She had her hands stretched out over the pit to warm them, and the linen cloth she had been given was still wrapped around her. Sol watched her as she opened her eyes and stared blankly into the fire. She watched it blaze and pop almost as if she was in a trance. He couldn't help but watch the fire reflect in her eyes as she stood there, at least until he was bothered by the sound of Serieve speaking.

"I can't believe you are such a coward, Sol."

Sol was pulled from his reverie. "I'm just not suicidal, like you," he replied. "I actually like my life, and don't want it to end just yet."

Serieve rolled his eyes as Sol spoke.

"Now you," Sol continued, "I can understand why you are so eager to die. You have no fun in life. Life is just a series of duties that you feel obligated to perform. It's no wonder you want it to be over with so soon."

Serieve's jaw dropped, "I do too have fun!"

"Yeah, of course you do. When was the last time you were with a woman?" Sol asked, turning and looking directly at Serieve.

Serieve was taken aback, almost embarrassed by the question. He tried to speak but nothing came out. He finally managed to spit something out. "Th…that's none of your business, Sol."

Sol sat back in his chair and looked at the fire again, "That's what I thought. You're probably still a virgin."

Serieve's feet hit the ground as he leaned up in his chair to look at Sol. "I…I…what does that have to do with anything?" Sol raised his hand and made a jabbering puppet motion with his fingers as Serieve spoke, infuriating Serieve even more.

"I just happen to think there is more to life than getting drunk every night, sleeping with every whore in town, and doing nothing important with my life!"

"They aren't all whores."

Sol leaned forward in his chair and locked eyes with Serieve. "If you love life so much, why don't you help me find a real way out of here, then go back home and actually do something that would make your father proud, instead of trying to be a stupid knight."

Serieve's eyes lit up as bright as the fire next to him. He drew back and punched Sol. Sol's chair toppled backwards to the ground and dumped him out onto the floor. Serieve jumped up out of his chair, walked over and stood over Sol, waiting for him to get up.

Sol hit the ground hard as he rolled away from the fallen chair. He turned over and looked up to see Serieve standing above him. Sol kicked upwards, hitting Serieve in the groin. Serieve's eyes bulged as Sol's foot hit its mark.

Sol stood up as Serieve began to sink to his knees, his hands darting to his crotch as the pain spread through his stomach. Sol was drawing back to slug the cavalier when he was suddenly jerked backwards and away from Serieve by Oather.

"Stop it!" Oather yelled as he stepped in between the two fighting men. The enormous man's voice sounded as if it made the entire building shudder. Serieve sank to the floor, holding himself. He stared hatefully up at Sol.

"He started it," they said in unison.

"I don't care," Oather growled as he pushed Sol back even further. The light push from the big man forced Sol back two or three paces and nearly knocked him over.

"This isn't helping," Oather said. He leaned down to help Serieve back up into his chair. Oather took Sol's seat and gestured for Sol to sit down on Oather's other side, so the two men would be separated.

Again, silence enveloped the room. Sol slumped back into his chair and looked at the billowing fire. The shades of orange and wisps of yellow danced in front of him and flashed about the dim room. In the far corner opposite where he sat, he saw that the wizard had taken a seat away from everyone else, and remained alone in the dark. He was wearing his hat again…where he hid that thing most of the time, Sol had no idea, but he was wearing it again and had it pulled down over his face.

Kicking his feet back up onto the stone hearth again, he turned towards Oather. "So what should we do?"

Oather didn't reply. His face was stern, completely absent of its typical joyfulness as he stared into the flames.

"Come on, let's hear what you've got," snipped Sol.

"I don't know."

"See," Sol exclaimed. "We don't have a choice. We have to get out of here. As fast as we possibly can."

"Is running always your answer, Sol?"

"Yes," Sol said, grinning. "No sense changing the tried and true."

"Do you really think you can just run away?" asked a deep voice that took Sol by surprise. It came from Zaroth, who had raised his hat. Sol could barely make out the old man's pasty white skin in the firelight.

"Certainly…we just wait until the army makes its way through this town and moves on. Then we'll make our way out behind it."

"You're a fool," Zaroth replied, his voice sinking deep and ominous as he spoke. "You don't get it, do you?" The wizard stood up and walked towards the fire, looking across the flames at Sol.

"The orb doesn't just raise the dead once to create a short term army…" he said slowly, looking in turn into the eyes of Sol, then Oather, Serieve, then the elf, then finally to his side at Andrea and Halistan. "It continuously raises the dead. If you knock a soldier down, it will rise up again and again until you are dead…then you, too, will rise and join them. Don't you understand, this is an impossible army to defeat."

It took a moment for Zaroth's words to sink in. Up until now, Sol hadn't really thought about the undead army. Avoiding it seemed like the easiest solution, but that solution was starting to seem more difficult than he had originally thought.

"I thought I could stop him from activating the device…I just had no idea how powerful he was." Zaroth's voice trailed into a whisper. "I fear that if we face him directly, we will most certainly lose."

Zaroth turned and stepped away from the fire and resumed his seat in the shadows. No one said anything. There didn't seem an easy way out, despite Sol's mind racing to think of a way to do it.

"No," said a voice. Sol jerked up to see who it was and saw Halistan standing in the glow of the fire. The young man clenched his right fist tightly. The fire roared up as one of the logs broke in half. The flames danced up between them. The fire bathed Halistan in light and made him look taller than Sol remembered.

"We can defeat him." Halistan spoke with a certain resolve in his voice which got everyone's attention.

"Just how do you…" Sol began to ask.

"We are going to fight." Halistan's steely gray-blue eyes looked down straight into Sol and pierced right through him. "We don't have any choice but to go back and put a stop to this once and for all."

"That's suicide," exclaimed Sol.

"There is no other way…" Halistan said looking directly at Sol.

"If we fight the army, we'll die for sure. If we try to escape through the forest, we'll die. Our only real choice is to go back and destroy the sphere."

Sol looked at the others, who were all watching Halistan. "What do you want us to do, walk back in through the front gate and announce ourselves? 'Oh, don't mind us, we're here to destroy your new toy.' Do you think he'd just stand by while we went in and hacked that cursed thing to pieces?"

"No," interrupted Zaroth. "You cannot touch it. Now that it is activated, it cannot be touched by mortal hands; otherwise it'll destroy you instantly."

"Great. Any other good news you'd like to share with us?" Sol asked.

"It can be taken apart, but only by magic…you must remember, it was created by a god. Only the most powerful beings can put it together, much less use it. So taking it apart is no small feat."

"This is impossible," whispered Khu-Rá. "We can't do this."

"Yes, we can," Halistan replied. "I know the rest of you do not believe in God, or even the Powers, but believe me when I tell you, we were not brought here by accident, and these people need our help. In their hearts, they are not bad people; they have just been the unfortunate victims of an ill-begotten curse, imposed by petty false gods who wanted to chastise the deeds of one evil man."

"What concern is it of ours, kid?" Sol snapped back. "We don't owe them or anyone, anything."

"I think you're wrong, Sol," Halistan replied, staring down and straight into Sol's eyes. "You, most of all, probably owe a great deal to the kindness of others. I do not know you, but something tells me that there have been others in your life that were there for you when no one else was. I don't pretend to know what kind of life you've had, but by the experience I see in your eyes, I would venture to guess it hasn't been an easy one. The fact that you're here means that someone…somewhere was there for you, picking you up when this world dealt you an insurmountable blow."

Sol didn't answer the young man nor turn from his gaze.

Halistan looked slowly around the room, "Those…those are the people we are fighting for. If this menace gets beyond this land, it will be those people that pay the price for our inaction. And I, for one, am not going to let that happen. Not today, not ever."

Halistan stood up straight and held his injured hand close again. The cloth wrapping his hand was now soaked in blood, but he didn't seem to notice. The fire died down and a restless quiet befell the room as the glow of the fire diminished slightly. The only sound came from the occasional pop and crackle of the fire and the muffled sound of rain falling upon the inn.

Sol stood and pulled the hood of his cloak over his head and marched out of the room, down the hall, and out into the rain. Oather sat up to follow, but Serieve grabbed his arm. "Let him go," Serieve said.

## 59. *Unyielding Compromise*

A bright flash of lightning streaked across the sky, followed shortly by the boom of thunder. It was still raining, but not as hard now. It was just sprinkling, which seemed to be about the best one could hope for in this land. As soon as Sol made it a few paces away from the building and into the street before he stepped in mud that went up to his ankle. With a jerk, he pulled his foot free and threw the hood of his cloak back to look up at the clouded sky.

Sol ground his teeth together as he walked. Behind him he heard the door open. Without even having to turn around, he knew it was Oather.

"You know," Sol said, "you really should get yourself a cloak. It's pretty wet here."

Oather came to a stop at Sol's right. He crossed his big arms as he too, looked up at the sky. "I like the feel of the weather on my face."

"You must absolutely love this place then," Sol replied. The two of them looked up at the clouds stirring above them, pushing to and fro with the wind.

"You know he's right," Oather said. "It's only a matter of time before that army reaches Tyric."

Sol didn't reply. He looked up at the sky and let his mind drift.

"Sol," Oather said again, trying to get his attention.

"Huh?" Sol said, dragging his mind back to the here and now.

"So, what do you think, Sol?"

"About what?"

"About-"

"You know, Oather, I was just thinking back about that treasure room," Sol said. "Even though we really weren't there long, I still got enough of a look around to bet that the old king there has enough to buy an entire fleet of ships."

Oather looked at Sol blankly.

"Seriously, think about it," Sol said again. He turned and grabbed Oather by the shoulders and looked him in his eyes. "If we did help these fools get back into the castle, they could attempt to stop the king, and that would at least create enough of a diversion to grab another chest or two of gold and head out."

"What?" Oather pulled away from Sol's grip and stepped back. "This is bigger than the treasure, Sol. What about the lives of the people of this town...what about the people back home. All of whom will die?"

"We're hundreds....maybe thousands of leagues, from there. Do you really think that army will make it all the way there? Come on, Oather, don't be so gullible."

Oather looked sternly down at Sol.

"Come on, Oather. This is easy money. We help them get back into the castle, the wizard can do whatever it is he needs to do to deactivate the sphere, and then we get the gold. We'd finally be able buy our own ship!"

Oather remained unconvinced. He stared at Sol, straight-faced.

"We'd also have enough to fix up the *Duck* and pay Tanner and Gretchen back," Sol said slyly.

Oather's eyes widened momentarily. Then he let out a sigh, "No, Sol...not this time." Oather's head drooped and he closed his eyes as he spoke.

"I can't help you this time, Sol." He took another step back. "I'm going to do my best to make a stand here and help these people."

"What? You can't be serious. Didn't you hear Zaroth? You can't beat this army! If you destroy one of them, it will just get back up again...the best you can hope for is to stay out of their way."

"I have to do what I think is right...and for our sakes, I just hope that Zaroth is able to destroy it before the army destroys us." Oather turned and walked away from Sol, returning to the inn.

Sol stood there and watched Oather walk back inside. He was completely astounded that Oather rejected his idea. He was caught somewhere between confusion and anger towards Oather at that moment.

"Oh, who needs you," he yelled as Oather re-entered the building. "If you want to die that badly, then go ahead!"

He looked up at the starless sky and the rain began to come down harder. Sol flipped up his hood and turned to walk back in, when out of the door walked Andrea.

"You need some fresh air too?" he asked her, a tone of anger still in his voice.

"Of sorts," she replied, "Are you going to help them?"

Sol was quiet for a moment as he thought about her question. "That depends."

"On?"

"On you."

"Why me?"

"I have a plan," he said, "but it relies on a few things, and you are one of them."

"How so?"

"It involves creating a diversion for the King as we make our way back into the castle."

"I see. And you want to use me as bait then?" It was more of a statement than a question. Sol stepped closer to her. She looked him straight in the eyes. Sol stared back into the young woman's deep hazel eyes.

"You could look at it that way." He smiled down at her. "I prefer to look at it more as the easiest of the tasks ahead of us."

"Why do you think it's so easy?"

"You're a beautiful woman, he's a man," Sol replied quickly, a wide grin spreading across his face. "You just walk in and talk to him, and I'm sure he'll melt in your delicate little hands."

"Until he loses his very short temper, and decides to kill me."

"No, no…from what I gathered so far, it sounds like he gets his power from that sphere thing. Once we destroy it, he'll be weak enough that we can kill him and we all go back home."

Andrea stood there, a less than satisfied look upon her face.

"Trust me, you will be the safest one of any of us. I give you my word."

Andrea looked up as she considered his plan, then looked away, turning away from him slightly. Sol stood there, watching her, gauging her reaction. She hadn't said no yet, so that was a good sign.

"Sooo," she began, "after this is over, how much treasure do you plan on taking back with you?"

"All of it," Sol replied without thinking, and cursed himself after he realized what he had said.

Andrea whipped around and stared him in the eye with a smile on her face, "I want half."

"Half? Have you lost your mind?"

"I think it's fair. I'll have the most dangerous job...you want me to walk right into the lion's den and distract him while you work. I think that is worth at least half."

"Five percent."

"Ha! I don't think so!" she spat back, "Forty percent."

"Okay, okay, I'll be fair...ten percent."

"Your plan is dead without me. I won't take anything less than a third," she scoffed.

A devilish grin crept onto Sol's face. "Okay, I'll give you twenty percent, and you have to give me a kiss."

Andrea's eyes flashed and her teeth clenched together. Then, suddenly, her features softened as she looked up at Sol. She smiled and looked deep into his eyes. Without saying a word, she reached up and slowly moved one of her arms around his neck. The other hand brushed his face as she drew closer to him. He offered no resistance as she took his hand and lifted it up and brushed it across her cheek, closing her eyes as she did so.

Her skin felt nice and soft. Sol loved the feel of a woman's skin and his body relaxed as she slid her body closer to his. Sol was in heaven. She was close enough that he could smell her, and she smelled wonderful. He opened his mouth, as her lips neared his own. He felt her soft and delicate hands slide through his fingers. She slowly took hold of his index finger and brought it closer to her lips.

Then she gripped his hand fiercely and bent his fingers back, nearly pressing them flat against the back of his hand. Intense pain surged through his hand and up his arm which forced Sol to drop to his knees. His eyes shot open to see the young woman staring down at him menacingly.

Her other hand grabbed his hair and she bent over so that her face was right in front of him. "Now I'll take fifty percent, and if you ever think about touching me, I will slit your throat and bath in your warm blood." Her voice took on a sweetly evil tone as she spoke to him.

"Do we understand each other?" she asked. Sol shook his head yes and she released his finger.

Sol shook his hand, trying to quell the pain that was still coursing through it. He stood back up as Andrea took a step back away from him and grinned.

"All you had to do was say no," he complained.

"I think it would be best if we kept this little…arrangement to ourselves, don't you?" she asked him, her voice returning to its previous, more innocent tone.

"Yeah. They might want a share as well."

When Sol and Andrea re-entered the parlor room, Oather had once again taken a seat next to Serieve and the two were talking. Zaroth was off in the corner, sitting in the shadows like he seemed to like to do. The boy was re-wrapping his wounded hand and the elf was standing near the fire, warming his hands.

They all stopped talking and looked at Sol as he and Andrea walked towards the fire. When he reached the fire pit, Sol stuck his hands out to warm them. He looked around at all of his companions and stopped when he made eye contact with Zaroth.

"Can you disable that…thing?" he asked.

"Yes," Zaroth replied, "but it takes time…and I certainly can't do it with Nicholas there."

"Don't worry about that," Sol said. "We'll take care of him." He looked to the elf standing across from him. "What about you? Can you help us, or do you want to die defending this town with these two?"

Khu-Rá thought for a moment, "I owe that young man my life," he said looking at Serieve, "My place is here, standing with him."

"Your choice." Sol looked at Halistan. "How about you, kid?"

Halistan looked up at him as he finished tying the bandage around his hand. "I will go with you. I am of little help in a battle, but I might be able to help get us inside the castle undetected."

"That is fine with me. This is what we're going to do…"

## 60. Backroom Deals

"Chop, Chop, Clank," were the first sounds that Sol heard as he stirred from his slumber. At first he thought he had a hangover, but he was certain that he didn't drink before he went to bed.

He rolled over onto his side to see out the window. People were scrambling about on the street below, carrying wood and tools and clamoring about making all sorts of noise.

He heard a familiar voice and saw Serieve directing several men to take a large plank down the street. Sol adjusted his view to try and see what was further down but couldn't see where they were going with it. It seemed the town was alive with motion, setting up barricades.

Sol sat up and felt on the floor for his cloak. After finding it, he rummaged around looking for the inside pocket that held his flask. He found it, popped the cork and took a swig. It was empty. Swearing under his breath, he realized that he must have actually drank it all before going to bed.

What a way to start a day, he thought, and headed out to see how things were going.

"You there," Serieve called to two men pushing a wagon. "Take that wagon to the end of the road, where they are building the barricade." The men turned towards the end of the road and began pushing the wagon through the mud again.

Another man approached Serieve, "Sar...da elf sen' meh ta tell ya dat dey ahr done barraca'in da eas' sie a town."

"Thank you," Serieve replied. "Let him know that if he has any people he can spare to send them this way. We need to finish the ditch and blockades on this side."

The man nodded and headed back the way he came.

"Look at you, bein' all productive. You should have woken me; I would have helped." Sol smiled widely as he approached Serieve.

"No, you wouldn't, Sol," Serieve replied as he directed more men carrying shovels to where the blockade was being erected.

"Okay, you're probably right, but it's the thought that counts, right?"

Serieve ignored Sol and walked towards the rest of the working men and women at the end of the road. Sol followed close behind him. They neared the end of the road, where it met the edge of the town. Several dozen men were digging a massive trench and planting very rough spears made from split wooden boards. The spears were little more than thin boards cut at a sharp angle to make a point, then stuck in the side of the trench to make a barricade. Behind it men stacked anything and everything they could rip from the insides of the surrounding buildings to make a wall.

"You realize, of course, that these will be entirely useless against that horde we saw last night, right?"

Serieve glanced hatefully at Sol, which made Sol grin.

"Also, that trench…"

"I don't want to hear it, Sol. If you're not here to help, then go away," Serieve growled.

Sol stood there silently, doing his best to look hurt, but failing miserably.

"Fine. Where's Oather?"

"On the north side, trying to do the same thing we are here, set up defenses," Serieve replied as he helped several men move some furniture onto the junk pile blockade.

Sol turned and started back down the road towards the Inn, where he veered right, in his quest to find Oather. He rounded the corner and his quest came to an end sooner than he thought. He nearly walked head first into his friend. Oather was at the front of a train of men carrying large planks of wood. Oather himself carried a couple of beams of wood that looked like they had come from the frame of a building, one beam on each shoulder. The men following him had a single beam carried by teams of two men each.

"There you are. I've been looking all over for you."

Oather grunted as he set down the large beams of wood. "Take those to Serieve and see if they can use them," he commanded the other men. They continued on, leaving Sol and Oather behind.

"Making any progress?" Sol asked. Oather wiped some sweat off his face, then looked back down at Sol.

"Some," he replied. "Probably a lot more if you helped us."

"We both know I don't do well with manual labor."

Oather didn't look amused.

"Well, yes," Sol shifted. Oather didn't say anything; he simply kept looking down at Sol.

"Come on, Oather," Sol's tone went from jovial to stern. "This is madness!"

Oather stood there.

"You know you can't win. Come with me to the castle," Sol said, almost pleading with his friend.

"And what? Face that monster again?"

"It's certainly better odds than facing that army."

"I don't think so, Sol," Oather replied with a sigh. "Thanks, but I'd rather take my chances here, where I know what I'm up against."

"Oather," Sol growled, like he was disciplining a child, "I don't want you staying here. If we can't stop this thing, then at least if you're with us, we can escape. Here...here you're trapped."

Oather remained quiet for a moment then cleared his throat and spoke up. "I know, Sol." He leaned over and grabbed the first massive wooden beam and lifted it upon his shoulders, then he grabbed the second.

Sol stood there watching his friend, grinding his teeth as Oather went on defiantly with his work. After balancing the planks on his shoulders Oather stepped past Sol and made his way down around the corner towards Serieve.

"Fine," Sol yelled as he walked into the street behind Oather. "It's your life, throw it away if you like."

Oather ignored Sol as he continued down the road.

Sol looked around and saw that he was standing in front of the Inn, again, and decided that he needed a drink. He entered the building and stormed his way straight back to the sitting room they had been in the night before. Sol walked in and this time there was no fire in the pit. The drapes were open, letting in light, making the room look completely different than it had when they first arrived. He hadn't even realized the room had windows last night.

Sol plopped down into one of the fire pit chairs, kicked his feet upon the hearth and tilted the whole chair back to rest on the rear two legs to a point where he was comfortable. He dug around in his cloaks inside pockets for his pipe and put it in his mouth, unlit.

"Where's a damn wizard when you need one?" Sol growled rhetorically, under his breath.

"They're never around when you really need them," replied a voice off to Sol's left. The response took Sol by such surprise that he inadvertently kicked and tipped his entire chair backwards, making him fall onto the ground.

Sol jumped up to see Zaroth sitting in one of the other chairs pulled over next to the window. The enigmatic old man was sitting and staring out of the window, puffing on a pipe of his own.

"How…what…?" Sol looked back and forth from the doorway to where the wizard sat.

"I like my privacy," Zaroth said as he watched Sol regain his composure. "I find a lot of times that it's easiest to be left alone if people don't know you're there."

"Well, you shouldn't sneak up on people like that."

"I didn't sneak up on you, you came in after me." Zaroth waved to Sol. "Come, have a seat. We must talk."

Sol looked quizzically at the seasoned wizard and cautiously pulled another chair away from the stone hearth towards the window and across from Zaroth.

"Talk?" Sol asked.

"Yes, there is much to discuss."

"Like what?" Sol sat down and eyed the old man, putting the unlit pipe back into his mouth.

"Arrangements."

"What kind of 'arrangements'?"

Zaroth took out his pipe and let go a puff of smoke that took the shape of a dragon and flapped its wings and flew away from him and flew about the room before finally disintegrating into a wispy little cloud. Sol watched the enchanted smoke, trying to contain any amazement he might have been showing. Zaroth leaned forward and looked Sol in the eyes. Sol snatched his attention away from the dragon and looked back at the wizard.

"Why are you really agreeing to this foolish mission?" Zaroth asked.

Sol sat there for a moment, looking the old man in the eyes, gauging him before answering. "I think you know, or you wouldn't be asking me."

"True," replied Zaroth, leaning back into his chair again. "Men like yourself are rarely hard to decipher."

"Hey, what's that supposed to mean?"

Zaroth ignored his objection. "How do you plan on getting the treasure back to the Empire?"

Sol actually hadn't thought that far in advance. Up to this point he had been more concerned with staying alive than anything.

"We're a very good distance from our land and by the looks of the fortifications these feeble-minded people are building, there won't be enough wood left for any kind of cart, and you can forget about getting these people to let you have a horse."

Sol sat there quietly. He wasn't sure how to respond. He didn't want to let on he hadn't figured that part out yet, but he had to say something.

"Sah," Sol heard from his right, which interrupted his contemplation of the wizard's words. It was the innkeeper's wife; he couldn't remember her name.

"Sah, whadja lie sum'n ta drin?" she asked in that gruff dialect of the townspeople. Fortunately, Sol could understand well enough to know what she was asking.

"Oh…yes…ale."

"An yew," she said looking at Zaroth who just held up his hand signaling he was content. Without another word she turned and headed out of the room.

"Hadn't thought that far ahead, had you?" Zaroth asked confidently.

Sol sat there in his chair, staring at the wizard silently. He was mildly frustrated by his lack of foresight, and even more so by having it pointed out by Zaroth. Moments drifted by and the old man went back to looking through the window at the townsfolk who were working away to defend their miniscule town. The wizard let out another puff of smoke that took the form of dwarf, then another, larger puff that resembled a troll which began to chase the dwarf around in circles before dissipating into thin wisps of nothingness.

"Why are you asking me this?" Sol replied, "I can't imagine you'd be discussing this with me out of the goodness of your heart."

Zaroth looked back at him, expressionless.

"What are you proposing?" Sol asked.

Zaroth removed his pipe and smiled at the young man. "I knew you'd understand me."

"Just spit it out, old man."

"I want that sphere."

"Not going to happen, grandpa," Sol scoffed. "We're not taking it away from one madman just to give it to another."

"If you want my help, that's my price. You can have all the gold, but the sphere is mine."

"What do you want with that thing?"

"Let's just say I'm a collector of sorts. I've been looking for that particular object for quite some time," Zaroth replied, taking another puff from his pipe.

"Well, you can't have it. It's far too powerful for anyone to have."

"I agree, and I don't need all of it, just pieces of it."

"Why is that?"

"I want to study it. It's only a threat when it's completely assembled. If even just one piece is missing, it cannot be activated."

Sol sat there, contemplating the old man's words silently. The old woman returned with a single mug which she handed to Sol. He took it almost by instinct, because he was so deep in thought he didn't consciously realize she was there.

She turned and left as Sol took a sip of the ale. The taste shocked him back to reality as he winced before drinking down the concoction. It tasted awful, and it was warm, but at least it was ale. Setting the mug down on a nearby table, he sat up, leaning towards Zaroth.

"Just one piece," Sol bargained, "and you help us get the treasure back to Tyric."

Zaroth exhaled another puff of smoke. This one did not take any whimsical form; it just drifted away from the old man as he stared at Sol.

"For each piece you help me acquire, I will transport you and one bag of gold back to your home."

"Deal." Sol smiled as though he'd made the best deal in history.

Zaroth leaned forward smiling, "I think we have an adequate arrangement, my friend." The old wizard raised his hand above Sol's pipe and sprinkled imaginary dust onto the pipe, lighting it for him. Sol took a puff, which he didn't expect as he hadn't loaded any tobacco into it yet. He smiled and nodded his thanks to the old man.

"I shall be here when you have prepared yourself and the others for our departure tonight," Zaroth said, his gaze returning to the work going on outside the window. Sol stood, taking another deep drink from the mug. His face contorted into an almost painful look as he finished it off. He set it down and began to walk out of the room. Then he suddenly stopped and turned halfway back to the old man.

"The smoke...how do you...."

"Morphing powder," Zaroth replied. From out of nowhere, he revealed a tiny cloth pouch and tossed it to the young man. Sol caught it and opened it.

"It's a formula taught to young apprentice wizards as more of an amusement than anything," the old man said as Sol got a bit on the tip of his finger and looked at it.

"Sprinkle some into your pipe and think of an image. It requires a lot of concentration so I doubt it'll be much use to you, but go ahead and try it sometime."

Sol disregarded Zaroth's comment, but it certainly didn't help his mood after talking to Oather. The young man was turning to leave when in walked Andrea and Halistan. They seemed to be snickering about something, but stopped immediately when they encountered Sol. The young man had new dressings on his wound, but he was still clutching his hand to his side.

He looked at Andrea sternly, "Are you two ready to leave?"

"No, but we can be soon," she replied. "Are we changing our plans and leaving early?"

"Yes, get what you need and meet me here. Let's get this over with."

## 61. Saying Good-Bye

Halistan returned to the parlor after getting his things and saw Andrea sitting near Zaroth. Halistan didn't know why, but he didn't trust the old wizard and wasn't particularly fond of him sitting near Andrea. She watched people working hard outside. He walked towards her, looking out the window to see if there was anything specific that she might be watching.

As he approached her, he heard several others enter the room. Halistan turned and saw that it was Sol, followed by the Burgher and another man that Halistan didn't know.

"This is Vego," Sol said. "Yaeva has instructed him to help us get back into the castle."

"Da, I can help you get back in, but I cannot set foot inside myself."

Sol looked to Halistan, "Are we ready to go?"

"Yes," Halistan replied, but then looked to the other two, making sure he hadn't responded incorrectly for the others, but they seemed ready as well. "Yes, we're ready to go."

"A'ight, let's go," Sol said as he gestured for them to follow him. He walked out in front of the Burgher and Vego. Halistan followed them outside, where five horses awaited them, all saddled and ready.

"See," Sol said, looking at Zaroth, who was just exiting the Inn. "We've got horses." Zaroth didn't reply, he simply walked to the nearest steed and got on. Vego took one of the lead horses, and due to his weight, had a little trouble getting up onto the saddle. Halistan silently felt sorry for the horse, having to carry a man of that girth.

Sol grabbed the reigns of his dark brown mare and kicked it lightly in the flanks to spur it to a trot. Halistan did the same, as did the other others. They made their way towards the blockade that Serieve was almost done constructing.

Sol stopped short of the barricade and looked down at Serieve. Oather and Khu-Rá were also there, helping to put the finishing touches on their wall of wood and junk. Serieve's shirt was covered in mud and sweat. He stuck the shovel into the ground and looked up at Sol.

"Good luck, my friend."

Sol extended an arm down towards Serieve, who accepted it. The two locked arms, "Save it for yourselves, you'll need it. We've got the easy job."

"I'll be lucky if you can actually do your part."

"Hey, elf," Sol called to Khu-Rá. "Keep an eye on these two. No telling what chaos they'll cause with me not here to stop them."

Khu-Rá acknowledged Sol's words with a simple nod.

Serieve looked to Halistan. "Did you get to those barrels as I requested?"

Halistan was momentarily confused before he seemed to remember what Serieve was talking about.

"Yes, they are done and ready to be used. Oather stacked them this morning."

Sol looked at Oather. Oather looked Sol back in the eyes but kept a stern look upon his face. "You watch over these guys too."

Oather replied with a grunt and a nod.

"Sure you don't want to change your mind?"

"No, I'm going to stay and fight," Oather replied. "Just do us the favor of working quickly."

"Will do," Sol replied, extending his arm to Oather. The big man clasped arms with his friend briefly before Sol withdrew and gripped the reigns of his horse.

"Let's head out," Sol ordered and spurred his horse into a gallop.

"Wait," Oather called out and everyone stopped and looked back at the big man.

"Do you have a weapon?" Oather asked Halistan.

"My faith will defend me."

Oather drew a dagger from his boot and tried to give it to the priest, but Halistan held his hand up to decline.

"Priests are not permitted to use blades."

"Why not?"

"They are instruments designed to murder, and we are forbidden to murder."

Oather looked baffled momentarily before walking over to his pack that was sitting near the blockade. He picked up the mace that he had stolen from the treasure room and brought it to Halistan.

"Take this."

"I cannot take this."

"Don't think of this as a weapon. It's not designed to kill; it's more…more of a giant meat tenderizer."

Halistan wasn't sure how to respond to the big man.

"Please," Oather said. "It would make me feel better knowing you at least had something."

Halistan gave in and accepted the gift from Oather and thanked him.

"Okay, we've wasted enough time," Sol barked as he turned his horse to head out of town, followed by Vego, Andrea, the wizard and finally Halistan.

In moments they were heading off into the distance. Serieve, Oather and Khu-Rá all stood there and watched until the others were no longer in sight.

As the village slowly disappeared into the distance, Andrea rode up next to Sol.

"Do you think we'll ever see them again?" she asked.

"Nope."

## 62. Into the Fire

"This way," Vego shouted to the others riding behind him. They rode through some of the dense, wooded lands of the realm on trails that would have been undetectable by even the most skillful rangers. To find them, one would just have to know they were there, and it was obvious that Vego did.

The sun set quickly and it was dark again…a state that seemed to fit this dead land. Sol followed Vego closely but each passing moment made it harder to see him. Unfortunately, they made more noise than Sol wanted, but he hoped that their speed would help counteract that.

Sol glanced back at the others who followed him, making sure they hadn't been lost. They had been riding for what seemed like hours and he was beginning to wonder if they were getting close.

Vego deftly whipped through a small clearing in the woods and pulled his horse to an abrupt stop on the other side. Sol stopped almost as suddenly to avoid running into the mystic, followed closely by Andrea, Zaroth and Halistan.

"What's going on? Why'd we stop?" Halistan whispered.

"Shhh."

The four of them sat quietly upon their horses. Sol closed his eyes as he listened to the night. Though it could not have been heard whilst they were riding, now that they had stopped, Sol could hear the sound of the legions of undead in the distance. Dry bones against rock, ancient and rusted armor clanking together as the horde progressed outward from the castle. The undead soldiers walked in unison, which made an ominous beat. If death were a sound, Sol thought, this is what it would sound like.

Sol dismounted, followed by Vego. Andrea and Halistan also began to dismount, but Sol held his hand up to stop them. Sol and the mystic walked out of the clearing towards the edge of the forest. They kept just inside the wood line in order to remain concealed while they watched the army make its way along the road leading away from the castle. A long line of glowing orange-red eyes was all that they could see, but it twisted back and forth all the way up to the castle gates in a never-ending procession.

"Look," Vego said, pointing to a small group of undead that had broken off from the main line and marched towards a farm some distance from the road. Sol watched as the complement of undead soldiers neared the homestead. They made no attempt to conceal themselves as they approached. Several made their way to the front and kicked in the door of the home while others smashed an axe through the window. There was a scream from inside as the skeletons overtook the home.

"We've got to help them!" said a voice that took Sol by surprise. It was Halistan, and he was rising to take off towards the house. Sol grabbed the younger man by the shirt and jerked him back.

"They're already dead," Sol growled. "What are you doing here? You were supposed to stay with 'what's her name'."

"You were taking too long, so she sent me to find you."

Another shriek resounded from the house as a young woman managed to dash out of the home, followed by several undead warriors in close pursuit. Halistan attempted to jerk from Sol's grip, but Sol held him tight. Halistan glanced back at Sol with a hateful stare.

"Let me go, Sol!"

"If you go, you'll expose us all," Sol replied, gripping the young man's shirt even tighter. Halistan turned back around just in time to see the woman get struck down by one of the skeletal soldiers. Her lifeless body slumped to the ground as the soldiers hovered over her remains.

The soldiers turned and marched back towards the home. Inside, lights flickered more intensely. Then fire erupted from one of the windows and traveled up to the thatch roof, catching it ablaze.

Halistan was still watching the poor woman who had been slaughtered when he saw her stir.

"Sol, she's alive," he whispered desperately.

The woman's lifeless body turned onto its side and she began to stand up.

"We have to go rescue her."

"Look closer," Sol replied grimly.

As the woman rose to her feet, she turned around--and her eyes glowed with the same light as those of the other undead. She walked back towards the road, joining the ranks of the other soldiers.

Halistan stared in horror, his mouth open in disbelief.

"We must be going," Sol said as he returned to their horses. Halistan stood there watching until Vego patted him on the shoulder.

Sol approached the clearing where Andrea and Zaroth waited.

"What did you see?" Andrea asked him.

"Trouble."

"What's that supposed to mean?"

Vego and Halistan emerged from the shadows and remounted their horses after Sol.

"He means they are unstoppable," Halistan said with a sigh. "With every person they kill, their numbers grow."

"Come on, let's go," Sol ordered, pulling the reins of his horse away from the direction of the oncoming army.

"Wait," Andrea said, "I think this is where we should part ways."

"No, we should wait until we are all closer," Halistan argued.

"She's right," Sol told him. "If we get much closer before she leaves us, the king will know for certain that she was not alone."

"How do we know that she won't be cut down like the people we just saw, Sol?"

Sol didn't reply, but Vego did.

"If there is anyone who's safe from that horde, it's her…he wants her, alive."

Halistan looked as if he wanted to contest the issue but no words left his lips. Andrea spurred her horse closer to Halistan's and looked him in the eyes.

"I'll be fine," she said to him. She stared at him reassuringly for a brief moment, before pulling the reins on her horse to guide it towards the road.

"Hold on, I have something you need to take with you." Halistan reached out and grabbed her by the arm. He quickly unpinned the small pendant he had on his collar. He held it out to her and she took it from him.

She looked at it and saw a small sun engraved on a metal disk.

"It's not much," Halistan said, "but I spent most of the night blessing it and it should help protect you. If it works, most of the undead soldiers should keep their distance from you. I don't know how long the enchantments I placed on it will last, so....do be careful."

Andrea pinned it to her shirt. "Thank you."

"Okay, time is short," Sol said. "Wait here for us to leave first. Give us to the count of one hundred before you leave the forest in case they come looking for us. I want as much distance between us as possible before you make yourself known."

Andrea nodded. Sol turned his horse away and headed further into the dense woods, followed closely by the other men.

## 63. Parting Ways

"One hundred," Andrea finished counting. She looked into the night sky, which was overcast and dark. Some moonlight was able to pierce the clouds, just barely enough to see by.

Without the others, she felt more alone than she had since she had arrived in this dreadful place. Pulling the reins of her horse, she spurred it into walking out of the forest. When she reached the edge of the woods, she could see the undead army marching on the road before her. They didn't seem to notice her at all. She urged the horse further out into the open. Her steed neighed and fought against her commands.

"Whoa, it's all right," she whispered to the horse. It calmed down, but still seemed reluctant to go any further. After she gave it a light pat on its neck, it finally did as she wanted. With some coaxing she managed to get the mare to walk closer to the road, until she was close enough to smell the dust and decay of the corpses walking in front of her.

Taking one final step, she spurred the horse onto the road itself. As she did so, the legions stopped and looked at her. They split and allowed her to pass through their ranks. Andrea's heart began to race as the undead soldiers stared at her with their glowing eyes and wide open mouths.

If it hadn't been for the distinct lack of facial features on most of their bony faces, she would have sworn they looked as if they wished for nothing more than to rip her from the saddle and kill her. Her hand reached for the Charm that Halistan had given her, and it comforted her somewhat. She breathed a sigh of relief and gripped it tightly as she forced the horse to begin walking down the road, right through the ranks of undead marching past her in the opposite direction.

## 64. Sneaking In

Vego took the lead ahead of Sol as they continued to make their way through the woodlands. The closer they got to the castle, the harder the paths were to follow. They were forced to a walking pace as their horses struggled with their footing through the forest.

Halistan looked up at the sky as they made their way. The dark cloud which spread out from the castle was directly above them now. The cloud seemed to assault the sky, pushing back the other clouds that stood in its path.

Halistan felt weaker under the cloud; as if invisible hands choked him more and more the closer they got to the castle. His hand throbbed again and reminded him that they had barely escaped the castle with their lives, and now they were voluntarily going back into that frightful place.

"This way," Vego called from the lead, as he led them down a ravine that wound around the side of the mountain. They followed closely behind him, their way lit only by the many bolts of lightning streaking through the sky in all directions.

They made their way to the cliff face on the side of the mountain opposite the main road to the castle gates. Vego stopped near a boulder and got off his horse.

"We're here."

"Where?" Sol asked skeptically.

"This…this is the entrance."

Sol looked around, "I don't see anything."

"You're not supposed to," replied Zaroth. "It's enchanted to look like a rock."

"Oh…I knew that."

After they all dismounted and readied themselves for the ascent through the mountain, Vego took the reins and led the horses away from the boulder. When he was a few paces away, he slapped the back end of one of the horses hard. The horse neighed loudly and took off, followed by the other three horses.

The commotion got Sol's attention as he whipped around to see what was going on.

"What in the nine hells do you think you're doing?"

Vego walked back to the boulder, in front of Sol, "We don't need them where we're going and if they stay here, his majesty might see them and know we are coming."

"We're still going to need them when we leave, you imbecile!"

Vego did not acknowledge Sol's response. Instead he turned away and walked towards the boulder. Without any hesitation, he walked into the boulder and vanished.

"Oh," said Zaroth, seemingly surprised. "That was simpler than I expected."

"What? Did you think the boulder was going to move or something?" Halistan asked.

"I wasn't sure. I expected at least a password or something. I don't know if I would entrust the safety of my tower to a mere mirage."

Inside the secret passage, everything was pitch black. Halistan stepped forward and bumped into a tall robed figure, which he assumed was Zaroth. He heard Vego's voice as he grumbled something and felt his way around. It took a moment, but Halistan heard the sound of metal clanking and scraping against stone.

"Ah," he heard Vego mumble. Then he saw a couple of bright flashes as sparks hit the ground. He heard Vego strike the flint several more times. Then all of a sudden light filled the passage and Vego stood up holding a lantern. There was a second lantern on the ground next to Vego. Sol reached down and picked it up and lit it from Vego's.

Sol held the lantern up to allow more light to illuminate the passageway. It was an ornately carved tunnel that led to intricately cut steps leading upwards and curving gently to the left.

"This was designed as a royal escape route in the event the castle was ever taken," Vego said.

On each side were alcoves filled with suits of armor that decorated the passage. They seemed to be an older style of armor than the ones inside the castle, Halistan noticed.

"Let's go," Sol ordered.

"I can take you to the entrance of the catacombs but no further," Vego said. "If I step one foot inside the castle, the king will know I am there, so I must not go in."

"Is the King's power over you that strong?" Halistan inquired; interested in just how in touch Nicholas was with the mystics. "Can he sense your very presence?"

Vego began to get short winded walking up the steps, and didn't answer right away. "Something like that, my young friend."

"Aye," Sol said. "Just take us as far as you can. We can make it the rest of the way ourselves."

Sol and Vego took the lead and continued the ascent. Halistan waited for Zaroth, who was a few steps back. Halistan clutched his arm close to this body, as his hand had once more begun to throb tremendously.

"Is it hurting again?" Zaroth asked, with little sign of emotion in his voice.

"Yes," Halistan replied. "It seems that the closer we get, the more it aches."

"That's what happens when you are burned with hellfire," replied Zaroth coldly. "It lives in the wound forever and increases in strength when you approach an evil source of magic. Personally, I'm surprised that it didn't consume you completely."

Halistan couldn't help but wonder what Zaroth meant by that.

"The few unlucky individuals I've ever seen burned with hellfire died instantly. You're very fortunate."

"I don't know if I'd see it that way," Halistan replied.

"Well, if it makes you feel any better, eventually it will consume you and you'll die."

That definitely didn't make Halistan feel any better.

## 65. *Ominous Approach*

Andrea managed to coax her steed up the serpentine road that led to the gates of the castle. Undead soldiers passed her on both sides, which made her horse very skittish. While most of the soldiers appeared to be human skeletons, she would occasionally see a beast that she couldn't identify.

The most recent had been the skeletal remains of a huge hulking beast that walked on two legs but had the skull of a giant dog--or a bear, she couldn't tell for sure. She could see that it had long talons at the end of its hands and she knew that she never wanted to see another beast like that again, living or dead.

The mare continued its long trek back up to the castle. She could tell the steed was frightened, because she felt it tremble when one of the beasts came too close to them. She gripped the charm that Halistan had given her and she could feel heat emanate from it.

"Just a little further," she whispered and patted the horse's neck, reassuring herself more than the horse.

Finally, she managed to reach the top of the mountain and approached the main gates to the Keep. Eerie purple lightning flashed through the ominous black cloud. A frigid breeze howled past as she reached the summit. It seemed to chill her to the bone and made her steed shake as it walked slowly with its head down.

On the Keep walls were what she had thought were gargoyle statues. She looked up at them and saw they had the same glowing red-orange balls of light for eyes as the rest of the undead around her. She knew then that they weren't statues. They looked right at her as she made her way through the main gates. She tore her eyes away from them and looked towards the castle itself.

More bolts of lightning streaked through the sky. Some strikes hit the castle, followed closely by the booms of thunder. As she stared at the castle, she thought that it looked different. At least it seemed different. It was darker and more dreadful, and almost seemed alive. The shape of the castle hadn't changed, but its features seemed to have sharpened. It was no longer just mortar and stone...it was now something more, something dark and evil. Goosebumps rose on Andrea's skin as she looked at it.

As she approached the giant double doors of the castle another large bolt of lightning lit the night sky. She caught a glimpse of a figure in the main window that overlooked the Keep grounds. She knew that Nicholas knew she was there.

## 66. The Trap

"Up ahead," Vego pointed, "the passage will split. We need to go right. To go left is certain death."

"Good to know," replied Sol, as he trudged forward up the steps.

Halistan felt himself breathing harder as they trekked. He couldn't remember the last time he'd needed to climb so many steps. The wizard was also starting to sound winded.

They came to the fork in the passage. Just beyond it was a niche in the stone that was large enough for several men to stand in. Sol turned back towards Halistan and the wizard.

"We'll take a break at that opening so we can catch our breath."

Halistan was glad for the rest, because his hand was really beginning to throb with pain. He took a seat on a step outside the niche and unwrapped his wound to take a closer look at it.

"May I see?" Zaroth asked, kneeling down in front of him.

Halistan extended his open palm to the old wizard. Zaroth callously grabbed his arm and pulled it closer, almost making Halistan jerk it back from the pain of being touched.

The old man examined the wound, paying particular attention to the holy symbol that laid in the middle of it.

"Interesting," mumbled the wizard.

"What?"

"It appears," the wizard began, "that your holy symbol seems to be holding the hellfire back, keeping it from spreading. This is no normal holy relic, where did you get it?"

"It's the Star of Salus-" Halistan began to answer but was cut off.

"The Star of Salus?" the wizard asked, sounding surprised by Halistan for the first time.

"I was taking it back to our carriage for Father Angelo when I was brought to this awful place."

"Hmmm," Zaroth replied, "and now it's fused to your hand. How...unfortunate."

Zaroth let go of his arm and Halistan began to re-wrap it in clean cloth. Zaroth stood up and watched the priest dress the wound.

"You should consider yourself lucky you had that. Without it, you'd probably be dead."

"You think so?"

"I know so. That tiny piece of metal has much in common with the relic that we seek to destroy."

"How's that?" Halistan replied defensively, "They don't seem anything alike to me."

"They were both forged by gods, and as such they both inherently contain great power."

"Except this is good and the orb is evil," Halistan said.

Zaroth pondered Halistan's words for a moment and rubbed his chin. "Under normal circumstances, I would disagree. Generally power is power. Its nature depends more on how it is used than on whether it is inherently good or evil. However, in this instance, you may have a point."

Halistan felt vindicated by Zaroth's explanation, but still didn't care for him comparing the Star of Salus to the orb.

"Let's hope the two never touch each other," Zaroth finished before walking away.

This caught Halistan's attention and he had to ask, "Why's that?"

Zaroth stopped and turned back towards him. "It's like you said. One's good and the other is evil. If the two came into contact it could be disastrous."

"You 'bout ready, kid?" Sol asked, looking back over his shoulder.

"Yes, just about finished."

"Good, let's go," Sol ordered. Halistan struggled against the wall to get to his feet as Sol and Vego led the way again, carrying the lanterns.

"How much further?" Sol asked Vego.

"Not much further."

They continued up the passage, avoiding several well placed traps that Vego pointed out to them. Finally, the steps leveled out into a room containing four unlit brass braziers, one in each corner of the room, with a stone door on the other side.

"This is where we part ways, my friends."

Sol turned and extended his arm to the mystic. Vego clasped it in return.

"Thank you for helping us get this far," Sol said. "I am sure we can find the rest of the way ourselves."

"This will get you into the catacombs and from there-"

"I know the way," Halistan interrupted. "This is close to the dungeon where I was held, and I'm sure I can find my way back from here to the treasure room."

"Good," Vego replied. He went over to the stone door and pressed a brick on the wall, opening the door for them.

Sol held up the lantern and walked into the catacombs, followed by Halistan and Zaroth. The passage exited into one of the empty alcoves that Halistan had seen when he was there before. They were in a larger room. To their right was the hall of kings and to their left was the staircase that led up and out of the catacombs.

Halistan began to feel as if he was getting his bearings once again. Then suddenly he heard the sound of bone and metal clanking against hard stone followed by the sound of Sol drawing his sword and yelling, "It's a trap!"

Halistan snapped back around and darted towards the secret passage. He could see a wicked smile on Vego's face before it disappeared behind the stone door, which sealed in front of him before he could reach it.

*\*\**

Vego removed a spike-shaped stone from the wall and slid it into a hole in the upper left corner of the stone door, preventing it from opening again.

"May the gods have mercy on my soul for what I've done."

He picked up his lantern and turned to make his way back down the escape route. His hands shook, and sweat poured from his brow into his eyes, blurring his vision as he tried to hurry down the steps without falling. He began panting from exhaustion.

He managed to make it to the guard post niche where they had rested before. From behind him, he heard the sound of stone sliding on stone.

He jumped at the unexpected noise and dropped his lantern, extinguishing his only source of light. His heart beat hard and he shook with fear. He touched the wall to get his bearings and continued his way down the steps when he reached the fork in the stairwell.

Vego was trying to feel his way along the wall so he could take the correct passage when he heard the sound of bony footsteps and the scraping of metal on rock. He turned around and saw two fiery balls of red-orange light, and felt the thrust of a rusty blade into his belly. He dropped to his knees as the pain shot through his body. He could taste the blood on his lips dribbling out of his mouth as he slumped down to the ground.

Straining to open his eyes, he could make out the outline of other figures surrounding him, all with glowing balls of red-orange light in place of their eyes. Boney fingers ripped into his flesh as he cried in agony.

## 67. Descent into Darkness

A bolt of lightning surged through the sky, striking the right-hand tower of the castle. It was instantly followed by a thunderous boom that startled both Andrea and her steed. She tightened her grasp on the reins, holding the head of the mare steady as they trotted forward.

"Shhh," she cooed to the horse, patting it on the neck, "it's all right." She looked back at the castle and felt goose bumps rise on her skin again. She knew the situation was more grave than she pretended.

She stopped directly in front of the castle. Its large oaken double doors were held together with bands of iron. Andrea dismounted from her steed and took the reins in her hand, more for her own comfort than to lead the horse.

She took small, very slow steps across the damp ground, dreading each step, until she finally reached the doors. She was reaching up to grasp one of the door knockers when the door opened by itself with a loud creaking noise. Inside was pitch black.

Andrea looked back at her steed and gripped the reins.

"I wouldn't normally bring a horse inside, but under the circumstances, I don't want to leave you out here," she said to the mare, and gently tugged at the reins for it to follow her in.

She had taken the first step into the castle when she heard the sound of leathery wings flapping above her. Before she had time to react, the reins were torn from her grip. She whipped around just in time to see the fiery orange eyes of two gargoyles sink their talons into the flanks and neck of her mare, causing the beast to buck in fear and let out a horrible cry of pain.

Without thinking, Andrea stepped towards the attackers, but was met by one of the creatures snapping its gruesome teeth at her, close enough to her face that she could smell the stench of decay that billowed from it.

She jumped back and dashed in through the castle doors, turning in time to see the horrible monsters rip her poor steed asunder. She braced herself behind the door and pushed with every ounce of her strength to close the door behind her, shutting out the monstrosities.

Andrea breathed a sigh of relief. She felt her heart beating rapidly in the dark. She gave herself a moment for her eyes to adjust to the darkness. The only light came from the streaks of lightning that shone through the windows from the outside.

She slowly stepped away from the doors of the castle. Andrea could barely make out anything in front of her, but still took several steps forward.

"Hello?" she called aloud. Her voice echoed through the halls of the castle. Suddenly, the exquisite chandelier above her, as well as all the candles around the room, all lit up. Andrea had to cover her eyes to shield herself from the brightness until her vision adjusted.

She stood on the red plush carpet that led to the staircase to the second floor. At one time it had been meant to welcome visitors into the castle, but was now darker than she remembered. It was a deeper purplish-red color, like that of fresh blood. It gave her the feeling that she was standing on a tongue and was about to be swallowed into the gullet of the castle.

"Is anyone there?"

A cool breeze brushed by her, chilling her to the bone. She pulled her cloak a little more tightly around her thin frame as she continued to look around. Andrea took a few steps forward, looking for any sign of life...but did not find a trace.

"Come upstairs," came a sound that was little more than a whisper in the darkness. Another chill went up her spine as she took a step along the carpet, towards the staircase. She gripped the wooden railing for support and found it to be cold, like touching a dead body. She resisted the urge to jerk her hand away. Andrea knew Nicholas was watching her, and she didn't want to show any fear to the demonic king.

Andrea slowly ascended the stairs. To her left was a corridor that led to a large open chamber that overlooked the castle grounds. Misha had told her that Nicholas loved to use that as a thinking room. If he was waiting for her, he'd be there. As she stepped through, new candles lit, and the old ones died again behind her, keeping only the area around her lit.

She took a breath and reminded herself why she was there, then stepped into the room. Nicholas was there, standing with his back towards her and looking out the window as another bolt of lightning flashed across the sky. She walked into the center of the chamber and stopped next to one of the high-backed reading chairs that decorated the room.

"I knew you'd come back," she heard him say.

Andrea remained silent.

Nicholas turned towards her. He looked different to her. Physically, he was still the same as she remembered, but there was something different about his eyes. They looked as though they could see directly into her soul, which made her uncomfortable.

They were separated by a divan and a small table. He took a step towards her and the furniture was swept out of his path by magic as he walked through the study. He stopped directly in front of her and looked down at her face. She lowered her head and looked toward the ground, as if ashamed.

"Tell me, my dear," Nicholas said with smug confidence, "what brings you back to my humble home?"

Andrea hesitated, intentionally pausing for dramatic effect, as well as giving her another moment to ready herself to play the role of the betraying lover who was crawling back to ask for forgiveness.

Nicholas raised a hand and lifted her chin. His skin was cold and lifeless, but she didn't resist, instead lifting her gaze until they were looking into each other's eyes.

"I...I was...wrong," she began. Just saying those words almost made her choke, but she continued the ruse.

Nicholas remained silent and let her speak.

"I never should have left," she continued. Her eyes began to water and she stifled back a sniffle.

"I...I was angry over the loss of Misha...and I reacted without thinking," Andrea managed to apologize. She wiped away a tear from her right eye.

Nicholas continued to look down at her, not showing the slightest hint of empathy.

"Go on."

Andrea faked another sniffle and took his right hand in hers. "I don't know what else to say, other than that I am sorry for what I've done."

There was a moment of silence. Andrea was beginning to think that Nicholas could tell she was lying. She desperately thought of anything else that she could say to sound more pitiful. She lowered her gaze slightly and whispered.

"I...I wish to ask for your forgiveness. You were so kind to me, and I repaid you with betrayal."

Andrea held his hands and looked up into Nicholas' eyes.

"Please, take me back," she pleaded, wiping more tears from her eyes. "Spare my life and allow me to live by your side."

Nicholas looked down at her for several moments. Andrea was almost certain that her subterfuge had been detected--but then he gently squeezed her hand in return.

"Shhh, my love," he replied, placing a finger lightly on her lips.

He wiped a tear from her right cheek. His features softened slightly as he brushed her skin, and Andrea knew instantly that he was falling for her deception. She fought back the urge to smile.

Nicholas led her towards the large window overlooking the castle grounds. She followed without hesitation or speaking a word.

Neither of them spoke. To Andrea, the silence was deafening. He let loose her hand and stood leaning on the window sill as he gazed out. The wind had picked up tremendously since she had arrived, and the pouring rain somewhat obscured her view below. It was not enough to prevent her from seeing even more undead scrape and claw their way out of the ground, joining ranks with the others that had done before.

She didn't understand how there could be the remains of so many men and beasts here. There seemed to be a limitless supply of them climbing out.

"Beautiful, aren't they?" Nicholas asked her.

That wasn't at all what Andrea thought. "Ghastly" would have been a better description to her, but she held her tongue.

"I know what you must be thinking, 'How do they continue to grow in number?' Am I correct?"

Andrea nodded, slightly unnerved by his insight.

"This plateau has always had a certain mysticism attached to it. Even before my forefathers conquered this land, it was used by men and beasts as a ritualistic meeting place. Beasts were sacrificed to the gods here, men worshipped gods and nature here, and when my ancestors came here, they slaughtered those that resided here. They buried them on these grounds and built this fortress on top of their remains as a symbol of their strength."

Andrea desperately wanted to tell him that she could now see that insanity was a hereditary part of his family, but she remained silent. It was imperative that she keep him distracted.

"You come from a powerful family. You must be proud."

Nicholas stood there, watching his army grow. More creatures, large and small, fell into the ranks marching out of the keep and down the side of the mountain.

"There is no need to placate me, my dear," Nicholas said condescendingly, taking her off guard.

"I do not know what you mean, my Lord."

"Look out at the army I have created."

Andrea took a small step closer to the window and looked at the monstrous horde. Below them, near the castle, Andrea could now see the remains of her steed. Seeing the poor horse's remains lying in heaps on the ground made her feel ill.

All of a sudden, the torn shreds of flesh began to stir. The parts slowly slid back towards each other until they were finally close enough to touch. Then they began to reform. Huge gashes remained in the skin where organs and entrails still sagged out of the torn hide, but the horse stood up again anyway.

After all that she had seen in the last day, she thought that this shouldn't surprise her, but it did. It was one of the most appalling things she'd ever witnessed. With glowing eyes, the mare stood and trotted towards the other undead. It was met by the skeletal remains of a soldier dressed in armor. The skeleton mounted the horse, drew its sword from its rusty scabbard, and rode into the ranks of the undead.

"Soon, they will begin their assault upon that pathetic little town," Nicholas said, with a sadistic grin. "When they do, all those within will be slaughtered and will be added to the ranks of my new army."

Andrea pursed her lips as she felt the anger well up inside her at the thought of the impending onslaught. She wondered how Serieve, Oather and their strange elf companion were doing.

"Do not look so troubled, my dear." Nicholas looked at her, a sinister smirk spread across his lips.

"Very soon, you will be the last woman alive in this land and not long after that, the world."

Andrea felt her emotions begin to flare up, almost uncontrollably. She took a deep breath, "Why are you doing this?"

"Revenge." Nicholas turned back to the window and smiled contentedly. "The gods thought they could punish me with impunity, but it is now my turn. Without the living to worship them, they will have no power. Then, after I have taken everything I possibly can from them, I will kill them for what they did to me."

"Do you think the gods will stand by and allow you to do this?" she replied contemptuously, letting her feelings get the best of her. She silently cursed herself for losing control because she knew it could be a fatal mistake.

"They won't have any choice. Now that the sphere is activated, not even they can stop me."

"Someone will stop you."

Nicholas let loose a boisterous laugh, then, almost instantly his demeanor shifted to menace as he lashed out and grabbed her throat. He pulled her close until they were face to face. His hate-filled eyes peered into her own.

"No one can stop me now," he growled, losing all of his civility as he growled at her. "Not the gods, not the townspeople with their puny little defenses, and certainly not your friends who have snuck back into my castle."

She suddenly felt her stomach twist into knots as she knew instantly that the scam was up.

Nicholas turned her head with his strong grip and pulled her ear close to his mouth. "Oh yes," he whispered evilly, "I know all about your little plan."

Andrea's heart sank even deeper, suddenly wondering if Sol, Halistan and Zaroth were okay…secretly hoping they were, but her hope was dwindling fast.

Nicholas released his grasp on her and she jerked away from him.

"I can smell the fear on you now, and it smells delicious," Nicholas said as he walked around behind her. She stood there silently, looking out the window, trying hard to suppress her feelings. She was consumed with desire to grab a weapon and try and kill him herself, but she didn't want to give him the satisfaction of knowing he was getting to her.

"I helped orchestrate your little plan, and while Vego is no longer of any use to me, he was instrumental in getting you back into my grasp, my darling."

Andrea continued to stare out the window. She refused to speak, somewhat by choice and somewhat prevented by the lump in her throat.

Nicholas gripped her shoulders in his hands and slid closer to her, again getting close enough to whisper in her ear. "They are all now dead. I had a 'special' little surprise waiting for them when Vego led them into the castle."

She leaned forward slightly and rested her forehead on the cold glass of the window. She knew all was lost now. If Zaroth was dead then there really was no one who could destroy the sphere and she would be forced to spend the rest of her days with Nicholas. The thought of the new life she'd have to accept nearly made her collapse in despair.

## 68. Line in the Sand

It was nearing nightfall, or at least as close as Serieve could tell as he looked up at the dense clouds that lingered above them. After a great deal of hard work, the townspeople had managed to blockade the main road into town as well as create a make-shift wall that encircled most of the tiny village. Granted, the innards of most of the buildings had to be scavenged. With a little luck, the fortifications would be enough to keep the oncoming army of undead from over-running the town, killing him and everyone else in the process.

Serieve, spattered with mud, stood near the eastern blockade as the last of the battlements were secured. The villagers seemed different to him now than they had been when they had first arrived. They still seemed weary and browbeaten, but something inside them had changed. Their attitudes were different and he could see it in every man, woman and child. They now seemed....hopeful. As if they actually had something to live for and were fighting for themselves, rather than being the helpless victims they were when he and the others had first entered the tavern.

"The barriers are complete," Oather said, coming up behind Serieve. Together they surveyed the work on the eastern front.

"Have all the trenches been dug and lined with spikes?"

"Aye, on both the western and northern parts of town. I don't know about the southern," Oather replied.

"Excellent. We'll check with Khu-Rá and see if his side is completed."

"Then what?" Oather asked, his stomach making an audible growl as he stood in front of Serieve.

Serieve smiled up at him. "I guess we should eat....it won't be long until the army gets here and we'll need our strength."

"Let us gather all the villagers. Have them bring whatever food they can muster and we'll have a feast."

"I believe many of the women have already made some food. I'll have them bring whatever they have ready and have some of the men set up some tables from the little wood we have left," Oather said as he clasped Serieve's shoulder.

Oather turned and headed towards the Inn, where most of the women had gathered. It was starting to get cold and Serieve now wished that he had a cloak. Serieve saw a company of men sitting in the remains of a house, warming their hands over a small fire. He called them to join him as he walked towards the center of the village.

In a matter of moments, townspeople were scrambling. Men were setting tables and creating makeshift benches to sit on from the leftover wood. Others brought chairs from inside the surrounding buildings.

Men, women and some of the older children carried out large pots of boiled meats and vegetables, and many trays stacked with loaves of flatbread. In no time at all, the tables were filled with food and people were gathered around.

Many goblets of water were poured. Unfortunately, most of the ale had been destroyed along with the tavern, but the water would suffice. Most of the townspeople took their seats. Yaeva took a place in between Serieve and Oather at their table. Everyone was ready to eat, and once everything was set, they wasted no time in filling their plates.

Serieve watched as Oather took a 'more than fair' chunk of meat from one of the pots and placed it on his plate and began to devour it. Serieve was astounded at how quickly Oather could put away food. He himself tore off a large piece of flatbread from a loaf sitting near him as he watched the people enjoy their meager banquet.

Yaeva took hold of a pitcher of water and filled a goblet and offered it to him. "You should say something," she whispered quietly.

Serieve thought for a moment and agreed that he probably should. He was, for all intents and purposes, the leader of this brigade, and he had learned from prior experience that it was the duty of a commander to address the troops before combat. Now was as good a time as any, he decided.

Taking the goblet in hand he stood up and cleared his throat, a little louder than necessary in order to get everyone's attention. Soon dishes stopped rattling and voices quieted as everyone looked towards him.

Serieve could see all their dirty and downtrodden faces looking up at him with a newfound glimmer in their eyes. Serieve wasn't exactly used to speaking in front of people like this, and for a split second he would have preferred being in battle already, rather than standing in front of all these people.

He cleared his throat again, this time more to stall for time as he thought of what to say, than to actually speak.

"Twilight is upon us," he began. He spoke as loud as he could without yelling so everyone could hear him, in the process, making his voice sound deeper than it usually was. The crowd of villagers and mystics were so quiet now that only the occasional drop of water could be heard splashing onto the wet ground.

"But this shall not mark our last night upon this world. As we sit here….the lord of this realm, the vile demon king, sends an army to bring about our destruction," Serieve proclaimed as he looked down at all the faces, young and old, staring back at him.

"He expects us to cower. He expects us to beg for our lives. He is sorely mistaken. We will fight! We will draw our line in the sand and he shall not cross! We may be but mere men, but our will is strong and our cause is just. We have labored long and hard this day and our reward shall be our lives as we stand our ground against the evil hordes and we shall be victorious!"

The villagers' excitement was barely contained as they heard his words. Serieve raised his goblet high, followed by all those that watched him.

"Drink with me! And know…if we are brave….if we stand united, powerful forces shall be by our side!"

Serieve drank from his goblet deeply and drained it completely. He was joined by all the villagers while they all cheered his words. In seconds, empty goblets were slammed down on the tables, followed by the joyful sounds of the people.

Serieve sat back down. Oather reached around Yaeva to slap Serieve on the back. "Good speech, Serieve."

"Thank you."

"I hope that you are right, my friend," Khu-Rá stated. "And that the powerful forces you spoke of are also doing well."

"You and me both, my friend. You and me, both."

Serieve took another bite of bread when Toran, one of the villagers who stood atop one of the buildings as a lookout, began yelling and calling to him. Serieve and Oather looked up at him. Toran was pointing at something in the distance.

"Here we go," Serieve said, taking a deep breath. "I hope we're ready." He stood and ran towards the guard, yelling up at him, "What do you see?"

"A man, sah, an ol' man 'proaches," Toran replied.

"Is he alone?"

"Aye, sah."

"Open the gate," Serieve ordered. Several men removed some of the large planks that braced the fortifications.

The old man ran towards the opening and rushed through as quickly as he could. He was elderly and panting hard from running. He was mumbling something, but Serieve couldn't understand it. Serieve grabbed hold of the old man and held him steady, looking him in the eyes.

"What is it?"

"Monsta's...comin'....mus' escape..." was all the man managed to get out before he passed out and collapsed.

The old man was helped by two other villagers who took him to the safety of a nearby building. Serieve quickly scaled a ladder against the building where Toran stood.

The dark cloud that flowed outward from the castle was nearly upon them. Under it, along the road leading towards the town, marched a line of soldiers that twisted into the distance as far as Serieve could see.

"Oather," Serieve called down, "Get the weapon!"

Without a moment's hesitation, Oather ordered a dozen men to follow him. They all raced towards the rear of the camp.

"Close up the gate and prepare for an attack," Serieve ordered the rest of the men on the ground. The marching of the oncoming soldiers could be heard in the distance. It sounded unlike anything he'd ever heard before. It didn't have the rumble of typical soldiers but was higher pitched and tinny sounding, like the echo of a thousand hammers drumming against a steel plate.

The cloud spread just ahead of the oncoming army. Bolts of lightning streaked through the sky above them, followed shortly by deafening cracks of thunder.

The army was getting closer, close enough that Serieve could see the sickening yellowish orange balls of flame that danced in the eyes of the undead soldiers.

Serieve looked down into the encampment. The women and children had fled to their hiding places. Serieve had never been religious, but he muttered a small prayer to himself asking the gods to watch over those he and his comrades were trying to protect.

Oather and the other men were coming up quickly towards the main gate, pulling on heavy ropes attached to a catapult they had found and repaired. It was a ratty-looking piece of weaponry that hadn't been used in years, or possibly even centuries, but Serieve hoped it would hold up long enough to get a few shots into the army's ranks.

Oather was in the lead, a thick rope over his shoulder, as he and the other men dragged the heavy weapon into position. The wooden wheels creaked awfully as they pulled it slowly along the muddy ground of the city until they were just a short way from the barricade.

"That'll be fine, Oather," Serieve called to him.

Oather dropped the rope and began to set up the weapon. Other men scurried towards them, carrying caskets of oil and pulling a cart full of large rocks.

Khu-Rá climbed atop the building with Serieve and looked at the oncoming host of undead.

"My men have taken their positions atop the other buildings and are ready," Khu-Rá reported.

"Good," said Serieve.

"I do not know what effect we'll have, but anything is worth trying at this point."

"I agree. Arrows themselves may not be effective, but I'm hoping these things are affected by fire," Serieve replied. He looked at the tops of the other buildings near the wall of debris, and saw several dozen men preparing for battle. They had their bows strung across their backs and some were kneeling next to buckets of oil that they were attempting to ignite.

They kept striking, but the drizzle in the air made it difficult. Finally, one man managed to get his oil lit. He then hastily dipped several cloth-covered arrows into the bucket to light and began passing them to others. In moments they were ready to fight.

Breathing a sigh of relief, Serieve turned his attention back to the approaching army. Now that they were within site of the barricade, they began to diverge from the road. They began fanning out, making a line parallel to the town's barricade. Serieve could see that the army was made up not only of humans, but also of the skeletal remains of huge ominous beasts, the likes of which he had never seen before.

One creature in particular, that stayed towards the rear of the horde, stood at least as high as, if not higher than, the building that Serieve stood upon. It had a giant horn that sprouted up from the front of its long, bony snout and rose up between the glowing orbs of its eyes. The monster stopped just outside the range Serieve believed they could hit with the catapult and lifted its weapon, an axe the size of a full grown man, to the sky. Serieve wasn't sure, but it felt like the beast was looking straight at him.

As the horde took their position, the wind blew and along with it came the smell of death. For the first time Serieve felt the pangs of doubt about their survival through this battle. He dared not show any emotion which might betray his lack of confidence to the others. He needed them to believe that he was certain of victory.

"Load the catapult with a boulder and prepare to release!"

Oather had just finished locking the catapult into position and loaded it with the largest rock they had in the cart. It was so heavy that it took Oather and two other larger men to move it from the cart into the catapult.

Oather signaled to Serieve he was ready.

"Release!"

Oather kicked the latch on the weapon, and instantly the entire rig jerked like a sprung mouse trap as the boulder was thrown into the air towards the opposing army. The aim couldn't have been more precise. The giant rock soared through the air and landed on the road, right where the undead split to make their line. The rock smashed down, instantly shattering a dozen or so skeletal soldiers, then continued to tumble forward, striking several dozen more skeletons as it barreled through their ranks.

Serieve grinned wide in satisfaction at the first strike. The archers that witnessed the attack cheered and relayed the good news to the others below.

"Great job, Oather. Load another and we'll hit them again!" Serieve yelled down joyfully. Then Khu-Rá pulled on Serieve's shoulder and pointed back out to the battlefield.

"Look!"

Serieve turned back and saw the scattered fragments of bone slowly beginning to slide back towards each other. In mere moments the broken pieces came back together, then formed larger pieces, and before Serieve knew it, the destroyed soldiers were standing back up again and rejoining the lines.

Serieve felt his heart sink. He turned and looked back down to Oather, who was in the process of winching the catapult back down.

"Don't use another boulder this time!" Serieve shouted from the rooftop. "Use a casket of oil instead."

Oather nodded in accordance and ordered the men to drop the boulder they were loading, and to bring the oil caskets instead. In no time they were ready to launch again. Oather was handed a torch. He lit the caskets, and then once again released the weapon.

The two fiery barrels tumbled through the air and again hit their marks, striking different points along the line of undead. They smashed into several skeletal soldiers and spilled their contents onto the crowd of undead, instantly setting them aflame.

For a moment the fire seemed to take a devastating toll. The fire spread to the crusty remains of clothing the skeletons wore and erupted into a bonfire. Serieve smiled with approval-- they had found a way to hurt the army in front of them.

A crack of thunder ripped through the evil cloud above them. The cloud began to churn and bubble in the air. Then, suddenly, it let loose a torrent of rain upon the undead army, which quickly doused the flames. Again, Serieve's confidence dropped as the undead army regrouped and stood in their line after the short shower stopped. It was almost as if they were taunting the defenders, allowing them to be hit just to prove that they were undefeatable. If causing fear and despair was their tactic, it was working.

Serieve heard several of the archers call down to the villagers, telling the others what was going on. He could hear fear in their voices. Serieve quickly took the initiative and called for the attention of the men.

"That isn't the last trick we have. They haven't beaten us yet," Serieve yelled, doing his best to sound self-assured. He pointed towards a small group of water caskets. "Oather, get one of the barrels from that lot there."

Oather looked up at Serieve, bewildered by the order.

"Trust me."

Oather went ahead and grabbed several barrels.

The men began winching the catapult down, preparing it to launch again.

"I do not understand your intentions," Khu-Rá whispered as he leaned closer to Serieve, "If stone and fire cannot hurt these monsters, what good will water do?"

"I don't know, but Halistan asked me to try this. I don't understand it either, but I trust him."

"I hope this does something, otherwise we'll lose what little morale the villagers have," Khu-Rá warned.

"I know," Serieve replied. He looked to see if the catapult was ready. Oather had just locked it into place; now he gave the signal.

"Release!"

Oather once again released the catapult and sent the barrels hurling high into the sky. Serieve, Khu-Rá and any villager who could get to a vantage point high enough to see over the barricade watched with anticipation.

The caskets tumbled erratically towards the undead army and soared past the line of undead. For a split second Serieve thought they weren't going to hit any enemy troops at all, but much to his surprise, one of them crashed into the skull of the horrific, towering beast that stood behind the line of undead troops.

The wooden casket smashed into pieces as it collided with the skull of the monster, splashing water all over the creature, as well as over a good number of soldiers that stood at its claw-like feet.

Instantly, the beast burst into white flames which rained down upon the other undead, catching them aflame as well. The beast arched its back and stomped around as if in pain. The more the creature lurched around, the more the fire spread among the other undead. After a few more moments, the giant hulking horror lurched forward and fell onto the ground.

Serieve watched intently, waiting for the monster to get back up.

A moment passed.

Then another, and another.

The beast did not rise.

The silence that fell over the battlefield was indescribable. It was if every creature, living and dead, held their breath waiting for what would occur next. But nothing happened.

"Weh destroyed eh!" Serieve heard one of the archers call down to the others in the most joyful voice Serieve had heard since coming to this land. "Weh keeled da biggin!"

Cheers rang from inside the walls. Serieve turned back to the undead horde to see them moving again. The victory was apparently short lived as the army regrouped.

Not waiting for the villagers to let loose another volley of the Holy water at them, the entire contingent of troops broke free of their positions and dashed towards the little fortified town, weapons held high.

Now it was time for the real fight to begin.

## 69. Andrea Finds Hope

Andrea felt the cold glass against her skin as she leaned against the window looking out. The coolness of the glass was comforting. What little hope that she'd had that Zaroth would be able to destroy the sphere had crumbled away.

Instead, as she rested her head, her mind quickly changed directions and frantically worked toward formulating her own escape. She knew she was trapped in this realm. As long as Nicholas was alive, she'd never be able to return home. She'd killed many men, and now she'd have to do the same to him, but even for her, she knew it would be no easy feat.

Her thoughts were interrupted by a blast of white light in the distance. A bright, intense, white light that shot from the ground up to the sky and lit it up for several moments. Despite its brightness, it wasn't hard to look at...at least for her. Next to her though, she saw Nicholas recoil from its intensity, like a shadow from the light. For a split moment, the look on his face almost showed pain as he raised his arm to shield his face from it.

Andrea heard Nicholas groan. He slowly stood upright again as she turned towards him. His face was burned slightly. The skin of his face was bright red and looked as if he had spent several hours in the summer sun at midday.

Nicholas looked at her, his eyes narrowing intently, and she knew he was furious. It was too hard for her to resist the pleasure she got from seeing him hurt in front of her, and she laughed as a wide, malicious smile swept across her face.

"You filthy whore," he growled, and backhanded her, knocking her to the ground.

The blow was the hardest thing she'd ever felt, but in her heart she felt it was worth it to see him pained the way he was. She looked up at him and he glared down at her. She felt the distinct, salty taste of blood on her lips. She smiled wide at him again.

## 70. *Attacked in the Castle*

Halistan hit the stone door hard with his good hand, cursing himself for being too slow to stop it from trapping them within the catacombs. He swiveled around to see who his attackers were. Both ends of the hall were filled with undead soldiers marching towards them.

Halistan did his best to ready the mace that Oather had given him, but with one hand being injured he only managed to drop the weapon onto the ground with a loud clank.

Sol had already taken point, facing down the soldiers coming down the side closest to them. "Zaroth now would be a good time for you to do something!"

Zaroth reached into a pouch on his belt and pulled out a handful of what looked like red dust.

With an underhand throw, he tossed the dust at the oncoming soldiers and bellowed, "Ignite."

The dust splashed onto the undead and instantly burst into flames. All the soldiers were soon engulfed in a cloud of fire. Halistan saw Sol smile in satisfaction for a quick moment before he saw the undead continue forward, seemingly unaffected by the flames.

One soldier was close enough to strike at Sol, which it did. In the arc of its attack, Sol was able to dodge, but the flames from the burning soldier caught part of Sol's cloak on fire. Sol whipped off his cloak and threw it to the ground as he parried an attack from another soldier almost in the same maneuver.

"Not helping, old man!" Sol growled as he kicked one of the undead square in the ribcage, knocking it to the ground.

"I'm open to suggestions," Zaroth hissed back at Sol.

The soldiers from the other end of the hall charged at them. Zaroth turned just in time to throw what looked like a blue egg at the oncoming forces. The egg hit the ground in front of the soldiers and splattered onto the ground, instantly spreading out into a sheet of ice that coated the stone floor. The undead didn't have time to react. As soon as they hit the ice they began to slip and tumble to the ground.

"That's only going to delay the inevitable," Sol shouted at the wizard. "Please tell me you have something a little more impressive."

Halistan saw the wizard fumble around inside another pouch, looking for something. He himself, meanwhile, managed to reach down and pick up the dropped mace. He held it weakly in his left hand, waiting for one of the undead to get its footing on the ice and stand up.

Finally, one did. Halistan took a swing but the undead easily blocked the blow with its shield. The force from the block rang through the steel handle of the mace and into Halistan's hand, making him drop it once again.

"Halistan," Sol yelled, "Put that thing down and do something useful!"

Halistan saw Sol manage to duck out of the way of two other undead striking at him. Another undead set its sights on Zaroth as he was rummaging through his pouch looking for something. The soldier's blade came sweeping through the air at Zaroth. Sol lunged at the undead; blocking the attack with his own sword but another soldier came up behind him and slashed him across the back.

Sol grunted loudly as the rusty blade cut through his skin. Sol spun around and brought his sword crashing down upon the skull of the soldier, splitting it in half, as he also fell to his knees.

The attack took Zaroth by surprise. He quickly looked up to see the other soldier in front of him. Zaroth pulled a wand from his pouch and held it out in front of him. Zaroth shouted something Halistan couldn't understand and all the undead around them instantly flew back out of the hall completely.

It was only a temporary victory, for as soon as they were knocked out of the hall, they began to slowly pick themselves up and come back for another attack. Halistan didn't know what else he could do. Looking down at his cloth-wrapped hand, he quickly began stripping the bandages from it.

To either side of him, the skeletal soldiers re-grouped. Halistan knelt down, one knee to the hard stone of the catacomb floor. He opened his hand wide as streaks of pain shot up through his arm. He grit his teeth in agony.

Halistan closed his eyes and began to whisper a prayer. He repeated the prayer over and over as the skeletal minions closed in around them. Suddenly, thin beams of light began to shoot out along the cracks in the floor from underneath Halistan's injured hand.

The undead continued towards them, weapons ready to strike. The light spread out underneath them. As it did so, each soldier touched by the light erupted into bright white flames. Moments later, scattered remains of weapons and armor came crashing to the ground as the light on the floor dissipated.

Halistan opened his eyes and saw a look of disbelief upon Sol's face.

"Great going, kid," Sol exclaimed, as he winced in pain from the cut in his back. He took a deep breath. "Now, just do that across the entire castle and we can call it a day."

Halistan, physically exhausted from the powerful spell, fell over onto his side and closed his eyes. Sol stepped over to him and extended a hand to Halistan. He looked up and took it as Sol pulled him up to his feet.

"I wish I was strong enough to cover the entire castle," Halistan said apologetically.

"You and me both, kid," Sol told him. "But seriously, you can do that again, right?"

Halistan was drained, but he still had some energy left. "I think I can. Once or twice more, at the most. After that, I will be too weak to do anything."

"Okay," Sol replied. "We'll try and be cautious."

He turned to Zaroth, "Fat lot of luck you were back there."

Zaroth straightened his robe, ignoring Sol's complaint.

Halistan knelt back down and picked up the dropped mace. It was obvious that it wasn't going to be much use to him on this mission, but Oather would probably want it back.

"Most of the spells I prepared for this journey are too powerful to unleash in our present vicinity," Zaroth replied in his typical condescending tone.

"Oh, that's what it is....your spells are *too* powerful," Sol scoffed.

Zaroth opened his mouth as if he was going to rebut Sol's sarcastic remark, but Sol cut him off.

"This was a trap," Sol stated, as if at a sudden realization.

"And your point?" Zaroth asked.

"You don't get it, this was a *trap*."

Zaroth continued looking at Sol as if he were trying to tell the wizard something insanely obvious, like that the sky was actually blue and the grass was green.

Then suddenly the implications of what Sol was saying hit Halistan like a solid right hook and his stomach instantly twisted into a knot.

"Oh, by God's grace," Halistan muttered. "Nicholas was expecting us."

"Exactly," Sol said, pursing his lips in anger. "The girl probably sold us out to save her own skin."

"No! She wouldn't do that," Halistan shot back. "It wasn't her, it was Vego. I saw the look in his eye as he closed the passageway behind us. He knew what was coming."

Sol thought for a moment. "You may be right."

"Come on," Halistan said as he took a step towards the staircase leading out of the catacombs. "We have to go save her!"

"Woah, kid. You don't get it. If he knows we're here, then he knows our plan and more than likely she's already dead…and that's only if she isn't the one who told him in the first place."

Halistan looked back at Sol and could feel the anger building up inside of him. He knew Andrea wouldn't betray them, but he also knew that Sol was right; there was little they could do for her.

Halistan's body slackened and he hung his head in resignation.

"Come on," Sol said. "Let's go. If he doesn't already know that we survived his little ambush, he will soon, so we must hurry."

Sol began walking towards the stairwell, followed by Zaroth. As Zaroth walked past Halistan he stopped and turned towards him. "There will be time to mourn later. Now we must make haste."

"Zaroth, you said you could lead us to the orb. Which way do we go from here?" Sol asked.

Zaroth reached into a pouch and felt around for something. The old man rummaged around for several moments before he stopped and closed his eyes.

"Something wrong, old man?" Sol asked.

"Possibly," Zaroth replied in a frustrated tone. The old wizard slowly pulled out two flat pieces of crystal. Each was a half-moon shape that looked like it used to be a single piece.

"That doesn't look good," Halistan said.

"This *used* to be a detector that I created to track the pieces of the orb. However, it seems to have been broken during my incursion with Nicholas."

"Can you fix it?" Sol asked.

"If we were at my lab, I could poss-"

"So that is a 'no'," Sol said sternly. "The wizard fails again."

"Hey!" Zaroth snapped back, "You try being kicked in the ribs by that monster. I doubt you'd have fared much better."

"Excuses, excuses. So how are we supposed to find our way back?"

All three men quietly pondered the situation before Halistan spoke up. "I was down here before and made my way to the orb chamber. I'm sure I could-"

"Great kid, lead the way." Sol said as he nudged Halistan forward.

## 71. Darkest Before the Dawn

"Ready yourselves, men!" Serieve ordered. Authority laced through his commands like the words of an old veteran.

He stood defiantly atop the building, watching as the horde blitzed towards the small town. His archers stood on either side of him, all watching in disbelief at the horrific sight of the undead creatures bearing down upon them.

"Everyone, ready your weapons and prepare to repel the attack!"

Immediately bows were tossed away and the sound of axes and clubs being snatched up filled the air. Serieve turned back and looked down at Oather and the battalion still inside the encampment.

"You men, on the ground!" Serieve pointed down at all the men standing around Oather, "Get your weapons and get up here and help us repel the climbers!"

The men scattered all around the camp and began to scramble to pick up anything they could use as a weapon. Some picked up left over pieces of wood, others managed to grab axes while still others had nothing at all, but they scaled up ladders to get atop the barricade to do what they could to help.

Oather drew his sword and began to follow them up when he caught Serieve's eye.

"Oather," Serieve called down to him as he was wrenching the catapult back to prepare for another volley. "Get the barrels of water we have left up here. It'll help us hold them off."

Serieve saw Oather nod as he yelled at two nearby men and they all three headed for the four remaining barrels. Serieve turned back to the battle just in time to see the horde slam into the ditch that had been dug in front of the make-shift barricade. Even though it had been lined with long spikes, it didn't seem to slow the undead soldiers a bit.

The first wave ran head first into the ditch. Snapped bones flew in every direction. Many of them became stuck on the poles that jutted through their bodies. Those impaled bodies were then used as a bridge for the next wave to climb upon.

Serieve turned back to look at Oather again in haste. "Hurry!"

The sound of the attack nearly drowned out the cavalier's voice. Turning back to his attackers, Serieve looked down and saw the bony soldiers climbing over each other like ants as they made their way up to the top of the battlements. They were getting so close that Serieve could smell the musty decay of their bodies. He could swear that he felt heat emanate from their fiery eyes as he kicked one of the first skeletons to scale the wall back down into the undead horde.

## 72. *Old Acquaintances*

"Well?" Sol asked Halistan, his frustration showing through his voice. "Which way is it?"

"I…I don't remember exactly," Halistan replied. "You have to remember, I was already lost when I came this way before…"

"You said you could find your way back to the study."

Sol was already irritated at being caught unaware by the undead soldiers. Getting lost now wasn't going to help that much. He tried to keep his temper in check, but he knew they had very little time before Nicholas himself would show up, and Sol didn't want to be around for that.

"I know, just give me a moment to get my bearings," Halistan said as they came to another turn.

Sol tried to look around to see if he might remember anything, but the lighting was dim and he couldn't really see that well. Every so often there was an oil-filled lamp attached to the walls of the castle, but they were so sparse that it was almost as bad as walking around in the dark.

"I….uh….think it was this way." Halistan pointed down a hall towards his left. "Or maybe it was straight ahead a little further…"

Halistan looked back at Sol, and he could tell by the look on his face that Sol wasn't happy.

"What about you, old man?" Sol snapped at Zaroth. "Got any tricks up your sleeve, or will you continue to be an utter disappointment?"

"If you call me old one more time…"

"This is no time for a debate, ancient one. I don't think you have enough life left to…" Sol suddenly stopped mid-sentence.

He turned his head to the side slightly, as if he were listening to something faint, and was dead still for a moment before Halistan broke the silence.

"What is it?"

"Shh."

Sol slowly and quietly drew his sword. "We're not alone."

Just ahead, out of the darkness, walked a lone figure. It was an older, world-weary man, wielding a long-sword.

"Lucian," Sol muttered.

"Stay out of our way," Sol hissed. "We're not here to fight you, so just turn around and walk away and we won't have to kill you."

"I'm not concerned about my safety in the least," Lucian replied. A sinister smile edged across his lips. "If I die, I'll just rise up and serve my master again....isn't that right, my pet?"

From behind the old servant came an all too familiar growl as four glowing orange eyes lit up the darkness. The massive, two-headed hellhound stepped forward. Flames danced around its jaws as it growled.

Sol felt his heart stop as he saw that horrible creature again. In all the commotion of facing what they would have to do to save themselves, he had completely forgotten about the frightful beast.

He readied his blade and squared off in front of Lucian. The man before him looked old and Sol normally wouldn't consider him to be much of a threat, but in the days since he had arrived in this land, he had found many things to be deceiving. He wasn't about to take a chance on Lucian.

"Run!" he shouted at Zaroth and Halistan.

Without any hesitation, Zaroth took off and pulled the young priest along with him.

"After them, my pet," Lucian ordered. "Do not allow them to get away."

The hellhound required no other instructions. It immediately turned and took after the other two men with a vengeance.

The hall became an orchestra of clamoring steel as Sol and Lucian's weapons clashed back and forth. Sol would strike and be blocked by Lucian's deft parries. Lucian's attacks could not hit their intended target due to Sol's quick dodges.

Sol tried every trick that he could think of, but he could not seem to get past the old man's defenses. He attacked and attacked and attacked, but not a single strike could meet its mark. What made matters worse was that Sol knew it was only a matter of time before fatigue would get the best of him. Conversely, and even more to Sol's astonishment, the old man seemed to be getting faster with each passing moment.

Sol knew that he had to do something quick, or he'd lose this fight. Lucian had already seemed to detect that his opponent was starting to wear down, and had intensified his attacks. Lucian struck a powerful blow down at Sol, which Sol just barely managed to block.

Both men's blades struck, and Lucian's bore down upon Sol. Sol's blade crossed the old man's, barely holding it back. Sol was tiring quickly now, but he summoned all the strength he had left and pushed Lucian's blade back, momentarily getting some distance from the older man.

Sol saw his opportunity as Lucian staggered back, and followed his push with a kick straight to the old man's abdomen. Lucian reeled from the blow and fell back.

Not missing a beat, Sol kicked the old man again, this time in the face. He knew that would only delay the old man for a moment. Sol looked down the corridor after his companions.

## 73. Defending the City

The wave of the undead minions climbed its way to the top of the barricade. Serieve gave another swift kick to the head of one of the skeletons as it pulled itself up. The head went flying into the distance and the headless body fell back into the sea of monsters making their way up the fortification.

"Where's that water?" Serieve shouted.

Oather was in the middle of hoisting a barrel up to a pair of townsmen at the top of the barricade. Hearing Serieve's urgency, Oather pulled the barrel back to his chest and with a tremendous grunt threw the barrel at the two men at the top.

It hit them with such a force that it knocked them down. Serieve and another soldier immediately grabbed the barrel and took it to the edge of the barricade. They set the barrel down and without a word, Serieve grabbed an axe from another man and struck the barrel over and over, cutting a chunk of wood from the corner.

"Pour!" he commanded the men around him, who instantly picked up the barrel and began pouring it over the edge just as the rest of the undead were getting near to them. As the water sprung from its wooden confines onto the skeletons below them, it erupted into a gigantic white flame. It looked like nothing short of pouring alcohol on a roaring fire.

Serieve looked to his right, where several other men had gotten two more barrels up to the top and had cut them open. As they poured the water over the edge, again the undead burst into flame and began to tumble back onto themselves.

"Keep'em coming!"

Oather threw up one last barrel to the troops atop the barricade, "That's all of them."

Serieve felt his heart sink. So far the holy water was all that had managed to affect the attacking force, and as he stood there, the last of it dribbled out and down onto the undead.

Serieve frantically calculated their next move when suddenly the mountain of undead that had scraped their way towards the top of their wall seemed to collapse in on itself. Most of the skeletons had dissolved from contact with the holy water. The few that remained mostly intact retreated to the main force away from the wall.

For the first time since the fighting began, there seemed to be a lull. Serieve could only imagine that the interlude was caused by the opposing force changing its tactics. He waited to see what they would do next.

"The-ah pullen 'way," one of the soldiers shouted down to the encampment, excitement resounding in his voice. Serieve stood unwavering and held his hand up to silence the troops.

It was true, the battalion of undead was pulling back from them, but he couldn't help thinking that the worst of it wasn't over yet. In the darkness of the night, the undead army pulled itself back further than Serieve could see. In the distance, he could still see the glowing points of light that emanated from the eyes of the ghastly force, but they were growing fewer and fewer. He couldn't figure out what they were planning next, so he waited.

Unfortunately, he didn't have to wait long. Suddenly, out of the shadows, he saw the shapes in the darkness of flying creatures that he could just barely make out. They were monstrous beasts, the likes of which Serieve had never seen before--giant creatures with bat-like wings, and arms and legs armed with sharp talons, and frightfully long sharp teeth. They carried other skeletal warriors with them and dropped them over the barricade and into the main encampment.

The skeletons crashed into the ground and splintered into a dozen pieces, but just as quickly formed back together, rose, and began attacking the defenders from inside their own stronghold.

## *74. Entrapment*

"Wha…Wait!" Halistan tried to say as he was virtually dragged down the hall by Zaroth, "Sol-"

"He knows what he is doing," Zaroth replied.

Halistan knew there was nothing he could do to save Sol now, and instead did his best to keep up with the wizard.

Behind him, he could hear the sound of swords clashing together and knew Sol was locked in a life and death struggle. After a moment, his and the wizard's pace began to slow. Halistan was trying to catch his breath when he heard the discouraging sound of claws tapping on the stone floor. He knew the giant, undead hellhound was still chasing after them.

With renewed zeal, Halistan began to run as fast as he could again.

"The beast," he managed to say in between deep breaths.

The two of them sped along as quickly as they could. They passed items in the halls, suits of armor and the like. Several times, Zaroth pulled over these furnishings in an attempt to slow down the monster that was rapidly catching up to them. The beast's agility had not been affected by its change from living to undead, and it easily dodged and jumped over the obstacles. Nothing Zaroth or Halistan did seemed to slow the monster at all.

They dashed down another hall, with the hellhound still close behind. Halistan was astounded at the sheer size of this fortress. It never seemed to end, and nothing they passed seemed at all familiar to the young priest. At least, not until the moment when they turned another corner and Halistan suddenly saw a light that looked like it emanated from an open doorway.

"That way," Halistan managed to say in between gasps. All the running was making him winded, and his heart felt like it was going to burst right out of his chest.

"What?" asked Zaroth.

"That's the study." Halistan pointed towards the light. He remembered that the door had looked exactly the same way when he and Andrea had found the others there.

"Great," Zaroth replied in between labored breaths. "Let's hope the door is strong enough to hold that thing out."

"I have a better idea," Halistan said as they reached the doorway to the study.

Zaroth rushed into the room, but Halistan stopped just outside. He frantically unwrapped his bandaged hand and knelt down in the middle of the doorway. He closed his eyes and placed his hand down on the cold stone floor and began to pray.

His hand began to glow as he spoke the words over and over. Then there was a quick flash and his hand stopped glowing.

Halistan snapped his eyes open and couldn't resist the urge to look up for the hellish beast. By the sounds that were coming down the hall, it was getting extremely close. Halistan looked up just in time to see the monstrous figure leap at him.

In sheer terror, Halistan scrambled backwards through the door of the study. Then, with a flash of brilliant white light, his spell took effect. Shimmering bands of light shot up from the castle floor and surrounded the monster, grabbing at it like vines of pure light.

## 75. *Command Decisions*

The winged beasts overhead were grabbing more and more of the undead and dropping them into the town. Serieve, now faced with fighting opposing forces on two fronts, quickly ordered a retreat from the fortifications.

"To the town hall!" Serieve shouted his orders at the men around him. He knew that they couldn't hold out long in their new situation, and he couldn't let the undead get to the town hall where the women, children and elderly were hiding. They would be slaughtered, and then they would rise from the dead and turn against his soldiers. Serieve quite frankly didn't think that these townspeople would have what it took to strike down their own wives and children, even to save their own lives. So saving them would have to become his highest priority.

"Wah 'bout da wahl, sah?"

"Forget the wall! Do as I said and get to the town hall!"

\*\*\*

Oather watched in astonishment as the skeletons that were dropped into the town began to stand up and attack the villagers. He leapt into action and cleaved a skeleton in half. His blade shattered the skull as it hit and continued its way all the way down and through its body, rending the undead soldier in half. That one undead was replaced by two more.

From behind him, he heard Serieve shouting orders to the men to head to the town hall. Oather whipped his blade around and struck down the two more undead, then smashed another that was about to kill one of his men.

The man, who was really no more than a teenage boy, looked up at him in shock as Oather pulled him to his feet and ordered him to the town hall. The boy stammered a "Thank ye," before he ran off.

The undead were growing in numbers. Worse yet, they were being dropped in between the barricade the townspeople were defending and the town hall they had to reach. Some of the men that had heeded the order early managed to make it past the undead and into the fortified town hall, but the rest were now caught, like Oather, on the other side of the growing mass of undead.

Serieve was still shouting orders for the men to break for the town hall as he made his way from the wall down to the ground. Then Oather heard another voice shouting orders almost directly behind him.

"The eas' wahl is open," shouted the Burgher. "We mus' leeve whah weh can!"

Soldiers stopped and looked. Cornwall was right; there were no undead blocking the route to the east gate, which would get them outside the city and further from the undead, but that would leave the town hall completely defenseless. The men didn't seem to know what to do, while the undead soldiers grew in numbers and began advancing towards them.

"You heard the commander's orders. Protect the town hall!" Oather's voice boomed like a cannon as he shouted at the men.

"De town is los', Weh mus' flee!" Cornwall shouted back.

Oather turned his back to Cornwall so he was facing the troops, who all almost looked like they were about to make a run for the gate, "We have to protect..." he began, but as he began to speak a sharp blade pierced his back, right through his left shoulder blade.

He fell to one knee and looked back to see Cornwall looming over him with a sinister look upon his face.

"Quick, go nawh!" Cornwall shouted. A few men did as he said and ran away while the majority watched in shock.

Oather reached around and pulled out the blade, which caused a terrible pain to shoot through him. He felt the rough texture of the iron dagger's blade as it slid out of his flesh, followed by the warm sensation of blood dripping from his wound. He was already soaked, so the wetness simply changed from a cold wet feeling to a warm one.

Oather's face turned red with anger and he stood back up. Cornwall stood before him as he rose. His vision turned red as he glared at Cornwall, and a look of sheer terror swept across the old man's face.

With a speed that could only be likened to a cheetah pouncing on its prey, Oather grabbed Cornwall by the throat and lifted him high into the air. Then he stepped forward and slammed the fat man down into the bowl of the drawn catapult.

Then, with a mighty kick, Oather hit the latch that released the massive weapon, instantly slinging Cornwall up into the air. As luck would have it, he managed to hit one of the undead gargoyles that was in the process of bringing more troops over the wall. Cornwall, the gargoyle, and the undead soldiers all were thrown through the air and fell outside the fort.

Anger still contorted Oather's face. He turned back to the remaining soldiers and shouted, "Fight them…or fight me!"

The men were so terrified by the sight of Oather standing before them that they smashed their way through the undead that blocked their path.

Oather was fully aware of the pain in his back again and the salty taste of blood on his lips. He started to slump over, but was caught by Serieve and Khu-Rá, who helped him get to the town hall. Once they got there, they were followed by the last few townspeople who had remained outside the building to hold off the undead. The door was then shut and barricaded from the inside.

## 76. Oblivion

Sol ran down the halls with Lucian right behind him. He was amazed that a man his age had so much strength, speed and endurance. *What the hell is this guy?* Sol thought. He was running out of breath, but he could still hear the old man right behind him.

Suddenly, he caught glimpse of a white flash come from a corridor ahead of him and to the left. He knew it must have been Halistan's magic, so he ran as fast as he could in that direction.

Sol tore around the corner and headed down the corridor, his saber swinging wildly as he ran. He looked up just in time to see the hellhound in front of him at the door of the study.

It seemed entangled in bands of light. In the doorway stood a figure that looked like Halistan, with his arm stretched out towards the monster.

Having no time to react before he was about to run into the trapped beast, Sol dived and slid on the floor. Sol felt the heat on his legs through his pants as he skidded on the floor and under the massive body of the beast. He saw its underbelly and caught a glimpse of the monstrous claws of the beast as it tried to free itself from Halistan's spell.

Before he knew it, he had come to a stop next to Halistan, just inside the doorway of the study. Sol looked up at the young man, who was concentrating intently on the hellhound suspended in mid-air in front of him.

Sol attempted to warn Halistan that Lucian was right behind him but his words were too strained from his heavy breathing to be intelligible. Sol looked up and saw a band of light whip out and snag Lucian around each of his wrists, his legs, his torso and his waist. Once they grabbed him, more bands lashed out and wrapped around him, just as they had done to the hellhound.

Sol looked at Halistan, shocked and almost impressed by the kid's ability. Halistan had a cold and detached look upon his face as he focused intensely upon the spell. Slowly he stretched out his fingers, and then drew them into a tightly closed fist.

Sol looked back at the beast and its master. The bands of light almost completely covered them, like cocoons that began to glow brightly and then suddenly burst into flame.

Instantly, nothing was left of Lucian or the hellhound. The flame dissipated in a flash, and along with it went all traces of the captives it had encompassed.

Halistan's eyes rolled back into his head and he collapsed onto the ground. Sol wasn't sure what the problem was at first. He knelt down next to Halistan and saw the boy was unconscious.

Sol lightly, but still sharply, slapped the young man to get him to wake up.

"Hal," Sol whispered, even though he didn't know why he was whispering. It just seemed appropriate. "You did it, they're gone."

Halistan didn't respond. "Wake up," Sol tried again.

The younger man slowly came to. He was still obviously disoriented, but that was good enough for Sol.

"Good job, kid…now can you do something to keep out any other unwanted guests?"

Halistan seemed to still be half unconscious, and simply groaned.

"Come on, kid," Sol pleaded as he pulled Halistan up to a sitting position. "You've done great. Just tell me that you have another trick like that up your sleeve."

Halistan's head wobbled back and forth as he recovered a little more.

"Wha…what?"

"Ah, there you are," Sol smiled at him. "Come on, what else do you have? We just need something with a little more range-"

"No," Halistan said, interrupting Sol's planning.

Sol looked back at Halistan. "What?"

"No," Halistan replied. "I'm sorry, Sol, but that's all I had left. I am completely drained. I can't cast anything else. I'm done."

Sol could see that the kid was starting to fade out again. He sighed as he realized that he probably wouldn't be able to get anything else out of him.

"Come on, Hal."

"Sorry…Sol," was all Halistan was able to say before he passed out again.

"Damn it," Sol muttered under his breath. He grabbed Halistan's arms and dragged him into the study and through the now open secret door into the treasure room. He dragged Halistan over to the far wall of the room and gently laid him to rest.

The sphere was now fully activated, and was an impressive sight to behold. It looked like a black sun hovering in the middle of the room. It was no longer a round block of onyx, but a glowing ball of darkness. Its surface churned and swirled with bluish gray wisps, and it radiated an eerie glow that made the whole room take on a different look.

Sol couldn't help but stare at the sphere for what seemed like an eternity before the wizard walked towards him.

"Get out of my way," the wizard said rudely.

Sol, still somewhat entranced by the device, simply stepped out of the way, but kept on gazing at the sphere. He leaned towards it and stuck out his finger, about to make ripples in the blackness of the orb.

"Don't touch that!" Zaroth barked as he slapped Sol's hand away, which snapped Sol out of his trance.

Sol looked sternly at the old man for hitting him. Zaroth looked back at him and gave him a sinister smile. "On second thought, please, go ahead and touch it all you want."

Sol very nearly went ahead and touched the device, but was saved by remembering what the old man had said about the sphere and how it would destroy you if you touched it.

Sol shot the old man a hateful glare, which seemed to actually please the wizard greatly. Sol stepped back and watched Zaroth for a moment.

"What are you doing?" Sol asked sharply. "Why isn't this thing shut down yet?"

Zaroth didn't acknowledge that Sol had even spoken.

Sol walked around behind the old man, looking at the sphere intermittently as he did so.

"Any day now, old man. It won't be long before the King knows that we're here."

Zaroth stopped and whipped around to face Sol. His demeanor gave away his irritation. "This isn't like loading crates, you idiot. In case you didn't hear me, this device was created by a God. You can't just de-activate it like you would blow out a candle. It must be studied closely so mistakes aren't made."

Sol stood his ground against the wizard. "You don't know how to do it, do you?"

Sol knew by the old man's defensiveness that he was not having any luck with the sphere, and his instincts paid off. Zaroth instantly shut up.

"Well?" Sol demanded.

"This is a very complex device."

"Damn it! I knew it. Is there anything you can do right, except kill innocent people?" Sol ranted as he turned and walked the other way around the sphere.

"Well...I...Err."

Then, as the two men argued, the wisps of smoke that swirled on the surface of the sphere were suddenly replaced by what looked like white fire that lit up the inside of the sphere. Red light erupted from its dark surface and burned like a fire within its depths.

"What the..." Sol muttered as he looked at the sphere in shock, "Did you do that?"

Zaroth looked as astonished as Sol, but he didn't answer. Instead, his gaze was intent on the sphere, as if he were trying to look into it. Sol came around and stood next to the old man.

"What was-"

"Shhhh," Zaroth snapped at him.

Sol shut up and stood back as the wizard went back to work. The old man closed his eyes and started whispering an incantation that Sol couldn't understand.

Sol looked back at the sphere. The bright light that it emitted began to fade. At one point Sol was almost sure that he could see images in the blackness of the sphere--images of a raging battle--but he couldn't be certain since they flashed by so quickly and then stopped entirely after a few moments.

Sol looked over at Halistan, who was still out cold. He began to wander back towards the entrance to the secret room, to check and make sure there was no one lingering about who would see what they were doing.

He had just taken up position to act as a lookout when another, but smaller, flash of purplish light pulsed rapidly from the sphere, accompanied by a very loud and deep humming sound. Sol jerked around the corner to see what was going on inside the treasure room.

The bright flashing light and noise seemed, to Sol anyway, like it was some sort of alarm or warning.

"What the hell did you do, old man?"

Zaroth didn't reply, but instead, he continued to look deeply into the sphere, still whispering the incantation.

"Is it supposed to do this?"

Again, the old man ignored him and kept chanting. Then, all of a sudden, the flashing and the humming stopped.

"Whew," Sol said with a deep sigh.

Zaroth stopped chanting and closed his eyes. "I didn't do that."

"Do what?" Sol asked. "Make the thing go crazy like that?"

"No," Zaroth replied. "I didn't make it stop."

## 77. Blissful Treachery

Andrea wanted this moment of elation to last as long as she possibly could. The angry, contorted face that Nicholas had as he looked down at her gave her a great deal of satisfaction. That moment would not last, though. He quickly swooped down on her and in an instant he had jerked her up by her arm, and grabbed her by the throat and lifted her up into the air.

Andrea hit and kicked him as hard as she could, but it felt like she was hitting a marble statue. She felt his grip tighten on her throat as she struggled in vain to breathe. His pupils began to swirl and change as she stared into them. They lengthened into long slits, like those of a snake, and turned yellowish green. His arms swelled and he grew several more feet in height, pulling her even higher into the air as he changed.

Nicholas' face contorted into a demonic visage. For a split second, she considered going limp, to see if he'd think she was dead and let her go but before she could implement the desperate plan she heard a loud noise. It was impossible to tell what it was, as it seemed to reverberate through the entire castle without coming from any one point.

Nicholas' grip relaxed ever so slightly as his attention seemed to divert to the sound she heard. He turned his head slightly, listening intently as if he were perplexed at what was going on.

In his moment of confusion, Andrea suddenly remembered the pendant that she had been given by Halistan. The young man had told her it might help her if she was in danger, and this definitely qualified. She had to act quickly; her eyes were already starting to see little pinpricks of light swirling around her head. If she didn't act soon, she'd be lost completely.

Just below Nicholas' grip, she could feel the pendant pinned to her. She managed to grab it and pull it hard and snap the cord that held it. She gripped it tightly and pressed it hard against Nicholas' skin. As the tiny bit of enchanted metal came into full contact with Nicholas, it erupted into a small, but bright, white flame.

Andrea saw Nicholas' head whip back around towards her just in time for him to see his arm catch flame. He dropped her and pulled his arm away, letting out a howl of pain at the same time. The roar was almost deafening to her and unlike anything she'd ever heard before.

She fell to the ground and gasped for air. The pendant fell from her grasp and her hands went to her painfully bruised throat. Andrea scrambled to get as far away from Nicholas as she could.

She looked back and Nicholas' eyes met hers as she glared at him. His eyes burned with rage and for a split moment she thought that he'd attack her again. She immediately began to look for the protective charm that she'd just dropped, but it was nowhere to be found.

Nicholas took a step towards her, but the noise emanating throughout the castle suddenly rang louder and his attention was diverted again from her to the sound. Then, all of a sudden, he turned and dashed out of the room.

Andrea managed to pull herself to her feet and stumble to the doorway. Nicholas was only in view for a moment as she saw him spread his large, bat-like wings and fly down the wide corridor.

From the direction he was going, she knew that he was headed towards the orb. This must mean that Zaroth had managed to reach the sphere. She took little solace in this, however, as Nicholas knew this as well and was heading there to kill the wizard.

She swallowed hard, which made her throat ache, and stepped out into the corridor. There was no way she could get to the room before Nicholas, but she had to at least try and warn them.

## 78. Sanctuary

Beads of sweat dropped from Serieve's brow as he and Khu-Rá managed to help Oather to a bench in the town hall. It was the same room in which they had been tried and convicted in before. Now, most of the benches had been commandeered and used in the village fortifications they had built. It was now mostly sparse which made the room look bigger than Serieve remembered it being.

A few soldiers sat on the floor of the room with them, tending to their own wounds, while two others barricaded the door. The few windows were boarded up and the only light came from a lamp held by one of the village men.

"Here, let me take a look at you," Serieve offered.

Oather leaned forward slightly with a painful groan to allow Serieve a better look.

"You, with the light. Come here."

Quickly, the dumpy, middle-aged man scuttled over and held the lamp up high to shine its light on Oather's back. The wound was deep, and though it didn't bleed as badly as it had before, it was still dripping steadily down, making a wide crimson path down Oather's back.

"Help me take this off him," Serieve said to Khu-Rá. With a little help from Oather, they managed to pull his tunic up over his arms and head, allowing Serieve to get a better view of the wound.

"It's not good," he said to Oather, "but it could have been a lot worse, I think."

Oather simply groaned in agreement, then spat blood onto the floor near his huge booted feet.

Serieve could hear a lot of commotion going on outside. He knew more undead were swarming into the village. Without him and his men there to repel them from the walls, they had surely scaled the barricade and were flooding into the area around the town hall.

He could hear all sorts of strange noises through the boarded-up windows; the sounds of clanking metal on dry, aged bone, and the loud crashing thuds of the larger beasts as they made their way closer. The walls of this building were the only things standing between the townspeople and oblivion.

Serieve took Oather's tattered shirt and began ripping it into long strips. He took the strips and made make-shift bandages from them. He rolled one into a ball and pressed it firmly into Oather's deep gash in an attempt to stop the bleeding, just as Sir Gavin had shown him to do during his servitude to the knight. The forceful push made Oather grunt as he bit back the pain. Khu-Rá took several other strips and began to wrap them around the barbarian's torso and shoulder to hold the bandage in place.

Serieve had never really given much thought to the gods, but he desperately hoped that his prayers would be heard. He could only hope that Sol had made it into the castle and was close to destroying the sphere. If he wasn't, it would just be a matter of time before the undead would break in and kill them all.

## 79. Dire Interruptions

The awful noise emanating from the sphere felt like a slap to the face as Halistan laid on the floor. He was drained of energy and his body surged with pain that stemmed from his arm. His whole body now felt as if fire were coursing through the veins beneath his skin.

He slowly managed to open his eyes. He saw Sol yelling at Zaroth, but couldn't make out what they were saying over the noise from the sphere. It was very apparent, however, that Sol wasn't happy with the older man.

Suddenly, the noise stopped and Sol glanced over at him. Sol must have seen that he was awake again because he ran around the swirling black sphere towards him. Sol knelt in front of him and looked him in the eyes.

"Listen, Halistan," Sol began, "I don't think we have a whole lot of time before we're going to have a lot more company."

Halistan couldn't seem to do anything but listen as Sol spoke to him. His mind was still swimming from the pain he felt. That, combined with his utter lack of strength, made doing anything but listening into an exercise in futility.

"What I need to know, Hal, is if there is anything you can do to help? We need to delay Nicholas just a little longer to give Zaroth a little more time."

Halistan looked blankly up at Sol. He tried hard to think straight. Spells, spells…what spells did he know off the top of his head, he thought. Food and drink spells…no, those wouldn't work. Traps, no, he was too tired, he just wanted to sleep.

Halistan laid his head back against the cold stone wall behind him. He needed to rest, just for a moment, but Sol shook him, grabbed his head and forced him to look at him.

"Come on, Hal, stay with me."

"I…I," Halistan began.

"Yes?"

"I cannot do any…" A jolt of pain surged up through his arm and into the back of his skull, making him grit his teeth hard. "I…don't have anything left."

"Come on, Hal!" Sol pleaded. "Anything will do."

"I might be able…"

"That's great, let's get you up and get to it," Sol interrupted as he began to help Halistan up to his feet. Halistan draped his arm around Sol's shoulders and was able to get his footing. He hadn't realized it before, but he was just a smidge taller than Sol. This whole time, he had felt like he was shorter than him.

"Okay, there you go," Sol said, as soon as Halistan was able to take a few steps.

Halistan glanced back at Zaroth. The wizard had his eyes closed and was chanting again, with his hands stretched out towards the sphere. This made him look as though he were warming his hands over an open fire.

Sol led Halistan towards the entrance to the treasure room. As they walked, Halistan felt some of his strength returning, and it was becoming a little easier for him to think straight.

"We should cast it here," Sol said, and pointed to the floor of the entryway, sounding as if he was an integral part of the spell. Halistan was able to stand on his own now. He still felt weak, but he was beginning to get a little more of his strength back.

He looked down at his arm, and though he hadn't realized it before, his hand and a good portion of his arm was now blackened as though they were frostbitten. Long dark streaks ran up his arm and under the sleeve of his shirt.

Halistan did his best to ignore how bad his arm looked and concentrated on the most powerful protection spell he could remember. He closed his eyes and began to pray.

Halistan could feel the symbol begin to heat up in his hand. It burned more as he spoke, and the holy energy poured from it as he cast the spell. The more power that coursed through it, the more the blackened skin on his arm burned. It felt as if someone had taken a red-hot piece of metal from a blacksmith's fire and applied it directly to his palm. His body trembled and beads of sweat ran down his brow and into his closed eyes.

He clenched his eyes shut and tried to ignore the pain, but it didn't help much. Then, suddenly, as quickly as the pain had begun, it subsided when the spell completed. The release from the intense heat coming from his hand was almost euphoric. His hand and arm still hurt, but for a split moment, he couldn't feel any pain at all.

He felt weakened again and thought he would lose his balance, but fortunately, Sol was there to help him.

"Woah," he heard Sol say as the other man grabbed him and held him up. "Okay, now let's put one at the main entra-"

Sols words were cut off by a thunderous roar accompanied by booming steps, coming from outside the study. Halistan looked at Sol, who looked like the blood had drained from his face as they both realized what the sound was.

"Here he comes," Sol yelled back at Zaroth, but Zaroth was so focused that he didn't seem to notice. Sol began pushing against the secret door to the study in order to close it. Halistan saw him straining as he put all his weight into the door, but it wouldn't move. Apparently, Sol knew how to open the door, but didn't know how to close it.

He watched Sol try pushing from all directions but the secret passage wouldn't budge. Halistan wanted to help him, but he was afraid that if he moved from the wall, he'd collapse. His head swam and exhaustion gripped him. All he wanted to do was sleep, even if just for a few moments.

Halistan reluctantly allowed his eyes to close, just to rest them briefly. Then he heard a crash at the door to the study. Halistan's eyes burst open and he saw a giant, muscular, red-skinned leg kick in the door. The massive door came off its hinges and fell onto the ground.

Halistan did his best to stand up and away from the wall. He lifted his hand up, pointing his holy symbol at the demon in front of him. Before Halistan could mutter even a single word, Nicholas backhanded him with his enormous gnarled fist.

Instantly, the world seemed to go black and time seemed to slow down or stop completely. Halistan flew through the air, although, it felt more like he was floating. He could hear loud noises all around him, but they seemed muffled and strange to him.

Then, he felt himself hit the ground. He landed shoulder first and he heard a loud crack as he hit the wall. His body went limp as he collapsed onto the cold stone floor. He felt blood pouring down over his lips. It was warm in contrast to the cold stone underneath him.

# 80. *Last Stand*

"You men," Serieve pointed to his right at a pair of teenaged boys who stood near the stairway on the left that led down to the halls detention block. They were no older than he had been when he first became a squire. They had been looking up at the ceiling, listening to the frightful sounds coming from outside. Both jumped as Serieve called to them.

"Get below and check on the women and children. Assure them that we are here and all will be okay. Barricade the door and do not, I repeat, do not allow anyone down there."

Both young men looked confused by the order but neither spoke. The terror they were experiencing was evident in their eyes but Serieve had to ignore that for the greater good.

"Now, go," he barked at them, and the two rushed down the steps.

Serieve stood and drew his sword again. Khu-Rá stood up with him and drew an elven short sword. Serieve would have thought it would have only been a ceremonial weapon if it were not of elven design. Elves were gifted in making their weapons functional in addition to ornate, something that set them apart from their human counterparts.

With a great heave, Oather too, rose to join them. He no longer had his sword, as he'd dropped it outside, but he stood with them nonetheless.

"We make our stand here," Serieve said confidently. As he spoke, a loud crash came from outside. It sounded like something huge had stepped on a house.

Serieve pointed towards the men to his left. "You there," his finger swept right, "if anything attempts to come through the door or the windows, hack it off and throw it back out. Do not allow any parts to remain inside."

His gaze went to each man in the room in sequence and they all nodded fearfully that they understood his orders. "Oather, you stay down here with them while Khu-Rá and I head up and help the men upstairs."

"Aye, cap'n," Oather broke a leg off the bench he had been sitting on to create a makeshift club. Serieve headed up the staircase that went up to the next floor, followed closely by the elf.

Before he could reach the top another loud crash rang in his ears. This time the whole building shook with it. Suddenly, above him, where a solid roof had been moments before, a giant hole now exposed him to the night sky. Outside the building, he could see a monstrous skeletal form stood and peered back at him.

Its giant bone head looked like the dried skull of a long dead cow, a giant cow with really big, sharp teeth and horns. Its fiery orange eyes looked down directly at him. It raised a tree-sized mace high into the air to take another swipe at the roof of the building.

Serieve was awestruck by the size of the monster and stood frozen in place. He just couldn't seem to pull his eyes away from the massive beast. It wasn't until he felt Khu-Rá push him out of the way and onto the floor that Serieve regained his senses. Debris from the ruined ceiling fell down around them.

"Thanks," Serieve said as he fanned away the dust and dirt that clouded the air around them. Khu-Rá nodded and jumped to his feet and prepared for battle again. Serieve envied the elf's energy. He didn't know if he was getting fatigued from the battle or what, but he was quickly running out of the will to keep fighting. Whatever it was, he was beginning to feel like all his limbs had heavy stones strapped to them.

He pushed himself up and got to his feet as quickly as he could, just in time to see the gargoyles flying overhead again.

"Those damn things just don't know when to quit," he grumbled. He saw another gargoyle, but this one was carrying several undead soldiers, which it dropped onto what remained of the roof.

"Incoming," Serieve bellowed to the soldiers behind him as he gripped his sword tightly and prepared for a fight.

Just over the edge of the hole in the roof, he saw two skeletal heads rise up over the opening. With a leap, each skeleton jumped off the roof and into the building. One landed directly on a soldier, impaling him with its blade as it landed.

Serieve struck at the monster with a fury. His sword broke through the dilapidated chain mail that the dead warrior wore, breaking bone in the process as it cut its way through the monsters skeletal body.

Then, before he could attack the other undead, another crash hit the side of the building, jarring the structure so much that Serieve nearly lost his footing. He caught himself just in the nick of time. He turned in the direction of the crash; he now saw an entire corner of the building was gone; torn away by the force of the monster's assault.

Out of the corner of his eye, Serieve caught a glimpse of Khu-Rá leaping ferociously at another undead intruder. His silver weapon flashed as it arced through the air at the creature, cleaving it into pieces. Serieve looked down at the fallen man nearest to him and saw him getting back up. Serieve realized that the dead man was lost to them and was now part of the undead army.

Serieve rammed into the newly-risen undead with all his strength. It flew back from the force of the blow much easier than he had anticipated. The undead soldier hit the other two skeletons just as they were beginning to rise again, and all three fell back through the hole in the side of the building.

Finally, they were rid of the intruders. If only for a moment, they were safe again and Serieve breathed a short sigh of relief. The moment passed quickly, though, as he heard the sound of new soldiers being dropped onto the roof above them.

"Quick," he shouted to his men. "Get down to the jail-- that's the only place we'll be able to fend them off!"

The men didn't need to be told twice. They dashed down the steps to the main floor and continued down the steps towards the dungeons. Serieve waited until the last man and Khu-Rá had descended. Before he could follow them, though, another undead soldier jumped down into the room. The way it landed, it was facing away from him. It was an arm's length from him and didn't seem to know he was behind it, but it stood between him and the stairway leading down.

Serieve reached into the pouch on his belt and palmed a small vial of water that he'd saved for just such an occasion. He gripped the small bottle in his hand tightly, then smashed the vial of holy water down upon the monster's head. Glass shattered, and the liquid splashed over the beast.

A small fountain of white flame erupted from the creature's brittle bones. The skeleton began to thrash about as if it were in pain as the flame spread to the rest of its body. Its weapons dropped to the floor as it flailed around. Serieve decided it would be best to not wait for its companions to arrive, so he ran past the monster and fled down the steps.

The main floor, he was glad to see, was empty. He could hear sounds of yelling coming from the stairway leading down. He hurried down the corridor to see what the yelling was about and heard several men pounding on the shut door. Serieve made his way to the front.

"What's going on here?"

"Weh canno' geh in!" replied an old townsman. He stood in between Serieve and the door holding a lamp.

Serieve turned and pounded on the door himself, "You, in there, I order you to open this door!"

Nothing happened. Serieve started to yell again when he could hear something on the other side of the door. It sounded like people moving and yelling far away from the door, although it was hard to tell from the other turmoil going on all around them.

"Oather," Serieve called back to the large man as he stood behind everyone else in the stairway. Oather pushed his way up to Serieve as fast as he could.

"Do you think you c..." was all Serieve had to say before Oather took it upon himself to act. With a deep grunt, the barbarian braced his arms on the walls around him and kicked mightily at the door, flinging it open with a loud crack of snapping timber.

Inside was a sight that Serieve was unprepared for. The undead had found the hole the adventurers had made earlier when they escaped imprisonment, and had completely filled that cell. Undead soldiers and beasts the like of which Serieve had never seen before were trying to squeeze themselves through the bars to get to the people within.

A mass of women had the children huddled into a corner at the far end of the room, holding them tightly in their arms as they screamed and cried. Several other women, as well as the soldiers Serieve sent down earlier and a few of the elderly men, all had makeshift weapons that they were using to hit the undead with to fend them off.

"What have I done?" Serieve muttered softly.

## *81. Battle for the Orb*

With great effort Halistan managed to open one eye. Everything was blurry, and the yelling he heard around him was unintelligible. His vision cleared slowly, just enough that he was able to see a massive creature walk into the study. With each step the floor shook. Halistan heard Sol's voice yell as he attacked the demon, but Sol's voice was silenced as Nicholas batted away his attack and struck him to the ground as well.

Halistan turned and tried to raise himself up onto his elbows, but soon realized he couldn't move his arm. A great wave of pain surged through his left shoulder. It wasn't like the searing pain from his wounded hand, but a sharp wracking pain that instantly brought tears to his eyes. Looking to his left, he saw a jagged bone sticking out through his ripped shirt, covered in blood. His mind swam uncontrollably now.

Halistan couldn't move and he could barely breathe. He tasted blood in his mouth. He coughed violently and the blood splattered onto the floor. Halistan strained to see what was going on. Wind whipped through the room, sometimes blowing Halistan's blonde hair into his eyes as he was trying to make out what was happening. On the other side of the sphere, Zaroth stood facing Nicholas. He heard a roar come from Nicholas as he took a single step towards the wizard.

Zaroth's hand stretched out towards Nicholas. From the tips of his finger poured grayish wisps of smoke that swirled into a disk that seemed to push Nicholas back, even as the demon tried to push forward.

In his other hand, Zaroth held aloft a blue stone. The wizard pointed it towards Nicholas and a great bolt of lightning burst from it. The light it generated was intense and lit up the entire room. The bolt struck Nicholas in the chest with a boom and a crackle.

Nicholas roared so loud that Halistan thought he might go deaf. The fiend took a step back to recover from the blast. Then, with an overhead swing, his mighty fist came down upon Zaroth's shield and destroyed it.

"Halistan!" he heard someone scream. It was Andrea. Her voice sounded horrible and strained. It was barely audible over the sound of the sphere.

She ran into the room and knelt next to him.

"Oh, what's happened to you?"

Halistan could hear the concern in her voice, although he was unable to reply to her. When he tried, he only managed to cough up more blood.

She grabbed him by his shirt and pulled him up off the floor to a sitting position. He grunted as the pain from his shoulder and hand both surged through him. He could see Andrea's eyes now.

"We need to get out of here. There's nothing more we can do now."

Halistan could only nod his agreement to her as she put his right arm around her shoulders and helped him to his feet.

## 82. Fallen Soldier

Serieve mustered every remaining shred of strength he had left and charged into the room. Near to the cell of undead, the two boys he had sent down earlier struck at the creatures that squeezed their way through the bars. He rushed to help them.

Just as he reached one of the boys, a grotesque beast reached through the bars and swiped fiercely through the air, catching the boy off guard. Serieve grabbed the boy's shirt and pulled him back to save him from the beast's massive, clawed, bony arm. The boy flew back and landed on the ground behind him.

Raising his blade high, Serieve came down on the beast and cut right through the appendage, which fell to the ground. Serieve swept up the severed arm and threw it back into the cell from which it had come.

As he looked up, several arrows zinged past him into the cell, hitting several undead that were forcing their way through the bars. The force of the arrow strike was such that it pushed them back but otherwise did very little damage.

Serieve saw the boy he'd thrown back out of harm's reach still lying upon the ground. He went to the boy's side to help him to his feet. As he knelt down, Serieve heard the thunderous crash of metal snapping like twigs. His head whipped around just in time to see the undead pour from the opening and into the room.

At once, Oather and the other men sprang into action. There was a clashing of sword, steel and bone. Immediately, Serieve rose and joined his comrades when he was pulled back by something grabbing his left arm. He looked to see what it was and instantly felt cold steel pierce his side.

Looking back in astonishment, he saw that the boy's face was shredded and blood dripped down onto his chest. To Serieve's horror, the boy's eyes were aflame and his hand gripped the blade that twisted inside of him.

## 83. Paying the Ultimate Price

Andrea pulled hard, attempting to drag Halistan along with her, but he wouldn't budge. Instead, he stood there looking across the sphere at the battle.

"Come on," she urged. "There's nothing else we can do here!"

Halistan didn't move, or even say anything. He just kept looking at the wizard.

She looked around him to see what he was staring at. Instantly, she saw Zaroth shoot a cone of flame at Nicholas. The monster drew back as if he were going to punch the old man. As the flame blew, the devil's arm instantly recoiled to cover his face from the fire, which arced up towards the ceiling and melted a hole in the stone. It had opened a hole in the castle ceiling, exposing them to the sky above them.

Andrea saw the old man dart a scornful look towards Halistan before yelling towards them, "I cannot hold him back much longer. You must do-" but he was cut off as Nicholas finally managed to get within an arm's reach of the wizard and grabbed him by the throat with both of his ghoulishly clawed hands.

Zaroth's eyes rolled into the back of his head momentarily. Andrea stood there, dumbfounded, as she watched Halistan open his hand and look at the tiny holy symbol. She didn't understand what the old wizard was talking about, but Halistan seemed lost in thought. His body was trembling as he stood just steps away from the swirling black orb.

"We must go, now!" she yelled as loud she could with her bruised throat. She looked back at the wizard, who had been lifted up into the air while Nicholas was choking the life from his body.

Then a figure ran towards Nicholas. It was Sol. He ran towards the devil with a speed Andrea didn't know he possessed. He jumped and sunk a dagger deep into Nicholas' back.

Nicholas instantly dropped Zaroth onto the ground, and the wizard's hands went to his throat as he desperately gasped for air. Howling in rage, Nicholas turned and swung at Sol. At first it appeared that Sol might somehow avoid the blow, but he didn't, and took the swing right across his face. The force of the blow threw him across the room and into the wall, which he hit with a loud crash. His body bounced off the wall and fell to the ground. Several shields and other pieces of armor that were hanging on the wall fell off and covered his motionless body.

Andrea stood there, confused at how horribly wrong their plan had turned out. She saw Halistan look towards the wizard, who was trying to stand up. The wizard looked back at him, "Halistan...do it!"

"Do...do what?" she asked, looking back at Halistan.

Halistan pulled his arm away from her and pushed her aside. She was confused, not knowing what the wizard wanted him to do. Halistan took advantage of her bewilderment. He reached out, open handed, took a few quick steps, and slammed his hand firmly down onto the sphere.

"Noooo!" she screamed, as she attempted to reach for him and pull him back before he could commit suicide. But it was too late. The moment the tiny star-shaped piece of metal touched the unholy orb, a great white flame erupted from the two artifacts. It instantly spread across the dark object and Halistan, engulfing them both in a bright white flame that stretched from the floor to the ceiling.

The blaze seemed to merge with the wisps of black fog that rose from the sphere and went up through the ceiling, changing the fog from dark gray to a bluish-white color.

Halistan and the sphere appeared locked together as they were enveloped in the bright flame. The orb rose several feet higher, taking the young priest with it as it lifted further off the ground. Halistan let out a horrific cry. His back arched and he screamed towards the heavens.

The intensity of the light became so bright that Andrea had to turn away and cover her eyes. From somewhere off to her right, she heard a furious growl. Before she could look for it, she was grabbed and thrown back. She hit the stone wall behind her with such force that she momentarily thought she was going to black out as she slumped to the ground. She was able to look up just in time to see Nicholas attempt to grab hold of Halistan.

As the demon approached him, a blast of white flame shot forth from the orb, hitting Nicholas in the chest. Nicholas howled as the flame hit him. As it had done with Halistan and the orb, the flame spread across Nicholas' entire body, engulfing him in the white fire. Then, all at once; Halistan, the sphere, and Nicholas exploded in a shimmering ball of white light.

As quickly as it had started, everything stopped. The flames subsided. The sphere stopped glowing and fell lifelessly to the floor along with the body of the young priest. The infernal device was no longer jet black, but had taken on a grayish-white color and was covered with a white powder. It made a loud crash as it hit the floor and shattered into hundreds of pieces. Nicholas, too, fell and crashed onto the stone floor of the castle and didn't move anymore.

Suddenly, everything was quiet. The wind stopped and nothing else in the room moved or made a sound. Halistan's body laid motionless in the middle of the hundreds of orb fragments, as the flames that covered his body slowly extinguished.

For several long moments everything was still and quiet. There was a calmness that Andrea hadn't felt in ages upon the room. She looked at Sol, who also lying motionless on the ground under a pile of shields, armor and treasure. Everything was quiet as she sat there for just another moment, not realizing she was holding her breath until she finally exhaled.

## *84. Respite*

Serieve dropped his weapon and grabbed the blade that was thrust in his side. The boy's strength had increased tremendously from being re-animated. Serieve struggled with the boy as the knife continued to twist in his side.

Slowly, Serieve began to win and the blade slid out of his flesh. It took all the strength he had left to hold the blade in a stalemate. The boy's flaming eyes glared at him menacingly.

Then Serieve saw Oather step up behind the boy, grab him by the shirt and throw him towards the other creatures that were pouring into the room. Serieve exhaled in relief at Oather's assistance and before he knew it, Oather had grabbed him and began dragging him towards the back of the room where the other men, women and children had withdrawn.

Oather let go of him as they reached the back wall. Serieve struggled to stand up. Only he, Oather, Khu-Rá, and a handful of villagers were left to stand between the women, children and elderly and the horrific undead monsters that stepped through the cell gates and into the room.

Serieve knew that all was lost. There was no way to get out of this room, they were surrounded by undead, and even if they could get out, the town was overrun with the undead horde and they'd never be able to get out alive. He no longer had his sword, but he did have the knife that he had been stabbed with.

"Ready yourselves, men," he said, without an ounce of regret. They all stood their ground as the undead marched towards them. The creatures had just stepped into range of their weapons, and Serieve saw Oather raising a blade high--and then the creatures stopped.

Serieve didn't understand why, but they all completely froze. Then, all of a sudden, the flames in their eyes extinguished like a campfire doused with water and their lifeless bodies fell to the ground.

"What the..." Serieve muttered under his breath.

For several long moments no one in the room moved. All was silent. Serieve unconsciously held his breath as he waited for the undead to rise again, but nothing happened. The deathly quiet was finally disturbed by the sound of a child crying. Behind him, he heard a mother pulling the child close and telling her that everything would be okay.

Finally, it was over. Serieve allowed exhaustion to overtake him. He fell backwards onto his butt, then laid back onto the floor. He let loose a great sigh of exhaustion and closed his eyes.

The next thing he heard was the sound of someone walking up next to him. He squinted open his eyes to see the elf looking down at him.

"You've been injured, friend." The elf pointed down at the gash in his side.

"It's just a flesh wound, I'll live."

"True enough," Khu-Rá replied as he sat down next to him.

Serieve opened his right eye and looked at Khu-Rá. "You saved my life up there. I owe you."

"It is I who owed you, remember."

The stoic look that normally occupied the elf's face was replaced with a smile. It was the most emotion he'd seen the elf display since they rescued him from being sacrificed back in the dungeons of Tyric.

"Then let's call it even."

The elf nodded appreciatively at him, then closed his eyes and they both finally relaxed.

## *85. Regrouping*

The ghostly silence was broken by Sol groaning as he pushed an ornate shield off his head and struggled to sit up. Andrea, although she was sore all over her body, slowly rose to her feet. Just a step away from her was Nicholas' corpse, and next to him laid the young priest who had given his life to destroy the sphere. She took a cautious step closer to Nicholas, and for the first time since she'd arrived, she felt a sense of relief.

She took another step around the fallen demon, walking closer to Halistan. He laid there, deathly still, as she approached him. Slowly, she knelt down next to the young man. His back was towards her, so she pulled him over so she could see his face. She'd seen men die--in fact she had been an instrument in many of those deaths--and it had never bothered her before. But this time, deep down inside, she felt a deep pang of remorse.

She looked down at his face. His eyes were closed and his skin was coated in a fine layer of white dust. She heard someone walk up behind her. It was Sol. He knelt down opposite her and looked down at the young man.

"He..he was brave," Sol said to her.

She slowly reached down and brushed Halistan's cheek. Sol put his hand over hers and held it still. Then Halistan's body convulsed. He coughed hard, flinging white powder into the air. Andrea and Sol both jerked their hands back from him as his body shook.

"Halistan?"

He coughed again, throwing more of the white dust into the air, making a small cloud between the three of them.

Andrea, momentarily forgetting herself, grabbed the young man's head and hugged it tightly. A smile crept across Sol's face as he watched her hug the young priest.

"Hal," he exclaimed. "I can't believe it, you're alive!"

Halistan coughed again, attempting to get a breath in between Andrea's tight squeezes. Reluctantly, she released her hold on him and let him go. Then, as he looked up at her, she slapped him across the face.

"Ow," he exclaimed, rubbing his cheek where she had hit him. "What was that for?"

"Don't ever do something that stupid again," she scolded him sternly, then hugged him again.

Halistan shot a confused look up at Sol, who simply shrugged and replied, "I don't know what to tell you, kid. I get that same reaction every time I go home."

Andrea couldn't help but smile at Sol's reply. She wanted to make a comment regarding some of the likely reasons for why he got slapped so often--she was sure it had something to do with his truly irritating nature--but she heard Zaroth shout behind her and her attention turned to him instead.

"Damn it all to the ninth quadrant of Hell."

She whipped her head around to see what the wizard was so angry about. He was standing in a pile of orb pieces.

"It's destroyed," he cried "Completely and utterly destroyed!"

"Wasn't that the whole point, old man?" Sol remarked snidely.

Zaroth shot him a glare.

"You know damn well it wasn't, Sol," Zaroth replied. "Or did you forget the little agreement that we made?"

"Agreement?" Andrea asked.

"Yes, well," Sol stammered as he stood up. "I knew I..uh…WE," looking at Andrea, "would need help getting all this treasure back home and so…"

"So you made a deal with the wizard, so that he could keep the sphere in exchange for helping you transport the King's treasure back?"

"Yes, well, you can forget it now," Zaroth fumed. "I'm going to get out of this god's forsaken hellhole and I'm never coming back."

Sol let out an irritated sigh as he reached down to help Halistan up. As Halistan offered his hand to Sol, she saw it was healed and quickly pulled his hand back to look at it. What used to be a piece of metal, imbedded in his hand, surrounded by a ghastly wound, was now whole.

Halistan showed Andrea and she could see that his skin had been fused with the tiny holy symbol. It looked as if it had always been that way. No sign of the previous wound at all. Halistan reached up once again and took Sol's arm this time.

Halistan began to help Andrea up when Zaroth darted towards them. He reached out and grabbed Halistan's hand and inspected it closely.

"That is simply miraculous," he said, in the most bewildered tone she'd ever heard from Zaroth. It was quite different from his usual arrogant tone, she noted. The old wizard peered closely at the priest's hand as he examined it.

"That should have killed you," he continued. "This...this is amazing."

He looked up at Halistan for a moment. "Don't get me wrong, lad, I'm glad it didn't. It's just unexpected...that's all."

"Oh my, the wizard was actually wrong about something," Sol replied sarcastically, which got him another irritated glare from the wizard.

Zaroth opened his mouth to reply but Sol quickly cut him off and pointed down at Nicholas' corpse lying upon the ground.

"So, what do you think we should do with him?" Sol asked as he lightly kicked at the dead remains of the King. "Are we even sure he's dead?"

"Nothing could have survived that blast from the sphere, not even a Byzmagth demon.

"A Byz..wha?" Sol asked.

"Are you sure that's what he was changed into?" Halistan asked, his interest suddenly piqued. Halistan stepped up between Sol and Zaroth for a closer inspection.

Zaroth knelt down to the corpse and with a great effort pushed the demon onto its back for a closer look. "You can tell by the skin, eyes and fangs," Zaroth pointed out to the young priest, who eagerly knelt down with him.

"Oh my," Halistan replied.

"For crying out loud," Sol said, rolling his eyes and walking away, "I wish I hadn't asked now."

"I've read about these horrid beasts, but I never dreamed I'd see one," Halistan said.

"Count yourself lucky. Few that ever have seen them, live to tell the tale," Zaroth remarked.

Andrea took a step back, closer to Sol. "You're crazy if you think I'm letting you get out of here with all this treasure," she whispered, winking at him with a sinister smile spreading across her lips.

Sol looked at her slyly. "Don't worry. If we can keep this secret, I'll find a way to get it out and you'll get your share....trust me."

"Trust you? Not a chance," she replied. "But see that you keep your end of the bargain."

## *86. The Others*

Halistan heard Andrea talking to Sol behind them. He couldn't make out what they were whispering, but Sol didn't sound happy. Eventually Andrea walked away from Sol and rejoined him and the wizard.

"What, exactly, is a Byzmagth demon?" she asked the two of them.

This was one of Halistan's favorite fields of study back at the church and he suddenly felt a rush to be able to explain it to someone as he looked up at her. "They are in the upper echelon of demonic servants of the service of Asumond, the Power, or demi-god, of Evil and the punisher of souls."

"One more time, kid, this time in words we can understand," Sol replied from across the room. Sol was filling a sack full of gems that he was picking out from several chests of treasure.

"Oh, err, of course," Halistan stammered, slightly embarrassed, as he tried to think of a better way to explain.

"When IAO created the 'Powers' or 'gods' to govern the world…" Halistan started to explain but was interrupted by Sol again.

"Zaroth, can you explain this quicker, I don't want a sermon, I just want to know what it is."

Halistan looked questioningly at Zaroth, who seemed entertained by Sol's lack of interest in what he was trying to say.

"They are very powerful demons. In fact, they are some of the most powerful servants of the evil god, Asumond. They're supposed to be immortal, but, apparently, even they have their limits."

"See, was that so hard?" Sol replied, looking at Halistan.

"The question still remains, what do we do with…it?"

"What does it matter?" Zaroth responded, "We're leaving. Let him rot here for all I care."

"I don't want it stinking up my treasure before I can come back and get the rest of it," Sol answered irritably. "Since you're not going to help me any longer, I'm going to have to make another trip here to get the rest of it."

"We need to bury it in consecrated ground," Halistan interrupted.

Both Sol and Zaroth looked at him like he was crazy. "Why do we need to do that?"

"Because that's the only-" Halistan began but was again interrupted, this time by Andrea.

"The bastard doesn't deserve a funeral," she spat. "All he did with his life was to make life a living hell for others."

Halistan heard the anger in her voice and wanted to argue, but thought it best to let it go.

"The others!" Halistan quickly realized that in their elation that they had completely forgotten about the others, and the town that was assuredly under siege by the undead army.

"You're right, kid, we need to get back there."

"It won't be any use," Andrea answered. "It'd take us the better part of a day to get back there again, and by then it'd be too late to do anything but bury the dead."

"That's not exactly true," Zaroth replied. "With Nicholas' control over this land broken, my magic should work normally again and I could transport us there."

"Then what are we waiting for? It's time to redeem yourself, wizard," Sol said. He grabbed his sack of gems and tied it to his belt.

"Everyone come close and grab hands."

Halistan stood up and grabbed Andrea's hand as Sol approached and took her other hand. The wizard took Halistan's other hand and closed his eyes and began to concentrate. It almost looked like the wizard was praying, even though he knew that he wasn't. He was beginning to wonder if he needed to close his eyes as well when everything went white and he heard a loud popping sound.

Suddenly his legs went numb and he fell to the ground. He hit the soil face first and was thankful that the ground was soggy and not dry, as he'd probably have busted his nose if it had been.

Halistan tried to open his eyes but when he tried everything was so bright that he had to immediately shut them again and open them slowly. The sun was out. The clouds that he'd grown used to blocking the sky ever since he got here were gone and he could feel the sunlight on his skin. His stomach felt ill suddenly, almost as if his insides had been scrambled up with a spoon. For a second he thought he might throw up, but he was able to resist the urge.

"Uugghhh," he heard from someone on the ground next to him. "I swear," Halistan heard Sol say with a hint of anger in his voice, "you have got to be the worst wizard."

He felt someone grab his arm and pull him up. It was Zaroth. "Oh, yes," the wizard said with a note of sinister joy to his voice, "for 'first-timers' there is typically some level of discomf...." He was cut off by a stern look from Sol, who turned his back on the wizard and walked away.

Halistan stood and brushed off some of the dirt and mud from his clothes. He saw Andrea doing the same. Sol didn't seem concerned with this at all, as he just simply looked around in awe.

All around them was the tiny town that they had left just a day or so earlier. It was completely destroyed. There were bodies, some of them residents of the town and some undead and other ghastly beasts, lying all around them. Buildings were in shambles, and the defensive wall that he had seen the others painstakingly creating were in ruin.

Most of the buildings looked like they had been hit by a tornado. Some had their roofs ripped off, and others looked like they had been walked through by something gigantic. Halistan had never seen devastation like this before.

"Hello," he heard Sol cry out at the top of his lungs. "Anyone there?"

There was no response. There was no sound at all. No movement aside from the light winds blowing around them. With the sun out, it made the little town look almost completely different. Even though it was mostly destroyed, it didn't have the weary gray tinge to it that it had when he was last here.

"I'm going to check the town hall, that's where they should be if there are any survivors," Sol said as he began walking in that direction. Halistan followed behind him with Andrea and Zaroth, but he could tell by the silence of the others that they didn't expect to find anyone alive. Sol marched on anyway.

The town was eerily quiet and Sol kept the lead as they approached the building. As they neared it, Halistan saw that a huge section of the upper floor had been completely ripped away. The debris laid on the street next to it. He couldn't begin to imagine what might have done that sort of damage to a building, but it had been done nevertheless.

The closer they got the more damage they could see. The scattered bones of undead soldiers laid all around the outside of the building. They must have been trying to break their way in when the sphere was destroyed, and them along with it. Halistan saw Sol pick up his pace so that he was almost jogging towards the building.

Just as he reached the main entrance, the door burst open. A giant foot had kicked it open, and out stepped Oather, carrying an injured woman. He was surrounded by kids, women and a few of the village men as he stepped out into the light. Behind all of them, Khu-Rá and Serieve also walked out. Serieve's arm was draped over the elf's shoulders for support.

Sol came to an abrupt stop as he saw the entrance fly open and Oather come out. Oather's face was grim and battle-weary. He stopped as he saw Sol standing in front of him. Not a word was spoken for several moments which, to Halistan, seemed like an eternity. Then, finally, Oather gently set the woman down. She quietly thanked him as he let go of her and took another step towards Sol.

Soliere, his face still showing no sign of emotion, took another step towards the barbarian. He was reaching his arm out to greet his friend when Oather snatched him up and hugged him tight. Sol's face turned red as he was nearly crushed by Oather's grip. A huge smile swept over Oather's face as he playfully squeezed his friend.

## 87. Mending Wounds

"So this is all that survived?" Sol asked as he and Oather found a place where the big man could sit down.

"Aye."

"What about Yaeva?"

"She is alive, probably with some of the other mystics. Most of their men were killed in the fighting, but the women are all back inside," Oather said as Sol removed the cloth from his wound, inspecting it.

"I don't see Cornwall anywhere, did he make it?"

"No. He and I," Oather paused, "we had a slight disagreement about command decisions…you might say."

This spiked Sol's attention. He flipped the cloth around to a side that was less dirty to re-dress the wound. "Oh yeah?"

"He wanted to run, and I ordered the men to make it to the town hall for a last stand."

"Yes, and…" Sol was completely engrossed in Oather's story now.

"Then when I turned my back on him, the bastard stabbed me."

"That son of a dung troll," Sol growled. "So that's how you got this wound."

"Aye."

"He's lucky he was killed in the battle; otherwise I'd kill him now," Sol spat angrily.

"He didn't exactly die in the battle."

This took Sol by surprise and his attention went back to his friend. "How did he die, then?"

"I killed him."

"You did?" Sol replied. He was unable to mask the astonished tone in his voice that Oather could have actually done that, but considering the circumstances it really wasn't that unlikely. "So what happened?"

"I picked the traitorous bastard up, dropped him on the catapult, and sent him flying to the enemy where he belonged."

"You did what?" Sol blurted in surprise. "By Qualinos' sword, I didn't really think you had that in you."

"Aye, heh di," came a voice from behind him. Sol turned around to see a teenage boy coming up behind him, helping Yaeva make her way towards them.

"Ye shoul hae seen haw brave Mas' Oathe was," the kid continued, talking faster than Sol had ever heard someone before. "Ne'er in my dae have I seen suh bravrae. Hay was rallae somethin ta see."

"Sounds like you're a hero."

"That he is, as are you, young man," Madame Yaeva said. "Cornwall was a coward, and his actions would have killed us all. We are in your debt, both of you." She smiled at them.

"Thank you," Oather replied.

"About that debt-" Sol began.

"Yes, my boy, you are more than welcome to all that you can take back," Yaeva said.

Sol's eyes widened like he was a child being given the toy he'd always wanted. "But I warn you, the route back to the Empire is a treacherous one, full of dangerous beasts, bandits and thieves. It's unlikely that you'd make it back with anything."

Sol was somewhat disheartened to hear that. "And just how long does it take to get back to the Empire from here?"

"The better part of a year," she replied and Sol felt his heart sink. "But don't worry, I'm sure you'll be able to persuade that wizard friend of yours to help you out." The old woman gave Sol a wink with one of her eerie double-pupil eyes. Then she and the child walked away towards the other mystics.

Sol wiped his hand across his face in frustration. If it really did take that long, there was no way he could get the treasure back without help from Zaroth, and the thought of begging the wizard for help made his stomach churn.

"Gonna do it?" Oather asked.

"Do what?"

"You know what."

"Yeah, I know. I just don't want to think about it."

"So what are you going to do?" Oather asked with a rather inquisitive tone to his voice.

"I'm not sure," Sol replied staring off, his mind racing trying to think of options. "Here, call the kid over and see if he can do anything about that wound. I'm going to think a bit."

## 88. The Souvenir

"There you go," Halistan said as he slapped Oather on the back where his wound used to be. There were so many people that swarmed him after he healed Serieve that it took hours to treat them all. He'd been at it all night and he was just now getting to Oather.

"Thank you," Oather replied, stretching his arms out wide, basking in the relief from the pain of his wound. "If there's anything I can do to repay you..." Oather began, but Halistan just held his hand up because he'd not hear of it.

"It's my pleasure," he replied back with a smile, "but oh, yes, speaking of repayment..." Halistan untied the mace that Oather had given him to use before he went to the castle. "I meant to give this back to you."

"Keep it," Oather replied. "Consider it a gift for healing me."

"I honestly don't think I'll have much use for it back at the monastery," Halistan said, looking down at the weapon he was holding.

Oather grasped the handle of the mace and pointed to the ornate head of the weapon. "This is some of the best craftsmanship I've seen on a weapon like this. If nothing else, you can sell it."

"But-"

"But nothing, I can't tell if this is ancient elven, or possibly gnome design, but it's good, I know that much. All I can tell you for certain is that it's old, and for it to be as old as I think it is, and still in this good a shape means it must be special."

Halistan stood there; quiet, because he couldn't think of anything to say.

"So, take care of it. Who knows, you might have a use for it someday." Oather patted Halistan on the shoulder and walked back in the direction of Sol and Andrea, who were talking near the ruined town hall.

As he watched Oather walk off towards the others, Halistan became keenly aware of just how fatigued he was. It all seemed to hit him at once. He was extremely far from home, with people he didn't know, fighting an evil that previously he couldn't even comprehend actually existed, and now he was simply exhausted.

He found a rock that wasn't covered in as much mud as most of the debris in the town and used it to sit down on. In the center of what was left of the village, many of the survivors were still huddled in front of the remains of a funeral pyre that had been created to burn the remains of their fallen loved ones.

Last night, he'd been asked to lead a prayer by the villagers for those they had lost. There were far too many to bury, so Sol suggested they burn the remains to honor them. Then he made a remark about how much experience the wizard already had in doing such things, which seemed in bad taste, but he didn't really understand what Sol was referring to. Zaroth just seemed to give Sol another menacing glare. Halistan didn't understand why Sol picked on the wizard so much, but he didn't think it was really that good an idea to upset a man like Zaroth. Nevertheless, the wizard did help start the fire for the townspeople after Halistan had given a small prayer in remembrance of the souls lost that day.

Not far from what remained of the slowly dying fire, Halistan saw Andrea and Sol talking to Zaroth. Sol seemed to be upset about something because his arms were flailing quite a bit as he spoke to the older man. It wasn't long before the trio resolved their issue and walked over towards him.

Halistan heard Sol call over to Oather, Serieve and Khu-Rá as he approached Halistan and gently kicked his leg.

"You awake, kid?"

Halistan opened one eye and looked up at Sol. He was awake, even though he wished he wasn't. "Yes, I'm awake."

"Good, the wizard has agreed to take us home rather than making us all walk."

"He...did?" This news came as a shock to Halistan as he didn't really think Zaroth did anything for the sake of being kind.

"Aye, I'm not happy about it, but I did make an agreement with Sol before we started this fool's venture. I'll uphold my end, even if I don't get anything out of it."

"Alright, so per our original agreement, I'll take my ninety-five percent and Oather and I will-"

"It was fifty percent." Andrea snapped at Sol.

"Stop!" Zaroth interrupted. "You all get one chest each. End of story."

Sol and Andrea both froze and looked at Zaroth.

With that being said, the wizard stormed off and left the group to say their good-byes to the townsfolk.

"What was that all about?" asked Serieve, who had walked up behind them.

"Long story, I'll tell you later," Sol replied.

"The mystics, along with the townspeople, are packing up and heading out."

"Do you blame them?"

"No, but I thought we might want to do the same. I, for one, have had enough of this place."

"Aye. Go get the elf. We have to make another trip to the castle, then we can go, and you're right, we should do it before the wizard changes his mind."

Serieve wasted no time in retrieving the elf, and returned before Sol even had time to light his pipe. Together, everyone in the group walked over to where Zaroth sat.

"Everyone's leaving. Perhaps we should get this done and get home ourselves."

"For once, I have to agree with you," Zaroth replied. "As before, everyone hold hands."

Everyone took hold of each other's hands until a complete circle was made. Then, like the last time they travelled, Zaroth closed his eyes and began casting the spell.

Then, with a flash of white, and a loud "pop" sound they appeared back in the castle's treasure room. Halistan again, instantly felt sick, like someone had hit him in the gut, but it wasn't as bad this time as it was the first time. This was probably because he was expecting it to some degree. He was able to remain standing though, unlike Serieve and Oather, who both hit the ground hard. Khu-Rá, on the other hand, didn't seem like it bothered him at all.

"I think I'm going to be sick," Halistan heard Serieve grumble as he tried to raise himself up off the floor with Sol's help.

"It'll pass, you big baby."

## 89. The Spoils of War

Unlike the town, the castle hadn't changed much with the death of Nicholas. It was still as dark and dingy as it had been when they left. The scattered white pieces of the orb littered the far end of the room. The only thing that had changed was that Nicholas' body was no longer in the room.

There was white dust around where the body had been, but it was no longer there.

"What the…" Sol mumbled as he drew his sword. "I thought you said he was dead," he hissed at Zaroth.

"He is dead," Zaroth replied. "I have no doubt that he still has servants in this castle who removed the body. So I would suggest you get your gold and we get out of here before they return."

Sol begrudgingly accepted Zaroth's explanation and put away his weapon. Then, followed closely by Oather, he dashed to the corner of the room with the largest chest and claimed it as his. Serieve found another chest, as did Andrea.

Halistan went to the chest nearest him and began to fill a small pouch with gemstones.

"Hey, kid," Sol said to him. "I thought priests didn't need money."

"I don't personally use it--the church gives me everything I need--but I plan to tithe this money to the church. It will find great use for it in helping the needy."

"Figures," was all Sol replied as he and Oather pulled the chest away from the wall and closed the lid. They heaved it with all their strength and only managed to move it a little. This surprised Halistan, given as big as Oather was. He wasn't sure if there wasn't anything the big man couldn't lift. After several strong pulls, they managed to get it pulled out and into the center of the room.

"Aren't you going to get any?" Serieve asked Khu-Rá.

"No, elves do no use gold to barter, only gems."

"There are plenty of gems here too, you know."

"Thank you, but I am fine."

Andrea had found a smaller chest that looked as if it was only filled with exotic gold and silver jewelry, but the chest itself was also probably the most ornate in the room. Serieve's chest rested on top of the enormous one that Sol and Oather had picked out. Soon, they were finished picking out what they wanted and rejoined the circle with Khu-Rá and Zaroth.

"Alright, everyone place their chests in front of them, within the circle, and then take hands again," instructed the wizard. "Andrea, my dear, where are you going?"

"Ondullus province, on the east side of the capital city," she replied.

"Get a picture of your home in your mind. Picture it as clearly as you can. Halistan, what about you?"

"The city of Valencia," he replied. "The northeast cathedral specifically."

"Khu-Rá?"

"Terrazzaz, the capital city of the Elven kingdom in the Great Mishivera Woods."

"Sol?"

"Oather and I are going back to the city of Tyric, to the *Lucky Duck* Inn near the wharf."

"Serieve?"

"Willumshire province, north of the capital city."

Zaroth closed his eyes tightly, as if he was concentrating very hard. Then he began to chant. Halistan felt a tingle flow through his hands. The spell seemed different this time than it had the times before. Zaroth chanted louder and louder, until he was almost yelling. Halistan looked around at the others. Most also had their eyes closed or at least had their heads bowed, like Sol, Oather and Serieve did.

While he waited for the spell to take effect, Halistan looked around the room; and just inside the secret door that led to the study, he saw something. It was Nicholas in his human form staring at him. A shiver went down his spine and his blood ran cold. Before Halistan could even speak, there was a blinding white light and a loud popping noise.

## 90. Back in Valencia

The next thing Halistan knew he was very disoriented and couldn't seem to get his footing. In fact, he could hardly feel his legs at all and his head was spinning. Fortunately, there was a metal railing next to him that he was able to latch onto and regain his balance.

He gripped the railing tightly and hung on until his head finally started to clear. This trip had been far more distressing than the others and Halistan was glad that it was over. He was never going to travel by magic ever again if he could help it.

It took several moments, but finally he started feeling better and could stand on his own. His head began to clear and the first thing he remembered was Nicholas. He had to do something. Nicholas was still alive.

Halistan sat down on the steps for a moment. Now that his head was clearing, he was beginning to doubt if he had really seen Nicholas, or if his imagination was just getting the best of him. He heaved a deep sigh of relief, and felt his heart rate slow down.

Looking around, he saw that it was a beautiful day. He was outside the cathedral and he was home. He'd never been so glad in his life to be someplace. He leapt to his feet and in front of him were the great oak doors of the northeast cathedral, the building he'd spent so much time in during his years of school, and which he considered to be his home more than any other place.

He ran up and pulled the massive doors open and rushed inside, almost running over Father Angelo in the process. As soon as he saw the old man, his face lit up.

"Father Angelo!"

"Hal...Halistan...is that really you?" Father Angelo looked at Halistan as if was looking at a ghost. "Where...where have you been? We've all been worried sick about you."

"I'm so sorry, Father. I don't know where I was."

"What?"

"I was gone…that's all I can say," he replied as he hugged the gray haired old man.

"But where?"

"A bad place, but I need you to do me a favor."

"Anything, you know that."

Halistan took a deep breath and tried to calm himself. This was a big request and he wasn't sure if Father Angelo would go out of his way to help Halistan with it.

"I need to speak with the Patriarch."

"His Holiness, but why?"

"I can't tell you right now, but I must speak with him and the council of elders just as quickly as possible. Do you think you can get me in to see them?"

"I…I guess I probably can," Father Angelo replied. Halistan grasped the older priest's hands to thank him. Father Angelo must have felt the star on Halistan's hand because he immediately pulled the hand forward to get a closer look at it.

"Great Alistair's ghost," muttered the old man as he adjusted the spectacles on his face to get a closer look. "What has happened to you?"

"I have so much to tell you, Father Angelo," Halistan said, as he and the Father turned and walked further into the cathedral and Halistan started to recant the series of events he'd just been part of.

## *91. Revenge is a Dish Best Served Cold*

Twilight overtook the city as Andrea approached the mansion that served as the assassin's guild headquarters. She had gone through a series of back alleys to arrive there without being seen by anyone.

Weeks prior, Andrea had come back to find her home razed to the ground and her servants killed. Axel had been tortured within an inch of his life and left for dead at her estate. He was severely delirious and she had barely got him to help in time to save him from certain death.

Now she was here to get revenge on the bastard responsible for all this, Jor'Dan. She was dressed in her black silk jumpsuit, which was more or less the accepted uniform of the guild members while on missions. It was form fitting, light and most importantly, quiet, which was a necessity in their occupation.

Fortunately, she kept a small cabin, not far from her estate, stashed with supplies in case of such an emergency. She was able to take Axel there so he could get rest and she could prepare the revenge she justly deserved.

She watched the headquarters building until the sun had fully set and darkness enveloped the city. On one of the many balconies, she noticed another guild member walk out several times, look at the night sky, then retreat back into the building. It was Chandra, one of the Chancellor's favorites, and a woman whom Andrea despised. She and Chandra had had several run-ins over the years, but never a direct confrontation. The guild strictly forbade fighting among its members, and to break a covenant of the guild invited certain death.

Getting passed her guild-sister might prove difficult, but that was a chance Andrea was more than prepared to take tonight. She patiently waited until Chandra returned inside, and then scaled the back wall. It was draped with vines and had provided an easy way for her to get in over the years. As she topped the rear balcony she stepped into a shadow that provided her access to peer through the windows of the guild.

It seemed there were not many members in. Several were downstairs, and only Chandra was on the second floor. Many of the members did not reside at the guild. Only initiates were required to live there as well as a few senior members and instructors. However, it was common for them to meet at the guild frequently, so Andrea was thankful tonight they were not there.

There were few lamps lit inside, which was a good thing for her, because she could blend into the shadows if she needed to. She felt the handle of the door, which was stiff and felt locked, but Andrea knew differently. With a strong jerk, the door opened. It had always been broken and seemed like it was locked shut, when it never was.

She could hear someone in the next room walking in her direction. There was enough light in the room that if the person came in, they would certainly see her, but fortunately, Andrea had another way out. On the wall next to her was a large painting. It reached from just above the floor almost to the ceiling. Andrea pulled it away from the wall. Behind it was a secret passage, which she quickly slipped into before Chandra was able to get back.

Few outside the Guild Masters themselves knew about this passage. It led directly to the Guild Master's room up on the top floor of the mansion. It had been shown to her by Cassiopia when she first joined the guild, and was meant as a means of escape for the Master in the event that the mansion was overtaken.

The passage was pitch black, but Andrea had spent enough years of her youth using it that she knew each plank of the steps perfectly, and could traverse them even if she was blind, if she needed to. She crept up to the wall where the passage ended. A slight push and she knew it would open, but she waited.

Putting her ear to the wall first, she listened for any sound at all. She could hear someone inside the room. Andrea heard the sound of some papers shuffling and a pen being set into an inkwell and then there was a soft knock at the door.

Then, she could hear the Chancellor's heavy footsteps walk over and answer the door.

This was Andrea's opportunity. She pushed open the secret door slowly and peeked outside. The room was very dim, with just a single lamp that had such a small flame that it barely gave off any light.

Andrea pushed the door and slipped inside. The room was long, with windows along the eastern wall, looking out into the city. The curtains were pulled shut. To her right was the Guild Master's desk, against the wall near the entrance to the room. Papers were scattered all about it in a most disorderly way.

*He's such a slob*, she thought.

At the far end of the room was the Chancellor's bed. Four large dark stained posts were draped with semi-transparent linen. Andrea crept slowly into the room and into a shadowy corner next to the large bed. It was getting late and she knew Jor'Dan liked to go to bed early. This far corner would give her the perfect opportunity to strike him when he was most vulnerable.

No sooner had she slipped into the darkness, than Andrea heard the handle of the room's main double door rattle. The right side of the main doorway opened and the Chancellor swaggered through. He was as cocky and arrogant as he'd ever been. Although now, he did seem to show even more confidence than normal.

The Chancellor walked closer towards the bed and slowly began to disrobe. He took off his boots and cloak, then his shirt and trousers, until he was left in a thin undergarment that only covered his manhood.

There was a tall mirror that covered the wall next to the bureau, at which he seemed to feel the need to turn and vainly admire himself. He turned his head so his chin was up and his eyes strained to look at his reflection.

Andrea decided this was her opportunity. She slid from the shadow towards him. She quietly snuck up behind him and let out a soft moan, so that he knew she was there. She reached out and delicately caressed his back, letting out another soft coo. She could tell he liked it; he closed his eyes and brushed her hand with his cheek as her hands went to his shoulders.

"I was hoping you'd change your mind and join me tonight, Chandra," he whispered. "See, it won't be so bad."

He reached for one of her hands but missed it as she slid it away and back down his back. He groaned again, lost in bliss. "Ohhh, you do that so well."

"Enjoy it," she hissed. "It's the last time you'll ever feel this way."

The Chancellor's eyes shot open in horror and she knew he recognized her voice.

With the speed that her years of training had given her, she kicked the back of the Chancellor's knee, making him fall to the ground in front of her.

Then, in one fluid movement, she wrenched her dagger from its sheath and at the same time slid her left arm around his head, pulling it upright. She whipped the dagger around in front of him, angling it up and pulling it towards her, thrusting the cold steel blade into the soft flesh of the Chancellor's neck and up through his skull.

His body shook and quivered, as she expected it to, but she held him taut until she felt the blade crack through the bone. His warm blood dripped down the blade onto her hand and finally he slumped to the floor in a lifeless heap.

Moments later, she had claimed her prize. She opened the door to the outer hall, her trophy in one hand and a sack in the other. Andrea slowly walked towards the steps that would lead down to the foyer of the guild, where her sisters were gathered. The upper level was dim to the point of almost complete darkness. She could hear her sisters whispering, wondering what this was about.

As Andrea neared the steps, she could see Chandra's feet as she walked closer to the other members at the base of the steps. Now was the time, Andrea thought, as she let loose the head that she'd claimed.

It hit a step half way down the staircase and bounced up, slinging blood around as it tumbled through the air. It hit another step, then another, and finally landed in the middle of the crowd of women.

A girl Andrea didn't recognize let out a fearful scream as the Chancellor's head came to a stop and its eyes looked at up at her with a hollow gaze. Andrea heard several gasps of surprise and horror as the girls looked upon the head of their former master. Andrea walked slowly down the steps, allowing all the other guild members to get a good look at her, allowing them to see the blood that dripped from her black silk clothing. She wanted them to know without a doubt that she had done this.

She came to a stop several steps from the bottom. This way she could look down upon them, signifying their place beneath her in this new incarnation of the guild. A guild presided over by her.

There was a long moment of silence. Andrea looked at each of them coldly, her gaze lingering a little longer on Chandra than on the rest. Most of them looked away from her, but Chandra stared back with abject hatred.

"What did you do?" Chandra finally asked.

"What should have been done a long time ago."

"The...the Emperor..."

"Will do nothing."

"Like hell," Chandra blurted. "He'll kill us all for your actions."

"He'll do no such thing," Andrea said coolly. "The Emperor, more than anyone, knows how this business works. He is a businessman and he'll get the message that the guild is under new leadership."

Again, there was silence until Andrea began to speak again.

"Chandra," she said as she tossed the bag onto the floor, "take the head to the Emperor. I want it there by morning."

A cold stillness settled on the room as all the other women looked at Chandra. At first the woman did not move. She seemed to be contemplating the order. Finally she swallowed, took a deep breath, knelt down and placed the head into the bag.

She turned and looked up at Andrea. Chandra reluctantly bowed her head to her new mistress and carried the bloody sack with her out through the front doors as she headed towards the stables.

The moments that followed seemed to last forever, as all the guild members heard their sister ride off into the night. Andrea stepped down to the main floor and joined the rest of the women, but none of them spoke. Eventually, Elitra stepped up towards her and asked meekly, "Are you sure the Emperor will not come after us for killing the Chancellor?"

Andrea looked down at the girl and smiled, "He's been at this game for a long time and knows how the system works."

Her confidence seemed to alleviate some of the tension in the air.

"For now, Elitra, I want you to go down and gather the initiates. I know they aren't asleep yet, despite it being past 'lights out'. I will be down shortly to explain things."

Elitra turned and quickly headed towards the initiates chamber. Andrea turned towards three of the trainers standing near her.

"You three," Andrea said as she pointed at them, "Come with me to my room. We have some trash to get rid of and some serious changes to make around here."

## 92. Brothers Reunite

Serieve stared aimlessly at the ceiling of the carriage he rode in. It was an immaculate carriage, in fact the nicest he'd ever seen. It was plush, with cushioned seats and gold trimmed windows with velvet drapes to block the sun…or the view of outsiders, if one wished, and it rode as smooth as a boat on calm waters. For all of its comforts, though, Serieve was bored, and a little concerned as to why he was in it in the first place.

All he knew was that he showed up at home, but his brother was nowhere to be found. Cate, the only servant still employed by their family, welcomed him home and as soon as he stepped into the parlor, he was greeted by six of the Emperor's elite guard. The captain of the guard told him that they were instructed to have him come with them.

He tried to dismiss them, but they were insistent on him accompanying them back to the capital city. He tried several times to ask what this was about, but none of the guards would respond to him. All he could manage to get from the captain was that they had orders to bring him to the castle, so there he was. They wouldn't even allow him to ride his own horse with them; he had to ride in this mobile prison. Even if it was a nice prison, it still felt like a prison nonetheless.

He peered through the window and saw that they had finally made it into the city proper and were headed towards the palace. His guards rode close by as the carriage made its way down the streets of the sprawling city. Serieve could see the palace drawing close, and in moments they were being welcomed in through the gates.

The carriage rolled up towards the front of the palace and came to a halt directly in front of the palace entrance. Serieve tried to open the door so he could get out, but as he suspected, it was locked from the outside. He could hear the guards dismounting and after what seemed like an agonizingly long time, he heard a click as the door was opened.

The sun hit him square in the eyes as he emerged, and it took a moment for him to adjust to the brightness of the day. When he did so, however, to his surprise he saw a majestic red carpet rolled out before him and a dozen or so attendants and guards surrounding him.

"Why have I...?"

Before he could finish speaking, a short dumpy little man in very fine clothes and a white wig approached him, "I am so dreadfully sorry, Sire, for this abrupt seizing of your person, but we were asked to bring you here the moment we learned of your whereabouts."

"By whom?" Serieve asked cautiously. He couldn't imagine that it had been the Emperor; otherwise, he would have been told so. Not that the Emperor would have any real reason to want to talk to him anyway.

The attendant drew in a deep breath as he prepared a long diatribe to explain the situation, but before the little man could get out a single syllable, a voice called from the palace entrance.

Serieve heard someone call his name and immediately jerked his head up to see his older brother walking towards him. Serieve pushed the little attendant out of his way and met his brother halfway up the carpet. As soon as he was close, he grabbed his older brother and hugged him.

"Wow, you've gotten stronger since the last time I saw you, little brother," Bourne said jokingly as Serieve let loose his grasp.

"Two years of hard training will do that to you."

"Has it been two years already?"

"Aye, two years and three months next week."

"I'll be damned," Bourne said with a smile. "How fast the time goes."

Serieve was genuinely happy to see Bourne. It seemed like ages since they'd seen each other last, but between Bourne's court duties and Serieve's training, it was understandable that they didn't get to see each other often.

"Gather my brother's things," Bourne commanded, "and take them to his room."

Immediately the carriage was unloaded, and all of Serieve's belongings were carried in. Bourne put his arm over his brother's shoulders as the two of them began to walk into the palace.

"Brother," Serieve began, "what is going on here? You're ordering people around like you own the place."

The two of them walked through the palace doors and past the palace guards. The interior of the palace was more majestic than Serieve could have ever imagined. The floor was white marble interlaced with gold. The walls were ornate granite and exquisite northland cherry wood. Serieve had never walked into a building so nice and it made him feel out of place.

"And what did you mean, to have them take my things to my room?" Serieve asked in a whisper, as though he was saying something he shouldn't have been.

"That's what I have to tell you, brother." Bourne smiled at him, then spread his arm out as if to point to everything at the same time. "This...this is all ours."

"What? Have you lost your mind?" Serieve replied in a whisper, keeping his voice low.

"There is much I have to tell you, brother, but first, there's someone I wish you to meet. I'll fill you in on the way. Come," Bourne ordered as he grabbed Serieve by the wrist and dragged him along.

Before Serieve could really comprehend what was going on, he was being pulled towards a massive set of cascading stairs that led up to the second level of the palace.

"While we've been apart," Bourne began, looking back at Serieve, "I've been filling father's position and I was chosen."

"Chosen...chosen for what?" Serieve asked, growing a little irritated with his brother's erratic behavior.

"I was chosen!"

Serieve momentarily lost his temper and jerked his arm out of his brother's grip. "Chosen for what, a swift boot to the head? Because that's how you're acting."

Bourne stopped and turned back towards his younger brother. With a wide grin upon his face, he placed his hands on both of Serieve's shoulders and looked him in the eye. "I was chosen by the Emperor to be his Heir."

Serieve nearly choked and his eyes shot open. "You...you were what?"

"You heard me correctly, Serieve."

Serieve's mind raced to take in exactly what this would mean to him, and his brother, and everything. Would that make him a prince, he wondered, as that and a thousand other questions went through his head.

"Now, quickly," Bourne said, bringing Serieve out of his mental tornado and back to reality. "I know he is currently free, and I want him to meet you. I've told him all about you."

"You what?"

"It's fine," Bourne attempted to calm him. "He's intrigued by you, so come on."

Serieve didn't have much choice in the matter. Bourne grabbed his arm again and pulled him along. Serieve couldn't imagine why the Emperor would want to meet him, even if he was Bourne's younger brother. Before Bourne had been selected Serieve was almost a nobody, and he didn't really feel that Bourne's new status changed that much at all.

Before he knew it, they walked into a huge covered balcony that had an ornate crystal chandelier hanging in it. The balcony presented a magnificent view of the royal tournament fields, where the Emperor was known for hosting jousts.

In the center of the room, near the edge of the balcony, stood an older, frail-looking man dressed in ornate red and black robes. He looked as though he were reading a letter. The servant held a burlap sack in silence while the Emperor read.

As soon as he and Bourne entered the room, Bourne immediately dropped to one knee, bowing to his master. Serieve quickly mimicked his brother, and they waited to be recognized by the Emperor before taking any further action.

Serieve was curious what his Majesty was reading, and thought he heard the old man laugh quietly as he finished the letter and handed it back to the servant. He then took off one of his signet rings and handed it to the servant as well.

"Take the sack to my office. Give her this and ask her to deliver it to her new Guild Master," Serieve overheard as they waited.

"Yes, my Liege," the servant acknowledged the order. "Will I be sending a message with it?"

"Yes," the Emperor said, taking a moment to think. "Tell her...welcome to the family."

He couldn't tell for sure, but the Emperor's tone did not sound happy. "God's speed," the Emperor said as he dismissed the servant, who quickly departed the room.

Serieve didn't think he could have possibly heard what he thought he did. It must have been taken out of context, he assured himself, and dismissed the thoughts entirely as the Emperor walked over to them.

"Rise, my sons."

Slowly, he and Bourne rose to address his Majesty.

"Lord," Bourne greeted the Emperor. "Please allow me to introduce my younger brother, the cavalier in training, Serieve."

Serieve nodded in reverence to the Emperor.

"This is wonderful," the Emperor replied. "I've wanted to meet you for quite some time now."

"Pardon, you're Majesty, but what do you mean? My brother was only appointed recently, wasn't he?"

"Ah, yes," the Emperor conceded, "I meant in the time that I've gotten to know Bourne. He talks about you all the time." The Emperor smiled again and patted Bourne on the shoulder which made his brother blush slightly.

"So, you've heard much about me these past few weeks?"

This got a reaction from his brother, who shot a glare at him, which Serieve knew was Bourne's way of telling him to shut up. Serieve quickly decided to change the subject.

"I would have come sooner, but news travels slowly in some parts and I have been training with Sir Gavin and have not had an opportunity to see my brother."

"Interesting, that you should mention your former master," the Emperor said, his head dropping sorrowfully.

"Wha...what do you mean, sire?" Serieve asked. Concern for his master made his voice crack slightly.

"Oh, didn't you know?"

"No. I haven't heard any news about Sir Gavin. Is something wrong?"

"Oh, dear boy, I regret to inform you that Sir Gavin was enlisted for a mission for the Empire and well...well, he was slain."

Serieve felt his heart stop and he momentarily felt it hard to breathe, but as he had been taught, he crammed his feelings deep down inside him where they could be controlled.

"How?" Serieve managed to ask. "How was he killed?"

The Emperor laid his hand on Serieve's shoulder comfortingly. "Let's not dwell on the details now. There will be a time and place for that later. Right now, let us rejoice in your return and your reuniting with your new family."

Serieve nodded in acceptance and the Emperor patted his shoulder reassuringly.

"We mustn't allow your training to falter though," the Emperor said as Serieve looked down into the old man's eyes. "I have already selected a new master for you, Sir Sonilauq. He is my personal guard, the captain of the royal battalion, and the most powerful knight in the realm. I believe he would be a much better instructor for you."

"I...I've never heard of him, but that is most gracious of you. Thank you," Serieve replied, but somehow it felt wrong for him to just be given to another knight like an article of clothing.

"Wonderful," the Emperor stated, sounding glad to be finished with the topic. "You'll start as soon as Sir Sonilauq returns."

"Oh yes? Where is he?" Serieve asked quickly. "A personal guard isn't personal if he isn't around."

"He..." the Emperor began but paused. "He is on a very important quest for me. Official business for the Empire."

"Forgive him, Sire," Bourne spoke up, apologizing for Serieve. Again he looked at his brother with a scowl which screamed for Serieve to shut up.

"There's nothing to forgive. He is very astute, and I like that." The Emperor smiled up at Bourne. "But I really must be going. I have some things that have come to my attention that I must address immediately."

"Of course, my Liege," Bourne said as he bowed respectfully. Serieve bowed as well as the Emperor turned and departed through a door on the far wall.

## 93. *Return to the Lucky Duck*

A bead of sweat rolled down Sol's forehead, downward along the bridge of his nose before finally dropping off the tip and landing on his leg. It was only mid-morning but the sun was out and it was getting hot. He hung his head while riding in the bumpy cart filled with horse manure being driven to the market in Tyric.

It had been more than two weeks since Zaroth transported them back. Only he didn't send them to Tyric and he certainly didn't send the chest of gold with them. They had ended up in a city called Styren, which was nearly a hundred leagues south of Tyric.

Sol should have known that Zaroth wouldn't send them to the right place. Sol was convinced that Zaroth had to be one of the worst wizards in the world. However, he was also sure that Zaroth hadn't sent the gold with them on purpose. It was just one last way for him to stick it to Sol, and Sol wasn't happy about it.

He and Oather had managed to hitch several rides along the way. They were nearly back to Tyric when Sol and Oather had run into Calin Lulkoek, and he had offered to give them a ride the rest of the way back into town.

Despite the smell, riding on a wagon hauling manure was better than walking. The full cart, pulled by a pair of asses, rocked slowly from side to side as they rode on. Without notice, the cart stopped and Sol slowly raised his head to see where they were. He lifted the brim of his hat to see they had finally arrived at the *Lucky Duck*.

"Here ye are fellas."

Oather hopped off the wagon, and Sol managed to drag himself off as well. His muscles were sore, he was very nearly broke again, and he was just not in a good mood.

"Good day to ye, and best fortunes," Calin said as he spurred his asses on again.

"Thanks for the ride, Calin," Oather called back, which got a wave from the old man.

Sol looked up at the familiar, swinging, wooden sign of the *Lucky Duck,* and was actually glad to be home. At least here he could get an ale and relax a bit.

Oather turned from watching the farmer ride off down the street and energetically opened the door and walked inside, with Sol following close behind. Once they were inside, what few patrons there were all stopped and looked at them as if they were ghosts.

Gretchen was carrying a tray of mugs back to the bar. She suddenly stopped and her eyes lit up like the yearly magic show above the capital city on Hero's day. Dumbfounded, she dropped the tray full of mugs and dashed towards them. She grabbed Oather first in a big hug, and then pulled Sol in as well. She gripped them both very tight as she squeezed them.

Finally, she managed to relax her grip slightly as she pulled her face back to look at them. Her eyes were red and watery, and Sol could tell she was glad to see them.

"What in all the realms happened to you two?"

Sol attempted to answer but she cut him off before he could say a word. "Don't you ever make me worry about the two of you on another one of your hair-brained schemes like that again," she scolded him before she hugged Sol a second time.

Gretchen wiped the tears from her eyes but she was smiling, which Sol didn't understand in the slightest.

"You said you were going to only be gone a couple of days, not almost a month. What were you thinking?"

"We sort of…" but before Sol could say another word, he saw Katrina emerge from the back kitchen carrying another tray, this one full of food. As soon as she came out, Sol saw her catch sight of him and Oather. Immediately she set down the tray and marched towards them.

Sol was shocked to see the girl. He thought for sure she'd have been fired by Gretchen by now. He was barely able to speak, but got the words out somehow.

"Katrina..uh…How are y-"

Before he could get out another syllable the young girl reared back and slapped him hard across the face.

"Ow," Sol cried and rubbed his cheek again. "What in the nine hells was that for?"

Katrina looked at him sternly, her eyes squinted just slightly. "You, Soliere Forrester, know exactly what that was for."

"Okay," Sol conceded, "I guess I did deserve that...a little."

Then, just as suddenly as she'd hit him the moment before, she leapt at him and threw her arms around him and hugged him tightly. She had more strength than Sol remembered, and it felt like she was going to tear his head from his shoulders. After a brief moment, she released him and kissed him full on the lips.

Sol's eyes shot open in surprise and a little shock, because Gretchen was standing right in front of them. Sol managed to unhinge the girl's arms and pushed her back to give himself some breathing room.

"Now that," she said as she looked at him in the eyes, "was for coming back home safe...but don't ever make us worry like that again."

"Um...Katrina," Sol stammered, his mind racing for an excuse for the girl's actions. "Don't you think that's a little forward, we hardly know each other-"

"Oh save it, Sol." Gretchen leered at him, as her right eye squinted and she pointed her finger at him. "Dear little Kat and I had plenty of time to talk while you were gone, and I've come to the decision that she'll be a fine addition to the family."

"You...what?" Sol felt the blood draining from his face.

"Oh, heavens, yes," Gretchen stated nonchalantly. "At first I was angry, and nearly fired her when I saw the note in my ledger, but after mulling it over and talking with Tanner..."

"Don't bring me into this, woman," Tanner called from behind the bar as he put several glasses up on the shelf.

"As I was saying," Gretchen resumed, "You're a grown man, and you have every right to follow your heart, and if your heart desires dear Katrina here, then so be it."

"Um...okay..." Sol managed to get out, completely dumbfounded by the situation. It'd never worked this badly before. *Gretchen typically fired these girls on the spot*, Sol thought. *Why in the world did Gretchen have to get a conscience now?*

"Oh, it'll be wonderful," Katrina said, latching onto Sol's arm.

"Yeah...it'll be a regular picnic," he grumbled.

Oather snickered and gave Sol a congratulatory slap on the back, "Too bad we couldn't take Katrina with us. The poor thing had to suffer without you all this time, tsk."

Sol shot Oather a stern 'Go flog yourself' look, who obviously was amused by this situation.

"What took you boys so long to come home anyway?" Gretchen asked, bringing the situation back to the time at hand. "We'd nearly given up on you coming back from those terrible ruins."

"We got a little sidetracked, that's all."

"Yeah," Oather erupted in an excited tone that Sol wasn't used to hearing unless Oather was talking about weapons. "We were taken to this weird land, that was all dark, and there was this evil demon, king, thing, and-"

"Oh my," Gretchen interrupted him, causing Oather to take a breath, "You boys will have to tell us all about it, but first you must eat."

Oather's face lit up, and Sol's stomach rumbled at the thought of food. He hadn't eaten much since getting set adrift after their sea voyage. Calin was kind enough to offer them their fill of some of the corn and tomatoes that he had with him, of which Oather had plenty, but Sol wasn't a big fan of vegetables and barely managed to force down a couple of tiny tomatoes.

"Come, have a seat at the bar and we'll bring you boys out something," Gretchen said as she ushered them to seats while she and Katrina went back to the kitchen. Tanner had two mugs of ale waiting for them as they sat. Sol quickly scooped up his mug and took a swig. It felt like ages since he'd had a good drink. Feeling the cool liquid pour down his parched throat was the nearest he could imagine to what it must be like to reside in the heavens.

He drained the mug as he pulled it from his lips and gestured for a refill from Tanner when he felt a tap on his shoulder. Curiously, Sol turned to see who it could be and behind him stood two men draped in dark black cloaks pulled over their heads as to shade their faces.

"Who are you?" Sol asked.

There was a short pause as one man pulled his hood back. "Are you the one called, Soliere?"

"Depends on who's asking?" Sol replied in a tone which betrayed how much he really didn't want to be bothered by strangers.

"Sire," the man began, "We have been sent here by Prince Serieve."

At the mention of Serieve's name, Sol quickly stood up. "Is this about the treasure?" Sol asked defensively, "If so, you tell him that we didn't get any either, the wizard sent us back empty-handed…"

The man stood there, silent, possibly even stunned. Sol couldn't tell.

"Wait…did you say 'Prince'?"

"Why, yes, sire," the man replied. "He is the younger brother of Prince Bourne, who was selected as the Emperor's successor."

Sol didn't know what to say. Dozens of interactions with their former companion were running through his mind. All he could do was turn back around towards the bar and take another drink from the mug Tanner had refilled for him.

"I'll be damned," Sol muttered under his breath as he took another drink and turned back towards the men. "So what does he want?"

"His Highness relayed how you and your companions saved his life-"

"Actually it was more…" Oather began to say but was quickly elbowed in the ribs by Sol who then motioned for the man to continue.

"Yes, well, His Royal Highness, the Emperor, wishes to repay you for your deeds."

"I think a reward is certainly called for." Sol's eyes were lit up like a child's in a candy store in anticipation of what was in store for him.

"The Emperor was told of your aspirations to start a shipping company, but knew you had no vessel," the man continued matter-of-factly, "Therefore, he has sent us to bring you the 'Excelsior', the Emperor's personal cargo transport ship."

Sol couldn't believe what he was hearing. His jaw dropped and he was speechless.

"The Excelsior is an elven crafted corvette. It's the fastest cargo ship in his majesty's fleet and he wishes you to have it. In addition, I and my companions will serve as your crew for the next six lunar cycles to give you time to acquire a crew for the ship. As you hire them, we will train them on the use of an elven vessel before we depart back to the capital."

Sol felt his heart beating and he couldn't believe what he was hearing. His body nearly trembled as he grappled with the thought of owning not just a ship, but an elven ship, which were renowned for being some of the fastest on the water. He wanted to grab the man and give him a bear hug but resisted the urge and instead turned to Oather who, by the shocked expression on his face, was in as much disbelief as Sol was.

"Do you know what this means?" Sol asked.

"Hopefully, it means you might actually begin to start paying off your tab," Tanner chimed in behind them. "These men have been here for nearly a week waiting around. Never would tell anyone what they were doing, but we've been curious. They paid their tab on time and didn't cause any trouble, so we didn't figure it was any of our business."

"Though, it would have been nice to know that they knew you boys were still alive," Gretchen said as she walked out of the kitchen carrying a tray of meats, cheeses and some bread which she promptly sat down in front of Oather.

"We apologize for that," stated the second man, who up to this point hadn't said a word, "but we were under strict orders to only speak to Masters Soliere and Oather, and to wait here until they arrived."

"How is Serieve?" Gretchen asked.

"I'm sure he's fine," Sol replied, not caring one bit if Serieve was really okay or not, "Now...about that ship."

464

# The End

I hope you have enjoyed this story. Volume 2 is under way and the tales of Sol and Oather will continue in The Orb of Chaos Vol.2: Fools Rush In.

In the meant time, if you liked this tale, please go back to Amazon.com and leave a short review so that others can hear what you thought of it. Thank you.

### *About the Author – M. Ray Allen*

Raised as a Navy Brat, I grew up living all over the United States. While born in Oklahoma, my family lived in Bermuda, California, Texas as well as a few other places in between. After High School, I attended the University of Oklahoma to be closer to my grandparents and close friends – The Clarks.

During my time at OU, my friend, Mark Blauser, and I stayed up one summer night drinking and talking about our favorite adventure stories (he's a Tolkien fan). I shared this tale with him and (to my surprise) he loved it. We were up until 3-4am talking about it before I finally crashed. The next day he came over (waking me from a hangover) and forced me to tell him the story again, but this time he brought a tape recorder and insisted we find a way to get this on paper.

So began the tales of Sol and Oather. It's taken a long time to pull it together, but it's finally done. I hope you've enjoyed it as much as Mark and I have but don't fear, there's more to come. This was just the beginning...

## *About the Artist – Mattijs Buma*

Born and raised in the small city of Gouda, the Netherlands. Mattijs has been drawing ever since he was a kid, but what got him to take art more seriously were the various anime shows he used to watch. That's when Mattijs started buying large numbers of art books, and really started practicing.

After some time though, he felt like this manga type of drawing was holding him back, so he started drawing things from life, and tried out different approaches to drawing. At that time he was also heavily influenced by art for videogames.

This eventually got Mattijs accepted into a course mostly dedicated to 3D art for film and games. As much fun as it was for him, the 3D aspect kept him from what he really loved to do, which was drawing. Mattijs quit the course, and went on to follow introductory courses at various art schools. He is currently still attending art school, working on various illustration projects on the side whenever he can.